THE
PLACEBO
AGENDA

A Novel

Forrest
Jones

The Placebo Agenda

Forrest Jones

ISBN (Print Edition): 978-1-09834-195-4

ISBN (eBook Edition): 978-1-09834-196-1

This is a work of fiction. Names, characters, businesses, places, events, locales, and incidents are either the products of the author's imagination or used in a fictitious manner. Any resemblance to actual persons, living or dead, or actual events is purely coincidental.

For Mom and Dad. Thank you for always being there
and believing in me. I am eternally grateful.

CHAPTER

1

An American blonde, draped in nothing but a silk sheet, ran screaming for help down an alley in Venezuela's Petare slum. The sheet snagged on the corner of a small house built from unpainted concrete blocks. She tried to grab it, but it held fast to a nail, refusing to flee with her. She turned her head and froze at the sound of footsteps behind her, her mouth and eyes widening. Abandoning the sheet, she continued sprinting down the stepped passageway, naked as the day she was born. Her cries drew stares from onlookers peeping out the windows of their ramshackle houses made of tin and brick, one house stacked on top of the other. Her sharp glances to see if her pursuer was getting closer cast a wave of fear among the curious.

She tripped at the sound of approaching footsteps coming from up the alley. The echo of her tibia smacking against concrete drew winces from a few neighbors—winces that evolved into widening eyes when the naked woman jumped back up and continued her descent despite her injury. Even hurt, she moved in an elegant way, with a touch of grace to guide her through hell. Still, the neighbors knew better than to jump in to help. They knew who lived up those stairs. And he was fast approaching.

A half a dozen or so armed teenage gang members sitting along the narrow stairway jumped to attention at the sound of a screaming woman, drawing their weapons by reflex at the hint of trouble. They stared up the alley ready to put the cries in the crosshairs, not trusting anything, not even a beautiful foreign blonde screaming at them in English.

"Shoot him! He's right behind me," the injured and naked American shouted, toppling toward them. A taller, older member in his early twenties caught her as if they were part of some amateur gymnastics move. "Shoot the bastard. You know who he is. He's not your fucking leader and doesn't have your back. Now shoot him!"

The gang members frowned. One tossed a cigarette down the steps, checking her out from head to toe, excited but wary. Despite the soft, golden, and perfumed rarity that had flown across their transom, he and his buddies were still confused and caught off guard.

"He'll kill us all if you don't shoot that fucking monster," she said in Spanish this time, apparently surprised at her command of the language.

No one said a word.

"You know he's not one of you. You know that deep down," she said.

Still no reaction.

A fresh bolt of logic shot through the young woman's head. "Just look at your shiny new assault rifles! A little pricey for street thugs like yourselves, right? You didn't buy them. He gave them to you. I saw a ton more up the hill. Think, you idiot pawns, and shoot him, or he'll do to you what he did to my husband!"

She reached for a gun, but the teenager backed away, refusing to let her touch it. Blood ran down her neck where an open knife wound pulsed in the afternoon September sunlight. It took about a minute for the gang to realize she was bleeding, their eyes fixated below her neck.

An old woman peered down the alley from a shantytown house above. Her eyes narrowed at the group of young men.

"You boys didn't do this, did you?" she shouted.

They shrugged and threw clueless glances at one another, and their confusion let the old woman know that this time around, they really weren't at fault for whatever crimes had taken place in her neighborhood.

"Get her out of here before he sees her!" the old woman screamed. She slammed her window shut.

"Jesus, look at you! You're naked! What happened?" the tall one who had caught her said, now grasping the situation.

"I got away. From that freak up there!"

"You realize what happens to gringas in here, let alone hot, naked ones?" he said.

The American woman tensed up.

"The police are even afraid to come in here. There's nothing that can save you," he added.

"I know that. I'll take my chances with you over him," she said, eyes darting from the young man back to the top of the hill.

"Did anyone touch you, you know, do anything to you?" another one asked.

"No," she said, her gaze fixed up the stepped alley. Sharp gulps and darting eyes let all know she was thinking only of her survival. "I got away first. Look, I'm not some random kidnapping victim. Something is going on up there that you don't know about," she said. She looked up, and the memory of her recent trauma hijacked her brain and took control of her body, throttling her sensory systems way past fight, past flight, and into panic mode. She started hyperventilating and shaking. "I can't breathe. I'm having a heart attack," she said, her eyes losing focus. A few of the armed adolescents laughed at her quivering body.

"Cut it out," the taller one, who had caught her, said to them. They shut up, and then he turned to the woman. "You're not having a heart attack," he said.

A shorter one with a shaved head, caramel skin, and blue eyes, donning a conspicuously new blue Oxford shirt, nodded, checking out her body. "You look fine to me," he said. He threw her a large smile, but his eyes narrowed. Nostrils flared. "Yeah, you weren't raped. You probably…"

"Look, idiot, he didn't rape me, but he was going to. I mean…" She took a moment to catch her breath, hoping to channel racing thoughts into some reservoir of logic in her head and comprehend something. Anything. "He didn't rape, but he… he did stuff! Oh God, sick stuff, to my husband, and, my God, there are more!"

Tears broke free from her bright blue eyes and took some stress and confusion away with them. She took a few very deep breaths and managed to calm herself. She looked up the hill and back at the gang. Then reality set in, and it wasn't a pleasant one. "My God. You're all with him!" She eyed each and every one of them. Her fear contracted as if withdrawing into some emotional cocoon, quickly transforming itself into something else, and exploded out in its new form—justified anger.

"Fuck you! You're part of this!" She took a swing at the taller one who had caught her earlier. He sidestepped her punch.

"Get her some clothes and get her inside," he said, as if he were dodging the hands of an infant curiously grabbing an adult's reading glasses as opposed to the flails of a confused woman fighting for her life. "I don't care if she's hot. If she's one of his up the hill, she's off-limits. And I don't want any trouble from the police or embassies," he added to no one in particular. He squinted. "Or worse. I don't want any trouble from up there."

"You definitely don't want trouble from up there, but we might already have it," interrupted a thin teen with curly hair and what seemed to be brand-new imported jeans and a designer T-shirt. "I mean she's got a point. Why are we getting free assault rifles and clothes? Nothing's free anymore, especially in this country." He smiled at the woman and spoke to her loudly in English so that everyone could hear. "She says Ricardo will kill us with these new guns he just gave us." He looked down at his own weapon, a Kalashnikov assault rifle. "See this bitch? This shit is Russian. Fuck you up," he continued in English, cocking the weapon. All flinched by reflex at the universal sound of a loading firearm.

The woman's eyes widened, sparkling with an idea. "Nice English! Good use of reported speech. I'm impressed. Let's see if you all can write as well. Give me a pen and paper. Now!"

The kid shrugged, withdrew a pen from his pocket, and grabbed a crumpled white fast-food bag off the street. He ripped it in half and handed the wrinkled piece of paper to the blonde. She snatched it from him and shoved another gang member against the alley wall, the young man's confusion whirled with pleasure at being pushed by a naked woman.

"Flex those pecs, kid," she said. She pressed the paper against his chest with one hand and wrote with the other. Before the kid had time to react, she had finished writing and tossed the pen down the alley, thanking God it was a felt tip. She read her message. It was clear and legible.

More echoes of flip-flops shot down the hill, sounding like bare fists smacking against soft, boneless meat.

"Dear God," she said, her jaw quivering. "Guys, sooner or later you're all dead if you don't kill him. Now is the perfect time."

A young man in his early twenties emerged from out of nowhere, no confusion in his big brown eyes at all, his calmness separating him from his peers. His long black hair was all one length and a little dated, like a style from the early nineties.

"You're not going anywhere," the young man said.

"Just let her go," the taller one, who had caught her, said. "This is weird. Why is an American woman here, and in Petare of all places? We're just asking for attention from the wrong people, and the police definitely will make a raid to investigate a dead gringa."

"Don't worry about it," this calmer one said, turning to the woman. He smirked.

"Fuck you," she said, throwing a punch at the apparent leader, who wore a faded tourist T-shirt showcasing the name and skyline of the city of Boston. "You'll burn for this. The rest of these idiots have no idea what's up there, but you do and I do." She looked at the small piece of paper in her hand, then back at the apparent gang leader's T-shirt and then into his cold and calculating eyes.

"Hey, Boston, get this note to a man named Street Brewer. Got it? Even if you're going to kill him. Let him see it first, and tell him it's all he needs." She shoved the scrap of paper into Boston's hands, broke free from the group, and bolted down the stepped alleyway. As she glanced over her shoulder, she said, "Remember, his name is Street Brewer. Get him that paper. You're a dead man, but that piece of paper may save Venezuela." Off she ran.

"Get her," Boston ordered his friends, annoyed that she was getting away. He jerked his head, ordering two gang members, including the taller one who had caught the girl, to move. He stared at the paper, shrugged, and stuffed it into his pocket. "Bring her the fuck back. She's limping. It shouldn't be too hard."

They nodded in obedience and then ran off in the direction of the fleeing nude blonde.

The ominous sound of footsteps stopped, and the American woman slowed to a halt, then turned around. At the top of the hill, an immense shadow of a man took shape. She gazed at the sight and fell to her knees.

"Please God," she said in a hoarse whisper, looking beyond the large man to a sliver of blue sky above the slum houses while puffy white clouds moved westward. "God?" she asked. "God, why are you not here?"

Nothing but silence.

The two young men drew closer as the meaty footsteps resumed. The shadow expanded downhill, but the woman held her gaze on the man. Then she looked downward and caught sight of the base of the alleyway, where a busier Caracas street bustled with commuters. Microbuses and motorcycles rumbled, though not loud enough to drown out the footsteps of the large man and his two armed minions heading her way.

"Please God, tell me what to do," she said amid surging sobs. She turned her attention from the sky to the approaching gang members. "Just shoot me, you cowards!"

They shrugged.

Out of the shadows, two enormous legs emerged, fat but powerful, and barely covered by white tennis shorts decades after their time. A faded navy blue T-shirt barely concealed a massive frame. The man had thick, curly black hair, like that on a figure carved in an ancient statue or adorned on a piece of pottery unearthed from antiquity. His dark eyes didn't scare her as much as the lifelessness behind them. He flashed a grin that matched his empty gaze, a smirk from someone who takes delight in making others suffer, a smile on an idiot tyrant relishing his first taste of power. One large hand pointed sharply at the gang, while the other pointed at the woman.

Clear orders from above. Get her, or else.

The woman looked away, her mouth tensing. No more eye contact with the giant. She bolted down the last of the stairwell and approached the street—pain, grace, fear, desperation, and resolve bundled into one beautiful broken body.

"We can't let her get away, morons!" Boston shouted from above. The two broke into a sprint and caught up to her, the larger one grabbing her shoulder. She snapped loose of his grip and exploded out of the slum and into the crowded streets of Petare, eastern Caracas. Shocked commuters took in the sight of the naked foreign woman. She was probably rich, too. Most foreigners in Caracas were, compared to everyone else these days.

One woman touched her shoulder. "My God? What happened? Let me help you."

A few men bolted into action to assist as well, fueled by a primal urge to save a woman in danger.

"Somebody help her," a pedestrian shouted.

The naked American woman turned in circles, looking at the crowd in a daze. A small commuter bus approached. She stared at it and then to the heavens. Blue sky. White puffy clouds. The bus drew closer, and she could make out the stops it made around town posted on the window, a neighborhood called El Silencio being one. She took in the confused expression of its driver and the crowd around her. Two faces broke free from the chaos and caught her eye, the two young men sent into action by Boston. They had her.

"Back upstairs, gringa," they said, catching their breath. The crowd bolted at the sight of the combination of male adolescence and automatic weapons, especially shiny new ones.

"It's over," the American woman said. "God, it really is." She took one last look up at the heavens. "I'm so sorry," she whispered. Then she dove hard, catching sight of the El Silencio placard while airborne. She went headfirst under the front right tire of the arriving bus, which bounced up on contact with her smooth body and down just as fast after driving off her skull, though not without damage to the vehicle. Her body rolled like a discarded potted tree crashing down a hill and then came to a stop on the curb, parallel with the sidewalk as if she had been hauled out that morning for trash collection.

The two young gang members paused to stare at the dead American woman. One nodded at her and smiled.

"Hey, problem solved, and no bullets wasted! We'll get beer or even some real toilet paper for this," the larger one said to the other. They turned around and ran back up the hill.

The man in the Boston T-shirt went back to report that the woman never got away.

CHAPTER

2

Street Brewer plowed through waist-high water between walls of saw grass somewhere in the Florida Everglades, enjoying the one-of-a-kind tropical wilderness on a late-summer hike. His childhood friends from Miami, Parker West and Turner Hickman, followed close behind and clearly weren't relishing Mother Nature as Street was. They were snapping their heads left and right, up and down, edgy about the many snakes and alligators likely teeming beneath the water's surface. Street was taking in the birds, the trees, and the open sky. He looked back and laughed at the nervous expressions on his friends' faces.

"We're not lost. Don't worry, I know where we're going. It just feels like we're lost," Street said. "Look around and take in the beauty of the Everglades. That's the point of these hikes. Keep your heads up and enjoy. Focus on the positive. Don't look down in fear and what-if the day away."

Turner ignored him, scanning the water for something that could bite him beneath the surface such as a snake, an alligator, or a crocodile. Even otters were known to attack people in Florida.

Parker stopped and stared at his friends. "This is too risky. Something could bite us," he said.

"Guys, you've missed so many birds, some of them rare," Street said, stopping to wait for his friends to catch up. "I saw a bald eagle a few minutes ago, something real, while your eyes were on the ground worrying about what likely scurried away in fear from our splashing around."

"You're used to it because you're out here all the time. I bet you see cottonmouths or rattlesnakes every time you're here," Parker said.

"Nope. Because I'm not looking for them," Street said.

"Hopefully we'll just run into one of those invasive Burmese pythons. At least they're not poisonous," Turner said.

Street saw he was a little nervous and edgy but not as jumpy as Parker.

"Actually, you'd rather be bitten by a rattlesnake or a cottonmouth. Painful but there's a decent chance you'll live. If one of those big pythons gets you, it could wrap you up and squeeze the air out of you with each breath you exhale, kind of like rolling up claustrophobia and suffocation and snakes into one big fear. Not a good way to go."

"That's bullshit. Even I know that. Burmese pythons won't attack humans," Parker said as he stopped to catch his breath.

Street laughed. "I know. Just messing with you," he said, not telling Parker and Turner that they walked just a few feet from one about half an hour ago.

Parker looked around, and Street saw he was eager to change the subject. "Street, did you lose your backpack? You came with a backpack and a smaller sling? All I see is the sling."

Street shrugged. "I think I only had this sling. Anyway, the car's up there beyond that hammock," he said, pointing ahead to a clump of trees jutting up from some saw grass and a scattering of bald cypress trees.

"I think you lost a backpack," Parker said. "It's gone, and there's no backtracking, either. There are no markers out here. No trees with signs. None of those spray-painted streaks that show where a path leads like they have along the Appalachian Trail. Speaking of trails, why couldn't we walk on one of those boardwalks today?"

"Too many people," Street said. He stopped and stared ahead. One cluster of trees was too big to be a hammock. Solid ground. The road was up there, nestled in the Big Cypress National Reserve. He pressed on.

"Why are you out here all the time? What do you do out here?" Parker asked, his curiosity distracting him from his fear of snakes. "Seems like you're hiding something out here."

"You'll never guess what it is with your faces glued to the ground keeping an eye out for snakes," Street said. You'll never guess anyway, he thought.

"Whatever," Parker said. "Sounds just like harmless frogs out here. Guess that's a good thing," Parker said.

"You mean those soft little throaty chirps?" Street asked.

"Yes. Frogs," Parker said.

Street didn't tell them that they were alligators, not frogs, and those little bellows could get a lot louder. No need to scare them unless they slowed things up even more. He was hoping they'd see the beauty in the freshwater prairies of the Everglades and the swamps in the neighboring Big Cypress National Preserve and not dwell on the scary parts of wild Florida. Baby steps.

A few minutes later, they hiked under the canopy of cypress trees, found a trail, and walked with greater ease. Not long afterward, they came to the safety of Loop Road, South Florida's answer to a country lane.

Back on dry land, Parker and Turner were drinking cold water in Street's Jeep. Street took a sip and stared back at the wilderness. Beyond the foliage, open prairies pockmarked by hammocks and thick vegetation jutted up out of this mysterious area known as the river of grass.

Street stepped off the road and headed back into the dark water. "I'll be right back."

"Where are you going?" Turner asked.

"Piss break," he said. He disappeared into the trees.

"There you go again, vanishing. No one's around here. Why don't you just piss off the side of the road?" Turner asked.

"Because there are people around," Street shouted through the thickets. He could hear Parker twirling car keys on one finger while trying to check emails on his phone.

"I don't see anyone," Parker said. "I don't see any signal bars on my phone, either."

"Me neither," Turner echoed.

"We're not alone," Street shouted from inside the cover of the trees. He came back out after a couple of minutes. "We're not alone, because we're being followed."

"What?" Parker and Turner said in unison. They snapped their heads around in search of something specific, like a car or person crouching in the trees and not snakes or alligators.

"You heard me," Street said, stepping up onto the road. He threw a backpack in the bed of his Jeep.

"You mean other hikers?" Parker said.

"No. I mean another car," Street said, staring at the backpack. "And thank you, Parker. I did leave a backpack out here. I ditched it before our hike."

"Screw this. Let's get out of here," Turner said. "I don't need some gun-toting swamp rat causing trouble in some pickup."

"It's a brand-new SUV. Black," Street said. "Definitely doesn't belong out here because it's too citified, just like its driver. You can tell by its paint job and tires and just by the vibe. Relax. It's probably just people who decided to come to the Everglades to take pictures or have a picnic, and they have no clue where to go, so they figured they'd follow the three dudes in a Jeep," Street said. Turner and Parker scanned the horizon. Street just stared calmly at the road in front of them.

"I seriously doubt they considered going picnicking where you took us today," Turner said.

"That's why they drove off. They're out of their element like most people out here," Street said.

"How do you know this? From your reporter's skills, or your outdoor survivalist skills?" Turner asked.

Street stared at the beauty of the trees, each leaf competing for the sun's warming light. He didn't tell Turner and Parker that the SUV had been following them all the way from Tamiami Highway, miles before they had left civilization. He wasn't exactly sure if it was a coincidence the SUV was following them or if it had begun trailing him when he was closer to home. He wasn't sure, so he let it go.

"Maybe a little of both. Relax, we're fine," Street said.

After a few minutes, both Parker and Turner had ceased jumping at every creak and forest noise like young golden retrievers hearing footsteps on their property. They began to relax, enjoying the calmness that came from post-hiking tiredness and ebbing concerns for their safety.

Parker glanced at his cell phone and tried to check for any missed messages. He walked around in circles in search of a signal bar, tossing his car keys in the air and catching them without looking in the process.

"You're going to lose your car and house keys, Parker," Street said. "And you won't find any cell phone signal."

"They're attached to a floating key chain, but you're right. Can you put them up? Catch," Parker said, tossing the keys way too high.

Street watched the bright red floating key chain and tailing golden keys sail in the air directly above him like an exotic bird flying with confidence that any terrestrial dangers were too grounded to be of any threat. The keys shot over the side of the road and disappeared with a splash.

"I told you." Street didn't give Parker time to even try to look for them. He'd get them himself. "Did you see where they went in?"

"Just in front of one of those four drains that go beneath the road," Turner said, peering down. "Actually, they floated in. They should drift through to the other side."

"You lost them, so go get them," Street said, knowing full well Parker wouldn't do it.

"Can't you just do it?" Parker said. "You're the expert at all this."

"At what?"

"Survival and shit," Parker said.

"Are you afraid?" Street asked.

"No," Parker said.

"Yes, you are. But I'll get them."

Street hopped off the shoulder and landed with a commanding splash in the waters of the Florida swamp. He disappeared underneath the bridge into the drainage culvert to the left. Turner was right. The keys had drifted through the length of the tunnel. Street came up with the keys and threw them to Turner, who caught them and handed them to Parker. Then something caught his eye.

Street peered back into the culvert, pretty sure there was a large alligator staring back at him. He looked up at his friends. Parker was short with green eyes and had fine reddish-blond hair, like a baby's. Turner had thinning brown hair, and he was one of those guys who appeared to be big and strong but was also overweight. He had a calm, intelligent way about him. Street, the tallest of the bunch, blond and blue-eyed with some weather around the eyes, looked up at them and then back in the drain.

"What's in there?" Parker asked.

"Looks like a gator," Street said. "A big one. Too dark to be sure."

"I say it's a log. Your torso is still intact," Parker said.

Street glanced up and watched Turner walk to the other side of the road, which was about twenty feet wide, if that, and peer inside each culvert. The four large cylinders underneath the road were there to direct water flow, especially during the rainy season. They were in the southern tip of Florida, cypress forests and a large moving river of grass otherwise known as the Everglades. River water broke over the soft rim of Lake Okeechobee and flowed southward, dipping into a slough here and letting a thicker hammock arise there. No matter how big neighboring Miami got, one of the world's greatest mysteries still lived and breathed silently just to its west.

"Anything?" Street shouted.

"Can't tell from this side," Turner shouted back.

"I'll give you twenty dollars if you go in there and confirm what it is," Parker said.

"Some friend you are," Street said.

"Why not? Do it. You feel alive when you're in a little danger. In fact, why not quit your wannabe Miami media job and move back to Venezuela, where the news you reported was interesting, unlike here. You were alive then, and everyone knows it's dangerous there. It's perfect for you."

Street squinted. He thought about his job as a reporter at *The Gateway*, a start-up media portal with limited readership, limited revenue, limited office space, limited everything—pay especially—except for the workload. He had been working there for close to two years now, earning just a few thousand dollars a year over the US poverty line for a family of four. It was a classic Miami start-up: the boss earned a good living, the rest earned peanuts, and it had a high turnover. Still, it was better than nothing. At least it kept his reporting skills sharp and kept him from having too much idle time.

"A job is a job. Do you have one?" Street said.

Parker said nothing. Street knew his friend's wheels were turning, especially when the topic of jobs came up.

"Something on your mind, Parker? Are we talking about my job decisions? About my professional past? Gonna bring that up?" Street continued.

"Yes, I'm going to bring that up," Parker said. "Working at *The Gateway*. You need out, and if it takes a little adrenaline to boost your job-search motivation, then so be it. Can you see that thing swimming around in there? I'll bet you a hundred dollars if you go in there and prove it's a gator, you'll come out pumped up and energized, your brain recharged and primed to rethink your job reality," Parker said. "Do it. A rush from a dare may be just the thing you need to get you moving again, and heaven forbid, start living a little and stop wasting your potential."

Street thought about it and shrugged. "Why is it that those without jobs always have the best career advice?" he asked, grinning at his friends. He approached Parker. Invaded his personal space. "Maybe you're right. Maybe it's time to get my résumé out there. In the meantime, shut the fuck up, start your own job search, and have a brew."

Parker lowered his eyes and saw a cold beer bottle jamming into his gut. He took hold of the ice-cold ale, which had a label he didn't recognize. Cool streams of water from the chilled bottle streaked with warmer sweat stains on his muddied hand.

"Where did this come from?" Parker asked, taking a sip.

"From Poland," Street said. "Cheers."

"No, I mean where did you buy it? Whatever. Thanks, man," Parker replied, checking out the foreign beer label. "You're all full of surprises."

Street stared back into the culvert and could make out the shape of the thing deep inside, though the darkness made it impossible to really be sure it was an alligator.

"One hundred dollars to feel alive, and it's not a lot of money," Turner said, standing shoulder to shoulder with Parker. "Parker's right. You thrive in dangerous places and sink when stagnant, like you're doing now. Just think about how much more you could have stashed away if you went along with your old coworkers when you worked at the big financial newswire in

Venezuela. Remember? That's always been on my mind, Street. You had a good job, but you avoided being too risky and look what happened."

"There's a difference between taking risks and breaking the law. That was the case in Venezuela," Street said, giving them his back. He stared down the rural road. Nothing. Not a sound or hint of a car or anything. Just the chirp of a cardinal in a nearby tree, a soft sound heralding the arrival of late afternoon and early evening.

"So take a little risk now and enjoy living. Take the bet," Parker said. "You may be wrong. After all, nobody is following us."

Street stared at Parker. Just stared at him. Parker was outgoing and vocal but often afraid of conflict, yet this time, he was holding Street's stare and showing no signs of looking down.

"Whatever, Parker. At least I had a good job then and still have something I can call work today."

Ever the diplomat, Turner chimed in. "That's enough. Here's how this is going to happen. Street goes in there and takes a picture of it with his phone. If it's a gator, Parker you pay him. He needs the money, and if it means going under a drain . . ."

"Technically, it's a culvert," Parker interrupted.

"Great. A concrete culvert," Street said, staring back at Parker, then nodding to Turner. "One culvert critter coming right up. I prefer crispy twenty-dollar bills, and if it is a gator, toss in a twelve-pack of this fine Polish ale."

"Deal," Turner said. "Why Polish ale?"

"To make you search for it. Now, throw me my phone. It's in my bag."

Parker scurried over to the Jeep. "Which bag? You've got several here. And why are you always out here with so many backpacks?"

Street said nothing and stared at his friends. Parker was unemployed, and Turner worked as a tenant representative for a big commercial real estate firm downtown—a job that locked him into money. Street knew Turner would have helped Parker out with a job, but Parker didn't have the real estate license needed to handle such work, and, more importantly, it took forever before those commission checks started rolling in. Turner was smart. Street was sure. Parker wasn't slow, either. Not as pensive and reserved as Turner, and sometimes he shot off at the mouth, probably because he was nervous and insecure about being unemployed. He was always trying to dodge attention away from finance-related and self-esteem issues, and that made him appear dumber than he really was. As different as they both were, they were united against Street that day. He was going under that bridge.

"It's the bag on the driver's seat. Grab my phone and toss it to me and not over the bridge into the swamp, please." Parker threw the phone underhanded, softball style, and Street caught it. He looked up to the sky. "Guess I need a new mess to get into," Street said to no one in particular. He adjusted the brightness of his phone and raised the volume. He checked it to see if he had plenty of battery life and then turned the phone over to review it in general, looking like a cop in an action movie fiddling with a handgun during a lull in a final scene gun battle.

"Back in a few." He bent over in the waist-deep water and plodded under the bridge. "Oh, and keep an eye out for that black SUV. It will be back." He was out of sight.

Street pictured the scene above and was able to make out bits and pieces of their conversation. Turner would be pacing between Street's point of entry and the other side of the road, looking for an SUV. Parker would be worried about being followed as well. They allayed their fears by focusing on Street.

"Should we go down there and check on him?" Turner asked.

"You want to follow him in there?" Parker asked.

"You owe him a hundred dollars for at least trying. You know he's strapped for cash ever since he came back home from Venezuela. Everyone knows he got fired and not laid off. Apparently, his work buddies hatched some scheme down there, and Street refused to go in on it. So they canned him fearing he'd blab about it."

Street eavesdropped a little more.

"You're right. We'll each pitch in fifty bucks," Parker said.

Street laughed.

"Well, let's just keep an eye on him," Turner said.

Turner walked back to the side of the road where Street would exit. He leaned down and peered over the side of the road. "Holy shit!" he said. "It's a gator!"

Deeper in the culvert, Street snapped on the phone's flashlight and pushed ahead. He heard Turner's muffled cries but couldn't make out the words. Then he saw the object in question and froze. It had moved a bit. Whatever it was, it had moved against the current since he saw it last.

"Did you just swim?" Street moved closer, shining the phone's light in front of him. The shape of the object was clear. The details of teeth and scales just below the surface were even clearer. Mystery solved. It was an alligator. Mystery yet to be solved: was it eight feet or ten? Either way, it was a big boy.

Street inched closer to the alligator and aimed the smartphone at the reptile. Its head moved sideways, its lateral eye getting a clear view of Street. He stared at the animal. It stared back, and Street snapped a picture. Success. Up ahead, he saw Turner far away on the banks of the creek staring inside.

Street turned off his phone stood in the darkness. The light coming in from the other end of the tunnel etched a clear silhouette of the gator's head. He stood there, staring at it. Then with one quick movement, he raised both hands to touch the top of the culvert. One hand cradled the phone, the other free.

"What the hell am I doing in here?" he asked the alligator. "Tell me that. Am I overcompensating for being chickenshit in the past?"

The alligator had moved sideways to get a good look at Street. It stared back at him laterally.

"Why am I asking this to something with a brain the size of a walnut? You're not going to help me, are you?"

The alligator said nothing.

"Screw it." He moved closer to the alligator and stared at it.

"Damn Turner and Parker. Bastards were right. I do feel pretty alive down here." With the free hand, he slapped the water. His hand landed on the surface with a meaty smack, as if he had struck the rear of a work horse. A couple of fingers scraped the gator's scaly back. The reptile roiled in the water in front of him, turned and swam out of the culvert. When the surface settled, Street saw the large and powerful tail snaking away from him and out of the small tunnel. Turner tiptoed away from the water's edge as the massive creature swam to the cover of nearby trees.

Street followed the alligator out from under the bridge, climbed back up onto the road, and crossed over to see his friends.

After a few seconds of processing, Turner spoke first.

"I can definitely vouch that it was a gator," he said. "Not sure how you got it out of there, but I saw it swim out with my own eyes." Turner stared at him. "We forget you have a crazy side to you."

"Well, I did move to Venezuela once," Street said.

After a moment, Parker handed Street the money.

Street took it. "Beer and wings are on me at my house." He walked to the back of his Jeep and stuffed the money into a backpack. Then he grabbed a Polish ale, cracked it open, and took a sip when he heard a shout.

"Stop!" Turner yelled.

"Whoa! Don't move another inch," Parker followed.

Street looked across the road. A black SUV, the mysterious follower, was overshooting a three-point turn. It was inches from reversing into a small curbside sinkhole the driver couldn't see and possibly falling over the edge into the swamp. One more lurch backward, and the vehicle would be in trouble.

"Don't move back another inch, or you'll go over," Street shouted.

The brake lights flashed on, and the car halted with a sudden jerk. White rear lights let Street know the car was still in reverse, though it remained motionless. He approached the truck and gave a respectful but solid knock on the back door.

"Move forward! Loop Road isn't a good place to be stuck, and getting a tow truck will take hours."

Street walked up toward the driver's window, expecting a simple greeting and small talk typical of these situations, which in the rural Florida Everglades would blend gratitude with a message as to who was armed and who was not.

Street stared at the window, which remained closed. All he saw was his reflection in the tinted glass. The SUV remained motionless, but the engine let all know it was alive and ready to move, similar to a big cat waiting for prey.

"Hello?" Street said.

Nothing. The vehicle remained still. After a couple of seconds, a slight jerk let Street, Parker, and Turner know the driver had shifted from reverse to drive. The entire forest seemed to jump at the changing of the gears, including Parker and Turner. Street took a step forward.

"Are you all right?"

Nothing from the SUV, save for the hum of the motor. A second later, it crept forward and then sped off at a surprisingly swift speed. Another second later, it slowed again, and the SUV honked. Both the driver's and passenger's windows rolled down. A man's hand jutted out of the passenger window, and a woman's shot out of the driver's window. Both waved in gratitude. Street took note of their clothes—a blouse of some sort and jewelry on the woman's hand. A rolled-up Oxford shirt sleeve revealed a middle-aged Caucasian man's arm. They were definitely not out in the Everglades to hike. Then the black SUV sped down the road. The driver's window remained open. Street saw a shadow of a face in the side mirror looking back at him. He couldn't make out any details. No eyes, no smiling teeth, no hair color to identify— just a shape. Then the window closed, and the SUV was gone. He took note of it. A Ford Expedition. Florida tags. Street stared at the tag numbers. He remembered them.

"Is that the one that was following us?" Turner asked.

"That's the one," Street said. "Whatever. It's out of here. And so are we."

Parker and Turner hopped into the Jeep, while Street made sure all the bags and gear were secure in the vehicle's bed. Then he jumped into the driver's seat and cranked up the engine.

Clouds were building above them. Every plant and animal and every square inch of water and life was either transpiring, sweating, or evaporating moisture into the air. A cool breeze aloft would collide with warm and wet air, and the sky would explode into a storm and drift over Miami, unleashing wind and rain in its way. "Good thing we got the top on," Street said. He sped off.

They headed east, and Parker eventually broke the silence. "Why did you go after that alligator?"

Street didn't say anything for a few seconds, and then he briefly looked at Parker in the rearview mirror. "Sometimes there's only one way out of a dark place, and that's straight through the monster. Why did you offer me that bet to see if it was an alligator?"

"To see if you had the balls," Parker said.

Street didn't say anything.

"Look, Street. We don't know exactly what happened in Venezuela, but whatever it was, you have to put it behind you," Parker said. "You have the spine. You just proved it to us. You prove it every time you come out here to the Everglades."

A hook of lightning let the swamp know the sky could absorb no more moisture. Time to send water and energy back to the earth. The first drops began to fall.

"He's right, you know," Turner said from the passenger seat.

Street's phone rang. Unknown number.

"Hang on," he said, answering the call on speaker.

"Hey, Street," an English accent came through.

"Ian? Is that you? Speaking of Venezuela—"

"You in that swamp pissing about?" Ian interrupted.

"You know me, boss," Street said. "How's Caracas?"

"I haven't been your boss in a while. We'll cut up in a few minutes, but I got some bad news."

"Shoot," Street said, waiting to hear whatever Ian, his old boss, mentor, and friend had to say.

"Violence is out of hand down here, everybody knows that, but now it's getting weird in some cases, even with all these protests and growing coup rumors. Seems less random. Americans are missing. This guy Roland Spradling has just vanished and is presumed dead, and his wife, Pennie, was found running down a slum stairwell screaming and naked. She jumped in front of a bus and killed herself before anyone could help. Another young couple—and these two I knew—Zachary and Deborah Tagle, are unaccounted for."

Street said nothing for about a minute. He glanced at Parker and Turner. "Old colleague," he mumbled. Then he turned his attention back to Ian, swallowing hard.

"Doesn't sound like typical express kidnappings," Street said. Anyway, I remember the Spradlings. He was in finance or accounting. I knew Pennie from Caracas and from here. She was from South Florida. Her mom lives not far from me. I haven't seen her in a long time but Jesus," Street said, taking a moment to breathe and stay composed, but he couldn't. "Jesus! Where did she kill herself?"

"Near Petare," Ian said. "You need a moment?"

"No," Street said, though he took a moment to process the information. Then he spoke more calmly. "Petare? Foreigners don't venture down there. Something's wrong. What do the Tagles do down there?" Street asked, sighing hard and regaining more composure.

"Zachary is in consumer products, or what's left of it down there. He wasn't just some brand manager but was in supply chain or something like that. Police know nothing, of course. The place is lawless. Anyway, I just thought you should know, in case you knew them well. Think twice about coming down here again. I know you've been thinking about coming back. Everyone knows that. Everyone knows you can't afford to live in Miami anymore."

"You're telling me not to come? That's like an engraved invitation to get me back down there," Street said.

"Are you sure you want that?"

"Come back down? Yes, I'm sure if there is an opportunity," Street said, clicking the phone off speaker mode.

"It'd be hard for you to get a job," Ian said. "It's hard for anyone, especially you."

"You still bringing that up? Look, I didn't want to get in trouble. I don't regret it."

"Remember where your play-it-safe attitude got you. How are they paying you at *The Gateway*?"

"Just keep me posted, Ian." Street hung up. He sighed again, exhaling hard. No need to keep his two friends guessing about the phone conversation they had just heard.

"Some people I knew in Venezuela were murdered. Another couple is missing. Details are murky. If it were random kidnappings, thieves would have them hand over their money and kill them right then and there, but it didn't go down that way. Nothing adds up, but then again, few things do down there these days."

Turner spoke first. "Street, I just heard you say Pennie Spradling is dead."

Street said nothing.

"When did you see her last?"

"I saw her in Caracas with her husband lots of times."

"That's not what I meant."

"I know what you meant. We broke up years ago. Just before she got married," Street said, looking in his rearview mirror. Nothing but empty road behind them and ahead. "It didn't work out."

"She was crazy about you," Turner said. "She felt safe around you. All that stuff about you never being able to afford her was in your head, dude. Money can't make a girl feel safe, and you know that. Self-doubts create sad, self-fulfilling prophecies."

They all rode in silence for a spell. Then Parker said, "Street, we're here for you, bud. It took balls living down there. Most people flee that place, but you thrived in it. Not sure why you can't muster up the courage to leave either that psycho girlfriend of yours or these lame jobs in this city and go back there or somewhere like it."

"First of all, don't badmouth Brianna, and second of all, we've all known each other since the first grade, and you know my situation. I need financial stability right now, but I am thinking about it," Street said. Both friends shook their heads and laughed.

"What's there to think about?" Parker asked. "You're withering away here, wasting your talent. You used to cover major events, economic crises, elections, and politics, and all sorts of crazy shit. Now you're writing about people leasing office space around town for a fraction of the pay. And why didn't you go along with your coworkers down there? They didn't get caught."

"It doesn't matter anymore," Street said.

"You were alive down there, just like you felt in that culvert," Turner said.

"It did feel good," Street said. "You're right. How did you know?"

"We know you."

CHAPTER

3

Street Brewer stared at his computer screen on a Friday afternoon just a few days after chasing the alligator out of the culvert. He was typing away like all journalists do—fast, focused and using simple vocabulary. He was working on a feature-length story on Latin America's economies, and the hard part of the work was over. He had finished the reporting, all the phone calls, all the live interviews, the follow-up questions, and had checked all his facts. The writing was the easy part. The downhill run after the uphill climb of reporting. He breathed a sigh of relief that the heavy lifting was over. Almost.

Brent Drum, his boss and publisher, stared at him from his glassed-in office at *The Gateway*.

"What are you working on?" Brent asked.

"Some light fiction," Street said.

"Plot synopsis?"

"Debt burdens and US interest rates. A little boring but relevant. Slow at first, but it ends with a bang, where I move into one of these empty offices and a graphic designer moves into another."

Street wrote and edited stories in the office's open room, a common area for the incubatory firm. Brent ran the business end behind Street in his small office with transparent walls. There were two other offices at *The Gateway*: one for Wallace Lockwood, the owner who lived in New York and rarely came to Miami, and another that also remained empty, of people that is. It had a desk with the latest hardware packed with all software needed to lay out and upload the publication online as well as handle photos and other imagery, and even prep it for printed editions when needed. It also served as a storage area for stacks of boxes with printed copies of the magazine that were distributed for free at big events or left in select high-traffic office lobbies. Copies of special reports and publications and pens, notepads, coffee, coffee filters, a water cooler, spare chairs, and a slew of other supplies left it too cluttered for human occupation.

"You'll have your own space in time, my young friend, in time," Brent said, noticing Street eyeing the empty offices. "So, tell me more about this story we're running."

"It's a nail-biter, a real page-turner on Latin American economies and US interest rates. You wanted it by Friday, which would be today," Street said. "It can't be late if it's on the editorial calendar. The advertisers are expecting it. No story, no money."

"When will you be finished?"

"In about half an hour. By the way, did you review my story ideas? My ideas for some investigative reporting around town? And all story ideas should be mine, you know? You don't want sales and editorial mixing. Conflict of interest."

"Not yet, chief, not yet. But trust me, *60 Minutes* will be knocking on your door to hire you in due time. You'll get full editorial control in a month or so. It's hard to let go of it, you know, to let go of being a one-man show, but your time is coming."

"So in the meantime, you want me to give an interview to your friends' companies who take out ads in *The Gateway* and pay us to host executive roundtables, which is where the real money comes in. I make your friends look good in a feature-length story fueled with wimpy questions. You and Wallace end up with money, but all I'm left with is a story sample that any real editor would laugh at."

"Come on! I only had to do that once," Brent said. "Sometimes you've got to be flexible to pay the bills, including your salary. Don't be such a purist." Brent's shaved head, tight goatee, and blue eyes could be intimidating one minute and jovial the next. He was a big guy. Not hulking but solid and athletic. One of those guys who came across smart and a little volatile. Like an intelligent but loose cannon all the other tough kids in high school avoided one day and made captain of the football team the next.

"Well I've got to finish this feature," Street said. "Remember the story pitch? US interest rates rise, and Latin American economies find it harder to pay their dollar-denominated debts? What that means for the local importers and exporters? What companies are doing about it? It's what our readers should know. Not exactly high drama but important. It's relevant news."

"Ah yes. We'll get to it, but I did want to ask you this one favor. Could you type up a quickie on Venezuela?"

Street shook his head. "Venezuela? It's the same story: poverty, despair, and violence, and that's before it gets worse."

"Worse?"

"There'll be a constitutional crisis down the road. There's always someone who calls out a tyrant these days, especially now that the country is in default and has locked itself into crappy long-term oil deals. Hyperinflation is out of control, millions of people are fleeing, violence is hellish, and food shortages have morphed into outright chaos. Pick your plague. The place has gone biblical," Street said, and stood up. He paced the room and looked out the window. "That said, I would go down for a visit and cover the conflict in person."

"So you like getting yourself into messes," Brent said.

"Story of my life."

"Did you like living in Caracas before it was a mess?" Brent asked.

"Caracas wasn't exactly the Garden of Eden beforehand, but it was okay. Run-down city but beautiful women. Baseball. Beer and lots of outdoor stuff nearby. Uncrowded beaches with palm trees bent over sandy shorelines. Green mountains dipping into the blue Caribbean. Pristine jungles and exotic savannahs with majestic mesas. Snow-capped Andes." He walked back to his desk and pulled a baseball out of a drawer and tossed it into the air, hurling it up not like a pitcher on the mound but in the same style a basketball player would use at the free throw line.

"Wrong ball for that sport, chief," Brent said.

"I'm not playing your game, boss," Street said. He caught the ball and stopped it with a smack. Then he thought about Caracas at night, with its twinkling city lights sparkling across the many hillside slums like distant fireworks. He wondered how despite the violence and imminent collapse of basic services, there must be some strand of logic keeping the country's head above water, one force like a narrow powerline that made the difference between a bright night and utter chaos in darkness.

"Without Finance Minister Hernán Bernal keeping that president in check, acting like a go-between with the opposition, probably this administration would be booted from the country. Still, I know about as much as you do, really," Street said.

"Well, you still know who's who down there," Brent said. "Good job. Hernán Bernal. Venezuela's pragmatic go-to guy. But did you hear? He's moved over to the position of foreign minister."

"For real?" Street stood and tossed the ball on his desk.

"It's just hitting the wire now," Brent said, staring at his smartphone. "I wanted you to type up a little something on it. But if you think it's trivial…"

Street checked the news on his phone. It was true. He paced the room in a quick but relaxed gait, still reading the news.

"Interesting," he said, scrolling on his phone. He looked at Brent and then back out the window. "Something's brewing down there. If the president needs him as finance minister, then it's to slow the country's descent into financial anarchy, which is the foregone conclusion of the century. If he needs him as his top diplomat, something's building on the foreign relations horizon," Street said. "That or the president is diverting attention away from something."

"This is why we need you," Brent said. "You know your shit."

"So does Bernal. He parachutes in wherever there's trouble because he knows how to work all sides in a conflict. Always has, from his days in Congress back to his days in the jungle as a guerrilla," Street said.

He thought about the pragmatic Bernal, the voice of reason in an otherwise disastrously dogmatic government. There was a sixth man on every team, one who could suit up and wear a million different hats in front of the cameras or behind the scenes or even covertly. That was Bernal. Loudmouths and spotlight whores come and go in any country or in any business. But the true intellectual, the true architect of power, sticks around and survives if he stays smart and flexible, and if he keeps his eyes open for what he can't see, rather than what he wants everyone to see.

"A total commie in my book," Brent said. "But you sound like a fan."

Street looked at Brent's reflection in the windowpane. "Not really," he said, focusing outside one moment and on Brent the next. "Yeah, he was a communist guerrilla, which is probably cool in some retro sense, but that was decades ago. He has lots of battle scars—burns and scars from a grenade attack. He wants stability today. He's tough on drugs in the country, or he tries to be."

"Bullshit. Everyone knows the Venezuelan military uses their country as a springboard to smuggle cocaine abroad," Brent said, as he leaned back in his chair and stretched out his arms, then yawned. "The president lets them do it so they'll stay rich and happy. Rich generals make for complacent loyalists. Without a fat, dumb, and happy military backing him, the president is powerless."

"As you just pointed out, that's the president covertly encouraging smuggling, but not Bernal," Street said. "Anyway, how long will that little game last? Not long. And smuggling injects nothing into the broader economy anyway. It just enriches the pockets of fat cats. The only thing that can save the country is higher oil prices, and the only thing that can seriously push up oil prices is a concerted effort by many countries to crimp supply," Street said. "That, or a war."

"Well, whatever. Anyway, I had a story idea that could get you back in Venezuela reporting for a few days," Brent suddenly said. "Sound good?"

"Let's hear it," Street said.

Brent stood up and walked into the common area, grabbed a chair, and sat down in front of Street. "This story's right up your ally. It's on nationalism and oil companies. Nutjob president down there nationalized all the oil fields a few decades ago. Some big oil companies fled and sued. Others stayed with just minority ownership stakes. Some weren't as outraged as you would think."

"Actually, everyone was pretty pissed off," Street said.

"Yes, whatever. It's old news. Anyway, there are still some foreign oil firms there holding minority stakes in wells they paid top dollar for. Knock on some doors. Find out if the ones that left are planning to come back. And then find out if the ones that stayed are in cahoots somehow with the government, and tie this Hernán Bernal thing into it," Brent said.

"Cahoots?"

Brent shrugged, then paced as if he were coming up with ideas for a movie script. "It's a yard sale. The regime seizes control of the fields to look like a hero to the people. But to seriously produce oil today, the president will invite foreign companies and their technology back and at attractive terms, because the state-owned oil firm is just too decrepit to do it on its own anymore. Everyone wins, especially the ones that never left. Who knows? They might even get the fields left over by the ones who bolted. What do you think?"

"It sounds very, I don't know—innovative."

"Innovative?" Brent asked.

"Sounds cool if we had a travel budget. Anyway, back to the feature. I need to finish it, and the angle about oil companies and the government is an ongoing story, if it's true. Nothing is going to change in a week. I want to write about Venezuela for sure, but I don't want to miss a story on the editorial calendar, lose money, and basically see us close."

Street paused for a minute. "And even if they were in cahoots with the government, do you think they'd tell the press, especially someone from a tiny outfit nobody outside of Miami-Dade and Broward Counties has ever heard of? South Florida is not exactly a Venezuela fan base."

"I still think we should strike now, and I can squeeze a travel budget out of the powers that be. Let's find out. Use your contacts, and I'll email you some of mine. I have an old one down there. I might hit him up for money to host a roundtable, so I won't approach him for a story. He's yours. Are you up for it? Up for some investigative stuff instead of reacting to everything around you like when you were a wire reporter?"

"You give me today to tidy up the Latin American debt story, give me a raise and one of these empty offices, and you've got a deal," Street said.

"Good," Brent said. "Except for the raise and the office."

"Brent, I gotta let you know that I might look for work elsewhere. I mean I know start-ups can take off and we all win, but…"

"I got it, I got it. We land this story, we expand our coverage beyond South Florida, and we finally begin to grow. Our market is small, mainly Latin American headquarters of companies based here in Miami, but we can grow with more hard-hitting stories, and I mean grow across the Americas."

Street didn't say anything. He opened a web browser and began checking out the price of airline tickets to Venezuela.

"Street, you worked at a wire service for years in Latin America before coming home here," Brent went on. "Your old company went bankrupt because the firm was too bulky, but we're sleek, meaning we'll grow, and when times are bad, we can weather economic downturns. And when times get really good, you get an ownership stake."

Street said nothing. He had heard promises of ownership stakes in the past and refused to entertain them until they became a signed and sealed reality. He checked his email, flight information to Caracas, and then he broke his silence. "By the way, how do you have contacts in the Venezuelan oil industry?"

"The guy running the Worldwide Oil & Gas office down there used to work in the United States years ago. I met him long ago at a western hemisphere energy industry conference."

"The one in San Diego?"

"That's the one."

"Where were you working?"

"A West Coast monthly business magazine in Oregon."

Street stood and looked out the window. The office was in a small building in downtown Coral Gables, a wealthy Miami suburb, facing Giralda Avenue, just off the city's locally famous Miracle Mile. He could see the airport. Planes swooped down just to the north, making their descent into Miami International Airport. He caught sight of one taking off. American Airlines, maybe headed for Santiago or Rio or São Paulo or the Caribbean. He didn't know. He just wanted to be on a plane and going somewhere.

"I'll do this story on one other condition. I go to Caracas for as long as I need. I do the interviews in person. No phone interviews. I travel for once. Also, you pay for another trip next month so I can follow up what Hernán Bernal is up to, or better yet, what the president has in store for him. Deal?"

"Perfect. That's exactly what I wanted to hear," Brent said. "See? We're already growing! But I need the story yesterday."

"I'll have it. Nicely recorded on my phone."

"Don't risk getting it robbed," Brent said, rooting around in his desk drawer. "Use the company's digital recorder."

"Thanks, but I'll use my phone or my own recorder."

"Not that boxy cassette player. I know you think it's cute, but it makes the company look bad," Brent said.

Street sometimes recorded interviews on an old cassette recorder, mainly for sentimental reasons but also to see how long he could keep using it. The old relic, given to him by an old relic of a reporter as a gag when Street was fresh out of college, could still record nicely. He used digital recorders and his smartphone at interviews to look professional, but especially in dangerous places, that boxy cassette recorder from another era did just fine, as long as his supply of tapes lasted. Street walked to his desk and took it out of the drawer. It was massive and old, so old that it was arguably cool again. He set it down and stared at the digital item Brent was offering.

"That thing is not traveling with you to Venezuela. Use this. That's a fucking order. And don't use your phone. If it gets stolen, *The Gateway* has to buy a new one, and I can't tell Wallace that."

"Wonderful," Street said. "Whatever, thanks. I'll use it and get us a good oil conspiracy story, though it may take a while to line up an interview. Oil executives aren't exactly media-friendly." He grabbed some pens, paper, and a few files from his desk. "You book the ticket, and I'll go," Street said. "I'm out for the rest of the day. I'll need clean laundry for the trip, and I'll give my Latin American debt story one final read before it goes live."

He headed out the door of the small office. Before he left, he noticed Brent pulling out a cell phone and dialing.

"Street's on his way," he heard Brent say.

Curious at hearing his name, Street stood in the doorway to listen in. The carpet and acoustics in the hallway outside of the office allowed for silent walking. The building's maintenance worker, who spoke no English, always tinkered on the wiring or lights or whatever else needed fixing just outside the door. The man scared the hell out of anyone in the office by popping in without making a sound. Look behind, nobody's there. Look again and there's a guy on a ladder changing light bulbs or painting something.

"Yeah. Should be down there sometime early next week. He'll come back with the right story, and that's your job, by the way."

Silence.

"He lived down there and has contacts. He can pick up other stories while he's in your neck of the woods down in Venezuela with the recorder I gave him, and I mean really important other stories, you know? The real stories. Oh, and maybe we can pick up a special Venezuela edition and add in this Bernal angle—and keep the company in the black."

Wallace on the other line, Street thought. Always worrying about costs. Was Wallace in Venezuela? Doubtful.

"Nope. He doesn't tell the whole world what he's working on."

Street listened for more.

"He's a Boy Scout," Brent said. "Probably never broke a law in his life. Keep an eye out for him. He's on the way."

Street frowned at talk of whether he had a record or not and then let it go. Brent was probably talking to his friend and Street's upcoming interview target. He walked off. The maintenance man moved quietly down the hall. Street nodded at him. The man nodded back in a deferential manner.

CHAPTER

4

Heavy traffic didn't bother Street Brewer that afternoon. He didn't even think about honking when a young woman in the car ahead of him missed a green turn arrow in order to attend to her urgent texting and giggling. He was off to Caracas, and before that, he had the weekend, a weekend with Brianna. He focused on the positive.

Forty-five minutes after leaving work, he parked at his building in Miami's Coconut Grove village on South Bayshore Drive, a sliver of road running alongside Biscayne Bay lined with sleek, luxury condominium buildings that overlooked sailboats, blue water, and swaths of green parks and bike paths. Autumn Crest Apartments stood out from the others. The six-story building was squat, unpainted, and downright dirty with black water stains streaking down the exterior, which made it look more like an unimportant bureaucratic office in an emerging economy when viewed next to glittery new condo towers. A misplaced suspect in a botched jail lineup. The balconies appeared to sag, making the building appear unsafe, though it was very sturdy, having weathered decades of hurricanes. Plus, the views made up for the cheap and outdated appliances, especially the old dishwasher, which failed to clean even breadcrumbs from a plate.

Street hopped out of the Jeep and entered the building by the laundry room. One dryer hummed away. An empty clothes basket rested on a large table, and a young woman in her early twenties wearing a dive-shop T-shirt was folding jeans and smiled at Street. Up on the fourth floor, Street entered his apartment, which was large—much larger than they made them nowadays. He walked onto the balcony and stared at the white-scrubbed sailboats moored off Dinner Key. Small, green barrier islands sprouting with palm trees gave them cover. The water was blue and calm.

From his balcony, Street caught sight of the marina dock were he kept his own boat, a twenty-eight-foot Whitewater center console fishing boat nestled in a slip between larger trawlers and sailboats. No matter how tight times were financially, he maintained his boat—a gift he bought himself when money was flowing. Time to grab some afternoon sun out on Biscayne Bay.

Before he could leave, the phone rang. He walked indoors from the sunlit balcony into the shade to see who was calling. It was Jenkins, his cousin from Sarasota, Florida, on the state's west coast. Jenkins was three years older than Street and always seemed to have legal issues. He was one of those guys who was constantly in some stage of prosecution—a night in jail for a DUI, or possession, or in some sort of pretrial release program, where he had to piss-test in a cup, or check in with a court official, though he was never sentenced. Though Street had fond memories of spending his childhood summers with Jenkins, as they got older, Street noticed that he was always out and about, always paying his bar tabs, always had a place to stay and always had money to pay bills but never had a real job. Street told him a few years ago over beers to go ahead and become a dealer because he looked the part. He used to think Jenkins never took him seriously. Until recently.

"Street, dude, I've been busted up here in Sarasota."

"Again?" Street asked, hardly paying attention.

"Yes, again, dude."

"What for this time? DUI? Public drunkenness?"

"Possession with intent to distribute."

"Whoa, Jenkins! That is serious!"

"Yes, well, you told me once to be a drug dealer."

Street laughed under his breath at the term *drug dealer*. He thought about the twentieth century stereotype of a pusher on a street corner hacking his wares from a trench coat.

"This isn't a time to kid around, Jenkins. I never said…"

"I'm not kidding. They found enough cocaine to put me away for a while."

"Wait, cocaine?" Street said. "Not pot?"

"Cocaine," Jenkins said. "But you have to believe me. I was in the wrong place with the wrong crowd. Look, Street, I wasn't the instigator. I won't go into the details."

"Not over the phone, thank you."

"Well, I called your dad. I know he's a lawyer and all, and I know this isn't his area of expertise, but I think he can help. No one on our side of the family can afford a good lawyer, so your mom and dad will be here in Sarasota to help and to catch up as well."

Street checked his phone. There was, indeed, a missed call from his father. He told Jenkins to hold on and checked the voice mail. It was true. His parents were headed to Sarasota and asked Street to keep an eye on their big house in Coconut Grove.

"This will pass. Just like all things," Street said. Another call came through. It was an unknown number. He ignored it and then stared out his window and across the bay. The low-angled sun enhanced the blue shades of the water, contrasting the bay with the whiteness of the boat hulls and sending sparkles of light to roll across the water and vessels.

"It's going to take some time to clear this up, considering I have a record," Jenkins said.

"Minor stuff," Street said. "Anyway, I'm going to Caracas to do some reporting," he added, jerking open the dishwasher, not really caring how hard the plates rattled with the door swinging down.

"Oh really? When do you leave?"

"In a couple of days."

"Are you taking Brianna with you? I haven't seen her in a while."

"Too dangerous."

"Good call. She'll be fine here. Tell her your no-good cousin Jenkins says hello. I will see you both when I am in town again."

"No more talking on the phone. Take care, Jenkins."

Street enjoyed a brief silence, and then his phone rang again. This time it wasn't an unknown number but Brianna. Street answered with a corny joke.

"Thanks for calling back. I'm in town for the weekend and want to seriously party. Let's go for six eight balls." Street kicked the dishwasher closed, waiting to hear Brianna's response.

"Jenkins?" Brianna said. "When did you get out of jail? Are you in town, and what are you doing with Street's phone?"

"Funny," Street said, blowing it off. "This is Street, not Jenkins. Ready for an afternoon boat ride?"

"All you guys sound alike," She said. "As to the boat ride? Maybe."

Street felt a little stung by her first comment but turned on by the way she said maybe.

"Maybe yes or maybe no?"

"Maybe I'm here at the marina now," she said.

The mix of jealousy, confusion, and mistrust at being mistaken for Jenkins vanished. Ten minutes later, Street was at his boat slip with a cooler of beer, water, snacks, and fruit as well as a backpack filled with towels and sunscreen. Brianna lay on the transom in a very small bikini, catching the warm late-afternoon rays of sunshine. Warm highlights in her dark hair streaked down to partially veil her bluish-green eyes. She turned her head, saw Street, and sat up. A man aboard a new sailboat in a nearby slip with his wife and three small children in life vests took a break from unloading gear from the boat and stared at Brianna. She made eye contact with him, and he stood up straight and jutted out his chest. Brianna smiled. The man's wife laughed at her husband's gaping jaw.

"You're late," Brianna said as Street arrived. "You need a new watch." She stood up, kissed him on the lips, took the cooler from him and sat back down.

Street jumped onto the transom of the boat. His side edged lower in the water, while Brianna's side rose. She hopped to her feet to avoid falling overboard, and the young man on the sailboat finally looked away from Brianna and turned his focus back to his kids and amused wife.

Street scurried to the driver's bench, started the engines, and let them remain in idle. He released the bow, spring, and stern lines. The boat was now free to move forward, backward, and sideways, though Street wasn't too concerned. There was very little wind and current that day to nudge the

Whitewater into the dock. He put the boat in reverse, backed out of the slip, geared into forward, and headed out to Biscayne Bay.

"Should we go to the sandbar?" Brianna asked.

"To the flats? Sure," Street said. "Let me just give the engines a quick run. You ready?"

"Ready!"

"Hang on." Street gunned the throttle and sent the sleek-but-heavy boat shooting across Biscayne Bay in the direction of Stiltsville, a small cluster of pastel homes built on stilts in the flats, which no one seemed to own anymore. He took in their soft colors and their allure of Miami's various yesteryears and continued toward the open ocean. A large sportfishing yacht crossed Street's bow several yards away. The driver, a short, fat man, stared at Street and then waved at him, nodding in recognition that he had come too close.

"It's all good," Street waved back.

The Whitewater sliced through the large wake. Brianna didn't even bounce. Off he charged toward the Atlantic, the smell of salt in the air getting thicker as the boat raced deeper into the open ocean and away from Biscayne Bay. Street ran the boat hard, giving the engines time to work out for about twenty minutes before circling back to the bay's protected, shallower waters and onto the Nixon Beach Sandbar, a flat just off Key Biscayne. It was often packed with people having cookouts on grills mounted on transoms while tossing footballs and paddle-boarding in the sun. That Friday afternoon, however, was quiet, with one or two other boats out, and they were at least a hundred yards apart.

Street killed the engines and let the boat drift. He reached into a cooler under the driver's bench and grabbed two beers, opened them, and handed one to Brianna. Then he walked to the bow of the center console, a bare-bones boat with little forward seating and low-rising rails, designed for serious fishing rather than for pleasure boating. He plopped down and relaxed.

"Might as well stretch out a bit," he said. "Cheers, Brianna." Their bottles clinked.

"Cheers, Street," Brianna said. She stared at the back of the boat and didn't take a sip. She sighed and looked across the bay toward the city horizon.

Her eyes sparkled and her hair glowed in the warm sunlight, but her expression soured.

"Street, can we talk?"

"Shit," Street mumbled.

"It's just that I noticed you have new outboard boat engines. They look expensive."

"They set me back a pretty penny, but it's all good. Three hundred horsepower each. Two-stroke engines. They weigh less than a four-stroke and have fewer moving parts. They get up to plane in a heartbeat. Both of them do!"

"Sounds just like you, Street. Light, quick, and off in a heartbeat. Street, those engines cost tens of thousands of dollars each when you factor in all the rigging and stuff, and you live in a creaky old apartment building. Why did you buy them when the last ones were perfectly okay?"

"They weren't perfectly okay."

"Whatever, you need to set your priorities, you know, get a decent-paying job and move into a better place. You're not in college anymore. I don't know what you earn, but I do know reporters in this town don't earn that much. I've done my homework."

"That makes one of us."

Brianna stared at the engines and then off into the horizon. "Street, I'm just saying your finances and career choice concern me. You live and dress like you're broke, and then you do shit like this," she said, pointing to the engines.

"My shitty salary is temporary, and you know I have savings," Street said. He stared at the horizon as well. A deep-blue sky and darker-blue waters let him know sunset was coming.

"Past salaries bought this boat and future salaries will help me tinker with it for years to come. Better a shitty apartment and a fine boat than the other way around, at least for now. Again, my current cash flow is temporary."

Brianna shook her head. "Street, things have been temporary with you for a while now, and I've known you for years."

"Look, we've been a couple for about a year or so, but we've known each other since we were kids," Street said. "Have you ever known me to fail? To just give up?"

"No, but one day you seem to be playing things too safely in terms of your career or where you pay rent, and then the next day, you're a little reckless with expenses, like with these engines. I don't know. It seems like you're hiding something from me."

Street stared off into the horizon. He thought about the alligator back in the Everglades. He thought about Venezuela and his aging apartment building. Then he looked at his boat. Its new outboard engines were fastened firmly to the stern, daring him to throttle them to the fullest and race to the horizon.

"I like what I do for a living. No one succeeds in doing what they hate. Faking it gets you only so far," Street said.

"And being a purist guarantees success?"

"I don't know," Street said. "Anyway, let's go back to dry land for some food and conversation. I've got some travel plans I want to tell you about," he said.

Two hours later, Street was eating fresh grilled dolphin and fries at the Grouchy Grouper, his favorite dive bar in Coconut Grove. Brianna sat across from him, nibbling on a shrimp salad. They ate in silence for a little while, and then Street spoke.

"I'm off to Caracas next week to sniff around for stories. If I land some good interviews that produce good clips, I stand a better chance of landing a higher-paying job or even lucrative freelance clients."

"That's all good, Street," Brianna said. "But that means that any real money, if it even comes, is light-years away."

"It's a start."

"Yes, and what if an offer comes from a big newswire at a Caracas bureau while you're down there?"

"One won't."

"What if one does? Where does that leave us? You'll abandon a steady high-paying but boring job for excitement and never come back. That's the problem, Street. I need someone who can navigate us to financial security and stability here in Miami."

"Stability," Street repeated with a slight head shake. "Everyone wants it. Doesn't really exist. Anyway, I'm trying. Don't I get points for effort?" Then his phone rang, an unknown caller appearing again on his smartphone. He screened it. "Define stability," Street said.

Brianna stared at him. "Minimum?"

"Yes, minimum," Street said.

"At least a three-bedroom, two-bath house with a pool in about a year, preferably in Coral Gables."

"You know, you were right about career risks and you were right when you said I need to work on my appearance and come across a little more mature. But a house in Coral Gables in my early thirties? Fewer people at any age are pulling that off than you think," Street said.

"What's that supposed to mean?"

"Financial security is important, but face it, most people in this town are making themselves appear richer than they are, maxing out credit cards or stealing from Peter to pay Paul. Appearances aren't what they seem. In fact, many are outright lies," Street said. "Appearances can be deceitful," he added.

"That's what I just said a little while ago on the boat. You're bold and adventurous to the point of being reckless one day and totally risk averse the next. You seem like you're hiding something."

"And so are you, Brianna," Street said.

Just then, his phone rang again.

"Maybe it's Jenkins," Street said. He looked at his phone. Another unknown caller. He ignored it. Nothing out of the ordinary, until it rang again. He picked it up and saw unknown flashing on the screen again. He wondered if a creditor was calling.

"Aren't you going to answer it?" Brianna asked.

"It could be for you. Do you want to answer it?" Street said. Brianna said nothing. Street answered with a curt hello.

"Street Brewer?" a female voice asked.

"Speaking."

"My name is Cyra Octavia Harred, and I'm an associate of Wallace Lockwood. I would like to—"

"Hi Cyra, can I get you to call me back? I'm in the middle of—"

"Out at dinner right now in the Grove, I get it. I'll call you back tomorrow. I thought I caught you alone. Just answer your phone when you have some time to yourself and when an unknown caller is ringing. Regards to Brianna."

"Whoa, whoa, whoa," Street said, scanning the bar. "Who is this? Cyra who?"

Brianna perked up at Street's obvious confusion. So did a couple of nearby patrons.

The woman had hung up.

Brianna frowned. "Who was it?" she asked.

"Not sure. A Cyra somebody. Said she was an associate of the owner of my company. She knew I was out with you. A little weird, and way too personal for another bill collector."

"A bill collector? And what do you mean by 'another' one?" Brianna's fork dropped.

"It's probably an identity thief." Street stared back at the phone in a frowning, curious manner, as if the phone would telepathically convey more information about the caller. He thought about the car that had followed him into the Everglades and began connecting the dots. Someone was following him. Amateur identity thieves, he thought. He hoped.

Brianna stared out the window. She took a sip of her water and looked at Street.

The temperature felt ten degrees colder from her stare alone. Better let her break the ice, Street thought. He knew what was coming.

"Street, I don't get it. One minute you're in a crumbling apartment, and the next, you're slapping on new boat engines, and now a bill collector."

"Again, identity thief," Street said.

"Whatever," she said, pushing her salad plate away. "I just can't figure you out. Your life is always going to be interesting yet always in disarray. Face it, Street. You don't belong anywhere."

"Well, I sure as hell don't belong on a bill collector's call list," Street said. "Anyway, like I said, nothing is permanent. Better economic times will soon translate into better times for normal people like me, and not just Wall Street players. I can feel it."

"I thought you said you were due for a raise months ago and an ownership stake in the company some time afterward?"

"I know. That's what I was told."

"Did you get that in writing?"

"You know the answer to that question. Look, I didn't want to turn down a job. I just took it on vague promises, knowing I was taking a leap of faith." He gazed into Brianna's eyes. She was stunning—like a dark, mysterious beauty from some forgotten corner of Eastern Europe. "Remember how we started going out? I was just back from Caracas. I saw you in that smoky little bar around the corner and we started talking. You said you wanted out of there, so I took you on my boat to see the moon. Remember that?"

"I meant to a nicer bar," she said. "And the moon was waning."

"Well, at least I got you out of there," Street said. "I stayed the course that night."

She looked at him, then turned away and mumbled something he couldn't hear.

Street glanced around at the tavern. The walls were decked out with nautical ropes, fishing nets, buoys and decorations such as license plates, public-service placards from decades gone by and pictures of patrons on the ocean showing off freshly-caught fish. There were also small, framed pictures of former regulars who had drunk themselves to death—old Coconut Grove characters who spent their waking lives on the water, doing odd jobs or in a tavern somewhere dreaming of a better life. The bar itself looked like it came from part of a large, antiquated ship plank. Sports always dominated the television sets, and the crowd was a mix of young to middle-aged professionals, college students, and a sprinkling of local color from near-homeless fishermen to aging hippies with leftist political views and elitist bank accounts. It's lack of pretense and its rustic, ramshackle ambiance made it a nice refuge from Miami's glitz and bravado, especially since despite its beat-up appearance, the entire place was always scrubbed clean, sanitized and up to code with an exceptional draft beer selection. The grilled snapper sandwich served on toasted garlic bread was so fresh that Street could have told you how high the tide was and whether it rained that day when the fish was caught.

The brief silence held the table. Street felt the energy rise and fall. Either she would forget about the topics of today's discussion, or she would escalate the matter into a full-blown argument.

Brianna looked around the place and then out the window. "You know, if you can buy new boat engines, why not buy a new car?"

"Because I like that Jeep. It's me," Street said. He sighed. "But maybe you're right. I need something a little less adventurous, something that better protects against the elements, at least for my passengers."

"Street, it's not that I want you to take me to every event in town in a shiny Italian sports car. It's just that I'm wondering how you're going to support me and our children living like this."

"Our children? Whoa. Brianna, I'm thirty. You're even younger. Children are a long way off," Street said. And so is a ring, he thought.

"I mean, I know you're smart and capable and you do what you love, but it doesn't look good living where you live, driving what you drive, and hanging out at the same place all the time."

Street took in her words. He thought about marriage for a split second. Then he thought about Venezuela and the alligator. Maybe life in a fine house in the suburbs wasn't for him. It was just a tether to a dull existence, some bygone tradition that didn't jibe with today's economy and times. He caught himself spiraling down into a mood of bitterness and took another pull from his beer. Then he put a stop to his negative thinking. He reminded himself that he would be off to see other parts of the world in just a few days, and then he felt better. He'd be a bigger man. Brianna was being honest about what she wanted in life. Time to do likewise.

"Look, Brianna, I'm sorry. I know that financial discussions can be stressful and all, but that boat is sort of my therapy these days, and I did get a good deal on the engines. And granted I need to move to someplace better but not someplace too expensive if it means giving up travel or my boat."

Brianna was about to speak when the phone rang again. Number and caller unknown.

He looked at Brianna. "Let's put it on speaker and listen to it together. I've got nothing to hide. Let's screw with this identity thief." Street answered the phone and placed it on the table in front of Brianna.

"Hello," Street said.

"Hi, Street. This is Cyra Harred calling again to discuss something that seriously cannot wait."

"You know I'm here with my girl. There's something we want to discuss with you, too. Opportunity is knocking," Street said, winking at Brianna.

Silence on the other end of the phone. Then Cyra said, "There's only one opportunity for you, Street, and it's this call. Consider it a head start to run for your life. And I mean literally run. Talk to me when you are off speaker phone, and I mean now. I know I said tomorrow, but it can't wait."

Street grew from curious to a little alarmed. She definitely wasn't a creditor. Identity thief was still on the table.

"Was that you following me in the Everglades last weekend?"

"Following you?"

"Yeah, like you're obviously doing right now."

"So you were followed. Were there two people following you? I bet there were two, right?"

Street stayed silent.

"There were two, right? One was a man. Was the other a woman? If you got a good look at either, we might be done here."

Street said nothing.

"Later tonight then. Call me when you're alone." The caller hung up.

A surge of anger shot across Brianna's face. "What was that? Call when you're alone? Why would this Cyra be calling you twice, using your first name only? And following you? Street, this is too much drama!"

"Using my first name only? Brianna, I think that's the least of my worries. That was not a bill collector, that was a criminal," Street said, tuning out Brianna for a second, frowning at the phone. He turned it off.

"Street, if you're being followed and now harassed by some jilted psycho bitch, then you obviously slept with her and are doing a crappy job at blowing her off. And now you're busted!"

Street stared into Brianna's narrowing eyes. It was all getting to be too much and then he started to laugh. "Wow. You concluded all that after hearing that short call?" Street said, making no effort to conceal his disbelief in the situation and Brianna's reaction to it.

A phone chirped again. This time it was Brianna's. A text message came.

"Is someone harassing you, too?" Street said.

"It's just Jenkins checking in."

"Jenkins? I texted him hours ago and haven't heard from him. Why is he contacting you and ignoring me? My father is helping him, not you. Tell that idiot to contact me," Street said visibly angry.

Brianna stared at Street and then back at her phone. She typed in something and put her phone away.

"What are you talking to Jenkins about? And when I called you earlier and you thought I was Jenkins, you asked when I got out of jail. How did you know he was arrested?"

"It's not a big deal. I'll just tell him to text you," Brianna said.

"It is a big deal. You're talking to my cousin without telling me?" He shook his head, stared at the television to unscramble his thoughts—a self-imposed momentary distraction. "Are you and Jenkins…"

"Street! Jesus, no," Brianna said, staring at him.

Street couldn't tell if the stare was angry at him entertaining the idea of her cheating with his cousin or angry in a defensive manner, angry at getting caught.

"If you're into image and impressing others, he'd hardly be a step up from me, Brianna. That means financially and in pretty much any other category, though I'm sure he can pass himself off to be more successful than he really is," Street said. "He's good at this whole image thing."

Brianna said nothing.

Image, Street thought. He took a good look at himself, and then at Brianna. Whatever message he wanted to convey to the world, Brianna wanted a different one. It wasn't a question of wavelengths; it was a question of waves headed in different directions in the ocean. Brianna wanted wealth, just like everyone did, but she wanted everyone to know it. Street knew he just couldn't be that guy. Not ever. That was one thing he was sure of.

"Brianna, this is goodbye."

"What?"

"I'm not the right guy for you."

"Street. Stop right there."

"Brianna, you know what I'm talking about."

"Are you dumping me?"

"Yes."

"Wait, I'm not good enough for you?"

"You're not right for me. I'm not right for you."

"No one breaks up with me."

"I'm not breaking up; I'm saying goodbye. Tell everyone you dumped me if that will strengthen your image."

She stood up. Her jaws were clenched and her lips were pursed. Then her rigid posture suddenly relaxed, which let Street know she saw his point of view and agreed.

"Maybe it's better I don't get any deeper into this financial and emotional mess of a relationship," she said.

"Well, you hit the nail on the head there. I do tend to get myself into some pretty good messes, personal ones, especially."

She didn't even look at him with some scenario-appropriate gaze to convey a decent goodbye. She just walked away and left the bar as if she would be right back.

Street watched her go. "Goodbye, Brianna," he said. He sat there for a few minutes and let his thoughts flow, processing getting branded as a reckless underachiever. Then he threw a wad of cash on the bar to pay the bill and added a 30 percent tip.

He walked out into the streets of Coconut Grove. Its green trees covered the neighborhood's bustling cafés. In the distance, Brianna disappeared into the noise of the village. Street watched her go.

"That was coming anyway," he mumbled.

He picked up his pace, wondering why Brianna fell for him in the first place. Yes, she was right. He lived in a nice area of town and had gone to Rollins College, a solid private school up near Orlando. On paper, he had that whole upper-middle-class Miami thing going on, but in reality he was always struggling, always jumping at the first salary that came his way. He never really took the risks needed to reap true financial, professional and personal rewards. He had settled for a beautiful woman who had different priorities instead of putting his heart out there and choosing someone truly worth dying for. Maybe he should take away some lessons from this latest relationship. He enjoyed taking Brianna out and appreciated the fine tastes they shared. And she was athletic and active like him. Maybe she was right.

Maybe it was time to say goodbye to his twenties once and for all and find a new line of work. But Brianna? Nothing would ever be enough for her.

"Probably best she's gone," he said to no one, walking back to his Jeep in a nearby parking lot on Grand Avenue. A bustling Mini Mart glowed across the way. Police officers hung out there as did drug addicts and alcoholics and young people on cigarette, beer, and vape runs.

Street pulled up to the window to pay the attendant. A placard on the window announced a fixed rate of twelve dollars for parking.

"Street! How are you?" the attendant, a fit man with pale skin, sandy-blond hair, blue eyes, and an unmistakably thick Cuban accent, asked.

"Awesome as always," Street said. He knew the man did farming work in the southern reaches of the county during the day and attended the parking lot at night to make ends meet.

"For you, five dollars."

"And as always, thank you," Street replied, handing the man a crisp bill. "You're too kind."

"And you need more money. More money, better car," the man said with a smile.

"I hear you," Street said, and he turned onto Grand Avenue, waving to the attendant. "If you, Brianna, my parents, or anyone knew how much I had buried in the Everglades, you'd all die of heart attacks," he said to the road ahead of him. "Just can't spend it yet."

He looked in the rearview mirror to see if he was being followed. There was no one. He headed home.

CHAPTER

5

Venezuela's president awoke. He opened his eyes, blinked, and then closed them again, preferring to keep them sealed when he reached for the smartphone by his bed. Eyes open or closed didn't matter really. He could feel it. Bad news was waiting on two fronts on his phone. Just get it over with. He picked up the device and checked the price of oil, which had plunged in Asian trading overnight while he slept. Bad news escalated on front number one. A Chinese purchasing managers' index came in far short of expectations. One of the world's largest consumers of crude oil and a major driver behind its prices, China was seeing its economy take a breather. Add to that, the world was awash in oil. So much supply and soft demand meant low prices, and that made for a nasty cocktail for a Venezuelan leader who was behind on his bills.

Low oil prices were not what he needed that week. The world was calling him out on his most recent election, which had given him a new term not too long ago, with Washington and Western Europe saying he had rigged it. Fresh economic sanctions from abroad were sending an already crashing economy deeper into chaos, and, worse for the president, some of those sanctions were hitting powerful people who were still in his camp. Food and medicine shortages were now turning the country into some post-apocalyptic nightmare, and millions were fleeing. And add to that, central banks overseas refused to give him the gold he had stashed away in foreign reserve accounts. Seeing fistfights in trash heaps across the city was common. Protests calling not only for his ouster but for his head were even more common, taking place almost daily, and all he could do was blame the outside world for the nation's violently spectacular economic collapse. Choose your daily life-threatening disaster. Today it was oil, the one thing that could save him.

He sat up and tossed the phone to the floor. He stared at framed pictures of his ex-wives, his sons and daughters, and a few of his supporters. What would they think about him, the president of Venezuela, now? He didn't even bother checking the local news to see how many countries had joined the camp calling for his removal. He also thought about his political challengers who were younger, more popular, and smarter than he was in the eyes of the nation and the world.

"Happiness. Where did it go?" he asked the two women sleeping next to him. Still in their own dream worlds, they did not reply. He shook his head and looked around the room. Printouts of yesterday's news stories with headlines announcing thawing US-Cuban relations and the Middle East's refusal to cut oil production to drive up prices were scattered on the floor, and depressed him even more. Don't even get me started on US shale producers flooding the world with even more cheap hydrocarbons, he thought.

Then the phone rang. Bad news escalating on the second front. Hernán Bernal was calling.

"I saw the data," the president said. "That and the additional sanctions from the US."

"I'm officially your foreign minister now, but just a few days ago, I controlled the country's purse strings, or what's left of them. You know how these things go, and you don't need to be reminded. Good news tomorrow will send prices shooting right back up. Don't panic yet," Hernán Bernal said over the phone. "But you know that. React calmly to low oil prices and security issues in public. Now is not the time for surprises. Price corrections are normal, and remember, we still have friends."

"We don't have friends as rich as the US, and, Hernán, I'm no idiot. The price is going to fall for good in the long term, which is not what we need to right this sinking ship. There's just too much oil on the market."

He stared at the young women in bed. One, a brunette, was motioning to the other, a blonde, to leave. The blonde got out of bed and scurried without a sound. The president turned his back for a moment, and within seconds the blonde was already dressed and closing the door slowly and silently. He waited to hear the click of the lock but didn't want to keep Hernán Bernal waiting. Then he turned his attention back to his phone and the most competent person in his administration.

"If only I could produce oil at ten dollars a barrel like they do in the Middle East," he said. "Fucking heavy, expensive Venezuelan tar." He stumbled into the bathroom, up to the mirror, and looked into his puffy red eyes.

"All I can say now, Mr. President, is that you might want to tone down the fiery rhetoric. We don't have money to buy allies in America's backyard like we did in the past, and anything you say can draw action from Washington," Bernal said. "We just need to keep the allies we do have, basically Russia and China, and we need to keep the military happy. Just keep doing what you're doing with our officers. I don't even want to know about the details of their extracurricular smuggling operations."

"It will work out," the president said, leaning the phone against the bathroom sink faucet. "The party's not quite over." He stared at himself in the mirror. Then he looked at the brunette, who had gone back to sleep. "Somehow, this party will go on."

He turned the shower on, gave the water a second to heat up, and wondered where he would be speaking in public that day and who would make up his audience. Then he remembered it was a group of supporters in Sucre State in northeastern Venezuela. Poor farmers and oil field workers mainly.

"I'll call you right back," he told Hernán.

The president showered, got out, and toweled himself dry. He left the water running in the shower—just left it that way—and thought about the new geopolitical reality. The United States had a new president on top of an ever-evolving Congress every year, it seemed. Plus, Washington's old enemies were thawing their beef with the empire to the north one day and rekindling it the next. Hard to stay a thorn in its side in such a liquid landscape. He wondered how the leaders before him dealt with shifting realities. How would dead strongmen and deceased dictators from Latin America and the Caribbean's days of yore deal with his problems today? Any advice from the grave would be appreciated. Nothing fuels political longevity more than basking in the global limelight, and serving as a proxy battleground between superpowers brings on some pretty good limelight.

He put on his clothes: dark blue fatigues and a solid-blue military-style dress shirt with a red undershirt.. He walked back into the bedroom; stared at the brunette.

Fuck basking in the limelight, he thought. I want to be the limelight, not have someone else shine it on me at their whim.

"Do you think we're going to have to round up supporters and bus them in this time? Another artificial crowd?" he asked the brunette. He crossed the room and entered the walk-in closet to put on his boots. "What do you think, babe? Can I even drum up the crowds like I used to on my own?"

"Am I your campaign chief? How the fuck should I know?" asked an older man's voice from the room.

He walked back into the bedroom. Instead of seeing a young brunette, the president saw Hernán Bernal himself, a stern face staring down at him. The brunette sneaked out the door. Bernal caught a glimpse of her leaving, nodded to her, and paced around the room. He picked up a discarded newspaper with notes scribbled all over it. He stared at it and tossed it back to the floor. Then he picked up a magazine, one called *The Gateway*. It was in English. Bernal frowned at it, scanned it a bit, and then tossed it on a chair.

Contrasting the fatigue-clad president, Bernal stood in a solid-blue suit, a crisp white shirt, and neutral tie with blue stripes. He was always dressed in immaculate suits, normally dark and matching his black hair. Hernán Bernal's coffee-colored eyes had a calm and almost pensive nature to them, although they could turn aggressive in a heartbeat; experience as a guerrilla and a diplomat kept his emotions compartmentalized and ready for retrieval whenever the situation arose.

"Hernán. Shit. I didn't know you were here. It's just that I know what's going to happen. I'll see all those people today; they'll remind me of my roots, and I just know deep down inside I'm going to fail them. I couldn't care less about what the world thinks of me as long as I can make life better for them. They'll see right through me."

"Expect me to believe that? Do you even know your own country anymore?"

"You're goddam right I do."

"I know you care about the poor. I really do. But I think you care too much about what your enemies and pretty much everyone else in power thinks about you as well. Plus, you've demonized everyone who supports the opposition. Look, I've worked with these people for decades, in Congress and in your administration, and not everyone is a corrupt oligarch."

The president said nothing. He slumped into a desk in the corner of the room. He looked tired.

"I need oil prices to rise. I can't stand in front of those people today and fake it. They'll know by looking at me that I can't deliver to them economically and tackle crime. I need money for new housing and new food programs for one." He stared at Bernal. "And that goes for everyone in the country."

"Mr. President, oil prices are important, but sooner or later, you will need to seriously change your economic policies to do exactly what you just said. That may mean reaching out to the opposition down the road to develop non-oil sectors of the economy."

"You know the research. Oil's day is coming to an end, and I mean in a few years. It's alternative energy. Climate change. All that shit is finally adding up," the president said.

"Tell me something everyone hasn't known for decades. Relax, though. Disruption takes time or at least a little longer than whatever some jackass with an economics degree and a crystal ball says. People will drive gasoline cars for a while longer."

"There has to be a way to boost our revenue by selling more expensive oil," the president said, looking up at the ceiling.

Bernal shook his head, silencing the president with a raised finger. "There isn't a way," he said, a tone of annoyance souring his voice.

"We need some conflict. Everyone knows conflict is good for oil prices. Nothing consumes more fuel than a good war machine."

"And nothing shatters a nation, its economy, and its people more than a war. No surprises now. Slow and gradual policy changes. That's my recommendation. Understood?" Bernal's face flared red but subsided.

"Understood," the president said.

"I'll see you within the half hour. Try not to keep your supporters waiting." Bernal left.

The president was alone at last. He looked upward. "If you're bugging my room somehow, put that in your file at headquarters. No war machine for now!" he shouted at the ceiling. "Nobody even knows where we are on the map." He shook his head. "Except, of course, when you tried to oust me in a coup, which failed miserably. Remember that?"

"What's wrong now?" the young brunette woman said.

The president hadn't heard her return. He watched her in her tight yoga pants climb back into bed.

"Why are you shouting at the ceiling again? And that coup attempt was decades ago."

"Have you seen the city streets? I just need a new revenue source to calm things down. I've got more proven oil reserves than anyone else on earth, and the US needs them. Their refineries are tweaked to burn my crude. Are you listening?"

The young woman checked her nails. "Everyone knows the US has to import our crude," she said, not looking up. "They don't want to buy pricey UK crude. Just clean up shop here and start exporting more stuff besides crude. Or, heaven forbid, try and make some peace with your enemies."

"Those stupid gringos are stuck with me," the president said, blowing off her advice. "And all this is their fault. They wouldn't give me a visa when I was campaigning, for Christ's sake! They wouldn't even let me in their borders until I was president of this fucking country. They've done everything to get me out of here, calling me a threat to democracy when they ignore the fact that I won in the biggest landslide approval in our history! They're still stuck in the Cold War," the president said. He stared at the young brunette, his mistress. Half his age but light-years beyond most around him in terms of wisdom.

"What are you talking about? Stuck in the Cold War? They really aren't," the young woman said, still not looking up. She began to text on her phone. "They're at war with themselves, just like we are, though to a much lesser extent." She tossed her phone down, hopped out of bed, grabbed a newspaper clipping off the floor, and started reading.

"Well, it doesn't matter. Geopolitics is all about conflict. Managing conflict, that is. Conflict is inevitable. It can't be stopped, but it can be managed," the president said.

"And are you going to manage it for the whole world?"

"No. Look, there's always going to be conflict, and the superpowers know how to keep people fighting elsewhere in the world and away from their borders, like in proxy countries. Sometimes things don't go as planned, but generally you can meddle or even invade someplace and create a little conflict where it's convenient for you," the president said. A wave of anger shot across his face.

"Damn it!" he shouted. He had forgotten to put on deodorant. He snapped off his dress shirt and threw the T-shirt across the bathroom. It bounced off the shower curtain and landed in the shower, immediately getting soaked under the still-running water. "Fuck!"

"Blood pressure, baby, blood pressure. You're gonna give yourself a heart attack. Americans get weary of conflict. Why do we want that job? We need friends, not enemies."

"How am I going to buy new friends when oil is in the crapper? They're fracking all over the US, and half the goddamn Middle East keeps pumping like crazy to steal market share and undercut us on prices for their American masters!" He looked over his shoulder at his mistress. "Did you hear me? You're one of the few people on Earth that I can trust."

"I think the whole country just did," the young woman said, not looking up from her newspaper. "Everyone from here to Russia did."

He stopped. Turned off the water. "What did you just say?"

"You heard me. Everyone from here to Russia heard you," she said, finally looking up at him.

Suddenly, a crack broke in the ice that had gripped his mood. "That's it!" he shouted. "Russians!"

He slammed the deodorant down, grabbed a fresh T-shirt that was typical of his martial attire, and put it on. Then the blue military dress shirt.

"I'll be the Russians' best friend. I've already given them rights to oil fields in return for loans and bailouts. I'll take it a step further and turn the

Russians back into Soviets, a true global empire!" A bolt of sunshine cracked depression's grip on his mood even more.

The woman laughed. "If you can't feed your own people and take them back to some glorious past that never existed, how are you going to turn the clock back and restore Russia to its former Soviet grandeur?"

"I've got ideas," he shouted. "Get dressed. You're coming with me."

The president set out from his room, his characteristic bright-red shirt shining from within. He dashed to his presidential limo and before long, he was approaching the presidential airplane, a Russian-made Ilyushin Il-96 loaned to Venezuela by the Cuban government from better days gone by.

"Let's get this speech over with," he snapped to aides and staffers upon exiting his limo, his young lover in tow. "We've got pressing issues abroad to deal with."

Getting to the airport and boarding the jet to fly to Sucre was a blur despite the hours it took for a sitting president, his staff and detail to fly. After a sunrise bout of depression, the president's mood continued to shoot through the clouds as he took off over the green mountains surrounding Caracas. All he could do was get to Moscow somehow and start building new ties with the Russians, and by that he meant military ties. He knew they wanted to be the Cold War superpower they once were, or close to it. Both countries had oil, and both countries suffered price shocks when oil prices dipped. Both would benefit from higher prices at the pump. Friends of a feather.

His mistress sauntered down the aisle of the airplane. The president grinned when he saw her dressed as a flight attendant. She looked good in the uniform, even though she wasn't qualified to be wearing it. Still, when he traveled, she traveled.

She handed the president a bottled water.

"Price corrections are part of life," she whispered into his ear. "Listen to Bernal and don't unleash any surprises. At least not today. Go slowly. Remember the people who put you in power. Don't lose touch with your own country."

"What have you done for me lately," the president mumbled after the plane landed. On the drive to the Sucre speech, while waving to the crowds who had gathered on the side of the road, he continued. "What have I done for the people? What have I done for my friends? Even my opposition? I'm about to do a lot more. I haven't lost touch with them." He stared ahead and frowned. "Staying in touch with them is the hard part. And that costs money."

High petrodollars from days gone by had bought him popularity in the past as he provided food subsidies, free medical care, and other perks. Discounted oil bought friends abroad as well. Now he'd have to step it up a notch with oil prices in the gutter. The rest of the world, the Russians especially, could come to Venezuela and do whatever they wanted. "You just wait, my loyal and disloyal people. I'll give you everything."

Conflict.

Before he knew it, all the pomp and circumstance leading up to his speech that day was over. The crowds were in place. The security measures had been taken, and the welcoming bands had stopped playing. He had made it to northeastern Venezuela, met some local dignitaries and supporters, and discussed some talking points with his aides. He knew US, European, and a host of other foreign intelligence agents would be monitoring his every word as they always did, but he didn't care that day.

Showtime. Finally, it was time to speak. He heard nothing but the sound of a gentle breeze and the hum of the amplifiers ready to carry his voice to the crowd before him and to the rest of the world.

"My friends and to those who don't consider me a friend," he stared out at the mass of hardworking but largely poor Venezuelans. "It's only fitting that I address you here in Sucre State, a state rich in oil but above all a state rich due to its people!"

The crowd applauded the cliché, sort of. It wasn't a sincere applause. Just bored fans going through the motions. The president thought how muted the applause would really be if many weren't drinking.

He went on. "The Cuban doctors brought in to work in the marginal neighborhoods in Caracas provided free medical attention. They worked in the capital's new healthcare facilities alongside our new schools, and they did their jobs well. Other revolutionaries helped spearhead literacy projects," he said and then paused.

"The literacy programs in Caracas are helping those that Big Oil multinationals wouldn't dream of helping. Foreign oil companies take our crude, produce it when it suits their bottom line, not our economy, and let it sit underground when we need it to be flowing. But lasting improvements to your neighborhoods come from leaders who care, those who act in your interests. Socialist grocery stores are selling healthy foods for far less money than a capitalist store would. That's all possible thanks to the foods you grow in this area of the country and sell to your brothers across the country! We will get through this foreign sabotage that has robbed us of our basic goods and services."

Another lukewarm applause, especially since store shelves were running empty. They'd heard this before, too, and the president knew it. Now it was time to drop the bomb. "Ladies and gentlemen," he roared to the crowd. "It has been said that I am a tyrant, that I care more for consolidating power than I do for my own people. They say everyone will turn on me now that the handouts are gone, and that it will get even uglier here in Venezuela. They are right, it is ugly. We have empty store shelves thanks to those who want you to starve and laugh at you from abroad, thanks to those hoarders who are really behind our problems, the capitalist oligarchs. They said we were done years ago when they tried to oust us via a coup backed by agents of the evil gringo empire. When they had me in jail, and when they briefly took power, it was you who demanded my release! You! The Venezuelan people! And what did I have to offer you in jail? Nothing! Who could I have bought off while I was in jail? No one! But you demanded my freedom time and time again, freedom from jail or from the economic crosshairs of an empire run by the insane megalomaniacs enslaved by a thirst for blood and money. So, I say, bless you, my Venezuelan brothers and sisters, and fuck you to the yanquis!" A roar erupted from the crowd; an applause much louder than it had been in a long time. Smiles swept across a sea of once bored faces. Heads nodded.

"Yes, I speak of the advances we have made in Caracas. And yes, I speak of the advances we helped to make elsewhere, but times change. And yes, I realize the sacrifices that you—my friends, my family here in Sucre State—make every day in the hot sun, feeding our families and running our oil operations day in and day out. Well, the time has come to shift some of the power away from Caracas and back home to you."

An applause burst up to the sunny skies. An energy shot through the crowd and into the president himself. He fed on it and went on. "Today, I am pleased to announce that a major project will take place on the shores of your blessed state. A project that will not only shift the focus of power and economic might from Caracas east to Sucre, but also from Washington and Europe to countries like Venezuela, to rising powers like Sucre State, right here in your own backyard! Today, I announce that Venezuela, with the help from foreign allies, will develop a major port that will create thousands of jobs and bring ships—both military and civilian—calling on Venezuela's shores. A major military outpost creating power and might not far from here at all."

The president watched the reporters speak rapidly into their phones, dictating one-liners that would flash Venezuela's grand plan to the world news. They hadn't seen that coming. Neither had the president's aides and staffers, who gulped and stared at one another. They'd heard nothing about it.

The attention fueled the president even further. "Oil tankers, cruise ships, battleships, aircraft carriers are all welcome in Venezuela! Need I mention how many jobs the port will create?"

The crowd let out another massive applause, which lifted the president's mood so high that he would barely remember the rest of his speech. He never revealed the foreign ally. That would remain undisclosed, even from the Russians as of now, though everyone knew the identity would remain secret for a few minutes tops. The president also sidestepped how much money it would cost or how it would be financed. He figured those little details and all the perks needed to get the Russians onboard would work themselves out as he went along. But the announcement would bring much-needed attention back to the presidential palace in Venezuela, and it would keep friends and foes alike scrambling to figure out what the man in charge of a big chunk of the world's oil was up to these days. And it would keep ambitious opposition politicians backed by Washington's intelligence agencies out of the limelight, and that was important.

By the time his speech was over, and after having promised twice the money he was supposed to allocate to local hospitals and schools in Sucre and neighboring Monagas State, the president was back on his plane and had his people calling to set up an official presidential visit to Moscow.

"I want a meeting with Russian president Adrian Sokolov next week."

Eyes grew wide, but the president ignored his staff's anxiety over the logistical impossibility.

"This is it, boys and girls," he said. "Moscow is going to rise to where it was in the Cold War, and we are going with them. With a port!" he said. All eyes focused on work, at tasks at hand. Nobody made eye contact with the man who controlled the fate of the world's largest proven oil reserves. A thin man, a staffer with a thin neck, chirped up after a small group of lower-level aides whispered into his ear.

"You tell him," the man snapped back to his cohorts.

"It's your job," a woman said. She stared at the president, made brief eye contact, and scurried a few feet away.

"Uh, Mr. President?" the thin man said. He swallowed. "You're due in Central America next week. Remember your tour starting with Nicaragua?"

"Come again?" the president said, sizing up the man. Wispy moustache. Paper-thin, cheap shirt draped over a bony frame, though somewhat taller than most around him.

"Next week. Central America."

The younger female staffer nodded in approval at the man. He stiffened his spine.

"Plus, do the Russians even know they're developing a major port right here in America's backyard?" he whispered back to the young woman, who blushed. Then her flirty, rosy cheeks went pale. Her eyes widened at the sight of the rapidly advancing Venezuelan president descending on her coworker.

"Run!" she whispered.

The slam of the president's fist knocked the staffer off his seat, startling everyone. The thin man flew like a wet towel hurled across the aisle. The president and those around watched the man sail to the wall of the aircraft, with the president smiling and everyone else horrified at the sound of the thump of his head against a chair armrest. The man went quiet, and so did everyone else. Even the white noise of engines seemed to hush in fear. But it wasn't over. The staffer sat up, rubbing his head. The president grabbed him by the neck and punched him. Not once but repeatedly, looking like a gorilla trying to jab the head off a tiny doll. The sounds of bone pounding on flesh echoed throughout the cabin.

"Are you telling me I don't know my own goddamn schedule?" He then kicked the slender man on the ground, lifted one large leg and smashed it down on his ribs. Crunches. More confirmation of some semblance of a bone structure. The pain would take weeks to fully subside. "Of course I know we're going to Central Asia next week," he shouted into the wounded staffer's face. "That's why I wanted to plan the trip to Moscow now, you stupid fuck! We can catch Moscow on the way back!"

By then a slew of men in suits had pulled the president off the staffer. Two burly security agents helped the man to his feet and led him to the back of the plane to nurse his bruised ribs and battered ego. One midlevel oil ministry official, a woman in a severe business suit, whispered to her colleague. "It's Central America, not Central Asia." The president glared at her, and all gazes dropped to their feet in submission. The president exhaled, knowing she was right. Time to calm down and make plans.

After a few moments, aides and even higher-ranking officials clutched papers and scuttled about. The president began to pace, fueled with the desire to grab global headlines again.

"I can't stomach anymore unrest. But I can handle more glory, and so can everyone else in the nation. I can see it now," the president said. "Long-range Russian bombers on military bases in Venezuela. Russian subs getting very used to tropical ports. Nuclear submarines, not the easily detectable ones that run on fuel. Submarines! Damn! I left that out of my speech. Let's just start out by bringing in some of those nuclear-capable, long-range Russian Tu-160 bombers to do some joint exercises. That'll get the blood flowing."

He paced about. A baseball bat and cap appeared in his hands. The team was Navegantes del Magallanes in Carabobo State. Nobody on the plane had any idea where it had come from.

"Uhm, sir?" the woman in the severe suit asked. "Are we relying too much on the Russians? Seems like they've got their hands full elsewhere."

"We'll need to prove to the Russians that we're their friends and offer them perks to come here. So let's start off by buying more hardware from them. We'll begin with hundreds of thousands of new Kalashnikov assault rifles for our army, add to the ones we already have. Then we'll explore tanks and helicopters. I've been keeping an eye on Sukhoi SU-30 fighter jets as well as Ilyushin Il-76 transport planes and some of those surface-to-air missiles," the president said, pacing even faster while practice swinging. "Let's secure a Russian-arranged loan to buy all this. We'll borrow from them to buy from them. In fact, let's get the Russians to pump in a few more billion dollars to improve our oil production. We'll also get some Moscow money to boost our gold-mining sectors. And let's see to it that they supply us with wheat."

"It's a good thing no one from the finance ministry is onboard. Christ, Moscow will own all our assets," the woman whispered to another female colleague, who blushed not out of amusement but out of fear. The president glared at them both but seemed to blow it off.

"If the US wants to ban the sales of military hardware to our nation, then fuck them." The president eased into his seat and relaxed. "An arms race . . ." followed by something inaudible were his last words before he dropped the baseball bat. He pulled out a magazine from the back of the seat in front of him. *The Gateway*. He opened it. Flipped through the pages. The woman in the severe business suit stared at it and its English headlines.

"Have you ever heard of that magazine?" she asked her colleague.

"Never," she said.

"Does he even speak or read English?"

"Not that I know of, thank God. Could you imagine? Eight hours on television one day in Spanish and then another eight hours the next day in English?"

The president closed the magazine and dozed off. Finally, everyone on the plane relaxed for the first time that day, except for one person. Foreign Minister Hernán Bernal walked down the center of the aisle from the back of the plane. The passengers scurried out of his way. He stared at the sleeping president, shook his head, and walked away.

"This isn't going to end well," he said.

CHAPTER

6

Street stared out of the airplane window eager to see green land appear on the horizon. Leaving the United States always made him happy. It was an adventure. Being a foreign correspondent was an adventure. He could report the news with ferociousness and without conflicts of interest. For the overseas correspondent, there were fewer friends or family members around that could stir up political leanings that would otherwise make a journalist bite their tongue or secretly beam in agreement when reporting the news. Overseas, Street thought, the foreign correspondent had access to top policymakers as well as business and labor leaders, and he could write from a more detached observational platform and even with greater curiosity than he would at home. Sure, he had less skin in the game, but he also offered the game a fresh set of eyes.

He sat in an aisle seat, flipping through hard copies of Venezuelan newspapers. Then he felt the aircraft slow a tad and begin its descent. He stared out the window and caught a glimpse of the country's lush coastal mountains. Caracas was in a valley a couple of thousand feet above sea level. Dense foliage covered a mountain range that separated the city from the Caribbean coast. The airport in Maiquetía clung to a strip of land wedged in between blue water on one side and seaside urban grit on the other.

When he cleared customs, Street grabbed his bags and headed out the door. The cab drive from the airport to the city went as he remembered. Up green mountains whose peaks were often hidden in clouds, through a couple of tunnels, and then through the outer slums of Caracas that towered above the highways with pro-government graffiti everywhere.

Caracas's slums always fascinated Street. Small, rickety houses with tin roofs stacked on top of one other, sprawling across the city's many hills. Hues of pink and orange splashed together like some impressionist painting. At night, the small streetlights twinkled, giving the hills a festive look. But it was deceptive, as they also simmered with gangs and armed government-backed militia, which made these slums some of the most dangerous in the world, especially for a foreigner. Even the police wouldn't enter some of them unless on highly publicized raids.

The cab headed east, and the wealthier parts of the city got closer. Swaths of green trees popped up, covering large houses, condominium towers, and even golf courses. Office buildings sprouted from the cityscape, though they were run-down and unkempt, as if they were in need of nourishment in a commerce drought that showed no signs of relenting.

The driver exited the main Libertador Avenue and stopped at a modest international hotel in Chacao, not far from the Plaza Altamira, a large public square. Street looked around. It was still the same old Caracas he had known years ago, and the same old plaza that had separated his apartment and his favorite cafés when he had lived there.

Street quickly ignored the past and focused back on the week at hand. Today was Monday, and he wasn't going back to Miami until Thursday. He would take off Friday to make up for the Labor Day holiday he was using for his interview at Worldwide Oil & Gas. Life was good. But first, he needed to take a shower and review his questions for the meeting.

After a short cab ride, Street entered the offices of one of the world's largest energy companies, which was located in a dated steel-and-glass building, a testament to better times in the past. He presented his passport, the only form of identification that would work in Venezuela for most foreigners, to the security guard, who quietly ushered him to the top floor, where a receptionist buzzed him in through the glass doors.

The lobby resembled any other in the global corporate world. Well-dressed people shuffled about, visible through glass on all sides. Typical leather lobby furniture filled the space. A few slightly dated business magazines, some in English and some in Spanish, fanned out across a no-nonsense table. Telephones rang in soft bursts from behind the receptionist's desk. The receptionist got up and shuffled Street past the quiet cubicles of diligently working employees to a corner conference room. She told him he would be attended to shortly.

Before he had left the United States, Street knew what the executive would look like—a silver-haired man in an expensive suit walking around with a look in his eyes signaling that he had too much to do. But instead of getting everything done, he focused on what, or who, could be blown off and what, or who, needed attention right then and right now.

The head honcho would be surrounded by young, nervous people keeping him on schedule. In today's case, the head guy would be accompanied by the company's public relations manager. She would be the first to welcome Street back to Caracas. And there she was, gliding through the glass doors and into the reception room like a breath of fresh air Street hadn't felt since he first hit puberty.

"Street Brewer. Ana Patricia Osorio Harding. Welcome to Caracas. I'll have the pleasure of introducing you to Juan Vicente Domínguez, head of the Americas region for our oil company," she said. "He'll be with us shortly."

Street took her hand, and stared into her eyes. "What was your name again?"

"Ana Patricia Osorio Harding," she said. "Patricia is fine."

"Street. Just Street. Last name is Brewer," he said. Then he did a double take. Long dark hair. Golden skin. A blend of confidence and playful amusement typical of a beautiful, smart yet humble woman with a good head on her shoulders. If you would have asked Street what she was wearing—a blue suit—he would not have been able to tell you. But he would have been able to spend hours describing her big brown eyes.

She looked at him for a moment, smiling, before snapping him back to earth. "Let's go to a different conference room. A bigger one. Plus, they might need to fix the lighting in this one."

They walked down a hallway lined with cubicles behind glass doors on each side. Faceless people worked at computers, crunching numbers and drafting reports. Pictures of children and spouses dotted the desks, little sprouts of humanity shooting up through the maze.

"How long have you been here?" Street asked Patricia.

"About a year," she replied, checking her smartphone. "I've got the calendar here open. We're on schedule."

She mumbled something to herself. They walked on.

"Where were you before here?" Street asked.

"Here, there, everywhere," she said. They made their way into a larger conference room with a stunning view of the Ávila, a large green mountain protecting Caracas from the Caribbean. Other than that it was empty save a long table, leather chairs, and a complicated phone in the middle that looked like some sort of digital feeding trough.

The door opened. The executive entered. He was tall and relaxed, and he carried himself as if he had been groomed to lead since birth.

"Street Brewer, I'd like to introduce you to Mr. Juan Vicente Domínguez," Patricia said.

Street extended his hand to Mr. Domínguez, who was probably in his early fifties, tan with gray hair shooting up from the sideburns. Fit and trim. Tailored suit.

"Mr. Domínguez. Thank you for your time," Street said.

"The pleasure is mine. Please, have a seat," Domínguez said.

They sat down, and Street pulled out the voice recorder that Brent had given him to use. He opened his bag, saw his trusty old cassette recorder and left it there. After some small talk between Street and Domínguez about where Street was from, who all they knew in common, and his flight to Caracas, a second of quiet fell on the conversation. Street knew it was time for the interview to begin.

"Let's get started. Do you mind if I record this? And also, we can do this in English or Spanish, whichever you prefer," Street said.

"We'll do it in English," Domínguez said. "I have an annual oil conference coming up. It will be good to practice."

"Ah, the one in San Diego this spring?"

"That would be one of them." The man spoke perfect English. He didn't need to practice. He was just being nice. Patricia, of the public relations department, clicked on her recorder as well. Street began.

"Okay, I'll dive right in. Your company bought several aging oil fields years ago. You bring in the money and know-how that Venezuela doesn't have to get the oil out. Everyone wins. Afterward, the government takes control of those fields and acts as the operator. You're still here. What's next?"

Domínguez didn't hesitate at all. "We stuck around with minority stakes, but now we're out. Sanctions from abroad may force the government to give us more say as to when to pump and when to export, but we are gone. We're done. We are going to take the money the government gave us and move on—cut our losses basically. Thank God we're not the target of any US sanctions that may come along if this government goes from horrific to apocalyptic. It's sad for Venezuela in the long run. This country lives off oil exports, and without our expertise, oil output will decline even further, and that means less money for the poor here, who are the big losers. And believe me, things here are going from bad to worse, and I mean horrific in the days or weeks ahead. Stick around."

"Why don't you stick around like others are? Other companies handed over majority control of their fields, took the money, but are staying. A little less is better than nothing. Why not just keep on pumping oil here?"

"And then what? The government takes even more control? Decides when we drill new wells or how much we can produce from the current fields? Or a crony friend of the president takes the reins of the oil sector and changes the rules of the game again? With Venezuela's inefficient and corrupt state-run oil company controlling most of the fields, remediation operations won't go well either when the fields run dry."

"Remediation?"

"Clean up after the oil is extracted. We've seen this before. The government won't do its part because it just can't or just doesn't want to pay to properly deal with production legacies of contaminated ponds and leftover oil-covered sands. Hydrocarbons and chemicals leak into the water supply, and then people near the field will get sick. Or the crops could die. We've learned a lot over the years, and we know how to do a proper cleanup and restoration job. We also know how much of a mess inefficient companies leave behind. So we lose control of the project, and then the government won't do its part to pay for that proper cleanup. And then guess who they'll blame for the pollution? You got it. The evil, foreign oil companies who are here to ravage the lands, poison the people, and then leave, counting the money in smoke-filled rooms back home, even if we weren't the operating partner in the project in the end."

That's good stuff. And I can quote him on all that, Street thought. This guy wasn't lukewarm about anything.

The executive went on. "The rules of the game keep changing in this country. The president is a thug. You know that oil companies aren't the most press-friendly of people, just by our nature. It's no secret we deal with shady governments and, to be honest, the press views us as evil Big Oil. We're an easy target, and we really have nothing to gain by talking about our business. But considering this administration and its disdain for the rules of the game, we're reaching out to speak to all of you to spread the word. This is no country for foreign investment."

Street dove in right there. "Let's talk about that. Let's say this same government that doesn't appear willing to step down any time soon decides in the future that it screwed up and needs the foreign oil companies back with their technology. So they auction out rights to drill for oil, develop the fields and produce under attractive terms, and by attractive, I mean attractive for you. You get a majority stake in the well, and you decide when to drill and when to produce, not when the government says. And let's say global market conditions make coming back here worth it. Would you reconsider?"

"No way. Not with this administration. Probably after as well. We are out for good, or for at least well past my lifetime. They can invite us back all they want, but trust is gone."

"Just like that?"

"Just like that."

"What about other oil companies? Are you in talks with anybody else about pulling out?"

"I won't speak on behalf of other companies."

"Fine. I'll rephrase. Are you the only company leaving the country now?"

"As far as I know."

"These are some pretty harsh statements. Aren't you worried you'll get kicked out of here or arrested?"

"No."

Right then Patricia stood up, pulled a cell phone from her pocket, and began dialing. It was not the phone she had used to check her schedule.

"Personal call. I'm sorry but it's very important," she said and left.

Both men watched her go.

"A little odd seeing the public relations person leave during the interview," Street said.

"It's all being recorded," Domínguez said. "Don't worry about it."

"Actually, let's just wait until she comes back in," Street said, not really sure why he reacted that way. Public relations people came and went during interviews at times.

"Fine," Domínguez said. He sat in quiet. Stared at the table for a second and picked up Street's business card. "So, how's Barry?"

"Who?" Street asked.

"Barry Drum? The publisher?"

"You mean Brent?"

"Yes. I'm sorry. Senior moment."

"He's good. He says you two go back," Street said.

"That's correct," Domínguez said, looking at his watch. He glanced at the door. No sign of Patricia.

"What was Brent like as a reporter?"

"He was good," Domínguez said. "Good reporter."

Street said nothing. Stared at his phone.

Domínguez spoke. "Are you going to be in San Diego this spring? We'd be happy to speak with you again. Can't promise you an interview with the global CEO, but you'll get something. I'll speak to you again if need be."

"That'd be great. I've never been to San Diego," Street said.

"It's nice. You'll love it. Beautiful city."

"What's that conference like? I hear anyone and everyone in the hemisphere's energy world is there. Isn't that where you met Brent for the first time?"

"Nope. Worldwide Oil & Gas is always there, but I've never been to this particular conference. Always pulled off in another direction," Domínguez said.

Street frowned. A second later Patricia entered the room and slammed her phone closed.

"Apologies, gentlemen," she said. "Or did you go on without me?"

Street spent the next half hour of the interview trying to get as much out of the executive as possible, considering the secret relationship between oil companies and rogue governments. When Domínguez told him all he would, Street switched to general questions about the current health of global energy markets and operations elsewhere in the region. When the interview started to wind down, which is the moment when the reporter realizes he got more or less what he wanted and the interviewee feels he got most of his message out, Patricia spoke up.

"Well, Mr. Brewer. Mr. Domínguez has to wrap things up here," she said.

Street took the chance to ask a few more questions with the hope of finding something new and interesting to fly over the transom. Nothing did, though. After Patricia reminded him a third time the interview should wind down, he closed it.

"I think I'm all set here. I've got everything I need," he said.

"Okay," Domínguez said. "You can follow up with Patricia here if you need anything else."

"Actually, I'll need your investment figures. How much you put into the projects you have here and how much you earmarked for future capital spending and cleanup efforts as well. If I'm going to write Worldwide Oil & Gas is willing to turn its back on Venezuela, I need to tell my readers how much money you've pumped into the country while not pumping anything out of the ground."

"You bet," Domínguez said. "I'd rather you use our official numbers instead of what I would recall from memory. I could get it wrong. Patricia, call Ricardo and have him email that info to you so you can pass it on to Street."

"Thanks again," Street said. "I can follow up with Ricardo myself. What's his last name?"

Domínguez stared at him and smiled. "Patricia will take care of it," he said. "Listen, I have to run. Follow up with Patricia for anything you need from Ricardo," Domínguez said. He grabbed a stack of papers off the desk and frowned at a large envelope.

"Bad news from the board?" Street asked.

"Nope," Domínguez said. "Just a letter from where I keep my money, which is in your country, thank God. Don't let anyone make fun of you down here, you know, tease you about your accent or laugh at your dancing. You gringos run a stable democracy and a stable financial system."

Street laughed, staring at the envelope sent from a company called Cornbridge Capital. He couldn't catch the address, though he saw it was in Naples, Florida. Interesting, Street thought. Probably some good hedge fund money.

Domínguez and Street shook hands as the oilman headed for the office door in that fast but relaxed pace typical of executives, doctors, and professional bartenders.

"Off to Texas?"

"Off to golf! Caracas Country Club. Gotta run. Got to talk about Venezuela's power structure on the green," Domínguez said. He left.

Street turned to face Patricia. She was in charge of spinning one of the world's largest oil companies in the Venezuelan and international press. Her voice was soft but firm, and she spoke English like a US national. Street had assumed she was from up east when he had called the number Brent gave him to request the interview.

"So, Street, when will this publish?"

"Next month's issue. October. We'll throw up a teaser on our site as well as in an email blast."

"If you need anything else, just let us know. You can get in touch with me."

"Will do. Just give me Ricardo's email and phone numbers to get those investment figures. I do appreciate it. I can go to the Securities and Exchange Commission website and go through the financials to get big-picture stuff, but I need the Venezuelan specifics to produce a good story."

"I don't have it. I'll have to dig it up. Quite frankly, I don't remember which Ricardo."

Street rewound the digital tape recorder and hit the play button to check the interview's audio quality. He heard some voices, his own at first. Once he heard Domínguez's voice come in clearly, he knew the interview was safely recorded, and he clicked the device off.

"Off the record," Patricia said. "You should definitely follow up on that Venezuela yard sale story with government sources. It's a good angle and really can't be ruled out. It gets a little old when reporters come in here and ask just about investing and hiring and OPEC. Kind of boring if you ask me. Those stories don't add any value anyway. Engage us."

Street nodded.

"Listen to your recorder. It's all there. If you need anything else, let me know," Patricia said. "Engage me for anything."

"Will do," Street said, amused at Patricia's corporate talk. Engage. Somebody had probably engaged her a long time ago. He blew off the thought. "I have it all memorized anyway."

"All of it?"

"Pretty much."

"So, are you one of those guys with a photographic memory? The kind who just sat there in high school and college? Took no notes? Never studied? Then showed up for the test and aced it? People like that annoy me," Patricia said, giving Street a wink.

"Pretty much. I mean I did study and learn everything. Except when it came time to take the test, I usually flunked. I don't test well. People who test well but aren't all that wise annoy me," Street said.

Patricia smiled. "You're funny," she said, touching Street on the shoulder.

He stared back at her, not even trying to conceal his bright-red blush.

"I do have a good memory. Pretty unshakable," he said.

He looked into her eyes.

She smiled back. Amused.

"It's Patricia, right?" he asked.

"That's right. Seems like there are chinks in your armor when it comes to memorizing names."

"Just your name, Ana Patricia Osorio Harding? Got a business card?" Street handed her his card first.

"Here," she handed him her card and yanked it back just before he took it.

"Wait. Let me write my cell down. I have a personal one, if you need anything."

"Write down Ricardo's, too. Whoever has the numbers is always a good source."

"Just stick with me for now," Patricia said, looking up at Street. "Nice try, though." She handed him the business card. "See you soon, Señor Street Brewer."

Street left. He stared at the card in the elevator. Her name. Patricia. Feminine handwriting. A bit of perfume lingered on the card. She was beautiful and down-to-earth.

Then he thought about Domínguez. Back to work.

"Golf," Street said, walking out of the office building. "Cornbridge Capital," he said in a whisper. At the foot of the Ávila, a few golf courses spread out like green roots shooting out from the base of the mountain and anchoring over the streets and neighborhoods. He remembered the president was going to have his government seize control of those private golf clubs like everything else, but he held back, mainly because he had allies who struck it rich when he came to power and joined those clubs. Even socialists like the taste of the good life. Sky-high oil prices in the past dampened revolutionary banter and sparked demand for silk ties and fine leather shoes, even when the cameras were rolling.

He withdrew his cell phone from his coat pocket outside of the building and dialed Brent.

"Your theory fell on its face. Worldwide Oil & Gas is out and won't come back," Street said.

"You got that on record?" Brent responded.

"Oh yeah," Street said. "The PR person, Patricia, said it was worth exploring, and we can, but Domínguez confirmed they won't come back at all. Even during future administrations."

"Well, I was wrong, but that's a good story anyway. File it."

"Will do," Street said.

CHAPTER

7

Not far from the Worldwide Oil & Gas offices, a man sat in a suite at a swank hotel in the posh La Castellana section of the city, enjoying a stunning view of the green Ávila Mountain while sipping from his first bottle of Bollinger La Grande Année champagne. He had only shelled out a few grand on the bubbly and a snack that afternoon. The hotel could import anything and give a lucky elite few the chance to shrug off Venezuela's dire economic woes. But the man had little time to wallow in the luxury. There was business to conduct, and right now he had a conference call.

"Let's get through this call quickly. I've got a young American couple to kill and some smuggling to plan this afternoon," the man said.

"We hope you're efficient about that elimination. Do it like we do it in the United States," an American woman answered. "That means it's done quickly and untraceably. Don't be sloppy like the Russians. No snapshots of assassins on airport security cameras. Such obvious poisonings and obvious decoys. We're the best at meddling, so do it like we do, and let someone else take the fall if need be. So be efficient. Pennie Spradling got loose, and even if it was just for a few moments, she was out of our sight and talking to people. So everyone dies, and I mean everyone who formed part of our agenda."

"Agreed," a Venezuelan woman answered in English, albeit with a thick accent. "Pennie got loose. Make sure you have the means to avoid any repeats."

"Don't dare question my tactics," the man said. "Fuck the US and Venezuelan governments. I'm in charge here. Anyway, I'll be brief, so I can get my work done and get you all up to speed. We got our traffic moving nicely from South America to the United States, right into Miami. That's where I come in, and I'm on schedule. Are the US and Venezuela focused on their roles? Do I need to step in and do your jobs for you both as usual? This call is the last one for a while to make sure everyone knows what to do. Don't ever fucking tell me my job again."

"All clear," said the American woman. "We find this call unnecessary as well."

"*Si, papi,*" the Venezuelan woman replied, emphasizing the Spanish term of endearment for a man or boy to irk the caller.

"*Papi?*" the man said, kicking off a pair of shoes that pretty much matched the price of his champagne. Anger wasted no time swelling up in his voice, as if the emotion was just as impatient as the man himself. "Be professional! This is a one-shot opportunity. The world has never seen a deal like this. One fucking shot at it. It's not typical."

"Sorry," the Venezuelan woman said, making little effort to conceal her laughter.

"Good," the man said. "What's going on in the States?"

"We've got people out everywhere working to make sure our little plan goes without fail and that business goes on as usual," the American woman said. "We've got assets and case officers pumping in enough intelligence to keep DC policymakers focused on the power struggles in Caracas that the entire US government will have zero time to worry about what's really going on in that hellhole."

"What about in Venezuela?" the man asked.

"Can't we discuss this in person?" the woman asked after a brief pause.

"No," the man replied.

"Fine," the Venezuelan woman said. "Hang on, *papi*." The American woman said nothing to the man on the conference call during the silence left by the Venezuelan woman's exit. Both listened to muffled sounds of the Venezuelan woman speaking to someone. A man's voice could be heard, though their conversation was indiscernible.

"I don't have all day," the man said, taking a sip of his champagne.

"I'm serious about that young American couple," the US woman said, taking advantage of the Venezuelan woman's departure. "You have to handle this in a way that nobody can get back to us. Americans die, especially lily-white upper-class ones like the Tagles, and the world starts paying attention, which is good, but we need the world to think they fell victim to Venezuelan street crime, not to us. It's harder than you think. If they don't venture out much, you can't just pay some thug to kill them and then off that thug."

"Trust me," the man said. "They'll be dead, and this will steer the authorities away from us. They've done their job for us. But now it's time for him and his wife to disappear," the man said. "I'll make sure we have the perfect red fish."

The American woman sighed into the call. "A red herring," she said.

"Whatever," the man said. "It will be brutal enough that everyone will suspect only a monster could think of such a thing. And that monster is on my private payroll."

"Good," the American said. After another minute, she spoke up anew. "Where is that idiot?"

"I'm sorry about that," the Venezuelan woman said coming back onto the phone, speaking in Spanish. "We're ready here in Venezuela to handle our end of the shipment. We've got all eyes on us while all eyes are off the Americans. But we gotta say that we're worried about your progress, *papi*."

"We've got the executions, the delivery and all logistics on schedule," the man said in Spanish back to the woman, a little irritation in his voice.

"Who's handling it? Who is this freak on your payroll?" the American woman asked. "And don't worry about the Spanish. I understand you."

"The right person for the job," the man replied. "The perfect delivery-man, and that's all you need to know."

"Don't patronize me. You know damn well who you're messing with, so tell me his name?" the American asked.

"Ricardo," the man said. "You've never heard of him."

"Good," the American woman said.

A young American couple crouched in the corner of a bedroom, trembling like children out of a fairy-tale nightmare. The husband, in his early thirties, teeth chattering, his right eye beaten to a pulp, his left hand broken, the bones in his forearm almost liquefied, stared up at a very real mountain of a man in front of him. The young wife, about thirty years old and unharmed, sat in fear beside her husband. There was a dead man about their age on the floor next to them, American as well. The body was naked and even singed by fire, though the couple refused to make eye contact with the corpse. Their minds were still charred from the image of the giant torturing the man before burning and decapitating him while making his wife and the couple watch. The dead man's wife managed to escape, but she didn't make it out of the slum alive, the sequestered husband and wife concluded. They had heard muffled conversations about a suicide, about diving under a bus a few streets below. Two American couples had entered the room, one remained.

The massive man, an enormous creature in his late forties with curly black hair like something from an ancient bust, peeled an orange and stared back at the couple from the edge of a bed, where he was seated. The woman's eyes scanned her captor's enormous body. Big, meaty arms like two skinned sea lions, very short white shorts, and enormous hairless legs. The large man hopped to his feet, and the young couple flinched at his sudden movement. He ate the orange plug and tossed the peel at the couple. He looked at himself in the mirror, turned sideways, and seemed to be either admiring his own figure or gauging any signs of weight gain. The short shorts rode up into the man's hind quarters. He flexed his ass muscles and stared at himself with each contraction.

A younger man stood on the other side of the bed, staring over the mountain's shoulders at the scared couple. This man was small, about twenty-one years old if that, with long hair, and wearing a T-shirt with the word "Boston" covering the front.

The large man looked back at the T-shirt and shook his head.

"Why do you wear those city of Boston T-shirts?" the ogre of a man asked in thick but working English, winking at the American woman in the corner.

"They were free. Probably came from the same charity in the US and made their way to this shithole," the younger man said in excellent English. "It's time now, Ricardo. We have to leave."

A phone's buzzing in Ricardo's shorts sent the young couple flinching again. The large man drew the phone out of his pocket and accepted the call. A man's face appeared on the screen, but the young couple couldn't make him out.

"Are we finally ready?" Ricardo asked. "Nice champagne, by the way."

"Do it," the man said. The screen went dark.

"Finally. Let's get this over with," Ricardo said. He stood and stared at the young woman.

"You. Up." The woman looked at her husband, who stared at the floor.

"I wasn't talking to your husband," the beast of a man said. "Now up."

"No," the woman said. She stared at the man next to her, her husband, who raised his head and gaped wide-eyed at the ogre. "For God's sake, do something!" she screamed.

The man looked back at the woman. "You saw what he did with that hammer," he said, rolling his eyes up into his head. "My bones are liquid," he managed to whisper.

"Then fucking kick him!" the woman said, turning to face their torturer. She shot out a roundhouse kick, which landed near his kidneys but failed to spark even a flinch on the large man's face.

The young man let his head sag, eyes draining of life and focus.

Bolts of rage shot through the woman's face, seeping out in high-pressure spurts through her eyes and clenched teeth, her wrath directed at Ricardo. She kicked the massive man again, though he dodged her foot with surprising grace and agility despite his enormous size and constricting white shorts. She threw another kick at the man and then exploded into a disorganized flurry of punches, grabs and fresh rounds of kicks.

Ricardo stared at himself in the mirror. Outside, the blue sky shone over the pastels of the slum. White kites soared into the air, contrasting nicely against the crisp blue sky.

"Animal!" the woman shouted. Punches and kicks landed across the ogre's torso, though he swatted her away with a powerful forearm smack. She fell down onto her husband, and sprang off him, kicking his liquefied arm.

"Get back up, or else," the giant said to the woman.

"Fuck you," the woman said, giving one last look at her husband, who kept his eyes and head lowered, fixated on the floor.

"Exactly," Ricardo said. "Fuck you." In a quick and fluid movement, he stood and grabbed the woman by the back of her neck, scooped her up, and slammed her down on the bed. He ripped off her white silk T-shirt and peeled her tan jeans off, as if he were field dressing a rabbit. The bra and the panties snapped off with little effort. The large man stared at her, and then the kid in the Boston T-shirt spoke up.

"Ricardo, we're supposed to—"

"Shut up," Ricardo said. He stared at the naked woman on the bed, tilting his head as if examining some curious piece of art. He took his shirt off, and then undid his shorts. On a bedside table, opposite from where the husband trembled, lay a large hunting knife. Ricardo took it and walked over to the shaking man. The husband cringed. He closed his eyes, his body language screaming in fear. Ricardo stood very close to him. The husband opened his eyes and winced at the fact that another man's penis was inches from his forehead.

"Take this knife," Ricardo said.

The man stared up with wide eyes. "What?" he managed to squeak out.

"Take this knife. Hang on to it. I won't need it when I fuck this woman, your wife," Ricardo said in surprisingly decent English for someone in a Caracas slum.

The American stared at the blade and then up at the massive man. Across the room on the other side of the bed, he caught a glimpse of the young man and also at a handgun pointed back at him and his wife on the bed. The American couldn't decide which was scarier, the gun pointed at him or the sick smile on the kid's face. He then extended a shaking hand up, took the large blade by the handle and stared back at Boston.

"If you think you're fast, go for it. You've got one good arm on purpose. Defend your wife," Ricardo said.

The man stared into the lifeless eyes of Ricardo, the wide eyes of his wife, and the taunting eyes of an armed Boston. His head dropped.

"Thanks," Ricardo said. He returned to the bed. The stunned woman crossed her legs, scooted far back to the headboard, and curled into a ball. In a matter-of-fact movement, the giant grabbed her by the hair and slammed her down on the bed, her body parallel to the small headboard and perpendicular to the wall. She lay on her stomach, her eyes peering over the side of the mattress just a few feet over her husband. Within seconds, the large man mounted her. The husband quivered, and a peep of a whine popped out of his mouth. Tears ran down his face when his wife snapped her eyes closed and gulped, which let him know that the giant was inside her. Slaps of skin against skin rang out across the bedroom walls. The woman's breathing picked up, then she swallowed again and went quiet, only short jerky breaths that were barely audible erupted from her mouth during each violent thrust, largely drowned out by the sounds of squeaking springs and mattresses croaking like a chorus of chirping frogs.

"Why did you give him the knife?" the man in the Boston T-shirt asked.

"He won't use it. He's a coward," Ricardo said, looking over at his friend while thrusting the woman.

"Isn't that right, Zachary Tagle is it? Are you going to defend your wife? She's good, by the way."

Deborah Tagle opened her eyes and stared at her husband with an expression on her face that screamed how did this happen sprinkled with a dash of do something now. Defend me.

In a few seconds, after bellowing out a large and powerful roar like that of a walrus, Ricardo was finished. The woman closed her eyes. Ricardo dismounted her and tossed her on the floor alongside her husband. The husband, Zachary Tagle, reached out to console his wife. She flinched at his touch, and pushed his hand away. She sat back against the wall, her knees up to her chin, and she began to rock.

Ricardo stood, walked over to the man, and extended a hand.

"I'll take the knife if you're not going to use it." Ricardo snatched it from Zachary, who just stared at the ground.

Ricardo then walked to the other bedside table. He grabbed another orange and sat there, peeling it. The room was large enough for a double bed, two simple side tables, and a dresser. On the side table closest to the door were two new laptops, a few tablets and smartphones in a neat stack. A television sat on a dresser directly in front of the bed. It was an older television set, somewhat thick and heavy. Ricardo grabbed a remote and flipped it on. International news was on. Outside, the Venezuelan neighborhood went about its business.

"Another orange? You're crazy," the kid said. "These two gringos are still alive. By now, we should have been—"

"Shut up," Ricardo said, sitting on the bed relishing in his nakedness. He sat that way for about thirty minutes. The woman, Deborah, buried her head into her raised knees. Zachary sat next to her, his back stuck to the wall, staring at the ground, moving in and out of consciousness. Ricardo walked out of the room and into a nearby kitchenette, the sound of his meaty feet pounding across the hard concrete floor echoed off the bare but clean, blue walls. A few seconds later he was back, opening a jar of peanut butter. He was about to scoop some out with his finger but stopped. He stared in the jar and then at Zachary Tagle.

"You're in the consumer goods business. Is this one of your brands?" Ricardo asked.

Zachary weakly nodded yes.

"Well, getting peanut butter and other goods inside the country is what you do best! It's why we hired you," Ricardo said, looking at Deborah. "That's why we hired you both."

Zachary looked at his wife as confusion swept across his face, chasing away his earlier appearance of fear and helplessness.

"What's he talking about?" Zachary asked, shaking his head. "Jesus, Deborah, what did we get caught up in?" Deborah ignored him, and Zachary didn't say anything else and just stared at the jar of peanut butter.

Ricardo took note of his gaze and raised the jar. "Very hard to find this stuff in Venezuela, even in good economic times, and especially in a slum like this one," he said in solid English. He dipped the large knife deep into the creamy peanut butter and licked it off both the dull and sharp edges of the blade while staring down at the smaller man.

"Want some?" he offered Zachary, holding out the jar.

Zachary just stared at him, and then he looked down.

"Your loss," Ricardo said. "Because you're going to need your strength." Ricardo screwed the lid shut on the jar of peanut butter, slammed it down on the dresser, walked over to Zachary and thrust the knife in front of his face.

"Up," he said.

Deborah lifted her head up from her knees, a bit confused that the command wasn't for her. She stared up at Ricardo. Zachary did likewise and stood up slowly. "Over here. Stand at the foot of the bed," Ricardo said. Zachary did as he was told.

"Now take off your clothes," Ricardo said.

"What?"

"I said, take off your clothes."

A wave of confusion swept across Zachary's face followed by a heavy punch from Ricardo's meaty fist. Zachary fell onto the bed, and Ricardo leaped on top of him. Ricardo's large arms threw powerful and surprisingly fast punches into Zachary's ribs and face in a synchronized pace. Then he stopped, stood up, and ripped off Zachary's button-down collar shirt followed by his pair of chinos. The young man screamed at each touch on his broken arm. Ricardo continued his assault. The boxer shorts ripped off with little effort. Then he grabbed Zachary by the hair on the back of his head and slammed him down on his stomach perpendicular to the wall so he would face Deborah. The man winced in pain at his hair being pulled, then squeaks of pain erupted into shrill cries of horror when Ricardo thrust himself inside of the man.

"Help!" Zachary screamed.

"Shut up," Ricardo shouted, jamming the man's face into the blankets, almost suffocating him with one hand. Slapping noises of skin pounding on skin echoed through the room. The man in the Boston T-shirt rolled his eyes and left the small house, the door slamming in his wake.

Ricardo lifted Zachary's head while in midstroke and jammed his face upright so he could look into his wife's eyes. Hers were lifeless, his spread wide open in pain and terror. After another walrus grunt, Ricardo was finished. He stood and threw Zachary on top of his wife. The throw was effortless, as if he were tossing a wet towel into a laundry bin. Zachary's head pounded into the wall, and he fell limp on his wife. She pushed him off, and he sat there trying to regain his wits and focus on the hell around him.

Ricardo, meanwhile, put on his shorts and a navy blue T-shirt. He walked to the bedside table, opened a drawer, and took out a wallet, a cell phone, and a stack of passports that he shoved in his pocket. He stuffed the laptops, phones, and tablets that were stacked on the bedside table into a large plastic shopping bag. Then he grabbed Zachary's ripped up clothes and then Deborah's, including their shoes.

"Well, it's been fun. Zachary, you've done a marvelous job here in Venezuela, especially when dining with opposition lawmakers and secretly recording them without even knowing it. But time's up, little man," Ricardo said, sliding on some flip-flops.

The kid in the Boston T-shirt came back in.

"Are you finished?"

"Yes. Let's go," Ricardo said.

"Who's next on our little hit list? The people we are supposed to kill, and I mean kill this time."

"A woman on Florida's west coast, another in the Palm Beach area, and someone named Street Brewer in Miami. A reporter, I think," Ricardo said, looking at the young couple. "Not sure if we get those jobs or someone in the US gets them. We might have to prioritize the delivery."

"Wait," said the man in the Boston T-shirt. "We were specifically told to kill these two. The other couple is dead. You killed him, and she killed herself."

"Oh yeah. That bitch. Pennie Spradling. You owe me some silk sheets for letting her get away. You should have tied her up better, especially considering that she saw the names on our little to-kill list and even went with us on one of our fishing trips back in Miami. She overheard our import-export plans. If our boss found out what she discovered, we'd be dead. Good thing we got her and her weak-ass husband back here by boat so they couldn't squeal. A nice boat at that. Talk about crossing the Caribbean in style."

"It's all good. She's dead," Boston said. He reached into his pockets for the crumpled-up paper she had given him. He withdrew it, stared at it, looked at the large man, and then put it back in his pocket. Whatever her ties were to Street Brewer, one fellow expat to another, were dead and buried now.

"Thoughts on these two?" the young man asked, motioning to the Tagles.

"Well, I was planning on leaving them here with the knife. Let them kill themselves out of shame. They'll turn on each other after what I just put them through. That was the point," Ricardo said. He gently set the hunting knife on a small, round kitchen table and turned to the younger man in the Boston T-shirt. "Or leave them to this East Caracas slum. Remember where we are," he added. "They'll be dead in minutes. Not like they're going to walk downstairs naked, speaking English. If they do, imagine what will happen to them."

"Sounds iffy," the kid said. "Most people here are decent folks. Good chance they'll get help. Remember, you're not from around here."

"Just let them walk out of here naked. I guarantee you that the boys down the steps will have their way with them and then kill them. Especially if we order them to," Ricardo said.

"No. Get it over with here and now. This isn't interpretive murder. Do it efficiently and do it right. Orders are orders."

Ricardo sighed. He looked down, and then nodded. "Fine."

He set the bag full of technology devices and their clothes on the bed and grabbed Deborah and threw her on the bed. He kneeled behind her, almost mounting her, and rested the blade against her throat. With one jerk of the hand forward and one jerk back, he thrust the blade deep inside her throat, carving up to somewhere behind her nasal cavity and then higher, somewhere behind the eyes, which were still open. Ricardo saw from a mirror in the corner of the room that the woman had a grimace of pain as blood flooded across the bed, an expression of terror and awe stuck on her face even though she was dead already. The husband died in a similar manner, twitching a bit, then going limp like a goat slaughtered by hand in some sort of religious ritual.

"Happy now?" Ricardo asked.

"Yes," the kid in the Boston T-shirt said.

After Ricardo showered, they left.

CHAPTER

8

Ted Bullard burst through the front door of the building in Naples, Florida, where Cornbridge Capital leased office space. He took a gulp of coffee in the midmorning warmth, high-fived the security guard and bolted across the lobby with a messenger bag and his coffee cup in one hand and a copy of a magazine called *The Gateway* jammed under an armpit.

"Afternoon, Mr. Bullard," the security guard said. "How are we today?"

"Nervous and happy at the same time," Ted Bullard replied to the security guard, an elderly African American with a bushy moustache.

"Ted's like that," the security guard said to another. "Everyone in the building says he's never relaxed but never frazzled either, just quickly moving along as if he's just reached cruising altitude."

Ted had important business at Cornbridge Capital that day, pressing business that would hopefully expand the hedge fund's $100 million in assets under management. And to do that, he needed to have his best employees out on the road. Ted, who'd helped launch the fund a couple of years ago, traveled the world often, searching for wealthy clients to park money in the fund when others had cashed out and left. He'd spend a week in Venezuela, a week in Argentina or Colombia or wherever, raising money to invest in highly exotic—and highly rewarding—asset classes that returned much more than a boring old mutual fund would.

His right-hand woman, Olivia Crawford, did a second-to-none job for him as a portfolio manager. She raised money for the fund as well, but she also ran the business. Whether on the road or running the show in Naples, Olivia never failed to shine. She held a master's in finance from Wharton. She was thirty-three years old and athletic, especially when it came to the water.

Ted liked athletic people. They tended to be driven, they knew how to compete and knew how to work on teams. Sports and other physical hobbies also kept bodies and minds focused. People who didn't work out lost concentration. They would daydream, gossip, or drink. Or worse, they would think too much and become people full of ideas, people who were great at starting tasks but rarely finishing them. He hated people who weren't action-oriented. Chin strokers need not apply to Cornbridge Capital.

Olivia could handle a boat out on Florida's west coast waters better than most of the men she had dated. She could dock in and out no matter what size the craft or how fast the currents and winds were moving. She could jump a wake on a wakeboard, surf in overhead waves when they made their appearance in South Florida's east coast waters, and would swim out in the water at night while nervous boyfriends waited safely on shore, dreaming of her long brown hair, big blue eyes, and soft skin.

That was also her downfall when it came to relationships, and Ted knew this about his protégé. She intimidated many men with her beauty, intelligence, and strength, and all the men in her life had left her for someone more manageable, playing that classic adolescent game: eject before she sees weaknesses and dumps you. Break her heart before she breaks yours. So it was natural for Olivia to take a break from rough seas and rough relationships and plunge into work instead, which made Ted very wealthy.

Ted took a sip of coffee and peered into Olivia's office. He walked in unannounced, donning his usual Tampa Bay Rays baseball cap and a goatee that always seemed to be just getting started.

Olivia stood and shook Ted's hand. "Well, hello stranger. Welcome back, Mr. Road Warrior."

"Great to be back," Ted said, taking her hand. "I hear you're spending too much time in the office. Just like my days on Wall Street. Where's the rest of the team?"

Olivia blushed. "The team? It's Labor Day. They're working from home. I'm just here doing some busy work and talking to overseas clients who aren't on holiday."

"Hmm," Ted said. "Oh well. I won't keep you long. I do apologize. I've been on the road for so long and have lost track of my own holidays. It helps if you're divorced and don't see your kids too often," he said. "Well, Olivia, you can bring me up to speed while I'm here."

He motioned her to a small conference room and asked her to have a seat. Even on Labor Day, she was appropriately dressed. Well suited, as an English colleague had described her once. Ted was in jeans, some kind of designer white T-shirt, and a tan blazer. He looked like a boss from a technology company on a casual dress day in the eighties.

"You know, we're one of the top-performing hedge funds in the area despite today's roiling ups and downs, and that's all thanks to you," Ted said. He entered the conference room and plopped down in a seat at the head of the table. Olivia remained standing.

"Thank you," Olivia said, opening a laptop on the large table. "I appreciate that."

"How's the sailing coming. Still enjoying the Gulf of Mexico year-round?"

"I am. But let's talk emerging markets. I have several concerns about our trading strategies given recent events—"

"That's great," Ted interrupted. "Because I really need for you to go to Chile. Just for a week."

"Excuse me?" Olivia said, crossing her arms. She was still standing. "That's not going to happen, Ted. I believe we have pressing matters here to address first. You are aware Chinese factory indicators have hit a bump in the road again, and emerging markets are not going to like that, especially those dependent on oil, which is sluggish. I haven't even started with currencies and the dollar's strength."

"Yep. Saw that. Another batch of disappointing data. That's exactly why I am sending you to Chile."

"Excuse me? Did I hear you correctly? You are sending me?" She shifted her weight to her heels as if ready to throw a counterpunch. "No one sends me anywhere."

"Duly noted. But we both need to travel now, and I mean right now." Ted sat back in his chair, stretched his arms, and stared up at the ceiling. "Some investors in emerging markets are going to run to more safe-harbor asset classes, including well-chosen US stocks," he said, tossing her a copy of *The Gateway*.

It landed perfectly in front of Olivia, as if positioned like a placemat on a fine dining table. She stared at it. Her unfamiliarity with what was on the paper was obvious. Ted took notice.

"I just downloaded this and printed it out for you. Check out the feature story on winners and losers in here. Looks like it's time to pick and choose assets a little more wisely, and not think that a rising tide will lift all boats. I've been on the line with potential investors in Colombia, and I am missing some calls from old friends in Chile. So I'm going to ask nicely if you can go down to Santiago and tell everyone who matters that they need their money parked in US capital markets or even in South Florida real estate, according to a friend of mine who runs this small magazine over in Coral Gables. The guy talks to everyone, so he knows his shit," Ted said, pulling out another copy of *The Gateway*.

He flipped through some pages and then set the magazine down on the table. "We need to pitch potential investors on the need for our selective global currency and commodities trades to complement stock positions, and you're the right one to do it! Tell the copper-rich Chileans all the reserves of the red metal in the world aren't going to save them if Asia isn't buying as much."

Olivia maintained eye contact with Ted. "Well, can't we get Pracy and Anderson on it first?"

Ted considered Pracy and Anderson, two young but soon-to-be hedge fund whizzes once they got that banking mentality out of their minds and started thinking like trading aces.

"Who am I going to call?" she asked. "I don't have strong relationships in Chile, at least not properly updated. And those two need experience anyway. They need to grow." Her cell phone rang. She stared at it buzzing along the table, moving a bit from the vibrations. Unknown flashed across the screen. She ignored it.

"I already have it covered," Ted said. "I'm going to give you a list of names, and you'll oversee this road show. Go down to Chile. See what you can dig up. In fact, start with Sebastián Ledezma, a copper mogul, smart and very slippery, a real mercurial old man. I'll get you his contact information. Even if he doesn't want to invest with us, get to know him anyway. Ask him what's going on. He's dialed into everything in Chile, a country you should learn more about, and he knows pretty much everything else going on in the region. Great storyteller."

"I don't know, Ted. I haven't done any research on him. I don't know his needs. His savings and income streams. If he earns largely local or foreign currency. His savings may all be in Chile, or they may be here. Our fund might not be right for him, and nothing is more annoying than a specialized hedge fund out spouting cookie-cutter sales pitches, which is what I feel you're asking me to do." Her phone rang again. The unknown caller was back. She let it ring without screening it.

"Then look at it as a research trip. If Sebastián isn't into us, then get some names from him," Ted said. "Do some homework on a market you know well but should know extremely well. Chile. We need to grow there."

"Just Chile?" She took a seat at the opposite side of the table from Ted. Not the end of the table but at the corner.

"Yes, Chile for now. It's in a class by itself in South America. It's somewhat insulated from shockwaves that can rattle the rest of South America, and it's pretty diversified. It's a good study. There's money there, lots of it, thanks to past booms in copper, which is due to cool if these Chinese numbers keep pissing everyone off. Quieter Chinese factories and construction sites need less copper wire."

"You sound like a journalist," Olivia said.

"Well, maybe I am in some other universe. Still, Chile's got a bright long-term future." Ted jumped to his feet, snapped his fingers, and looked out the window. "Go down there, take a couple of days and drive up along the central coast. You'll think you're in California. Or even better, go sailing for a day or two way down south. It's September, and an early spring is approaching. You might find you like it and who knows? Next year, you'll sail around the tip of South America, around Cape Horn. Go meet Sebastián."

"Where are you going?"

"Me? Colombia, and then Brazil. Want to switch?"

"Not right now," Olivia said, a smile coming to her face. She'd spent a little time in Chile earlier in her career in equity sales nearly a decade ago. She had mentioned to Ted once she enjoyed the change of seasons. Ted saw her wheels turning.

"The spring is different in Chile than it is here on the East Coast," Ted said. "Santiago may be in early bloom. Flowers budding in the afternoon sun. The days getting longer and warmer, people wearing spring clothes along the tree-lined city streets. Bustling cafés. Long afternoons. All that."

"One condition," Olivia said. "When I get back, I want Pracy and Anderson stepping it up around here."

On top of acting as the portfolio manager, Olivia ran the investment selection committee, and took charge of sales and communicating with existing clients. Pracy and Anderson were following in her footsteps. They formed the core of the team, while other full-time and outside parties handled accounting, legal counsel, regulatory issues, and other matters.

"You got it."

"I'll book a flight leaving tomorrow out of Miami," Olivia said.

"Don't forget your in-flight reading for the plane ride," Ted said. He motioned to the magazine across the table.

"*The Gateway*?" Olivia said.

"It's out of Coral Gables. Decent reporter, that Street Brewer. The publisher has some good insight into the hemisphere. It will fill you in on some news from the region. Again, check out the lead story on Latin American markets being less tied to the US economy. Good stuff."

CHAPTER

9

Street left the Worldwide Oil & Gas office building and did another quick rewind of the digital recorder in the taxicab. The recorded voice of Domínguez and that of his own came in loud and clear. He even remembered all of it by heart, and he typed up some standout quotes in his phone while the cab flowed through traffic. The day was going without a glitch.

The driver dropped Street off at the Plaza Altamira. The large public square was a meeting ground for anyone and anything, ranging from young lovers to opposition political rallies. It was decorated with blooming flowers, park benches, a stately obelisk and fountains. Surrounding buildings that Street remembered still stood, although they were more worn out. He stared into a fountain pool and saw the reflection of blue skies and puffy white clouds as memories of yesteryear, when he used to relax on Sunday afternoons, came flooding back.

Then he noticed a thin man walking about the plaza, talking on his cell phone. The man glanced at Street, made eye contact, held it, and looked away. He was of average height with a reedy build and bushy gray hair, and he wore a tweed blazer and khaki pants. Street pegged him as an academic or a government economist of some sort. Smart and strong but not a leader—not enough charisma to be a politician. Definitely behind the scenes. He paced about a bit just far enough away that Street couldn't hear his conversation. The man stared at Street, stared at him for too long. Street stared back.

"Can I help you?" Street asked in Spanish.

The man said nothing, though Street heard him tell whoever was on the line to hold on, also in Spanish.

"Seriously, can I help you?" Street repeated himself, a little annoyed.

The man was up to something, but he was no common criminal, that was for sure. His body language suggested he was out of the ordinary, a foreigner like Street. The man smiled, snapped his phone off and into his coat pocket, and walked away.

Street watched him dart toward a nearby subway station, flicking his pen as he made his way, and thought nothing of it. Then Street saw it was five o'clock. Time to go meet his old boss Ian Collins.

He mounted the stairs of El Techo, a bar and grill just steps away from the pen-clicking man in the plaza. He had spent many a night here a few years back. After working late, he would pop into this cozy US-style tavern full of expats and Caraqueños alike. It was a two-story place, but most people ate and drank upstairs, hence its name, El Techo, Spanish for the roof. It could pass for a US corner pub save for the cloud of cigarette smoke.

He pulled the door open and bumped his chin, distracted by a young model or soap opera star leaving the restaurant, and muttered a curse word under his breath.

Speaking of curse words…

"Street fucking Brewer!"

He heard his name carry across the bar via a heavy northern English accent, blotting out the clink of happy hour. Clad from necktie to shoe in Armani, Ian Collins crossed the bar, grabbed Street's hand, shook it hard, and then lodged a beer in it.

"Welcome back to Caracas," Ian said, a broad smile stretching across his face.

He could pass for someone aged thirty thanks to his baby face, though he was really north of fifty. Black hair cut short over skeptical but smiling blue eyes. Neck like a bull. His skin remained white with a constant luster. He sized up Street in his conservative blue suit and blond hair.

"You stand out like a turd in a punch bowl in this town, mate. You look like you're oozing with dollars and unarmed at that. You'll be robbed for sure once we leave here. Always assume people are watching you. You remember that."

"Ian Collins," Street said. "Still knows what's best for everyone, and well you should. How long have you been here now? Twenty years or something?"

"Something like that."

"You look good. I guess you should after more than two decades living in the tropics, free from London's expenses and taxes," Street said.

"I knew from the day I first met you that you would move on."

"Nah. I liked it here. The death of our company sent me home, not the chaos. You know that," Street said.

They stared at each other, then each looked away. Street sat down at the solid wooden bar.

"Anyway, I always knew you were bailing. I can spot the short-timers," Ian said, lighting up a cigarette.

"I don't know. Maybe," Street said. "So, are you here for much longer? Wife ever going to make you guys move back to London?"

"No, mate," Ian said. "We're not going to London."

"Why not? No interest?"

"No wife. We split." He took a drink.

"Sorry to hear that. What happened?"

"We just drifted. Most of my savings drifted with her. That's it."

"Jesus, what did you do?"

"Cheers, Street!" Ian said, rolling his eyes. "She wanted the UK, and I wanted Caracas. We both saw wealth and adventure outside our native countries. The grass is always greener and all that."

"I'm sorry, Ian," Street said.

Half Dutch, half Irish but raised in northern England, Ian was Street's former bureau chief when they worked at the wire service years earlier. Ian was now a freelance writer with regular clients, including specialty energy publications in the United States and Europe and a few business magazines and online news services. When a fresh crisis popped up and pushed the country center stage in the global spotlight, Ian would either report for the world's major news outlets or appear on television sets in live interviews to brief the world on what was going on and make sense of the catastrophe.

Nobody had sources like Ian, no one in the foreign press, that is. Ian was a reporter's reporter—fearless, tough, and as smart as they come. He was often the first to break stories in Venezuela, like surprise oil output cuts or plans to publicly jail opposition leaders.

Before excelling on the job, Ian excelled in academia at the London School of Economics, where to the surprise of many, he championed leftist causes. While a self-described socialist, and a staunch one at that, Ian often pointed out that communism failed because it arose in rural countries like Russia and Eastern Europe, morphing into some sort of strongman hybrid form of an oligarchy in the process.

Odd words for a reporter who covered capital markets for bankers and traders and did it so well, Street thought, though Ian was likely trying to get a rise out of Street for being an American and stopped short of seriously endorsing Marxist doctrines. And to really break the mold, Ian opted for Armani and Ermenegildo Zegna suits, tailor-made at that, rather than windbreakers and plaid shirts typical of union bosses and leftist politicians in the region. Ian Collins was in a class by himself.

"The United States is perfect for communism. Lots of industries, constantly improving technology, widening income gaps, educated people angry at watching their standards of living erode, while the rich get richer," he told Street over drinks after work one day a few years back. His comments, even if in English, raised a few eyebrows. No need for translation. Street was used to it.

"So, how's the leftist cause?" Street asked that afternoon in El Techo, unwinding from his interview at Worldwide Oil & Gas. "How is Venezuela's model of socialism?"

"These guys in power? They're no socialists, just do-it-both-ways populists who say they're champions of the left but pay their lenders right on time, or at least they used to before they fucked that up," Ian said. "Just like anyone who ever ran this country. They throw oil money on the most pressing problems, you know, give people subsidies or made-up jobs of some sort so they'll line up drunk and happy at the next election. Ideology is dead. It's all branding, and with no new areas of economic activity to cultivate, no structural changes at all, and with crude prices falling, I'm worried, Street.

I've been talking to lots of people, and this place is going to implode soon. It's gonna be bad unless the president can muster up a miracle." He paused and then glanced at Street. "I mean really bad."

"How bad is really bad?" Street asked. "He's got buddies in Moscow and elsewhere that share his goals that can lend to him."

"Really bad? Who knows? Venezuela is in a class by itself. Anyway, the president can't borrow much more," Ian said, taking a pull from his beer and lighting a smoke. "There's only so much any of us can borrow."

Street said nothing, taking note of Ian's pricey garb. "Borrowing is like everything else. One form of it may go out of fashion, but the power of lending to and then controlling another never goes out of style. Nice getup by the way, Ian."

"Thanks, bro," Ian said, clinking his glass to Street's, not making eye contact but checking his phone.

Street made note of his blend of American and UK slang, hybrid idioms that creep into any expat's vocabulary, changing anything from nouns to describe kitchen items and household goods to insults.

Street saw Ian open up a bank app. He couldn't make out how much was in whatever account that was on the screen, but he did see that there weren't too many numbers.

"Times pretty tough?" Street asked.

"They're tough all around," Ian said. "Nothing's permanent, dude." He looked at Street. "How are you holding up? Financially, that is."

"I'm getting by," Street said.

"Just getting by? I thought so."

"Well, apparently I'm doing better than you," Street said.

Ian said nothing.

They caught up for an hour or two, small talk mainly, until Street noticed that the same man from the plaza—the one talking on the cell phone and clicking his pen—was now inside the bar and seated across the room at a nearby table made of dark wood. Street stared at him, and the man met his gaze. This time, Street held it for a while with resolve since he was obviously being followed or studied somehow. The man had eyes like coffee beans and comfortably worn skin that was a little pale and loose but not sickly, as if he had just had his skin laundered and put back on, though the tropical heat and city grime were loosening it a bit. The man kept Street's stare, sipped what appeared to be water, and then quietly stood and walked off, clicking his pen.

"Did you see that guy?"

"What guy?"

"That man. He was just over there, clicking a pen. Staring at us. He's been following me around all afternoon," Street said. He thought about the black SUV in the Everglades and the mystery caller back in Coconut Grove.

"So you still paranoid? Man, you came to the right city," Ian said, taking a pull from his cigarette and looking across the bar. "Maybe a little paranoia is a good thing."

"I'm not paranoid, even though you told me to be just a few minutes ago," Street said, clearing his head of thoughts of being followed either in North or South America. "Anyway, I'm drawing interest. I don't trust anyone in this city."

"Not even me? I'm your old boss." He glanced up at a television set.

A baseball game was on. Baseball, Venezuela's athletic obsession. The Miami Marlins were playing the New York Mets. Marlins were up six to four. Sixth inning. The game bored Street for a bit, so he glanced back at where the man with the pen had been. A young man and woman, both in pinstripe business attire, occupied the table now. They sat reading menus while discussing the day's events in emerging bond markets. Their suits were so alike that they resembled employees in a fine clothing store as opposed to wealth managers, which they clearly were, judging from their conversation.

"There are few people I trust down here. But I guess you're one, Ian. Who else can you be wary of but depend on at the same time?"

And just then, a pair of large, brown eyes captured the attention of all in the bar. Beautiful, brown hair cascaded down a soft neck. Men sat up straight. Women frowned, as if by reflex, out of jealousy or grudging appreciation. Ana Patricia Osorio Harding entered the bar and crossed the room.

"Street Brewer. Good to see you have a life beyond oil platforms, refinery outages, double-skinned tankers, and futures markets. Figured I'd find you here."

"Good to see that you have a life besides working at the only major oil company that signs deals with only squeaky-clean governments."

She smiled.

"Please join us," Street said. "This is a friend and former colleague . . ."

"Ian Collins," Patricia said. She smiled at Ian and extended her hand.

"Patricia, I'm sorry, what was the last name?" Ian asked.

"Full name is Ana Patricia Osorio Harding. Just Patricia is fine. Please, tell me you haven't forgotten me, Ian? Remember when I was a young public relations manager at the oil company? You tore our last boss up? You didn't even write a story afterward. Showed up for an interview just to taunt our guy."

"Of course! Ana Patricia Osorio Harding," Ian said, stressing her last name.

"You know who I am, Ian," she said.

"Let's get Patricia something to drink," Street said. "What would you like? I hear they make pretty good rum in Venezuela."

"Polar beer, if there's any left on the shelves."

The bartender brought over a glass of Polar. "*Salud*," Patricia said, raising her glass, making eye contact with both Street and Ian. She sat down at the bar. Street sat in the middle, Patricia to his right, and Ian to his left.

Street dove in. "These shortages suck," he said. "Run low on tampons and toilet paper, okay. But run low on beer? Not happening. Anyway, I thought the interview went well. How did I measure up? Did I ask the right questions? Did I miss anything?"

"You interviewed Worldwide Oil & Gas already?" Ian asked. "Street, why didn't you inform me first? I have a few questions for that cockwomble capitalist Domínguez." Both Street and Patricia dismissed him with smiles.

"You did well, especially with that bit about our company and the government in cahoots, where we get kicked out and then get invited back in for a yard sale. Very original."

"Well, it's not so far-fetched but thank you," Street said, shifting his body to face Patricia.

"Nothing better than a creative story, and not something cut-and-dry like you guys used to write," Patricia said. "You remember asking to know changes to output and all that boring shit. Still, though, we're not in bed with the government. But stick around. Keep digging. You never know who's in bed with whom."

"Well, you can never let the facts get in the way of a really good story," Street said.

"What are you talking about?" Ian asked, suddenly interested in the fact that Street had a theory that didn't sound like Street's. "Street doesn't believe in theories or conspiracies or any bullshit. He just tends to dwell on present facts, which get a little dry at times. You were always too reactive."

"Maybe I'm boring, but I don't want to be that guy at the water cooler full of crackpot conspiracy stories."

"Street here believes that Venezuela forced out the foreign oil companies, so the government looks like a champion for the poor. Later, when the government needs oil revenue because it doesn't have the money and up-to-date technology to produce in aging fields, it'll open up those wells and invite the oil companies back to the country at attractive terms, so they'll bring that foreign technology with them and drill away and produce. Pump fresh petrodollars into company coffers. Everybody wins," Patricia said.

"I don't really believe it. But I wouldn't rule it out. Anyway, it was my boss's question, not mine," Street said, pulling Ian's box of cigarettes from across the bar. He stared at them and then pushed them back.

Both Patricia and Ian studied Street as if they were taking part in some sort of marketing focus group or in a behind-the-scenes psychological test.

"I haven't had a smoke in ages," Street said. "Just being back here rekindles old habits, you know? Surroundings and all that."

"Very self-aware," Patricia said. "I like that. Anyway, I haven't heard of any secret deals between the Venezuelans and Big Oil or the Russian government other than the president's nonsense, but if I do, I will let you know."

"Who said anything about Russians?" Street said. "Are we talking oil or that port deal the president alluded to? Or am I missing something?"

"Relax, chief. Russians are all around. Everyone knows that," Ian said. "They set up shop here a long time ago. It's common knowledge that their military is well established in the country. They now have a toehold in America's backyard, and some fresh eyes and ears on their investments here."

"Ideology takes a back seat to money any day. Anyway, I'm not on this trip to write about Russians," Street said. "I'm just asking the questions that are on the minds of the Miami business community and my boss. Speaking of bosses, I'll need some government sources to counter what yours told me today," Street said to Patricia. "Both sides of the story and all that. Know anyone who is some bombastic loudmouth who will counter everything Domínguez said?"

"That's kind of a wide net in this administration," Patricia said, laughing. "Who have you spoken to on this trip so far? Anyone in the government?"

"Just you for now."

Another quiet befell the group. Street glanced at the television. Marlins were still ahead. Street looked over his shoulder and scanned the bar. "Hey, Patricia, when you came in, did you see a thin man in the corner over there? Clicking a pen? Looked a little out of place?"

Patricia scanned her surroundings. She shrugged. "Nothing."

Street shrugged as well and looked back at the baseball game on television. "That's quite an arm," he said.

Patricia and Ian stared up at the television as well. A break from keeping the conversation going.

"Speaking of arms," Street said. "Is Venezuela still on a weapons spending spree?"

"Pretty much," Ian said. "Last I heard, they were stocking up their army and gangs in the slums with a fresh batch of Kalashnikovs. Russian. The good kind."

"I heard that," Street said. "Pretty soon they'll manufacture them here as well, if they aren't already doing so now—at least that's what I heard far away in Miami."

"You heard that? In Miami?" Patricia asked, eyes wide. Street thought she looked pleasantly surprised.

"I bum around in the Everglades a lot. I come into contact with some real gun nuts or gun enthusiasts, depending on your voting bias. There's always someone trying to get ahold of a Russian-made Kalashnikov, and Russia's pal Venezuela isn't too far away. People talk about these things,

Venezuelan expats included. Anyway, they'll start manufacturing them here if they aren't already."

"Interesting. What else have you heard, Street?" Patricia asked.

"That's about it really. Venezuela is still pumping out lots of cocaine to the US and sending subsidized oil to Cuba despite US sanctions," Street said. "A buddy of mine in the coast guard says they're working on internal studies to gauge smuggling."

"Interesting," Patricia said. "And?"

"Well," Street said, feeling a little confident because he had captured the interest of a beautiful woman. "He said based on their research and intelligence, the percentage of narcotics consumed in the US that's actually smuggled in from abroad could drop. Like by a lot. People will get high off more chemicals manufactured at home like meth or bath salts or God knows what else. Stuff shipped in from China, too. Smugglers in this neck of the woods are taking note. And so are drug lords. They'll try and get what they can while the demand is there. It's all economics."

"Fascinating," Patricia said. "You say your friend is with the coast guard? It's not Horacio Suárez is it? I have friends in the coast guard."

"No. My friend Alfredo Lino. Anyway, let's not talk about work anymore."

"Agreed, because I have to go," Patricia said. "Have a good evening, and Ian, make sure Street gets home at a reasonable hour. Be safe. They say the streetlights will be going out soon, meaning this dark city will literally be dark earlier than normal." She gave Ian a peck on the cheek goodbye. Same with Street. His kiss lasted longer.

"Oh, and one last thing about work, Street. If you want to balance your story with a public official like you just said, there's an exec from the state-owned oil company who hangs out drinking coffee up in Petare about now. He's not too outspoken, but he is smart and could help you with your oil witch-hunt story. I'll text you his name and contact info," Patricia said. "And, Street?" she added. "Call me if you ever feel you're sick and tired of *The Gateway*. I know it's a small gig with no hopes for much growth or even an ownership stake, so maybe I can help with some contacts."

"Thanks, Patricia. I appreciate that," Street said, a little caught off guard by the offer but interested anyway.

She paid the tab for all three in cash. The bartender brought her change. She handed the man a tip and watched the baseball game for a minute longer. Marlins were still up.

"Later, boys," she said, and walked out.

Both men watched her go. Street watched her for a little longer. And then it happened. She turned around, smiled at Street, and walked out into the night.

"Forget it, mate," Ian said. "She's married."

"I know," Street said. He sighed and glanced up at the TV a few minutes later. Game over. No final score. Someone had changed the channel.

"Does she know how you really lost your job?" Ian asked. "How you got fired not long after I left? That you weren't let go due to slashed payrolls? You were allowed to spin your dismissal to downsizing and bankruptcy, but let's remember, there was a six-month window between when you were shown the door and when everyone else got sacked."

"No. And she won't know, nor will anyone else."

"What were you thinking? Why didn't you go along with it? Too afraid to take a little risk? I turned out okay."

"Well, it looks like you're broke today, Ian. Anyway, I was squeaky-clean and employed. I didn't need the money."

"Look where you ended up. In fact, look where you are now. You're probably going to have to help bail that dumb fuck cousin of yours out of trouble," Ian said. "Don't think I don't know what's going on. At any rate, you'll always need money because you never take career risks."

"That's enough, Ian," Street said. A couple of bar patrons turned their heads. Even if they didn't speak English, they could easily catch Street's tone of voice.

"Street..."

"Just shut up right now."

"Okay. I've overstepped my bounds."

"Ian, that's enough."

"Agreed," Ian said.

He motioned to the bartender and ordered a shot of tequila. He didn't offer Street one. The bartender approached with the small shot glass glistening on a black tray, eyeing both Ian and Street with a slight air of suspicion. He set the glass down on the bar as if the drink were some kind of pricey gem, and stared at Ian, wondering whether he could afford it. Nobody wanted drunken foreigners running around bringing attention to themselves.

"Thanks," Street said to the bartender, who snapped back into an air of humbly fabricated servitude and walked away drying his hands with a bar towel.

Ian took the shot and stared at Street. Street stared back at Ian and then down at the empty glass.

"Something bothering you, Ian?"

"Get out of here, Street. It's not safe," Ian said, looking as if he were delivering bad medical news.

Street laughed. "It's never been safe here. For decades. I know it's worse now and all that, but come on. Get real. Venezuela was never the oasis people said it was before."

"I didn't mean tonight. I meant after this trip, don't come back. Ever."

"What?"

"I'm serious."

Street stared at Ian. There was something different about him, as if he were suffering from a sadness or a lack of confidence that was seriously atypical for the fearless reporter that had taught him everything. As if he were in trouble, and Street was next.

"Ian, something's wrong, isn't it?"

Ian slammed his beer and took a sip of a glass of water.

"No, mate. Nothing at all. Just be careful."

About five minutes passed. Both Street and Ian glanced at the television set and their cell phones, not saying a word, until Street broke the silence.

"Look, let's turn over a new leaf and get out of here and go get a news story. I need a government source, and if Patricia is right, at this hour, that guy from the national oil company has paid his bar tab and will be enjoying coffee and cake at this little place down in Petare. I know who Patricia was talking about. Let's go get him."

"I know who he is, too," Ian said. "He grew up on that end of town and was pretty much anonymous until the world discovered he had a brain and a flair for financial engineering."

"That's the guy," Street said. "Let's go talk to him. I need him. I can't work at some low-paying job like the one I have at *The Gateway*. I need to get out there with some good clips, and good clips are measured by one thing, and you taught me that, Ian."

"By who is talking to you," Ian said. "And what he's saying, of course. Anyway, your boy pops into this little coffee shop after happy hour to enjoy a little dessert. It's right there, not far from the subway station. Nice little rustic place that kind of stands out. Let's go find him. He'll probably be there tonight with baseball on, and he'd be a great source for your conspiracy theory."

"I don't care how dangerous it is, I'm going in there tonight. We'll be reasonably safe as long as we're near the subway," Street said.

"You're right. Early evening rush hour is still in full swing, so we'll be fine at this hour. As long as you don't go up into the slums," Ian said.

Street stared at the front door, his image of Patricia leaving still fresh in his mind. He felt the calming elixirs of the beer run deeper in his veins, relaxing more and more of his muscles. He then ordered a cup of coffee to wake up a bit. The suspicious bartender brought it over, relieved they weren't ordering more shots, and set it down as if it were an item Street could afford. The man nodded and walked away. Street stared into his coffee mug. It was often rare to see American coffee in Venezuela, but El Techo had it. He wondered if they had made a fresh pot when Street had asked for it or if someone else in the bar or restaurant had ordered coffee. He was getting bored.

"I need a jolt of caffeine so I can stay sharp when we get robbed or hassled by the police. I don't have the funds these days to pay off some idiot cop for imagined infractions."

"That's not going to happen. Not to a foreign journalist," Ian said.

"Well, it might."

Ian nodded as he swallowed even more beer, enjoying the fact that he had struck a nerve. He motioned to the bartender for a last shot of tequila and the bill.

"Don't be so paranoid. Forget the past," Ian said.

"I'm working on that," Street said. "Let's go."

They walked down the stairs out of El Techo. A cool evening breeze met them in front of the Plaza Altamira. Street was happy. A longer night out on the town was due. After all, when would he be in Caracas again?

"Let's go to that coffee shop in Petare. Let's see part of the real Venezuela and find that source. Show this town I still have what it takes."

"There's the old Street."

To the east, millions of lights in Petare, one of Latin America's largest slums, twinkled across a massive hillside, firing up for the evening like some wild carnival that was opening for business.

10

S treet and Ian descended the steps into the subway. Despite the city's gritty appearance, the subway station was clean, its floors swept that night and its tiled walls scrubbed to a welcoming luster. They boarded the train and headed east to Petare, hoping power outages or maintenance issues wouldn't disrupt the night.

Though known for its massive slums, Petare was also home to remnants that embodied South America's majestic past. Something about the white and yellow walls and the old streets conjured up images of a vibrant history and captivated Street. Barred windows and tiled roofs. Horses clopping on cobblestone streets alongside old Spanish buildings. Ladies in stagecoaches. Dreams of commerce, of global trade, of extending an empire from Spain. Gold and silver. Agriculture. Romance. Chivalry.

Street and Ian found two yellow plastic seats available on the subway. "This will be a good thing. You're gonna get some keen quotes for your story," Ian told Street in Spanish. "If he speaks to you on record, then you've got a solid story."

"I guess, whatever. It will be good to get out of the Chacao district," Street answered back in Spanish. They spoke in Spanish so the other commuters would understand them and wouldn't think they were sitting alongside lost foreigners with limited time in the country. That would make everyone nervous—outsiders drawing attention to themselves in a part of the city where they shouldn't be. Images of armed robbery and stray bullets can make for an unhappy commute.

"After we find that source, I'm having me some of that counterfeit whisky while we're here," Ian said. "I've got to try that shit."

"It's terrible. You're gonna need new kidneys and a liver after one shot," Street said, staring out the window into the passing blackness of the tunnel. "A European in an Italian suit and a Yank with a briefcase. We'll be robbed for sure if we wander too far away. This isn't England, Ian. A fistfight isn't the worst thing that could happen in this area of the city if we get too crazy. You know that."

"Nothing's going to happen," Ian said. "We're just going to walk on about a hundred yards, and then we'll be safe. Coffee for you, and some counterfeit whisky for me. Sure, the bottle will say Johnnie Walker on the outside, but God knows what kind of rotgut swill will be inside. Or maybe they'll just slap a cheap brand on it, like Manager's Whisky."

"The Manager's Choice? The Manager's Dram? The good stuff from Scotland?"

"No, Manager's Whisky," Ian said. "It's a cheap brand. It has an English name, but I've only seen it here. God knows where they make it, or even what it really is."

Street listened to the hum of the subway. A few passengers looked at them but paid them no real attention. Tired commuters mainly. Street thought about the man clicking the pen at the bar. Then he said in English, "Something doesn't seem right about this city anymore. Or this night. Something's off. This trip is weird."

"You just need to get used to being back here. You know you can't come home again. This is the best idea all night."

The metro came to the Petare stop, and the doors opened. Street and Ian left the soft colors of the tiled metro station and rode up on the escalator. They exited the station. Street looked at the hills, which were no longer large and far away but bustling under the night sky. Power lines and hanging light bulbs snaked up the narrow streets. Swarms of couriers and commuters on their motorcycles, some new and shiny, some old and rickety, zoomed about in the bustle amid the early evening rush. Some motorcyclists were working as makeshift cab drivers, ferrying friends and strangers to their destinations in the chaos. The energy of a Friday sizzled just as hot as it did anywhere else.

"Plenty of places nearby," Street said, shouting over the noise.

"This way," Ian said. "I see it. It's actually just at the foot of the hill." He pointed to a nearby café up the road, a well-lit place with a busy take-out window.

The noise of the street vendors hawking their wares dimmed a bit as they headed up, away from the subway entrance. Ian had taken off his suit jacket and thrown it over his shoulder. Street squinted and saw a café. It did look nice, but it was a bit farther up the road, farther away from the metro station than he had imagined. They walked past several busy street corners crammed with street peddlers and pedestrians and retail outlets selling clothes and other basic consumer products. It was still reasonably safe where they were. The streets were so bustling and crowded that even if they didn't blend in, the sheer mass of humanity would hide them from anyone more than two feet away.

"Hang on," Ian said.

Street looked over at Ian. He had a cigarette and was trying to light it. The wind kept blowing out his matches.

"Do you still have a lighter? Mine's about to die."

"Nope," Street said. "I haven't had a smoke in ages."

"I have to light this out of the wind," Ian said. He turned off the sidewalk and headed into a slum entrance and walked up a few steps along a narrow stairway, where he was still reasonably safe. Street tensed a bit at Ian entering the slum, but he knew he was just a stone's throw from the street, and all would be fine if he lit his cigarette quickly. Fortunately, a curve in the alley blocked any view of them from those who might be hanging out above.

He flicked the lighter, but eddies of wind kept finding the flame and blowing it out. Ian climbed the stairs even farther and sought calmer air deeper in the lee of the slum walls. Small children emerged from their colorful shantytown homes to stare at the foreigners. Street thought Ian looked like a politician, stumping in an impoverished area. Suit coat off. Sleeves rolled up. The works.

Ian lit his smoke and they were about to turn around when they heard a shout.

"Gringos!" a voice shot from above. They looked up. A plump, older woman, whose smooth tanned skin had wrinkled into a frown, stared down at them from a window above. A look of disdain.

"Wait right there," she shouted. They did, honoring a universal instinct among young men to behave and stand up straight in front of a matronly figure. Street couldn't help feeling that he was going to get a lecture about something, safety no doubt. A few seconds later, she waddled out of her home and down the narrow stairway donning a flowery dress and an apron. She stormed over like an approaching hurricane, spinning in their direction with a gradually increasing resolve. Street thought it would have been fitting if she had a rolling pin or a skillet in her hand, ready to chase them away. Both just stood there, feeling like two mischievous boys who had been caught red-handed in some schoolyard prank, though they were trying to figure out what for.

"What the fuck are you doing here?" the woman shouted in Spanish, her word choice catching Street and Ian off guard. She stood there, short but firm and upright, her face jutting up into Street's.

"Just lighting up a smoke," Ian said. "Too windy out there."

"Rich foreigners like you two don't take walks around here. You do that back near the Plaza Altamira or wherever the fuck it is you came from," she said, still sizing up Ian and Street although she wasn't even five feet tall.

Street intervened. "We're meeting a friend for coffee, and we wanted to see the historic Petare." He stared at Ian, even got in his face a little. "Can we get out of here please? This isn't funny."

The old woman frowned at Street. "The historic part of Petare? Get real. Plus, there are historic parts in your own countries you should see first. What are you here for? Drugs? A Venezuelan girlfriend you'll leave one day once she's no longer exotic? Get out of here, dipshits," she shouted, shooing the two away. "Get back on that metro and stay where you belong. You have no idea how dangerous it is around here."

"Look," Ian said. "We're just checking things out on a nice evening. We apologize," Ian said, leaning forward and speaking into the breeze. "And we're just a little lost."

The old woman shouted, "Not a little lost, but very lost. You're not safe here. Out! Fuck off!" That was enough exploring for one night. They headed down the hill. As they reached the end of the alley, Street turned back and made eye contact with the old woman. She shook her head. Then she smiled at them both, a sincere motherly smile, looking out for two dumb boys. She turned and disappeared into her world.

Street and Ian walked down the stairs, broke out of the neighborhood, and made their way to the wider street. They turned right. "That was good for a laugh," Ian said. "Come on. Let's forget the café and the oil source and head back to the safer side of town and grab another round. We don't need any trouble. I'll buy," Ian said.

"Agreed," Street said. "Maybe we can find some Manager's Whisky."

Back up the hill, the old woman shooed some teenage girls away. A few boys made their way down. She knew right away which ones were bad news and which ones were armed. In this case, all of them were armed. She looked at them, sighed, and walked back to her home. From her apron, she withdrew a cell phone. She dialed. "It's Maria. Ian was just here. With the American. What's his name? Street? Ian said they were just a little lost." She hung up.

CHAPTER

11

Ian and Street headed through the sprawling streets of Petare back to the subway. Even more street vendors were hawking clothing, electronics, and pretty much everything else they could find in the still-early evening. Police officers, pedestrians, children, and hurried commuters flowed past one another quickly, eager to unwind for the evening.

Street took in the city energy, and then shook his head. "Thanks Ian. Not only did we risk being shot, but we weren't even tough enough to take on the grandmothers in this part of town. I'm feeling really good. If only Brianna were around to see this."

Ian laughed. "Did you see how the neighborhood girls were checking you out back there?"

"They were curious as to who the two foreigners were," Street said.

"Maybe so. Let's find a liquor store and head back to where we belong."

A few street peddlers selling counterfeit products snatched up their wares, and obvious pickpockets began to dash through the crowd like excited birds, one after the other fleeing in a flock. Cops approaching to crack down on fencing, Street thought.

Street relaxed at the sight of the suspicious characters fleeing. The arrival of cops would keep the gangs away from the streets and up in the hillside slums, even if only for a few minutes. Still, he didn't want to hang out for too long. Cops could be dangerous too.

"Let's get out of here," Street said. "Let's just get a cab and head back and have a drink at the hotel bar. Forget the metro. I want out of here."

"Metro's just up the corner. Quicker to take it than wait for a ride. Let's avoid this raid and cut through this square," Ian said. They hurried through the streets into a fairly well-lit square just off the main street. Few people were in it. Street walked ahead at a brisk pace, glancing left and right, forward and behind as he moved along. Most of the people had fled with the arrival of the police cracking down on petty theft, drug possession, or even selling pirated goods. The empty streets were a bad thing, as there was less humanity to shield them from danger. Both Street and Ian felt a wave of relief as the entrance of the metro grew larger.

"Back to our safe zone," Street said.

"Agreed," Ian said.

Then they heard loud words, loud words clearly directed at them both.

"You two, stop right there!" a man's voice ordered in Spanish.

"Again? Really?" Street said.

They both turned and faced a national police officer. Decked out in what appeared to Street to be some sort of bluish camouflage uniform, the officer stood smiling. He was short, had dark-brown wrinkled skin, and a bit of a moustache. He was fairly old for a street cop, and fat as well. Yet he was backed up by two other officers who were both so young that their uniforms didn't seem to fit, as if they were two school kids dressed up in their fathers' gear. The ringleader paced over in a calm, relaxed manner, a smile stretching from ear to ear. To Street, corrupt cops looked the same wherever they were. It was the insincere smile. The government had long overhauled the once highly fragmented Caracas police force, yet these guys didn't get the message, especially the fat one, who still harbored the mindset when small bands of rogue police officers patrolled—and terrorized—the city.

"Over here, foreigners. Let's go. Step it up."

Both Ian and Street knew they were screwed. Clichés are bad news when getting robbed, especially abroad. *We're all friends here. No problem, sir, no problem. This situation is a bit complicated.* Pick a cliché. Things weren't good.

"We were just headed to the metro," Street said.

Ian nudged Street to shut up. Unfortunately, no clichés came.

"You two are fucked," the officer said. He circled Street and Ian, motioning them to a small courtyard nearby that would be largely void of pedestrians. "Tell me, idiots, in what area of town are you staying?" the officer said, pushing the muzzle of the pistol into Street's chest.

"I'm staying in the Chacao-Altamira area. My friend lives here. He has a national ID card, and I have a passport with a valid tourist visa. We have the proper documents," Street said in Spanish.

"Just as I thought," the policeman said. "You're no strangers here. You speak Venezuelan Spanish, and you know how bad it can be to be out and about in this city without documents. Plus, you know what area of town a foreigner should be in and"—he motioned to the mountain of slums behind him—"shouldn't be in. What is it you were looking for here? Cocaine? Marijuana? Either you have it, or I'm planting it. Maybe even some spy stuff, too."

"We hear the whisky is good on this side of town," Street said. The officer shook his head and began to walk around them.

"I find that a little hard to believe. Anyway, it seems to me that things are going to get a little complicated."

Both Street and Ian sighed in relief at the cliché.

"This is going to be a fairly routine shakedown. How much money do you have on you?" Street asked Ian in a hushed tone in English.

"I've got euros and pounds. You've got dollars. Enough to keep us both out of jail," Ian said.

"Not likely," Street said.

"Shut up," the dumpy officer shouted. Both Ian and Street shut their mouths.

"Breaking the law in Venezuela is just as much an offense as it is in your so-called civilized countries."

"Come off it, then," Ian said.

"Seriously," Street said. "We haven't done anything at all. We don't have any drugs. We haven't robbed anyone, and we don't have rare birds or orchids stuffed in our clothes to smuggle abroad and sell. This is bullshit. You want to search us, then search us. You think you got something to ticket us with, then ticket us. If you have reason to arrest us, then arrest us, but just don't fuck with us!" Street went off in Spanish. "How much?"

A baton wacked Street's back. He went down, grimacing in pain, though laughing a bit. The hit was more of a warning than a blow designed to cause serious injury. He stood back up. By now the two younger officers had their guns drawn. That didn't worry Street as much as their blank stares. Few things are scarier than a very young man with an automatic weapon and the IQ of a fern.

"You fucked up, boss," the cop said, spitting on Street's shoes.

Street spoke up. "Look, officer. You seem like a rational man. There has to be some way out of this. We don't have anything illegal on us. Surely there must be some way we can work this out. We are truly sorry for what we have done," Street said, his hands raised.

"And for what we have left undone," Ian mumbled. Street snickered.

The corrupt cop seemed a little pleased. "Well, I would hate to ask you for your IDs only to see you've lost your passport. You know what kind of a nightmare that could be, you know, trying to leave Venezuela without a passport," the cop said, pacing behind Ian and Street. He snatched Street's briefcase. Rooted around. Found a passport with a visa. A ninety-day tourist visa. The cop went on. "But then again, it would be illegal to work here on a tourist visa." He rooted around in the bag, found the digital recorder, rewound it, and listened to the interview in English.

"Interesting," the cop said, putting the recorder in his shirt pocket. "Not sure what kind of work you were doing here but something that sure merits more than a tourist visa."

He looked at Ian and snatched his wallet from his pants. "And I can only guess where you work. How about I just toss your IDs and arrest you both for walking around undocumented? Let you rot in a Venezuela prison for a while before we hand you both over to the military for smuggling or espionage."

"Smuggling? Here? Look, how about twenty dollars? Twenty for you and twenty for those two and then we go. Everybody wins," Street asked.

"Fuck you. This isn't the nineties. Try five hundred dollars," the cop said, motioning to himself and the other two officers.

"Jesus, don't lowball him, Street," Ian said.

The officer didn't say anything. He just stared at Street.

"Great. Five hundred dollars for the three of you to split," said Street. "Forget going to an ATM and having me withdraw money. The only thing you'll get from us there is the weak local currency. The money is not in my briefcase. Root around in there all you want. I have it on me. In my shoe."

The cop glanced back at the two officers. He motioned for them to back off a bit. They did. "Five hundred," the cop said.

"Whatever," Street said. He reached down into his sock and took out five one-hundred-dollar bills and handed them over. The cop smiled, pocketed them, and shouted back to his two subordinates. "Two hundred dollars, boys," the cop said, giving Street and Ian a slight wink at their shared knowledge of his own personal windfall of three hundred dollars.

They smiled back. Blank smiles.

Street relaxed. Not for long.

"All of you, just stop right there," a voice from out of nowhere shouted in neutral, calm Venezuelan Spanish from what seemed like in all directions, definitely over a loudspeaker. Street, Ian, and the cops turned and were blinded by several flashlights that popped on at once.

"That's enough," the deep voice sounded. "Everybody show me your hands. And that means you three officers as well."

Street and Ian did as they were told. The three national police officers did as well. Street never heard them place their guns on the ground. But he did hear a chorus of assault rifles clicking to life all around him from behind the glare of flashlights and blinding car headlights. The vehicles surrounded all of them.

"We're either saved or extremely screwed right now," Ian said.

Even the national police officers knew something was up beyond the ordinary. The lights gave way to several uniformed men dressed in green fatigues. The Bolivarian National Guard of Venezuela. They were tall, speedy, and moved like trained soldiers, unlike the three national police officers. They quickly seized Street and Ian, and had them place their hands on the hoods of unmarked cars that hadn't even been there a second ago. One official in civilian clothes looked calmly at a smartphone, scrolling through pages as if he were a medical doctor outside a patient's room. Tall and thin, he had very dark skin and short, wiry, brown hair. He wore blue suit pants and a white shirt with a yellow tie. The jacket was probably back somewhere in the office. He glanced over. His green eyes flashed to Street and Ian. He looked down at the three police officers and shook his head. "Idiots," Street heard the man say.

"Us or the cops?" Street asked. Who was this guy? Is he with the national guard? The police? Street wished he had more money set aside for a fresh round of bribery. He had another five hundred dollars in cash back in the hotel, which he wanted to put right back in the bank when he got home.

A few of the uniformed military officers spoke to the man in civilian clothes, who nodded calmly. He walked over to the national police officers, who were now disarmed. "You three, give me the money the American gave you," the man said. Street recognized the same booming voice from the loudspeaker moments earlier.

The fat police officer handed the money over to the plainclothes official, who counted it and then shook his head.

Street, meanwhile, stopped counting at fifteen men and seven women in green fatigues. He glanced at the top of the nearby buildings and saw more officials, both female and male, with guns drawn on Ian and him. Police on the roof? Who did they think he and Ian were?

"All of it. I know he gave you five hundred dollars total. I saw the whole thing go down. Hand it over to me," the plainclothes official said.

The officer shrugged and rolled his eyes. The two young officers stared at each other and then angrily at the fat man.

With a speed Street had never seen, the plainclothes official whipped a pistol out. A .45. Big and powerful. The barrel jammed hard at the temple of the corrupt street cop.

"All of it. I'm serious. Don't think I won't execute you right here. This whole neighborhood would rejoice."

The cop did as he was told.

The plainclothes man took the rest of the money and waved it at the younger officers. "When you shake down foreigners, be sure you do it with someone who splits it fairly." He walked over to the dumpy police officer and leaned down to stare at him. "What business do you have with these two foreigners? Anything legitimate? Did they commit any real crime?"

"No, sir," the dumpy cop said.

"Then drag your sorry asses out of here and go catch some *malandros* up in those slums, that is, if you're not too afraid to go up there," the official said. "And give me that digital recorder."

The fat cop drew it from his shirt pocket and handed it over. Then the law enforcement trio gathered their guns and trudged away, looking like a losing baseball team headed back to the lockers.

Street felt relieved and a little curious at the same time. One, he knew he wasn't dealing with corrupt cops anymore but with trained professionals, yet on the other hand, what would an armed squad of military personnel want from Street and Ian? And who the hell was this guy in street clothes?

It seems the thin officer with green eyes was reading his mind.

"I guess you may be wondering why I am here. So I'll tell you. My name is Pérez, of the, well, let's just say I am with your friendly neighborhood police department. Or the military. Or the finance ministry. Or the tourism board's welcoming committee. It doesn't really concern you. And second of all, we have idiots running the country who may overhaul civilian and military intelligence services again on some other half-cocked whim just to be a thorn in the side of your government, Mr. Brewer."

"How did you know my name?"

"It's my job. We've been following you," Pérez said, stuffing the money back into Street's shirt. Pérez turned to face Ian. "And you, Mr. Collins? What brings you here to the slums with Mr. Brewer? Not a lot of oil executives here to provide you with some real market-moving news regardless of what you might hear."

"We heard there are," Ian said.

"Wonderful. Care to make something else up? Just like you did when you erroneously reported Venezuela damaged its own refinery to hike the price of oil and stick it to the empire?"

"That was a good story, mate," Ian said. "Care to comment on it?"

Pérez walked closer and stared Ian in the eyes. They were both the same height—tall. While Ian had the body of rugby prop, Pérez had that of a marathon runner, lean and lanky with long arms. And anyone who has been in a fight knows that a lanky arm can move faster than a bulky one. Pérez shot a jab into Ian's gut, timing Ian's breathing first to be sure to push the diaphragm up high, punching as much air out of Ian's lungs as possible. It worked. Ian fell over, completely unable to breathe.

"Comment on that," Pérez responded in perfect English. He turned to Street. "Surprised? I was trained with the US military in Panama. Spent some time in New Jersey, Iowa and other places too. Now get up. Corrupt cops here in Caracas are the least of your worries," Pérez said. Four armed officials came forward as if on cue and shoved Street and Ian hands down on the hoods of their unmarked cars and cuffed them.

"What did we do? What exactly are we being detained for?" Street protested, his anger rising. "This is bullshit. I'm in town with a valid visa, writing stories for *The Gateway*, a news company where I work back home. I can vouch for all of it. Fine, it's a tourist visa, but I'm not getting paid here, so technically I am not conducting business."

Pérez walked forward and met Street's glare. "Who said I was charging you for anything? I'm going to take you, as you would say, downtown for questions. Or am I going to take you to spend the evening in a Venezuelan prison? Yes, a prison. We'll skip what you call county jail and send you straight to a Venezuelan prison. They're pleasant. Very pleasant. Would you rather be gang-raped and then have someone set you on fire? Or how about being gang-raped while being set afire? You get some real kinky tastes in our prisons," Pérez said.

Street shut up. He knew silence was best and that he was innocent. A few minutes had passed, and Street and Ian were hurled off to separate cars, blindfolded.

The passenger door slammed shut. Then the driver's door. The engine started. Movement. It can't be too bad, because we haven't done anything, Street thought. Pérez seemed rational enough. At least Street had his cash back. Not sure why he gave it back to him for the ride to the police station. Why not confiscate it and release it with him later? Would seem to be standard protocol anywhere.

The bump of the roads and the hum of cars around him lulled Street into a rhythm that calmed his nerves even more. He thought and thought and thought what he could be arrested for. Drugs for sure. Though it seemed a little ridiculous. He just arrived yesterday and was in Caracas the whole time. In fact, the whole trip is pretty much verified. Check the records at the office building of the oil company. Check the airport records. Listen to the interview on the recorder. The entire conversation with Domínguez at Worldwide Oil & Gas would be on it. They could have it for all he cared. He already downloaded the interview and emailed it to himself and Brent earlier as a backup.

Drugs, Street thought. If he were a mule, he would be holed up in a hotel somewhere, waiting on a phone call like something out of a cheesy movie. Or realistically, he'd be on Venezuela's Margarita Island on a sailboat, waiting for the delivery, not running around drinking with his friend Ian and hanging out in slums as peace corps volunteers or religious evangelists would do. Did they think he and Ian were down here looking for hookers or for drugs for personal use? They wouldn't have sent in a unit like this for that.

The automobile came to a stop, and the driver and the passenger hauled Street inside a small building. He didn't know where he was, just that it was far from Petare. Probably farther west and closer to the downtown area. He didn't hear screams and shouts echoing from all around, so at least he wasn't in jail. Just a room. When the blindfold came off, Street felt pretty good, at ease even, though armed military officials were all around him. They had the expression and body language typical of trained military servicemen no matter what country. One with clear brown eyes, almost transparent, and a recently shorn head, stared at him. Another taller man with coffee-colored eyes did likewise; no hostility in his stare, just professionalism. Their man was contained. Street sat there and waited. Not long afterward, Pérez returned. Street chuckled when he put a file down on the table in front of Street and offered him a cigarette. Just like in the movies. He declined the offer.

"So," Pérez began. "What brings you to Caracas?"

Street shrugged. He had absolutely nothing to hide. "Tourism. Plus, I had an interview for a story I'm working on."

"So you're in Venezuela conducting business without a proper business visa?" Pérez asked, pulling a handgun out and staring at it, as if it were a new-model cell phone just released onto the market.

"I'm not conducting business at all. No transfer of money of any kind. I'm just writing some stories. When I say business, I mean I write about business. Can I go now?"

"No. You can't go yet," Pérez said, putting the gun back in the holster slung under his shoulder. "Let's backtrack. You say you were here to conduct interviews. Who did you interview?"

"Just one so far. The head of Latin America at Worldwide Oil & Gas. Juan Vicente Domínguez."

"Ah yes, the one who is so enamored by our illustrious and gentlemanly president."

Street remained silent.

"Our president is an idiot, of course. You won't get arrested for agreeing with me on that," Pérez said.

"So why am I under arrest?"

"You're not yet. You're here for questioning. Every time our beloved ruler opens his mouth, we find ourselves more at odds with your country and your friends in the region. That threatens our nation's security and that threatens my security, and worse, it threatens my daughter's security. You know how that feels, do you? To have your security threatened?"

"Not really, no."

"I'm sure being a foreigner here in Venezuela in the past made you feel a little threatened at times," Pérez said.

"Yes I do. I was robbed here once at gunpoint. Made the mistake of trying to get to a party too quickly. The cab driver offered to wait until I went inside, but a friend of mine paid him, and he drove off. As it turned out, everyone else at the party must have decided to head on out by the time we got there. We were late. Rang the doorbell. No answer. So we walked down the street, down the hill. We thought it was a nice neighborhood, but apparently, pockets of it weren't. And two guys popped around the corner with pistols and took all our stuff, or at least my stuff. My friend's thief was relaxed, shifting through his things. He gave my friend his passport and keys back.

My guy took everything and was getting nervous. They missed a nice chunk of loose bills in my friend's pocket, however. We eventually found another cab and went straight to the nearest bar. That said, I feel more threatened now than I did then."

"You felt threatened and feel so now because you went along with something probably against your better judgment."

"Everyone does. I thought you meant you knew what it was like being threatened from abroad. What it's like to live under constant threat of attack. Personally, I wouldn't know. It's kind of weird. People say I'm too risk averse, yet I chose to live and work here. From one extreme to the other. Anyway, how did you know I used to live here years ago?"

Pérez said nothing. He then asked Street to focus on the day and to describe his actions through the day. Street went through it again and again. He arrived on the plane, checked into his hotel, and went to the oil company for an interview. Drinks afterward. He told Pérez everything, back and forth and over again, including how many people he had come into contact with, what all social and work-related matters were conducted.

After the third hour, the relaxation that came out of the initial fear had morphed into annoyance with all the repeated questions. Even when a polygraph machine entered into the room, Street remained calm, relieved to tell the truth to a nonhuman judge. He knew the polygraph would back up his story when it rolled in with the coiled cords and the pins and needles ready to scrape across the paper. They strapped him and attached probes to any area of his body where lying could betray him, making Street feel as if he were being prepped to run a stress test in a doctor's room.

The person who ran it, a wiry man with glasses that resembled something from the mid-twentieth century, came in and sat behind him. He had that whole military intelligence look to him: green uniform, short hair, unassuming nature yet definitely physically fit. Street didn't know when they turned the machine on.

"We'll begin with some control questions. We're going to ask simple questions, and then we'll ask you to convey a falsehood."

Nice phrase, Street thought. *Convey a falsehood.*

"Let's just do this. I really have nothing to hide," Street said. He knew the answer to the first question before it was asked.

"State your name."

"Street Brewer."

"Are you currently in Venezuela?"

"Yes."

"Are you currently in or near Caracas?"

"Yes," Street said.

A few more questions like that continued.

"I want you to answer 'yes' to the following questions," the man said. "This is known as a stimulation test. You will deliberately lie so we can make it easier to determine when you are actually telling the truth. If you try and beat this, then your results will not be accurate, and we will assume you have been lying about everything."

"Are you currently in Colombia?" the man asked.

"Yes," Street responded. He heard pens scratching across the paper.

"Are you in the United States?" the man continued.

Street took a breath. Exhaled. "Yes." More scratching. Fine, he thought. It looks easier in the movies. The machine caught his lies, Street guessed. It didn't take too long before the questions really began, this time those searching for the hard truth.

"Did you have contact with Ian Collins this evening?"

"Yes."

"Where did you have drinks?"

"At El Techo."

"Here in the Federal District? Or the one in Mérida? The college town out in the Andes in western Venezuela?"

"Neither," Street said. "Technically the one by the Plaza Altamira is in the Chacao Municipality, which is in Miranda State. It's neither in the Federal District or hundreds of miles away in the Andes. Sort of like Arlington is in Virginia and not technically in the District of Columbia."

The polygraph made no sound.

"Did three police officers attempt to coerce money from you?"

"Yes."

"Have you ever conducted business with a police officer here?"

"No." That question was pretty open-ended, Street thought.

"Did a man named Pérez return your money?"

"Yes."

"Do you believe Pérez to be a legitimate Venezuelan authority?"

"Define authority. Is he police? Military? Who is he?"

"We ask the questions here," the man continued.

Such lines of questioning continued for a while, and Street suspected that the order of the questions had been predetermined. Some direct and to-the-point questions were mixed in with those that were a little open-ended, and those were sprinkled with gotcha' questions here and there.

The man went on.

"Have you ever consumed cocaine?"

"No," Street said. He saw it before. Wanted no part of it. Turned people into lunatics. Cost too much as well.

"Have you ever consumed marijuana?"

"Yes," Street said. He tried it a few times in college, though he didn't like it. Thought it was a silly drug. Made him paranoid.

"Have you ever sold drugs?"

"Yes," Street said.

"Explain."

"I sold off a bottle of painkillers when I had my wisdom teeth taken out in the summer after my high school graduation. I don't like painkillers. They make me nauseous."

"Is that it?"

"Of course not. I've sold drugs lots of times. One broken finger, one dislocated shoulder, and two broken legs. Accident-prone playing football. Injuries weren't serious enough for me to take those awful painkillers. My pill-popping friends were happy."

"Okay, that's enough. Back to yes or no questions." The man went on.

"Did you come to Venezuela yesterday?"

"Yes." Street was getting bored by now.

"Did you visit Maiquetía or any other coastal cities besides Caracas?"

"Nope. Hopped on a cab and came here today."

"You didn't go by Margarita Island or any other offshore Venezuelan territories first?"

"No."

"Have you spoken to anyone besides Ian Collins or employees at the oil company where you conducted your interview?"

"Yes," Street said.

"To whom?"

"The bartender at El Techo. I may have told him I was switching to coffee. I may have said hello to the hotel staff."

"Mr. Brewer, did you attempt to buy narcotics here in Venezuela for the purpose of use?"

"No."

"Did you take delivery of narcotics for the purpose of exporting abroad?"

"No."

"Did you attempt to buy wildlife to smuggle back abroad?"

"No."

"Are you working for a narcotrafficker or for any illicit organization?"

"No."

"Have you ever smuggled drugs out of Venezuela and into the US or elsewhere?"

"No."

"Are you a US government intelligence officer or agent?"

"No."

"Let me backtrack. Are you a US public official here on police, military, diplomatic, or other business?"

"No."

"Are you here on contract by US or other sovereign officials?"

"No."

"Are you here to arrest and extradite any Venezuelan national?"

"No."

"Do you work for any other government?"

"No."

"Do you work for a civilian intelligence or forensic accounting firm?"

"No."

"Do you work for a multilateral financial institution such as the International Monetary Fund, the World Bank Group, or the Inter-American Development Bank?"

"No."

"Do you work for a private financial institution that is also a creditor to the sovereign nation of Venezuela?"

"No."

All the while, the polygraph remained silent.

The questions went on for a little while longer. Then they stripped the polygraph probes off him. The man stared at the paper, frowning. Then, Street was left alone in the room for a while. One came in with a cup of coffee for Street and left. He checked the clock on the wall. It was four in the morning, and he was beyond exhausted. But for the life of him, he couldn't figure out why he had been detained. Then Pérez returned.

"Mr. Brewer, if you're a US military or law enforcement official here to snag a drug dealer out of Venezuela without going through the proper channels, you and your superiors will find yourself in a world of hurt. And more importantly, if you're seeking to ship drugs out of Venezuela, you'll end up in one of our prisons."

Street stared at the man and said nothing.

"But your story checks out. So does your polygraph. So does your hotel room. So does your briefcase, and so does Ian's messy but generally accurate take on the day. We see you entered the country yesterday through airport security cameras. Your tourist visa matches the time when the airport filmed you entering. Even in your interview, we can hear references to the same time—yes, we listened to your digital recorder. Many drug smugglers look just like you, foreign kids in search of more money. Plus, you speak the language and know the city. But we've got nothing on you, and further-more, I don't know of too many drug traffickers or government officials who spend the evening drinking like you and Ian do, admit to selling drugs in the past, and then go running around through the slums for no reason. Being a friend of Ian Collins's is foolish to begin with," Pérez said. "Off the record, you picked a pretty dangerous slum to enter. I wouldn't go in there myself, at least not without an army to back me up, and I mean that literally. So you're free to go." He opened the door and instructed an officer outside to gather Street's belongings.

Street stood and walked up to Pérez. He faced the man. "One thing I don't understand. Who obviously tipped you off that I was in the Petare area of the city up to no good?"

"I don't reveal my sources," Pérez said.

A man brought in Street's briefcase. Street checked, and all was inside, including the digital recorder, passport, wallet, and all of its contents.

"See?" Street muttered. "I'm just a journalist."

Pérez stared at him. "I'm still not buying all of this. Something's just off, and I mean really fucking off, and I don't like it. If I'm being played somehow, you know, part of some plan that I don't know about, I swear to God I'll ruin the careers of those who're responsible, no matter how powerful they may be, you understand me?" he said.

"Yes," Street answered.

"Good. But just out of curiosity, anything else you might be working on down here? Never hurts to ask. Maybe we can help each other out."

"No. I'm out of here. I'm going back home." The security escort took Street to an unmarked car outside of the office. By sunrise, Street was asleep in his hotel bed. His wallet, money, watch, passport, and voice recorder were tucked deep inside his luggage.

CHAPTER

12

After leaving Street and Ian at Techo, Patricia walked down the Plaza Altamira. She ordered some ice cream from a vendor, a chocolate cone, and sat in the cool and quiet evening before heading home. Her car was parked on a tree-lined side street a block over from El Techo. She finished her ice cream and stared in the direction of her car. She shook her head.

A few minutes later, Patricia turned the ignition of the small Ford Fiesta and shot up the hill. Not even a mile away, she turned toward the rust-colored brick building and was home. She looked up at her condo. It could have fit in any city worldwide. Sparkling new. Bricks and cleanly polished glass. No water stains. She drove through the gate, waved hello to the guards in their official blue uniforms, and parked. She walked through a small patch of gardens and went up the elevator to her floor. The top floor. Panoramic view of the city.

George, her husband, would be waiting. George Maldonado. Aged forty-one. MBA from Kellogg. Undergrad from the University of Pennsylvania. Double Major in Economics and Political Science. Good grades, too, and a string of other academic accolades followed by a string of never-ending great ideas that rarely materialized.

Patricia opened the door, and there he sat at his computer at the kitchen table.

"Hi, honey! I just had a great idea for a new business tool that's going to revolutionize the way flowers are sent to the United States from Ecuador," he told her, not raising his eyes from his laptop. "Blockchain!" He typed away, looking committed and stern, as if he were about to send an email out to a team of lawyers and accountants providing last-minute marching orders.

Patricia saw he had already switched to red wine from coffee. Hopefully, he made it to two o'clock in the afternoon this day.

"I can either sell this idea to the industry or cover it in my magazine that I'm gonna launch."

"Hi, George," Patricia said. She put her keys on the entry table and walked to the kitchen table. She looked around. A nice three-bedroom condominium. Nice by US standards. Marble floors. New appliances. She preferred hardwood floors, though. But she focused on the positive.

"I think the Chilean airline, Ecuadoran growers associations and Miami import-export companies are way ahead of you on that one, cryptocurrencies and blockchain notwithstanding," she said.

George slumped in his chair.

"Did you look for something meaningful to do today?" Patricia asked. Silence.

"Like for a job, maybe ?"

More silence. Followed by some semblance of a shrug, eye movements and an opening jaw. His body language told Patricia he was thinking of a story to tell her instead of retrieving memories to provide an answer.

"Did you even call Domínguez? It's not every day that you have access to a top executive at a global oil company. I mean normally these guys take in young engineers who study abroad and groom them going up. To get an outsider in a support role is something people would kill for."

George took a sip of wine. He looked up. "Stop attacking me," he said in a huff. A defensive huff. He stood up abruptly and stormed out, quick-paced and childlike.

Patricia watched him. He was a big man with broad shoulders but a thin neck. Big, meaty arms and a small head. He had handsome features, including a strong chin, and while his black hair retained the color of youth, it was receding, which made his head appear even smaller. If he'd lose twenty pounds, he'd look good, almost as good as he did ten years ago.

He came back in a little more relaxed, and Patricia studied his big, square frame and wished it packed more strength to match its size. He sat down. His composure regained. Patricia was amused for a minute. He looked as if he worked at a funeral home, and was calmly and quietly discussing arrangement costs for an unprepared family.

"You know I can't sell out and ignore my supply-chain expertise and my journalistic endeavors," George said.

"Journalistic endeavors?" Patricia asked, pouring herself a glass of wine. At least she had ten hours of work under her belt. "Journalists get out there and crank. They read the news. They write the news. They make phone calls. They do press summaries. They go to press conferences. They doorstep people in hallways and sidewalks. They interview like crazy. They're constantly writing and not talking about it. But with your background, and with my connections, why not try something more suited to your abilities? You're an executive. That leaves oil and consumer products here, or what's left of them. Maybe automobiles. Take your pick!" She looked at him and his moist, needy eyes, and swallowed her wine. She sat down next to him and put a hand on his knee. He looked down.

"I know you may feel down. I know how it is to be at a crossroads in life, especially when you're trying to figure out your next move in this chaotic country, and I will support you. I'll do anything in my power to stand by you to watch you succeed, so I can applaud from the sidelines as you do it yourself. And I swear I'll scream to the world and point to you and tell everybody, 'That's my man.'"

George raised his head and looked at her.

Patricia continued. "But you have to take that first step. You need to make it happen." She kissed him on the cheek, stood up, took her glass of wine, and walked away. Then she looked back at him. "And you need to do it soon." She left him there at his computer, alone with his thoughts and dreams.

She walked into their bedroom, took off her blazer, and placed her purse on the bedside table. Street's business card was peeking out of her purse, and she thought about what it might be like for a young American man traveling in Caracas. She recollected the interview and how he had peppered Domínguez aggressively but respectfully with questions. He wanted the answers. Wanted a good story. She liked how Street went for what he wanted. He wasn't out to get Domínguez or anyone else. He wasn't out to make them come across as stupid or up to no good, but he wasn't there to give them free press either. He was just engaging the company, finding out where the story was, and having fun with it.

She looked at the card and walked around the room. Everyone on earth experiences fear, but Street didn't let fear get the best of him. Patricia kicked off one shoe, then the other, and glanced at the closed bedroom door. George sat on the other side in the den out of her sight. No shame in being afraid to do something, but to work through it and get what you desire, that takes guts. Street had them, George didn't. She threw her coat off onto a nearby chair. There was goodness in George, and she saw enormous potential, but sooner or later, she wanted a man who was confident, courageous and independent. She set the card back on the bedside table as she undressed, then picked it up again and stared at it.

"Street Brewer," she said aloud. She looked at herself in the mirror and then at Street's card, taking in his number and office address, wondering what his desk looked like, where he went for coffee nearby and for cocktails after work. She breathed in and out. Then she heard a beer can snap open in the kitchen. Heard a cigarette lighter click and caught a whiff of smoke that crept in under the door. She turned off the light and climbed into bed. She stared at the ceiling in the dark. A soft glow from her phone lit up the bedside table to her right. A text had arrived. It was from work. Routine. She ignored it and was about to put the phone back down but didn't. Instead, she checked the time. It was only about nine in the evening, but she was tired. George would be on his computer for a while, so she had the room to herself.

She deleted the text from work and began to type a new one. This time to Street Brewer.

Street Brewer, maybe we can have another drink before you fly out of here. This time just the two of us.

She was about to press send but thought otherwise and deleted what she had typed. She turned on the television to a news show that was discussing the state of US politics. Gridlock. Whatever.

Patricia checked her phone again. No new texts or messages of any sort.

Mr. Street Brewer, be safe in Caracas, she thought. She put her phone down and began to doze off in front of the television.

CHAPTER

13

The Venezuelan president boarded his official aircraft, took a seat, stared out the window, and began daydreaming. Taxiing down the runway at Maiquetía Airport never got old for him. Not just a few days ago when he headed to Sucre State, and not today with the green mountains disappearing into clouds on one side and the Caribbean Sea on the other.

As a kid in southern Venezuela, he had often marveled over maps and yearned to fly but was too poor to go anywhere. He dreamed of playing baseball in the US major leagues—in New York, Atlanta, Chicago, Los Angeles, Boston; spring training in Florida. All were places where he would have killed to fly to and play ball. Those dreams were long gone, and so were his aspirations of gaining popularity in the United States. "Fuck the gringos," he mumbled.

The captain had just told the passengers to keep their seatbelts on when the president jumped out of his seat and took center stage. He paced the aisle, glancing at spreadsheets with official government data, inflation rates figures jumping off the page. There was no way he was going to release the true data. In fact, he wasn't going to release any numbers at all. Nor was he going to give the United States an inkling of how bad things really were in Venezuela. He knew he couldn't fudge the numbers either. Everyone would call him out. That left him one choice: find a way to be powerful and execute it quickly.

"We're going to steal the word 'gringo' and use it to call ourselves, and the world can look up to us," he said, folding the reports and shoving them into the sleeve of his coat crumped up on an aisle seat. "In fact, I am officially stealing the word 'gringo' now. It's no longer reserved for North Americans or Europeans. We're going to turn it into a proud word. From the *green* hills we *go* to the world to spread socialism and equality," he said in English. "I'll make the country stellar again, opposition be damned."

Aides and staffers stared at each other and then at the president. Nervous nods of approval ensued.

The president jumped back in his seat and stared out the airplane window.

"And to say I don't know my own people. Fuck you, Hernán," he mumbled. "I haven't forgotten where I came from."

The plane gained altitude, and Venezuela's coastal green mountains gave way to the deep blue sea. Then he heard Hernán Bernal's voice—the voice of the man who had turned him from a firebrand thug with nothing but raw popularity into a world leader with political clout, at least when oil prices were high.

"Still dreaming of how you're going to make everyone in Venezuela love you? One hundred percent approval rates? A champion to every poor person across the globe, no matter the consequences? The savior of the national economy?" he asked.

The president turned to face Bernal, his right-hand man, his new foreign minister clad in, as usual, a solid-blue suit.

"Still dreaming about how you are going to eradicate the planet of poverty and save the world from capitalism? Everyone will love you and praise your name for all eternity?" Bernal asked.

"They will love me. This isn't just some power trip. I've got plans," the president said, slumping in front of the older man looking down at him. "They should be crazy about me, and that goes for the opposition as well."

"They will, but as I've said, now is not the time for surprises," Bernal said, taking a seat near the president. "Remember the boy who cried wolf."

The president got up and paced the plane. He poured two Scotch whiskies and handed one to his friend, who had touched a nerve by calling him out on being detached from his base.

Hernán and the Venezuelan president grew up on the same side of the fence politically, but they came to run the country from two vastly different corners of South America's political left. While the president of Venezuela came of age in the legitimate military, serving under officers who favored ties with the United States, Hernán Bernal started out as a Marxist paramilitary fighter in the Venezuelan jungle decades earlier. The two never crossed paths, as Bernal was much older. By the time the president of Venezuela was a high-ranking military commander, Bernal and the rest of the Marxists had long laid down their arms and joined the mainstream political system, mainly trying to get as many ideological sympathizers elected to Congress as possible.

Good with explosives and even better with his brain, Bernal tossed his guns to his feet with the promise that as a lawmaker, he would have a shot at turning Venezuela into a more leftist state. He did well, winning support from labor unions, teachers' guilds, and others who opposed selling off control of the oil fields to US energy companies—or selling off steel mills or telecoms or aluminum producers or hotels or any other state-owned industry for that matter. But since previous administrations, one after the other, had all been in the US camp for decades past, all Bernal could do was sit back in his little niche in Congress and vote against anything capitalist. He would always end up watching with his arms crossed as one state asset after the other hit the auction block and fell into the hands of foreign corporations, pretty much a requirement for bailout money from the US-controlled International Monetary Fund at the time. That scared labor unions big time, as US giants or their subsidiaries took control of more and more of industrial Venezuela.

Bernal didn't feel that capitalism was evil. In fact, sometimes capitalist ideologies were in order. He was pragmatic like that. So while the winds of US corporate muscle swept the world's emerging markets, Bernal didn't try to swim against the tide. A state could still be socialist, foreign investment could still be welcome, and the working class could still live comfortable lives. Whoever spent billions of dollars buying bits and pieces of Venezuela were free to do as such, but they'd better get used to tough labor laws while Bernal was around, especially when it came to layoffs and severance pay.

Always kind to his base, welcomed by business leaders and even by his opposition, Bernal demanded, and got, respect. During the toughest of congressional debates in decades past, Bernal would bring in boxes of potato chips, candies, and crackers for his fellow lawmakers, even if he knew he was debating a lost cause.

Bernal dressed like a US banker, and there was one reason he wore suits day in and day out, even at outdoor photo shoots, where the president himself was donning a tropical guayabera shirt. Hernán Bernal had been horribly burned; his chest, shoulders, and back were scarred for life. His skin looked as if it were a wildly flowing stream of lava that had finally cooled in a chaotic mold. A nice souvenir from a firefight with rival guerrillas back in the eighties along a porous Colombian border.

A column of rogue Colombian guerrillas had been muscling into Venezuela to sell their version of communism along with cocaine bound for the north. Bernal and a few others fired on them to keep the cocaine business out of Venezuela. A firebomb from the cocaine-financed narcoguerrillas seriously wounded Bernal, pushing his life and his purist ideology close to death. But the wounds had tempered him somewhat.

He knew the president was letting the country's military smuggle drugs, but times were different now. Economic implosion was the true enemy these days, and that required his attention in financial and diplomatic theaters. Scars and the president's need to be in the spotlight at all times kept Bernal downstage in the public eye, and even though he held high-profile positions, he was happy to let others have the limelight day in and day out while he steered the country away from further collapse each day before he could have his morning coffee. He took a sip of Scotch that had been offered to him by the president, a man who was both his superior and his protégé.

"I think on this trip to Moscow, we should make the announcement that we and the Russians are going to finance this infrastructure port together on top of announcing details surrounding some soft loans from Moscow that we're going to get to import Russian hardware," the president said. "We'll stress the naval aspects. What do you think?"

"First of all, *salud*, Mr. President," Bernal said, raising his glass. He took a languid sip.

The president looked at him, as if he were waiting for instructions.

"Second of all, we'll thank the Russians for meeting us on such short notice," Bernal said.

The president nodded.

"When we arrange the financing, I think we should first—"

"We'll start off using the latest loan proceeds to buy firearms," the president interrupted. "We'll need more and more Kalashnikovs for our army, both imported and fabricated in Venezuela. Then we'll talk planes and armored vehicles. We can tap other funds too, even after we get this Russian line of credit. We need more military upgrades."

Bernal let the president voice his thoughts. Sometimes it was good to wait and let him run his course.

"Yes, Mr. President. I agree, but let me caution you on policy. Too much defense spending could spark an arms race in the region. And you know the Americans will arm their allies in Colombia to the teeth as long as the government there keeps its pro-Washington stance on drugs and guerrillas, which it always will in exchange for a flood of financial aid. Frankly, I don't much like any side in Colombia, but Bogotá does have access to US money, and Washington's pockets always run deep. Plus, they'll ship in much more modern American weapons and technology, much better than the stuff we might be seeing on this trip. Furthermore, too much defense spending could divert money away from social programs. People want to see hospitals, schools, and food on the shelves, not weapons. Let's not forget that we've already signed just under half of our US oil refining and gasoline distribution company to the Russians as collateral for badly needed cash. We don't want to come across as desperate for more, even though we are." Bernal paused. "And what did you mean a few minutes ago when you said that this isn't some power trip and that you had plans? What plans?"

"Forget it. We'll find more financing to get what we need," the president said. "That means both keeping our old US equipment in action and buying from suppliers elsewhere."

"Any plans go by me, Mr. President, especially when it comes to this port. I see the big picture like you do, but on the flip side I have knowledge of sovereign finance and markets and the pitfalls and politics that come with them. You don't. So I sign off on anything announced when it comes to Venezuela and Russia."

The president stared at Bernal long and hard, and then nodded. "Agreed."

"Anyway," Bernal went on. "We can only borrow so much, especially with our horrific economy. All I'm saying is, let's make the announcement about the port, the jobs it will create, and keep mention of finance and any other arms on the broad level without going into details," Bernal said, his face turning a little red at having to remind a sitting president over the need to act stately. A vein popped up on the side of his neck, as if it were going to probe the conversation.

Visibly annoyed, the president jumped up and poured another Scotch.

Bernal caught on to the president's quick change in mood and said, "The Russians need foreign investment in their energy sector just like we do, and foreign investment means western investment, so they won't want to make Europe or the United States uncomfortable by arming Venezuela too quickly. In fact, I'm surprised Moscow signed up to this port deal so quickly. Suspicious, in fact."

The president sat back down and stared out at the early stretches of the Atlantic Ocean.

Bernal went on. "Russia can't antagonize the US too much. We can welcome them to Venezuela, their diplomats, their money, and their military, but let's not get carried away and start a war, Mr. President. And let's not trust the Russians too much either. That just goes without saying. Remember, a big country will treat a little country like a little country, even if that little country is its friend."

"We're sort of aligned," the president said. "All producers want higher prices."

"Not all. The Arabs are pumping for next to nothing in terms of costs, especially on land, where it's cheap and where their big fields are. Remember that. The Arabs produce for cheap, so they can afford to drive down prices by flooding the market with oil and put us and the Texans and many others out of business. We are not all aligned."

The president sat back and stared out the airplane window. "So, we're still just a small country," he said.

"Yes," Bernal said. "But a small country in a changing world."

The president withdrew into thought; shook his head.

"The key to true success is developing human capital and innovation," Bernal said.

"Yes, but that costs money and moreover, takes a long time. We're dealing with a crisis right now."

"No matter who saves the country, no matter what creditor or nation helps bail us out, there will be pain paying back those debts any way you look at it," Bernal said. "Think about the future. Craft some policies that will provide long-term substantial and sustainable gains for the people, even after you are long gone and can't take all the credit for it. That way, we can avoid cycles of booms, busts, and bailouts." He took one more sip of Scotch, stood, and placed the half-full glass on a seat tray. He walked away.

They landed at the Sheremetyevo International Airport, and the president of Venezuela was chomping at the bit to get deals done. The door to the fuselage opened and down below in the pomp and circumstance, Russian president Adrian Sokolov stood to greet the president of Venezuela. It truly was a red-carpet welcome, very rare with the president himself, instead of the foreign minister or someone else important, waiting on the tarmac. Military and other distinguished figures stood at attention. Cameras flashed and dignitaries applauded.

President Sokolov was everything that the president of Venezuela wasn't. He wore fine suits, not military fatigues. He was tall, athletic, pushing seventy, and still largely had black hair, obviously not dyed as noted by random streaks of gray. He had green eyes, hard but softened by an easy-going smile typical of a man who made people feel at ease when he was commanding them.

"Mr. President. The Russian people appreciate your continued interest in our country and your respect for our industries and services," Sokolov said, shaking the president of Venezuela's hand. "I'm confident our business ties can grow as the global economy relies more on emerging leaders like ourselves."

The Venezuelan president responded. "You mean when we tell those dipshits in Washington to go fuck themselves?"

A wave of discomfort flashed across Sokolov's face, though Bernal was impressed by how quickly the Russian leader regained control of his expression. Bernal knew that everyone in power had heard of the Venezuelan president's lip, and some had reservations about being associated with him. This Russian leader apparently knew who he was dealing with but probably cared little about what people thought about him standing shoulder to shoulder with the world's biggest sovereign loudmouth.

"Something like that," Sokolov said.

Sighs of relief exhaled all around. After brief welcoming ceremonies, both presidents and their teams rode in their motorized details across Moscow. Bernal looked through his window and out across the city. Then he saw those familiar spirals jutting up into the sky overlooking the Moskva River: the Kremlin.

"I've finally arrived," the president of Venezuela whispered, staring out the window.

Bernal nodded, noticing the president was like a kid at an amusement park for the first time, zeroing in on choosing his first rides of the day. The Kremlin, where Soviet power brokers spent the Cold War plotting both against and sometimes with the Americans, overlooked Moscow's Red Square, Saint Basil's Cathedral, and the Alexander Garden.

"Venezuela will soon be the Kremlin of the Caribbean," the president said.

Someday, Bernal thought. Someday.

While the Venezuelan president and Sokolov took off to hold formal meetings and discuss what Venezuela was and wasn't going to buy, and what to say and what not to say to the press, Bernal and Russia's foreign minister, Andronico Popov, prepared for a more private conversation. No aides, no advisors, no staffers save for one—a thin man with bushy gray hair and a tweed jacket. The man introduced himself to Bernal as Peter Bogdanov, a weapons and logistics expert at the Ministry of Defense. Bernal shook Bogdanov's hand.

"Welcome, Minister Bernal. Foreign Minister Popov will be with us in a moment. Please have a seat here," Bogdanov said.

Bernal took in his surroundings. It was a typical room for power brokering—large leather chairs, big tables, dark wooden walls, and portraits of past heroes.

"Thank you," Bernal said, and he sat down.

Just then the door burst open and a man entered. If one had called central casting and asked for an old-school Russian power broker, Popov was not it. He was not a bull of a man in slick clothes with thick gray hair, cigarette in one hand, and a vodka in the other. He was the opposite. Andronico Popov was tall with thick red hair, and was perfectly suited. He walked in a quick but relaxed pace with an aura of health about him.

He looks like he was once a European tennis champ, Bernal thought.

"Minister Bernal. Welcome to Moscow," Popov said with an extended hand.

"Thank you. The pleasure is both mine and Venezuela's."

They sat down in two large leather chairs. Bogdanov, knowing his rank in the room, sat behind Popov in deference to the two foreign ministers and stared at Bernal, who was checking out the quality of the chairs. They were nice. Bernal made a mental note to review the chairs and desks back in Venezuela to make sure everything was up to par when foreign leaders came.

Bernal began. "Well, Mr. Popov. Venezuela would like to thank the Russian Federation for our most recent credit line. Our military will be better equipped to deal with guerrilla groups spilling over the border from neighboring Colombia. Venezuela is considering investing in Sukhoi fighter jets as well as Ilyushin-76 and Antonov transport planes, S-300 air defense missile systems, among others, once we finalize the total package. That's down the road. Park some Tupolev Tu-160 bombers at our airport in the meantime." Bernal took a sip of water. "But for now, the Venezuelan government is ready to announce to the world purchases of up to several billion dollars in weaponry for the infantry at first, starting out with a fresh batch of Kalashnikovs."

138

"I'm listening," Popov said. "You seem to be going overboard on missile defense systems, but whatever."

Bernal went on. "Secondly, we, the Venezuelan government, will announce military purchases to the public once we finalize the terms and the final amount. But we'd also like to hint at more future collaborations in both military deals and in the mining sector in particular. That will get the press buzzing. But today, we are only tapping Russia's credit line for the equipment I just mentioned."

"Agreed. We don't need the Americans running to Bogotá, stocking them up," Popov added. "We can't anger the Americans too much. They're upset enough with our ties to Syria, where we're moving lots of weaponry, but on the flip side, we can't close off foreign investment in our own economy."

"And thirdly, I have good news here," Bernal added. "Initial studies show it's feasible for Moscow and Caracas to develop naval facilities at the port on the Venezuelan coast that would best serve Russian naval fleets. Sucre State is one option we've proposed."

"Go on," Popov said. He made eye contact with Bogdanov, the man in the tweed coat.

"You'll have a foothold in the Americas."

Popov was silent for a good fifteen seconds. He rose. Paced to the window. Stared out. "Can we be frank here, now that everyone is gone and there are no staffers, aides, or any other eyes and ears of Washington?"

"Of course," Bernal said, looking at Bogdanov, wondering why he would wear such casual attire to a meeting of senior officials.

"We see value in a deeper friendship with Venezuela. We all know the United States will never be the superpower it once was. And we all know countries like us and China are now driving more and more of the global economy. Times are changing, and if the US doesn't wane from its soapbox peacefully, things could get rough. Yes, the US will always be a force to be reckoned with, just not the only one. But when we rise, our friends rise, and there's the problem."

"What are you saying?" Bernal asked. "The problem isn't the US?"

"No. The problem is with our friends. We're a little uncomfortable with your president's—how should I put it—totally inappropriate public comments and outbursts, especially in times as the global power balance realigns and things get uncertain. Sometimes he gets out of hand, his shoot-from-the-hip announcement of a port being one example, unveiling it before we approved, let alone basically even knew about it. We understand he needs to blame Washington for everything to stay in power and keep that popular base happy. That's his business model. We get it. But let's remember one thing. We try to keep the number of loose cannons with which we do business at a minimum, and we do conduct a lot of business with the United States and its allies. Remember, if he's out, our Venezuelan assets could be at risk.

"Now, I know it's hard for you as a diplomat, as a career politician, and as a rational man to hear such blunt talk from your Russian counterpart. I know it's hard, especially since you have contributed to the Russian-friendly causes when I was an infant. But I also know that you wear many hats. Many, many hats. I just want to make our position clear. Your sovereignty is our backyard."

Bernal sighed. "While he appears bombastic at times—"

"He called the US president an asshole in public and on record. He said capitalism ended life on other planets. Do you want me to go on?"

"He's more pragmatic than he appears. Yes, he talks and spends too much, and that affects our debt ratings—"

"You're in default."

"We will always pay our bills to you." Bernal sat up in his chair to reposition his creaky bones, though his gaze remained fixed on his counterpart. "He mouths off too much, but in the end, he does the right thing to at least keep the military in our camp and us in power, and you with oil assets on your books."

"I understand. Anyway, my comments don't go out of this room and aren't designed to scrap business between our two countries. I'm just conveying information here, you know, keeping the lines of communications open and keeping publicly announced fiscal surprises in check. And speaking of fiscal spending, I don't want to know how he keeps his military brass loyal, at least not from you. I know that must be killing you inside."

"I see," Bernal said.

"Well, I will report to my president that we are in agreement on all points, Mr. Bernal. The base is a go-ahead. Venezuela will handle the bidding process to companies interested in building the infrastructure."

"Agreed."

Both men shook hands, and Bernal said, "I will see you at the press conference."

"Sounds good, Hernán," Popov said, sizing up his Venezuelan counterpart. "You are a respectful man. I understand where you come from. I think I know your true intentions. My question is, do you know your president's?"

Bernal left the room.

CHAPTER

14

Not one minute after Bernal left, Popov turned to Bogdanov and glared at him. "Nice wardrobe choice. Even that necktie is wrinkled. You look like a fraternity brat at some eastern US university."

"I just got off the plane from Venezuela. No time to change. We need to talk right now."

"Okay," Popov said, annoyed. "Talk."

"The Venezuelan president isn't telling Bernal everything."

"There's the shocker of the century!" Popov said. "Bernal doesn't want to know everything the president is doing. All my people in the field tell me that. Can you tell me something I don't know?"

"Venezuela is planning some smuggling of some kind behind our back. We don't want to be involved in any dirty dealings in South America, but they may be involved in drugs to help pay their debts," Bogdanov said. "We don't want this port to be some springboard for narcotics or something."

"No, we don't. But we're in on this port deal," Popov sighed and put his hands on Bogdanov's shoulder. "Relax, Bogdanov. It's our port. It's for our military. If anything, drug dealers are going to veer away from it. Let them smuggle that shit from elsewhere in the country."

"Fair enough, but I just get the feeling the Venezuelan government may be involved in something really bad," Bogdanov said. "Or parts of it are."

"How do you know this?"

"I talk to Americans down there. You know how this goes. Some of them feel something's up as well, which may include their own."

"What?"

"Too early to really brief anyone on anything specific, but I just don't want us to get wrapped up in something, well, something really fucking bad."

Popov began to pace. He opened some curtains and peered out a window. Nothing going on outside.

"I like Bernal but not this Venezuelan regime. So stay on this. Just don't tell me anything yet. I don't want to know what you think, just what you know."

"But it's not—"

"Did you hear what I just told you?" Popov said, walking to the door, annoyed and fidgety. "We're dealing with the US on multiple fronts, from Ukraine to Syria, and now it looks like Venezuela will become our new proxy battleground. Whatever it is, just keep us clear of any drugs." Popov left, slamming the door behind him.

"It's not what you think it is," Bogdanov said to no one in the room. He sighed and withdrew a small spiral-bound notebook and a pen from his coat pocket. He made some notes and stared at the curtains where Popov anxiously had peered earlier.

How do I get a meeting with the right person to find out what Russia needs to know? He reached into his coat pocket for a pack of cigarettes, rolled his eyes, and withdrew a stick of gum. Guess I'll have to speak with my go-to girl in the US Central Intelligence Agency.

He drew a phone from his pocket and dialed. It didn't take long for a woman to answer.

"What's going on? If we're going to work together, I need to know everything," Bogdanov said, a little smile on his face. "I'll show you mine, if you show me yours."

"Don't think I don't see you checking me out. I know you want what's mine," the woman said.

Bogdanov could sense an amused smile on the other end of the phone.

"Anyway. I've got people on the ground peppering all assets to figure out what the Venezuelans are really up to, including Venezuela's help in

America," the woman said. "Jesus, I'm spying on my enemy and homeland at the same time."

"Drugs? Arms?" Bogdanov said.

"You know as much as we do at CIA headquarters in Langley, Virginia," the woman said.

"I guess we both know that Venezuela needs higher oil prices right now," Bogdanov said. "That's true for us, too. Everybody knows that."

"And low oil prices must make you nervous. Heaven forbid the current Venezuelan regime would go under, especially after all you've done with them. It's been a good investment for you so far. Moderate loans, say a few billion here and a few billion there in exchange for some nice oil assets in Venezuela and in the US. But if the opposition ousts him, you'd lose peanuts in the loans, which would be a slight headache, but you'd be in litigation forever fighting for assets with creditors holding defaulted bonds, which would be a major headache. So it's back to oil prices to supply that idiot in Caracas with petrodollars to keep his military and cronies permanently happy and the opposition at bay. That or a shitload of cocaine. Anyway, it'd take a miracle for crisis-racked Venezuela to move the global oil market on its own. Is that what you guys are up to? Spook the world and send prices on the rise? That port announcement won't do that at all."

Bogdanov reached for another stick of gum, taking in all his frenemy from the CIA was telling him. None of the information was new, of course, but the fact that she was reminding him meant Washington may be stepping up its game with the opposition in Venezuela. Still, Russia had the edge. The opposition was always fragmented and rife with disagreements. Nothing he knew led him to believe they'd zeroed in on someone, at least not yet. That'd be a game changer.

"Well, my dear Cyra Octavia Harred, thanks for the heads up. I'll just keep sharing with you what Moscow wants you to know, especially about our port. And here's a freebie. We're gonna land some Tu-160 bombers on Venezuela's coast as part of joint exercises most likely. Nice photo ops. Anything you can give in return."

"I know I'm not the only US mole you deal with," she said. "Who's your other handler, Peter? Who else are you talking to?"

"I don't have a handler. You know that," he replied.

"Just tell me something I don't know." She hung up.

Something was up, and Bogdanov didn't like it one bit. American espionage was getting messy, but that didn't bother him as much. But Russia being part of a ruse did bother him. Big time. He threw the gum into a nearby waste bucket, took out his wallet, counted some money, and peeled off a few bills to buy some cigarettes. He made a mental note to speak with his CIA contact, the lovely young Cyra, at their usual marker location when he was back in Caracas. With all the oil producers out there, how could one country push up oil prices by itself and to the point that would pump real money into Venezuela's coffers? It'd be a miracle, or something worse. Miracles come with their prices.

CHAPTER

15

Olivia Crawford landed at the Arturo Merino Benítez International Airport just outside of Santiago, Chile, on a Tuesday morning. She took in the snow-capped towering Andes to the east, shining high above the country's capital. It was September, and an early spring was spreading across the southern hemisphere, fresh winds blowing the air pollution away. Olivia hailed a cab after leaving the glassy airport terminal and was off. She knew Chile would soon be in bloom with temperate flowers not always found in tropical South Florida. If only she had spent time in the city during the cold, rainy winter. Then she'd really appreciate the burst of spring.

But it was time to forget about the weather and time to go pitch the fund. She'd start with shrewd mining barons. With Chile being the world's largest producer of copper, parts of the country were rolling in money due to strength in the metals markets over the past years. The red metal kept making gains after gains as Asian countries bought more and more to develop their booming economies. If there was a need for copper wire to go into new office buildings and houses in China, Chile was only happy to supply it. And all that money made many mining executives rich, some foreign and some Chilean, like Sebastián Ledezma, chairman and CEO of Tarapacá Mines, located at the tip of northern Chile, and Ted Bullard's target investor. Olivia's cab headed his way.

Across town, at about noon, not long after Olivia left the airport, Sebastián Ledezma popped open a fresh bottle of Macallan 25-year-old Highland single malt Scotch whisky. He took a sip, staring at the bottle, which sold for over $2,000 in the United States. He savored the fine malt and took in hints of peach, blood orange, and wood spice. He cherished the coconut and vanilla flavors, and of course, the lingering peats, wondering how he made it to age seventy-seven without high blood pressure or high cholesterol. He weighed two hundred fifty pounds, gave up cigarettes only ten years ago, and ate whatever he wanted. Despite his lifestyle, which was somewhat devoid of exercise, he got a clean bill of health with every visit to the doctor. Plus his hair was still predominantly black and youthful, and he had never had to use the words 'erectile dysfunction.' His prostate was as soft as they come.

"It's all in the attitude," he said, smiling at himself in the mirror, slicking his hair back. The little bit of gray had started to appear only about a decade ago. He then waddled into his closet and checked out the latest in his quiver of Savile Row suits he'd bought during his many trips to London.

Not far from his sprawling mansion over at the Mandarin Oriental, near the Avenida Presidente Kennedy, which resembled a US interstate, Sebastián was due to attend a cocktail party and dinner for mining executives from around the world that night. Granted it was about six hours from now, but he wanted to spend his day watching market news on television and taking more than enough time getting ready while sipping whisky. He was the keynote speaker, and he would deliver an address on how he developed a billion-dollar copper mine not only ahead of schedule but within budget several years ago. Bankers financed him and loved him. Even his critics who said he'd fail ate their words.

Sebastián had gotten lucky while drilling for copper when he found ample underground water sources to supply the operation with water in the northern Chilean desert, where some spots have no recorded rainfall. As soon as the cash started flowing in, he expanded the mine, betting demand would increase down the road. Because the mine was thousands of feet above sea level, he built a slurry pipeline to get the wet copper concentrate, a sludge mainly, down to sea level at the mine's port, where ships waited to haul it off to smelters in East Asia.

He grabbed a yellow legal pad with notes and rehearsed aloud what he really wanted to say in his speech that night. He wanted to rub it into his peers.

"Too many miners, like most of you out here tonight, have tried to do it all. You're making Grade A copper cathodes ready for trading in global markets, yet you suffer from price swings that punish your profit margins after investing all that money into smelters. Forget about doing it all. That's why you're seated at tables, and I'm up on the podium. I extract the rock and sell the concentrate to you guys, the refiners, locked in at a very nice price. I'm sitting pretty. You guys deal with all the headaches to make the final product and suffer the fallout from market whims. You suffer; I find my niche and prosper. Life is good."

But he knew full well he wasn't going to say such things.

A few hours later, he summoned his driver at his home in Santiago's Lo Barnechea District, and he was off. The city was glowing in pleasant late-afternoon sunshine. His driver moved slowly between the city buses and a slew of cars. Sebastián flipped through an older copy of *The Gateway* that someone had left in his office, and read an article on how private equity funds were stepping in and financing small businesses across the region when banks refused to approve loans.

"Nice article, Mr. Street Brewer," Sebastián said.

At the cocktail party before dinner that night in one of the many fine salons, Sebastián met with several US, Canadian, Chinese, Japanese, and Australian mining executives and promised one-on-one meetings with each one of them that week. They were all eager to be part of Sebastián's next venture, eager to tap his brain and grab even the slightest glimpse of his thought processes. To Sebastián, they were all an open book. Big Canadians and Americans. Polished Asians. Husky Australians. He could walk into an office anywhere in the mining world, spot an executive, and immediately know which route they had taken to get to the top, either the MBA from the United States or the burly guy who worked his way from the pits up. They were all at the hotel that evening, and they all looked the same, except for a lovely young woman, obviously American, and a true breath of fresh air. He could spot foreigners a mile away due to their body language alone.

"And that is quite a body," he said aloud. She wore a blue pinstripe business suit over a lighter-blue blouse with the collar overlapping the lapel in the style typical of businesswomen all over the world. She was speaking with a few mining executives and bankers in an open area just outside of the main banquet hall. Crisply dressed waiters shuttled back and forth with trays full of red and white wines as well as pisco sours, a cocktail made from a grape brandy popular in Chile and in Peru. A large tray on a stand with a purple-stained white cloth served as a table for those to set their empty glasses on. It didn't take long for a member of the wait staff to haul it away.

"Who's that rose among thorns over there?" he asked a young American reporter texting nearby.

"She's not one of us. She's a hedge fund manager from Florida. Name's Olivia," the young reporter responded.

"I'll have a chat with her," Sebastián said. He turned to leave and then glanced back at the reporter. "Thank you. Oh, and here's a little nugget for you. We see copper prices cooling a bit in the short term, but in the long term, they'll rally again. We're off to New York soon to talk about financing new greenfield projects in Chile and Peru. The whole industry has been too cautious."

The reporter immediately dialed the copy desk in New York, dictated a short lead, and added Sebastián's comments. Moments later, copper futures across the world jumped, and so did stock prices in Tarapacá Mines.

Sebastián walked up to the pretty young American, smiled, and extended a hand. No Latin American greeting kiss. Take charge with a handshake. Let her know that you know that she is an American. "Hello there," he said in perfect English, British English that he learned as a child in London.

"Hola," Olivia replied, and smiled back, taking his hand.

"Sebastián Ledezma," he said.

"Olivia Crawford," she replied. "I'm supposed to meet you."

"You're not a financial journalist, I presume."

"Hedge fund manager," she replied.

"Interesting. What brings you to Santiago? Need some new money?"

"I'm with Cornbridge Capital, and yes, today we do."

"Well, I don't qualify. The money in my family goes back quite a way, so I am not exactly new money," Sebastián said.

Olivia laughed. "Old money, new money. I'm just here to prove to you that money makes money. Is that a good cookie-cutter response?" she asked. "Anyway, you're familiar with Cornbridge Capital, I hear. If so, I'd like to ask for some time this week to discuss global investing opportunities tailor-made for high-net-worth Chileans such as yourself," Olivia said.

"Is that so? Didn't hedge funds get the world into trouble a few years back?"

"Not ours. At Cornbridge, we invest in conservative venues only. If you're looking for a really high-risk venue that comes with an insanely high return, we're not for you."

"Sounds like Ted Bullard," Sebastián said.

"That's him! Boring but safe," Olivia said. "Ted told me to keep an eye out for you. I have a list of target clients, but you're my white whale. How do you know Ted?"

"Perhaps we should have a meeting tomorrow at my office. I know Cornbridge, and I could bring a few friends and business associates."

The ice was broken. "A meeting would be great. What time?"

"Three o'clock tomorrow," Sebastián said. Both took sips from their drinks and enjoyed a moment of silence.

"Hmm," she mumbled.

"What's that?" Sebastián asked.

"It always surprises me how different Chile is from the rest of the region. It's prosperous, and it works, most of the time at least."

"No coups and cocaine? The product of a benevolent dictator from the twentieth century?"

"At least no cocaine," Olivia said.

"That's not altogether true," Sebastián said.

"Cocaine? Here? I thought most of the coca paste came from Peru and Bolivia, while most of the refining into cocaine took place in Colombia."

"That's true, but you're forgetting the very thing that you just brought up."

"What's that?"

"What did you just say about Chile?"

"That it's prosperous and stable," Olivia said.

"Exactly. And how would you describe Peru, Colombia, or Bolivia?"

"Not exactly prosperous or stable but not unstable," Olivia said, standing back a bit. "Colombia is looking pretty good these days. Anyway, I see your point. A ship from a stable economy will raise less suspicions among US officials than a ship from a known drug-producing country."

"Exactly," Sebastián said, taking a sip of his fine Scotch. "I ship out a lot of copper from ports in northern Chile, many of which shuffle out products from Bolivia, where more and more cocaine refining is taking place these days. I don't need that on my ships, so I keep a close eye on the ports and everyone using them. I want nothing to do with drugs."

"So you snoop. Do you share your knowledge with authorities?"

"Somewhat. I know US spies track my copper data to basically gauge Chinese demand and know how healthy they are. That's fine, but I don't want trouble with the law or with those who break the law, like Mr. Manuel Rodríguez, one of the largest producers of the raw coca paste in the world. He lives in a lovely mansion way up in the mountains near the Chapare region of Bolivia, where most of the coca paste comes from. Today, he's moving more of his raw paste to refineries in Colombia through nearby ports at Antofagasta, Arica or Iquique as well as by air and road, but he also refines at home. That way, he taps the US and European markets as well as the thriving crack cocaine market in Brazil. Did you know Brazil is one of the world's largest consumers of crack? We track his every move, including his rumored plans to set up makeshift refineries in South America and as far north as Honduras and Guatemala with the help of local authorities, of course. I know of one high-ranking military official in Honduras who's facilitating this. Freddy Velázquez. That makes it a national security concern for you. We don't want any of his money in our financial system, or any of his garbage smuggled on our ships," Sebastián said.

"I like that," Olivia said, shifting her purse on her shoulder. "A diversified cocaine baron versus a billionaire regulator. How else do you track these things?"

"Everyone knows the top distributor, Mexico, is fighting a war on drugs. It's in the news all the time. One top cartel guy gets killed, another takes his place and immediately becomes ready to make a name for himself in part by squeezing his suppliers. So the South Americans reroute the cocaine when the Mexicans get too demanding. But to where exactly? Well, to find out, just track the crime rates. If you see murders on the rise in the eastern Caribbean, in places like Trinidad and Tobago, or in normally quiet places like the Bahamas, you know that more drugs are moving back through Florida. Track other things as well, like movements of certain goods. I have an equity stake in one of the local ports that ships in and out general cargo, so I look for hikes in the movement of acetone, acetic acid, and calcium chloride, and other chemicals needed to turn coca paste into refined cocaine. I also track imports of camping gear and microwave ovens. Anything that suggests someone wants to set up a lab in Bolivia or Peru and away from the prying eyes in Bogotá or Washington. Then I pay people to make sure it stays away from where I do business."

"It's a shame my country consumes so much of this stuff and fuels this industry," Olivia said.

"Any international fund manager needs to know that money is clean, especially considering the constant stream of new regulations and tax laws out of Washington," Sebastián said. He took a sip. "Now, just a couple of things. One, when you meet my friends and pitch us on your fund, please realize that all of us in emerging markets are painfully aware that a thirty percent return on nothing is nothing. Also, please, no more securities backed by bad US mortgages, and lastly..."

"Yes?"

"How about another drink?"

"Sounds wonderful," she said.

A waiter appeared out of nowhere and served them both.

"Cheers," they said. Their glasses clinked.

Two days later an ecstatic Olivia returned home to Naples. She had just signed up two very well-qualified investors along with Sebastián Ledezma to pump some fresh money into Cornbridge Capital, and a much-anticipated sailing regatta was still far enough around the corner to get some practice time on the water. She walked into her office after a good night's sleep on the flight home, and there was Ted, smiling with a gift basket flowing with cheeses and red wine.

"Olivia," he said. "Welcome back. California reds in this basket. To complement the Chilean wines I'm sure you snapped up duty-free."

She smiled, almost like a blushing teenager. "For me?"

"You're a sweetheart. Sweet as a person, and sweet for our fund. Right guys?"

Pracy and Anderson looked up from their cubicles and gave a thumbs-up, almost in unison.

She smiled at the two young and preppy twenty-somethings. Short, dirty blond hair. Tan skin. Both of them.

"Walk with me to my office," Ted said.

They entered his office, and Ted sat down behind the desk.

"So how did Chile treat you?"

"It was wonderful. Sebastián was great!"

"What did you talk about?"

"Investing, wine, and cocaine."

"Start off with cocaine, then the other two get better," Ted said, laughing. He slouched in his chair but remained fixed on Olivia. "This should be good."

"He was telling me something about how coca farmers in Bolivia and Peru are shipping coca paste out on ships from northern Chilean ports in Antofagasta, Arica or Iquique. Then they unload the paste for refining in Colombia and even in Central America. Either way, there's no record of ever having docked at any Colombian ports along the way."

"Interesting, but we know this already," Ted said, stroking his chin.

Olivia frowned. "We know this? Cornbridge Capital follows this stuff?"

"Yes, we do follow this. We don't want dirty money in our fund."

"Well, then you don't want any business from Manuel Rodríguez in Bolivia."

"Who?"

"Manuel Rodríguez. Sebastián said he was a big producer of coca paste in the Chapare region of Bolivia. He's setting up cocaine refineries in Honduras and Guatemala. A Honduran military guy named Freddy Velázquez is overseeing it there."

"Duly noted," Ted said. "We've got contacts in Honduras and Guatemala. Now we know who to scrutinize. Thanks Olivia. Any word on copper?"

"He said Asia demand may be cooling, but it's temporary."

"Hmm," Ted said. "Good job! Take the day off. Go sailing!"

A few minutes later when he was alone, Ted drew a cell phone from his office drawer and dialed. "Yes," a woman's voice on the other line answered.

"Manuel Rodríguez in Bolivia."

"Ah yes, the Bolivian coca paste producer," the voice said. "What's new?"

"He's refining more cocaine at home, bypassing Colombia and channeling it up through Mexico or directly."

"We know this. That's not going into any briefings."

"Yes, but this is new. He's opening refineries in Honduras and Guatemala these days. We got a name. Freddy Velázquez. Honduran military. Helping out with it somehow."

"That is new. Nice work," the voice said, and she hung up.

CHAPTER

16

Olivia sat down at her desk and her cell phone rang. She didn't recognize the number and screened it, wondering whether it was a client or a robocaller. She waited for a voice mail. None came. Robocaller, she concluded.

She walked into Ted's office, saw he was on the other line, and indicated she was stepping out briefly but would be right back. She left the office, glad that she didn't live too far away to drive home for her gym bag. She was a little angry at herself for not working out at all during her trip to South America, so it was time to make up for lost ground. Yes, she could have waited until after work and then get the gym bag, but even a fifteen-minute delay at that hour could mean missing her CrossFit class. She drove through light traffic in Naples, arrived home, and entered her condo. Her eyes were still adjusting to leaving the outdoor sunlight when her cell phone rang again, an unknown caller.

She answered.

Before she even said hello, a female voice at the other end of the line cut to the chase. "Is this Olivia Crawford of Cornbridge Capital?"

"Speaking," Olivia said, setting her keys on her granite counter. The sun shone warm and comfortable on the white and pastel buildings by the tranquil blue Gulf of Mexico, a sliver of which was viewable from her kitchen window.

"This is Cyra Octavia Harred. Let's just say I'm a legal counsel for one of the investors in your firm. I'm not going to tell you who, of course, but I suspect there is something you need to know about your place of work," the voice said.

"Who is this?" Olivia asked.

"Cyra Harred. Who I am is not important. But you could be raising money for the wrong people. That could get messy, especially when you're taking foreigners' money and telling them it's going for one thing when, in reality, it's going for another. That's what I am calling to find out."

"Who is this? Are you sure you have the right person? This is Olivia Crawford of Cornbridge Capital."

"I'm pretty sure. I'll know in a minute. Is your fund manager's name Beryl Phelps?"

Olivia relaxed. "Sorry, but you have the wrong fund. I'm going to hang up now."

"My apologies. It's just that my client is well diversified, and I need to conduct more background checks into his or her business partners. I'm often left in the dark, amazingly. I'm playing catch-up here, so work with me. Now, I am going to give you a list of names. Is there a Matthew Merrill at your fund?"

Sigh. "No."

"Is there a Phillip Wade?"

"Nope."

"Brent Drum?"

"No."

"Ted Bullard?"

Olivia paused.

"I'll take that pause as a yes."

Olivia frowned and hung up. I'm being harassed, she thought. Or robbed. She rushed to make sure all the doors and windows were locked and then stood alone in her kitchen. She put the phone down and looked around. Everything was normal. No sign of a break-in or stalking, which helped her lower her thoughts out of the clouds and back into a decision-making reality. All her sailing plaques and trophies were in place in her two-bedroom, two-bath condominium. She took further inventory. All the silver was there. The hidden safe in her closet was there, untouched. The dial stuck on three where she always left it. She opened it to be sure. Spare cash there. So was her passport and the key to her bank lockbox. All her jewelry and important documents were there.

She blew it off as a prank caller or an identity thief. All she knew was that the caller was tracking her via her cell phone. She didn't have her number broadcast on the web anywhere. Plus, she stayed away from social networking sites. Still, if they could find her number and knew where she worked, then they probably had access to other details about her life. Olivia rushed to her computer and quickly reviewed her checking, savings, credit card, mutual funds, and some higher-yielding investment accounts. All were normal. She then dug through her email and checked all the names. Nothing from Brent Drum or any other names the so-called Cyra Harred offered.

"Legal counsel," she said aloud. She knew who the investors were in the fund, and each would be getting a phone call really soon. She also considered maybe it was someone tied to previous investors. She didn't know everyone who had money with Cornbridge before she came on board.

She returned to work, closed her office door, and picked up the phone. Ted was out of the office, so she called him. "Ted. It's Olivia. We need to talk," she said.

"What's up?" Ted asked. "Pending meltdown in China? Conflict in the Middle East?"

"Harassment," Olivia responded. "Crank call," she went on. "A woman. She said she was legal counsel for an investor, but I found it odd she didn't know the name of the fund's manager. That would be you. All she said was that we were raising money for people who aren't who they say they are and wanted to confirm your name. I didn't give up anything of course. She asked if the manager was a, let's see, a Beryl Phelps, a Matthew Merrill, or a Brent Drum or something like that. She did get to Ted Bullard, but I said nothing. Something was off."

Silence on the other end.

"Hello? Are you there?" Olivia asked.

"I have no idea who these people are," Ted said on the other end of the phone. "First of all, are you safe? Do you feel threatened? Tell me what I can do."

"I'm fine, I guess," she said. "There's not much you can do."

"It's an identity thief. Change your passwords and ignore whoever it is," Ted said. "Look," he added. "It's either a hacker or a prank. Maybe some rival fund trying to rattle us. Someone who has an interest in seeing us unwind. Don't worry about it. Just tell me if it happens again."

Olivia said she wouldn't worry, and she pretty much blew it off. Her relaxation wouldn't last. She was sitting at her desk in the evening when unknown flashed on her phone again.

"He blamed these calls on a competitor, didn't he? Downplayed everything," the voice claiming to be Cyra Harred said.

"What?"

"That's what he'd do. I'll go so far as to bet that you didn't even ask Ted what he thought about all this," Cyra said. "And I know he's going by Ted Bullard based on your pause on the phone when I mentioned his name. I found that out pretty quickly anyway. I am just studying your reactions to my intrusions. I am fairly transparent. You'll soon see."

"He said it was a prank. And now I am apparently being pranked again. Harassed more like it. I'm going to call the police. If you're the lawyer you say you are, then you'll appreciate the shit that's headed your way," Olivia said.

"That's an excellent idea. Do it. Call the cops. But call Ted first. Ask him if he knows anything about young foreign professionals disappearing in Venezuela. Ask him if he has any information about Russians investing in Venezuelan infrastructure. Study his reactions. Do it. Then call the cops. Tell them Cyra Harred told you to."

"I will. What's the name of your firm?"

"Harred, Harred, Harred, and Harred."

"Well, Cyra, you're going to jail, jail, jail, and then prison." Olivia hung up. She was about to dial the police but called Ted first via video conferencing on her phone. Ted answered immediately. "That Cyra woman called back. She's a psycho bitch. I told her that I was going to call the police if she kept it up."

"Good idea. Do it. What else did she say?"

"She said to do just that. To call the police. She also told me to ask you about young professionals disappearing in Venezuela. I don't know, something about Russians in Venezuela. Gibberish, basically. I know this is scary and all, but she sounded cool and collected. Almost prepared. I'm calling the police."

"Prank or not, this is getting annoying. If she calls again, let me know. In fact, I'll call the police myself. This is my fund, and your safety is my responsibility. I'm going to take the lead on this. Just turn your cell phone off for now."

"Ted," Olivia asked. "Is that your real name?"

"Don't let her get inside your head. This is what identity thieves do."

"I don't think she's an identify thief. Seems off. And why are you telling me to turn my phone off? Shouldn't we keep it on in case she calls again so we can bust her somehow? Maybe get a trace, track the timing of her calls or something?"

"Look, Olivia, I will take care of this. I promise you."

Olivia just stared at him on her phone and then hung up.

More calls came through that evening, including one identified as unknown, though Olivia screened them all to avoid conversing with Cyra. Even if an investor called from abroad, Olivia let the call go to voice mail. After she received two more calls from an unidentified caller, that was it for Olivia. She called the police herself.

"9-1-1. What's your emergency?"

"Someone is prank-calling me. Can you trace my most recent call?"

"Please don't use this emergency line for nuisance calls."

"Just listen to me. A woman claiming to be Cyra Harred says she's legal counsel for an investor in a hedge fund where I work. Won't say who the investor is but keeps asking strange questions about my boss not being who he says he is and to ask him about people disappearing in Venezuela. I know it sounds like gibberish, and I know I am rambling. But it's like she's watching me. I'm sorry. My name is Olivia Crawford. I run a hedge fund called Cornbridge Capital."

"Well, is there a number that she left? Can you see the number calling you?"

"It says unknown. Can you trace the last calls on my cell phone? I have the times that she called."

"We can't do that now, but we can maybe arrange for that later. But first, where are you? Are you alone?"

"I am alone. At home."

"Lock your doors."

"Already done. Listen. On second thought, I don't think this is some stalker or identity hacker. This person seems intelligent. She seems to be snooping for something beyond my bank account."

"Is there any evidence of forced entry in your residence? Is anything missing?"

"No, I've already checked."

"If there is such evidence, would you call us and ask us to dispatch a police officer just to be sure? To answer some questions? File a report?"

"I don't know. Maybe I am overreacting. It's just that I get the feeling that I'm being watched."

"Well, we don't normally get involved over prank calls, but this time we'll get involved. A squad car is on the way."

The officer arrived. The conversation with the police could have been scripted for any television show.

"Are you currently dating?" an Officer Parks asked.

She couldn't tell if he had a New York accent or a South Boston accent, though she dared not ask and risk offending him. He was wiry, scrappy, and tough, yet he was meticulously neat. He wore a trimmed moustache and sculpted his hair way too much with mousse and a blow dryer, like those hard-nosed, street-smart bond traders up in the Northeast did, Olivia thought, a bit amused.

"I don't think we can track previous calls at this time, though the appropriate authorities will ask your cell phone provider to monitor your calls going forward," Parks said. "But let me ask just a few routine questions. Any ex-boyfriends or girlfriends who might be behind this?"

"No ex-boyfriends, and I don't date girls," Olivia answered.

"Any disgruntled coworkers? Distant relatives?"

"None." Olivia didn't have any enemies or suspect anyone of threatening her.

"Have you noticed anyone following you at work? Maybe at the gym or at the bah?"

"A bah?"

"You know, a bah. Sorry. I forget I'm down south. A bar," Parks said, going out of his way to ditch whatever accent he had.

South Boston, Olivia guessed.

"Nobody. Look, I think the best thing is to download an app that will track this sort of thing," Olivia said.

"Maybe. We'll also monitor it on our end. Let us know if something out of the ordinary does pop up. It's probably a prank, but you did the right thing by calling us. After all, they do know your name and something about where you work," Parks said.

He left, the scent of some strange aftershave trailing behind him.

And that was that, Olivia thought. After calling the police, she relaxed and walked around her condo. She could afford bigger, but she bought all she needed. She looked at a few photos of college sweethearts and sailboats on her fireplace mantel and thought about an upcoming regatta. "It's going to be nice to be out on the water again," she said aloud.

After checking to see if all the doors were locked, she grabbed her phone and dialed Sam McBride, an old boyfriend.

"Sam?" she said. "It's Olivia."

"Wow. Long time," the young man answered.

"How are you, Sam?"

"Good, I guess. How about you?"

"Not so good. A little freaked out. Been getting crank calls and don't want to be alone."

"You? Afraid? Come on."

"Believe it or not, I am. I just don't want to be alone. Can you come over? We can talk, have a few drinks."

"And then I end up on your couch. Friend-zoned again. I'll pass. Call the cops. This is a job for a boyfriend." Sam hung up.

"Great," Olivia said. She dialed a few more men from her past with the same results, and she dozed off on the couch with all the lights on. Alone.

The next afternoon she was at her computer at the office, winding down the day. She opened a web browser and typed in *Ted Bullard*. Links on various individuals popped up. So did links to executives in various industries. She typed in *Ted Bullard* and *hedge fund*. A link came to Cornbridge Capital. The site had bios on Olivia, Brent, Pracy, and Anderson. No pictures. No phone numbers. Olivia was okay with that. Cyra knew Ted worked there, Olivia thought. She was gauging her reactions to the questions all along.

Let's see, she thought. She started a Google search for Beryl Phelps. A couple of links to friendly faces on Facebook. Not much on Beryl Phelps and the finance world. A quick Google search for Brent Drum. A couple of people scattered here and there. There was a Brent Drum at *The Gateway*, the publication. She clicked on *The Gateway*'s website and went straight to the "About Us" section. She clicked on Brent's profile. He's the publisher of *The Gateway*, she read. Past stints include publisher of *The Oregon Business Chronicle*. Time spent at financial newswires in Belgium and elsewhere in Europe. Studied at Denison University decades ago. Majored in economics and political science. No picture.

Then she clicked on Street Brewer's profile. Editor. Spent time in Venezuela. Studied at Rollins College, a good private school near Orlando, and graduated about a decade ago.

She studied the masthead. Art directors and distributors were listed but not included in the core staff. Back to the home page. The "Contact Us" link jumped out at her. She dialed the telephone number listed on the page. The phone rang only once and went straight to voice mail.

"You've reached *The Gateway*. For Brent Drum, press one, for Street Brewer, press..." Olivia hung up. Nobody there.

Back to the "About Us" section. She clicked on Brent Drum's profile again. At the bottom was an email link. She clicked on it and wrote "Subscription" in the subject line. She typed in a few sentences about getting a subscription, mentioned that she had some questions about events and to please respond. She pressed send. Off the email went. Immediately, an out-of-office reply came back. Brent Drum was traveling.

"Nobody is manning the ship at *The Gateway*," she mumbled. At the bottom of the email she saw more of Brent's info. The general office number and a cell phone number.

She dialed the cell phone number. Ringing. Ringing in her ear. Ringing somewhere else. More ringing in her ear. Ringing down the hall in the conference room.

She hung up and walked to the edge of her office, noticing her heartbeat picking up. She peered into the hallway, which was empty, and retreated to just inside her office door. She dialed the number again, this time from her cell phone. Ringing in her ear. A phone down the hallway rang again. In unison. She hung up. Immediately her office phone rang, piercing the silence and startling her. She answered.

"Olivia Crawford," she said.

"Uh, Olivia. It's me, Ted. Meet me in the conference room. We need to discuss—"

"I'll be right there. Just give me a minute," she said and slammed down the phone. Immediately the phone burst to life anew, ringing again and startling her even more. This time, it was a Miami number, the same one from *The Gateway*'s "Contact Us" link.

"Olivia Crawford speaking," she said.

Silence.

"Hello?" Olivia said.

"Hi, my name is Karen Whittaker from *The Gateway*. I saw a missed call from this number and wanted to return the call. Our apologies for missing you."

"I was interested in, uh," Olivia said, trying to come up with an excuse why she had called *The Gateway*. "I was interested in taking out a subscription and organizing some events."

"Okay. Well, I will put you in touch with Brent Drum, who handles those matters, though he's in a meeting right now. Or you could just do it online. I handle public relations and other sales-related matters for the magazine but as an external vendor on contract. I will surely tell Mr. Drum that you called. May I ask from where you are calling?"

"Cornbridge Capital in Naples. You're in sales and marketing and can't handle a subscription and events request? I will call back," Olivia said and hung up.

Toward the end of the day, after a brief meeting with Ted on perfunctory office matters, Olivia checked her phone as she had all day. No ringing. No creepy calls. She did call the cell phone of a Brent Drum at *The Gateway* several times, though it went to voice mail each time. She was still nervous about the harassing phone calls, with a woman named Karen Whittaker now possibly involved, though she couldn't be sure that it was the same person going by Cyra Harred on other calls. Whatever the case, she felt more confident knowing she had names and phone numbers of people at *The Gateway* whom she suspected as either the culprits or tied to them somehow. She was amassing information on suspects that she could report to the police. Add to that, her phone had been quiet. A typical, event-free evening was coming to a close. Life was returning to normal. Then, after hours of apparent calm, she noticed a little icon showing that she had a new voice mail.

She dialed into her voice mail. It was her mom checking in. She deleted the message. Right when she deleted it, the phone rang again. The name "Mom" flashed on the screen. Olivia relaxed and took the call.

"Hi, Mom!"

"Olivia, it's Cyra again. Sorry to have your mom's name flash on the screen when the incoming call is mine, but you need to listen to me, so I resorted to some technology that's over your pay grade to make it seem like your mom is calling. Don't screen me again."

"Oh my God," Olivia said in a whisper.

"Officer Parks is a good man but can't really help you. I know I said go to the police, but to be honest, no police force on earth can protect you from what's after you."

Olivia froze.

Cyra went on. "I may be able to help you. I just need to know if Ted Bullard ever mentioned the name Brent Drum, or any other name. Anything. I can't go into detail on the phone, but he had you talk to Sebastián Ledezma in Chile because he couldn't go down there himself due to his real line of work, which is not running a hedge fund. I will tell you in person later. The walls have ears, so I am going to hang up. Do not screen my calls. I'll be in Naples to talk to you about this as soon as possible. Do not be afraid of me. But don't isolate yourself until then. The worst thing right now is for you to be alone."

She hung up. Fear froze up everything inside her, making it hard to breathe. After about a minute in shock, she felt her blood thaw just enough to resume flowing through her veins and carry some bits and pieces of logic back to her brain. No time for panic, just planning. How did this Cyra know she had spoken with Officer Parks? How did this Cyra know she had been in Chile talking to Sebastián Ledezma as if she knew him personally? How long had she been stalked?

"I'm being bugged. Right now," Olivia whispered. "This woman has eyes and ears everywhere."

She looked all around her office. She looked at the lights, the phone, the pictures on the wall, her closet. Everything seemed to look back at her. She stood up and gathered her things. Then there was a knock at the door.

"You okay?" Ted said, entering her office. He saw Olivia standing at her desk. Bag and purse in hand. Water bottle tethered and ready to go. She was wild-eyed and defensive.

"Ted," Olivia said. Sharp breaths shooting out of her nervous mouth. "She called again and said all this stuff. She knew about Chile. Knew I spoke with Sebastián. Ted, I called the police last night, and she knew the name of the officer who came to my house! I'm out of here. I'm going straight to the police right now, and I want this entire office and my house debugged, and I want whoever is doing this caught and thrown into prison! Even if that means you!"

"I have no idea who this person is, or what she's talking about! So you're right. Let's go right now. I agree. I don't like this either," Ted said, staring around at the walls. "Were the police helpful?"

Olivia said nothing and then nodded.

"Good," he said. "Let's tell them everything in person."

"Everything," Olivia said, pacing. She looked out her office window. It was getting dark, and the parking lot was empty except for a dinged-up pickup truck. Its headlights were on, but it wasn't moving. She couldn't make out the driver, though nearby streetlights revealed the silhouette of very curly hair.

Olivia looked at Ted. "This is different than simple harassment. I'll tell the detectives everything she told me. Like that you're not who you say you are. That she is coming down here to give me more details about you and someone named Brent Drum, and that you sent me to Chile because you can't go down there at all because of your real job. I looked up a Brent Drum online. Found one who works at *The Gateway*, a Miami media company. I called and spoke with a Karen, and I heard your phone ringing when I…"

"No idea what's going on here either," Ted interrupted her. "My phone is in my bag, anyway. Jesus! Someone has been in the office."

Olivia tensed up. Ted looked behind him into the hallway and then back at Olivia.

"There's no one here now, but this is too much. Let's get the fuck out of here. I've stood idly by for too long while people from my team are being harassed. In fact, I will walk you to your car," Ted said. "I'm going to make sure you are taken care of. The worst thing right now is for you to be alone until you are safe in your condo with an armed police officer outside tonight."

"I appreciate that," Olivia replied. Ted watched her visibly relax after waves of suspicion rolled across her face. He gave her some room so she could pass him by and exit the office.

"Big plans for the weekend? Going to do some boating?" Ted asked.

Olivia smiled weakly, but still it was a smile. "Yes. It's going to be nice to get out on the water and away from all of this."

"Ah," Ted said. "Around here or over on the East Coast?"

"Haven't decided yet," Olivia said.

"Sounds nice. I know you swim well."

"Yes, I do. I love the water."

"Not me," Ted said. "I'm a terrible swimmer outside of a pool. I get seasick on docks."

The humid Florida air slapped them both across their faces as they left the building and made their way to the parking lot. Ted glanced around. Not too many cars left. Just Olivia's MINI Cooper and his own white Porsche 911.

A worn pickup truck remained parked in idle in the corner of the parking lot. Its lights were on, though it was still hard to see the driver.

"I don't like this," Olivia said, staring at the pickup.

"I don't either," Ted said, also staring at the pickup. Then he looked at his own car, which was listing at a sickly angle as all cars with flat tires do.

"Jesus!" Ted shouted. "Would you look at that?" His rear right tire was as flat as they come.

"I don't like this at all," Olivia said. "You don't suppose this has anything to do with our crank calls, do you?" She circled Ted's car. "Let's get out of here in my car. I'll drive you home or even to the police station if needed. We'll call 9-1-1 from the car if he follows us."

Ted knelt down to get a better view of the tire. "It's been leaking like that since this morning. I should have taken it in. Doesn't matter, though. I want us both out of here right now." He scanned the parking lot. The outdated pickup truck, an old Ford, remained in idle about a hundred yards away. A second later, it twitched into gear and began to inch forward. It approached Ted and Olivia, and stopped. Olivia walked beside Ted, and they both faced the approaching car.

"Stay behind me," Ted said, stepping in front of Olivia.

The truck's passenger-side window rolled down. It was hard to make out the details of the driver. A shape but not a face. A large outline of a head and shoulders at that, but the shadows concealed any details. There was nothing but silence. Not a peep came from inside. It inched forward again, and both Olivia and Ted flinched in response. Then the truck sped off. It came to the edge of the parking lot, hooked a left, and was gone.

Olivia exhaled. Her body became visibly relaxed. "Let's get out of here now. I'll give you a ride," she said, pointing in the direction of the pickup truck.

"Olivia, I don't want you to go out of your way. It's far away. Don't worry about it. I will get an Uber or a Lyft. Because of you, the fund is doing very well. With billions in assets under management and with stellar returns, I can afford a ride. I want you inside and safe."

"Seriously, Ted. Save that money for a drink. I don't trust shared rides now. Get in," she said, pointing to her car. The truck was up ahead on a road adjacent to the parking lot at a stoplight. The light turned green, and the truck drove out of sight.

"Well, if you say so," Ted said. "Let me just grab one thing out of my car." He unlocked the door and grabbed a leather messenger bag and then closed the door. "I can't tell you how much I appreciate this. Not too many people would give their boss a ride these days." Ted opened the bag and rooted around in it.

Olivia checked her surroundings and looked back at Ted, who held a cell phone up for her to see.

"Good thing the heat in the car didn't ruin it," he said, throwing the phone back into the bag.

Just then, Olivia's cell phone rang, and a number flashed across the display. Miami area code. She didn't recognize it. She held it up to Ted, who shrugged.

"Answer it," Ted said, checking his own messages.

"Olivia Crawford," she said, putting the phone on speaker.

"Hi, Olivia. It's Karen Whittaker from *The Gateway* in Coral Gables. We spoke earlier. Do you have a moment?"

"Well, if I could call you back..."

"Actually, I'm calling not about magazine matters but to inquire about investing in hedge funds. See, my day job is kind of a hobby to pass time. That's why I was so bad at booking events or handling subscriptions. My husband is a doctor, an orthopedic surgeon who specializes in a very profitable field of practice. After we hung up, I got to thinking and did a little research. I just want some of your time to talk about alternative investing—and hosting events, of course," the woman named Karen said with a chuckle.

"I see," Olivia said. She gave Ted a thumbs-up and pointed to the phone, whispering "new money."

Ted, gave her a thumbs-up back, and motioned to her to throw him the car keys.

Olivia tossed them to Ted, and he opened the door and slid into the driver's seat. Olivia did likewise in the passenger's seat while remaining on the phone. Ted set the messenger bag beneath his feet. Then he adjusted the seat to his size and did the same to the rearview mirror. He started the car and listened to Olivia's conversation.

"Well, my husband and I are pretty conservative investors. Maybe too conservative, and nowadays we want to take on a little more risk, now that we have some money to gamble. Anyway, I was calling to get your advice on how to approach going about selecting funds."

"I see. Well, we could arrange a meeting of some sort—"

"Hang on," Karen said. A moment later, she was back on. "Yes, I'd like that. You have my number. Write down my email address."

"Give me a second to get a pen," Olivia said, taking a pen out of her purse. "Okay."

Karen gave her the information and then thanked Olivia for her time. Olivia hung up.

"New lead?" Ted said.

"Looks that way," Olivia said, staring out the window. "Have you ever heard of the name Cyra Harred? The woman who keeps calling me?"

"I've never heard of her," Ted said. A minute passed. He glanced at his phone in the bag. It was dark. No caller ID notifications glowing on the screen. "Look, I don't blame you for not trusting a soul, not even me. We're gonna get to the bottom of this."

"You're goddamn right we will."

More time passed. Both seemed to relax a little. Ted broke the silence. "This is some car. I was a bit of a motorhead in high school. Won't tell you stories of grandeur of rebuilding a '65 Shelby but did manage to keep a fine 280ZX in shape for longer than most models. My niece is turning sixteen really soon, and her father and I want to surprise her with a new car. This one would be a good choice."

Olivia said nothing and continued staring out the window. Ted was headed south on Highway 41, the Tamiami Trail, which stretches all the way across the state over to Miami. Then his phone rang. He glanced at it. Unknown flashed across the screen.

"Looks like we're both making statements, and by that I mean statements at the police station," Ted said. He screened the call. "I've been getting unknown calls for days now. We're going to the cops tonight in person."

"Looks like you missed your turn to the police station and your house," Olivia said. "You just blew by Collier Boulevard."

"Damn it!"

His phone rang again, but this time he fished it out of his bag and answered it.

"Hi. Pracy."

Olivia's body visibly relaxed.

Ted spoke for a few minutes about perfunctory office details. A commercial real estate tenant representative suggested they move. As assets under management grew, so would support staff. The health insurance provider wanted a word as well. They'd deal with it tomorrow. Ted clicked off the phone and stared ahead into the darkness.

"Okay, so I missed the turn. I had to take Pracy's call. We'll just take San Marco Road down to Marco Island. I'm exhausted," Ted said. "But your safety comes first. I know where there is a police station in that area."

"Ted, I'm not comfortable on this road," she said.

"The next stop is the police station, right there on Marco Island, right down San Marco Road," he said.

Minutes later, Ted pulled off Highway 41 and onto San Marco Road, which was flanked by walls of trees and thick underbrush. Ted accelerated down the road. Canals ran close along both sides of the road.

"It's so dark," Olivia said. "Go faster. In fact, get us a speeding ticket." The absence of city lights kept the forest black save for a ribbon of a glow from Naples to the north.

"So, what's your take on these crank calls?" Ted asked, really picking up the pace. "I want off this road, too."

"Who knows? I just want to make sure whoever it is can't hurt me," Olivia said.

Ted was pushing ninety miles per hour.

"We're getting close. You'll be back in the driver's seat in a few minutes. Jeez. It's after nine," Ted said.

He looked at the rearview mirror. Headlights shone about a hundred yards behind him. He looked ahead of him. No oncoming traffic. When he looked back at the rearview mirror, the headlights were narrowing the gap.

"Look behind me and tell me what you see," Ted said.

Olivia's head snapped back.

"Someone's really coming up on us fast," she said. "Really fast. I hope they pass us."

"That makes two of us," Ted said.

Within seconds, the headlights were close to the bumper, and in a millisecond, the headlights made contact with the bumper.

"What the hell!" Ted screamed.

"Shit," Olivia whispered. Her body tensed and remained taught.

The vehicle slowed down for just a few yards and then screamed beside them, overtaking them in the left lane. An old pickup truck, the same one from the office parking lot, passed them. Ted flashed his brights. An enormous head with curly black hair emerged from the driver's side window and stared back at Ted and Olivia. Both caught sight of a brief, empty smile. Then the head submerged into the truck. The passenger side was empty.

Olivia gripped her seatbelt. "Slow down, Ted. Let him go, or just turn around, or just do what you have to do to get us out of here."

"There're no cops around here. I just want to get somewhere where there are cops, which is right down this road," Ted said.

"We can't stay on this dark road with that psychopath!"

"And go back? There's nothing but miles and miles of swamp and mangrove forests back that way."

"Just turn around fast, and fucking do it!" Olivia shouted. "There's always a cop car back at the corner of San Marco Road and the Tamiami Trail at night. He should be there or somewhere nearby by the time we circle back. It's a known speed trap."

"You're right," Ted said, breathing heavily. Red taillights suddenly brightened on the truck up ahead. It was slowing down.

"I know a way out of this." With a flick of his wrist, Ted lunged the MINI Cooper off the right-hand side of the road, flooring it.

"Ted, what the hell! Oh my God!" Olivia's scream escalated into a soundless panic.

The tires' screeching went silent when the car flew off the grassy shoulder in a small area void of trees and then off the canal bank. Fully airborne and shooting off into the darkness, the car's nose almost pointed upward for an instant.

Ted looked over the hood as if it were a roller coaster, waiting for that inevitable thrill as his stomach dipped with the moving vehicle. Olivia's mouth was wide open next to him, her arms locked straight out in front of her against the dashboard, as if she were part of the car.

"Wow!" Ted screamed.

"Oh my God," Olivia echoed.

The car slammed into the dark water of the canal. Like a black sheet yanked upward, the water shot across the glass. The car bobbed a bit before emitting hisses. Bubbles shot up alongside the sinking metal.

"Oh my God. I hit the turn too fast! I'm sorry, but I will get us out of this. Just hang on," Ted said. He glanced around and took some deep breaths. "You can't open the doors until the water rises inside and the pressure equalizes. My window is cracked so it won't take too long. Also, that monster may still be out there. Just hang on."

A wide-eyed Olivia managed to turn her head and stare at Ted. A brief nod in agreement. It was still rather warm inside the car, though Ted could hear Olivia's mouth jittering. They both felt a little bob of weightlessness as the car began to sink. A gentle thud jolted Ted and Olivia as the front tires hit the bottom. When the rear tires followed suit, Ted moved around in his seat. Olivia looked out her window. Nothing but blackness save a few lights from the dash. The surface was just above the roof of the car. The temperature inside began to drop.

"Wait here. We are going to get out of this," Ted told her.

"Wait here? Where am I going to go?" She began clawing away, jerking at the door handle, yet the door was locked. Water was shooting through Ted's window and through the AC vents as if it were jutting out of mini hydroelectric power dams. Ted took in the coolness of the black water covering his ankles, and then his knees, and eventually his waist.

"The car is going to flood. Then we can open the doors and swim to the surface once the pressure subsides. But you won't be able to push open the door until the water calms. Fighting it will drain you of your energy. You can swim well, so you'll have to hold your breath, and up we go. That's the easy part. The hard part is that we have to pray to God he didn't see us," he said.

"Oh God! We're going to die," Olivia said.

"No, we're not. I have something that can save us."

"What is that?" Olivia asked.

"A small air tank."

"What?"

From the messenger bag between his legs under the water, Ted pulled a small pony scuba tank, a compact unit built for emergencies but perfect for his task at hand. The tank held three cubic feet of air and was small enough for him to stash in his blazer. It would give him fifty-seven surface breaths.

"Okay. Pressure outside is easing. We'll get out when the water reaches the car ceiling. Take a deep breath. I'm going to help you with that seatbelt and then open the door, then give you some air. Don't ask why it's here, but thank God I have it. We'll head to the bank opposite the road. Are you ready?"

"Ready," she answered.

They hyperventilated, and then the water covered them both. All sounds of panic went quiet underwater.

Ted slipped the regulator of his pony tank in his mouth and stretched his hand across to Olivia's seat. He found the seatbelt latch and locked both hands on it. He took his first breath of air. Stay relaxed and take them slow, he thought. You have a task at hand. She may be in good shape and might thrash about.

She did. Both of her hands clawed into Ted's, trying furiously to break his grip on the seatbelt latch. She punched and punched hard, but it was useless.

Ted had her. He wondered if she was staring at him wide-eyed while he drowned her. What color of blue were her eyes again? Does it matter? Whatever, he thought.

With no air and fading strength, Olivia spent her last spurts of energy punching at Ted's arms. She even hit his face once and almost knocked out the pony tank. Her lashing exploded and then she went limp.

Ted felt her arms drift up a little and then her posture softened even more. Drowning was a calm affair, and the panic before let Ted know the water had not yet reached her lungs. He touched her open mouth. She was dead. No movement at all. He could feel her soft hair float to his face like a drifting ink blot in the water. Quickly, he undid the seatbelt and pulled her lifeless body closer to him. Then he undid his seatbelt and floated a bit, taking care not to use up all fifty-seven breaths too quickly. He let himself drift with his back to the windshield, pulling Olivia's body before him into the driver's seat, both bodies moving as if taking part in some dance. He got her into the driver's seat and fastened the seatbelt around her. Good job, he thought. Any samples of trace evidence of him in the car like fingerprints, hair, or other fibers would be so waterlogged that it would be unlikely the authorities would find them or even suspect what really had just happened. Any bruises or cuts she took on by clawing at him would be irrelevant by the time police got around.

Ted figured he had taken about thirty surface breaths when he opened the driver's door, floated out and then closed the door behind him to make sure that when the car was discovered, it wouldn't look like another person was there and had escaped and left the door ajar. He drifted out into the canal and floated there in the blackness. Natural threats to his safety such as reptiles would be long gone after a car plunged into the water, seriously disrupting the nighttime ecosystem. But he waited. No flashlights overhead. No muffled calls for help above the surface. No gathering crowds. Just darkness. He swam up feeling confident until panic struck him, causing him to suck in a few extra surface breaths. His messenger bag. The one that had held the pony tank. The one with his phone inside. He had left it in the car. No mistakes, he thought. The local police would be able to easily track it to him. His wallet was in it as well.

Ted did a backflip in the water and went back down. His swimming arms whipped in the black water. Eventually, his left hand slapped some metal and it didn't take too long for him to feel his way back to the driver's door. He opened it and thanked God he had kept it unlocked. He swam over Olivia's lifeless body and straddled her, as if he were involved in some sort of morbid lovemaking. He reached beneath the seat and felt about, ecstatic when he felt the handle of his bag. Then he floated out of the vehicle, pulling the bag as if he were playing a childlike game of guiding it through the water without touching anything before it left the car. He made sure to close the door behind him again. When he broke the surface, Ted reckoned he had used about three-quarters of the air in the pony tank.

A car whipped along the road up above. That was good, he thought. It didn't stop or even slow down to rubberneck. The view of the canal was obstructed by trees save for small openings here and there. Nobody heard or suspected anything. No witnesses. No gawkers. He came ashore on a flat, grassy area under the cover of the bushy side of the road. He opened his messenger bag and pulled out a sealed plastic bag. He cracked the bag open and pulled out dry clothes. Unidentifiable gray sweatpants and a white brandless cotton T-shirt. Running sneakers with no identifiable brand of any sort. A blue baseball cap to cover enough identity without making him look suspicious. Wallet and keys as well. His phone was safe in a bag of its own. It took him all but a couple of minutes to slide out of his wet clothes and into dry ones, and add a dash of mosquito repellent. He grabbed his wallet, phone, and keys and shoved them into his pocket. Then he jammed his wet clothes in the messenger bag and was off. He stuck close to the canal bank at first and made sure he was out of sight. Twenty minutes must have passed since he had driven into the canal. It seemed like an eternity.

Almost two miles away from the crash, he took the wet clothes out of the messenger bag and buried them under rocks in the canal. A while later, he grabbed some more rocks, crammed them into his bag, and tossed it into the canal. It sank. Then he popped up onto the road and began to jog.

He ran down the road for a while. He was at a bridge when the first car passed him, paying him no attention. He crossed the bridge and saw a small set of docks to the right and what he assumed was a water treatment tank of some kind to the left. Closer to civilization. Onward he pressed into Marco Island. Civilization appeared and quickly became super luxurious. A few dog walkers here and evening strollers there. The late-night walkers weren't even out yet.

By the time he was jogging under a lighter canopy of Marco Island nightlife, there was still evening bustle to make him even more anonymous. He made it to a hotel that overlooked the Gulf of Mexico.

A few minutes later, an old pickup truck pulled up alongside him, the same one that had run into his bumper when he was driving with Olivia. Ted opened the passenger-side door before the car could stop, and he hopped in.

"Turn around and let's head east to Miami," Ted said.

The large man, who looked like a fairy-tale ogre with curly black hair, took a U-turn.

"There are more fun ways to kill," the man said, speeding up. "Why not have fun with her? Is her body still warm back there?"

"Be serious. Anyway, excellent job using a nudge to my bumper to signal where the deep part of the canal is, Ricardo. We crashed at the perfect spot. The only spot where a car can be totally submerged. Cost us a small fortune to dredge a little added depth, and with nobody looking." Ted took his phone from his pocket. "I need to contact someone to tow my car out of the Cornbridge parking lot," Ted said. "Give me a minute."

They drove along in silence until they came to the site where Ted had gone over the side. They stared at the spot. Only still, black water. No evidence of any kind, not even disheveled soil.

"She can sleep there for a while," Ted said. "Too bad we had to kill her and not let her live in ignorant bliss. If this Cyra Harred knows about what's going on and is calling them, then they all have to die."

Ricardo nodded.

"They all have to die," Ted repeated himself, letting the hum of the engine and the darkness of the passing swamp hypnotize him. "Anyway," he said, snapping back to reality. "It will be days or even weeks before anyone discovers that car."

Ricardo nodded.

Speaking of Cyra Harred, it's time to deal with her once and for all, Ted thought. "She better pray she kills me before I find her," Ted said aloud after a few moments of more intoxicating silence. For the first time in hours, he was relaxed.

"Okay, we're good. Let's get to Miami. I'll hole up there tonight and develop a slew of alibis regarding my location," Ted said. "How is the delivery coming?"

"It's done."

"Then why are you here?" Ted said.

"To help you, boss. If anyone is getting killed, I should be involved. The big man wants to make sure you've got everything under control."

"Oh he does? Well, what do you think? Did you see the car with two folks fly off in your rearview mirror and only one person get out? It's all handled. Now you get back down to Caracas and make sure there are no loose ends that need attention."

"You got it," the large man said.

"Great," Ted muttered, staring out at the warm, humid blackness that covered the swamps as they sped down the Tamiami Trail. "Nothing like the Everglades!" he said, lightening the mood. "Isn't there a good barbecue restaurant around here?" He could already taste that Carolina vinegar-based pulled pork barbecue.

"There's no time, Ted," the ogre said. "Is it Ted, or is it Brent? Which one are you today? You go by Ted Bullard in Naples and Brent Drum at *The Gateway*, right?"

"That's correct, my big friend. That is correct. Since we are headed to Miami, I'll start going by Brent Drum for the rest of this little road trip."

CHAPTER

17

S treet Brewer inserted his earphones into the digital recorder, pressed play, and stared out the window on the flight back to Miami. He transcribed the entire interview verbatim, saved it onto his laptop and uploaded a copy to the cloud as well. Still, he played it again to see if anything jumped out at him, to see if he had prioritized something a little lower than he should have. He listened for a few minutes. Nothing leaped out. He stared at Miami-Dade County as the plane landed. It was so flat compared to Caracas, or most other cities for that matter, but it was clean and organized.

After landing, going through customs, and a short cab ride to Coconut Grove, Street was back in his apartment. It felt abandoned. Even the neighborhood roads and avenues felt a little vacant for a weekday afternoon. As far as he was concerned, nobody was in town, which would give him a day to acclimate back into a US mindset after having settled into an expat mentality. It was hot out. Very hot and humid too, unlike Caracas's eternal spring. Yet his place was cool and dark, very welcoming when he arrived home.

It was messy, as usual. Jeans, flip-flops, books, and neckties lay strewn across the floor. The hum of the air conditioner was the only noise. Time to clean it up and grow up, he thought. You just interviewed the head of a major oil company for Latin America, and you still live like a college student. Surely you can do better than this. He opened the blinds and let the sun inject a little natural energy and life into the cool, stale air. He got to work, throwing out old papers and other documents lying around. A beer can here and a soda can there. Within half an hour, he had his dirty clothes in a hamper, the sheets changed, and his bed made up.

Then he sat down on his sofa in the living room. He placed his backpack on a small hand-me-down coffee table. He took out the digital recorder, removed the earphones he had used on the airplane, and pressed play. He listened to the interview again. He didn't know what it was, but something about the whole encounter at Worldwide Oil & Gas was odd. He listened through the first few minutes of the interview. There was nothing out of the ordinary, just small talk at first. Then the questions began, and Domínguez confirmed the company's exit from Venezuela. He was clear on that. Brent's story idea was the dead end.

Brewer: "What about other oil companies? Are you in talks with anybody else about pulling out?"

Domínguez: "I won't speak on behalf of other companies."

Brewer: "Fine. I'll rephrase. Are you the only company leaving the country now?"

Domínguez: "As far as I know."

There was a pause in the interview. He heard some shuffling. Patricia had left the room to make a call at that point. Street remembered the phone. Some throwaway cheap thing. Not the large smartphone she had used minutes earlier to check her email and verify the conference room in which the interview would take place. She had said that one was a work phone and the other personal, the latter not being a priority. Something she wouldn't miss if she were robbed. He let the recorder play and picked up his pen and began to take notes.

"This is the part where someone lies to me," Street said aloud, writing down on his piece of paper. He noted the time during the interview down to the second. "Barry Drum, not Brent Drum. Get the name right, Domínguez. Also, why did your friend and my boss, Brent Drum, lie to me? Domínguez said he's never been to the San Diego industry conference," Street continued writing notes in long hand. The interview ended.

"I'm missing something," Street said. It seemed like they were trying to get their stories straight but one was wrong about the other. Oh well, Street thought. Memories get fuzzy with age.

Street went back over his notes. Then he thought about the numbers. He needed the investments, the money the company pumped into a country it was so adamant about leaving. No business story was complete without numbers. He drafted up an email to send to Patricia. Subject line: "Ricardo." Then he wrote the email.

Dear Patricia. Thanks again for the meeting with Domínguez. I just wanted to follow up and ask for the investment figures. Domínguez said to write to you and remind you to ask Ricardo. I don't have his last name.

Street was about to press send, and then stopped. He picked up the phone. Dialed. It was Patricia's direct line. But he held back on sending the call through. He then opened up the Worldwide Oil & Gas website. Big company websites were all the same, with promises to build a better and more sustainable tomorrow for our children, or something along those lines. It didn't take long to find a list of subsidiaries. He scrolled down, way to the bottom, where the Venezuelan office was. There it was, a general switchboard line. He dialed that number, and the call went through.

"Good afternoon and thank you for calling Worldwide Oil & Gas. For English, press one." Great, Street thought. Phone voice—a horrific global export. Street went through the motions and was asked to dial in the first three letters of the employee's name.

He studied his keypad to see which buttons would allow him to dial letters. Button two for ABC, button three for DEF and so forth. Generations were familiar with the technology by now. He dialed button seven for PQRS, button two for ABC and button eight TUV to start spelling Patricia's name. The voice came back and told him to press one for Patricia Gutiérrez Zambrano. Press two for Patricia Osorio Harding. He wondered why she never went by Ana Patricia and just Patricia. He liked it nonetheless. Street held off on dialing her and went back to the switchboard. Juan Domínguez Vicente was also on the list. Time to get a Ricardo.

He dialed PQRS-GHI-ABC. Press one for Pia Alejandra Palacios. Press Two for José Manuel Ricaurte Errázuriz.

"Good lord!" Street said. Then that was it. No more names. He had the phone voice repeat the names that would bring up a Ricardo. The lovely young Pia Alejandra Palacios and the stately José Manuel Ricaurte Errázuriz. No Ricardo. "He could be new to the company," Street said. He dialed zero for the operator.

"Good afternoon. How may I direct your call?"

"Yes, good afternoon. I'm calling from the Houston office. My name is James Jamerson. I need to speak with Ricardo in accounting. I don't have his last name."

"Just a minute please," the voice said. The line was quiet. He was on hold.

Do they do this everywhere for shits and giggles? Street wondered. He scratched down the names Pia Alejandra Palacios and José Manuel Ricaurte Errázuriz while he waited.

"Thank you for calling Worldwide Oil & Gas. How may I direct your call?"

"This is James Jamerson, again. May I speak with Ricardo in accounting?"

"Let's see," the woman said. A pause.

"I'm sorry, but I have no Ricardo in accounting."

"Maybe he's not in accounting. Just dial me into any Ricardo. I'll take it from there."

"Let's see again," the woman said. Another long pause. "I'm sorry but there is no Ricardo employed here at Worldwide Oil & Gas in Venezuela," the woman said.

"I was there last week. I was told to contact him to get some information."

"I'm sorry, sir, but this list is always updated. There is no Ricardo here, and I don't see any changes to the number of employees. I believe you've been misinformed. Now good day."

"Thanks," Street said. He hung up and dialed Patricia's phone number written on her business card. She answered.

"Hi, Patricia. Street Brewer."

"Hi, Street. How are you? Where are you?"

"Good. Miami. Yourself?"

"Doing well in Caracas."

"I'm just calling to say hello and to follow up. You said you were going to get that data from Ricardo?"

"Ah yes," she said. "I haven't gotten it for you. The problem is that Ricardo quit the day you interviewed Domínguez, at least that's what I was told. Domínguez told me about a distant relative coming into some money back in Spain. His ship came in, and now he's gone—no two-week notice. He just bolted. But anyway, I will see to it that you get your data," she said.

"Really?" Street said.

"Yes. Really," Patricia said.

"What a shocker. I wish my ship would come in."

"Me too."

"Me too? You mean you wish your ship would come in, or do you agree with me and wish that my ship would come in?"

"I mean whatever," she said. Street could sense a smile on the other end of the call.

"Well, if you're in Miami, I'll take you out on my ship," Street said. "It's not much of a ship, just under thirty feet, but the view is incredible."

"I'd like that. But only on a calm day. I get seasick on boats. In the water I'm fine, but not tossing about on the surface."

"Right. So how long was Ricardo employed there?" Street asked.

"Not sure. I don't remember him too well. He may have been a consultant here to do specific work on the financial side of things and not on payroll and in the system. Domínguez doesn't tell me everything. So, do you need anything else besides the figures? You will have them today. In fact, just stay on the line with me. I'm typing an email to Domínguez now as we speak. I'll take you through this in real time."

"Thanks," Street said.

"There we go, email sent," Patricia said. "So, how's it going? Keeping busy up there in Miami?"

"Trying to," Street said. "How are things down there?"

"The country is just like you remembered it. Peaceful and stable," Patricia said.

Street smiled. He stared at a picture of Brianna on her Facebook page. He saw she had unfriended him but didn't outright block him, a passive-aggressive move on her part. She probably did it the night she left him. She had a new profile pic, a nice one of her standing next to someone, though that someone was cropped out. Clearly another man. Even more passive-aggressiveness. He closed the browser and listened into the phone.

"Anything yet?" he asked. "I bet you my numbers get here in two seconds."

"Huh," he heard her say.

"What's up?"

"It's here. Your numbers are here. Broken down by country. Everything you need in Venezuela and elsewhere in South America. Wow. Here are some pro-forma profits, too."

"I'm that good," Street said.

"I'm forwarding them to you now," she said. "There. They're off." A few seconds later, they popped into Street's inbox. He opened the attached Excel spreadsheet. Healthy investments. Hundreds of millions of dollars invested in acreage put up at auction by the former government for Worldwide Oil & Gas to reactivate marginal wells decades ago and everything since then. Investments made prior under previous administrations as well.

"Good stuff. Thanks, Patricia." Then he said it. "How long has Domínguez been in his post? I need to account for that in my story."

"I'll find out exactly," Patricia said.

"Just need to check my facts. My publisher, Brent, says they go way back and met at a San Diego energy conference, one that Domínguez says he's never been to."

"Maybe your boss was wrong," Patricia said. "Maybe he's often wrong. Does he seem to be forgetful and short-sighted?"

Street didn't know what to say. "I don't know. Anyway, thanks for the numbers," Street said.

"No problem," Patricia said. "I still think you may be wasting away there at *The Gateway*. Anything else?"

Street saved the file on his computer and on the cloud and then closed the spreadsheet. His inbox remained open. In it, he saw an old message from Brianna. He shook his head. He was about to say goodbye to Patricia when he felt the urge to complicate his life again.

"One more thing. Do you ever get to Miami?"

"Everyone in Venezuela does," Patricia said.

"Good. I'll take you out next time you're here. Just to say thanks. Plus, you seem pretty down-to-earth. Kind of a rarity in this town. If you're not married, of course."

"Okay," Patricia said. "But I'll pick up the tab and expense it, and I'm kind of on the other side of a marriage."

"Kind of?"

"Far enough on the other side of marriage for you not to worry about wrecking my home," she said with a light and breezy laugh.

"That's great!" Street said. Then he caught himself. "I'm sorry. It's not great. I mean it's great you'll be in Miami—"

"I know what you mean," she said.

"Done deal. Get ready for dinner. And expense it to Ricardo. Surely he has the money to pick up the tab after having worked for an oil company and having his ship come in from distant relatives in Spain," Street said. "Just kidding, of course. This one is on me."

"I'll see you when I get there."

Street hung up and glanced at the clock on his phone. Time for an afternoon coffee. He walked over to the kitchen and opened the cabinet. Coffees and teas were organized perfectly. Salts and syrups and dry goods were stacked in order of height. He snatched the coffee.

The remote control to the television was on the counter. He turned it on and scanned through the movies. A movie from the sixties was on, with a scene mocking the plastics industry. Street turned up the volume and focused on the dialogue while he popped a coffee pod in his machine, and within seconds, coffee was flowing into his mug. US television blending with the scents of US coffee was the perfect recipe for getting back into US thinking and getting the expat mindset out of his system. A career in plastics. Something they laughed at, something they branded as fake. That's great. Baby boomers making fun of good careers and industries. He took a sip of hot coffee.

I'd love a career in plastics, he thought. Everyone his age would. If DuPont called up and said, "Street, we're going to pay you to write up reports on petrochemical and plastics markets and give you a good salary with insurance and dental," he'd be all over it. He stared at the television and thought about the baby boomers. And we're the entitled ones.

Plastics, he shook his head. They're derived from oil, and you can't get away from oil. We drive with fuels that are derived from oil, some medicines require oil, women wear cosmetics made from petrochemicals, and we even use plastics to make digital voice recorders and cell phones. He picked up the recorder and phone and stared at both. Then he tossed both on his couch and glanced at the clock.

It was six in the evening. He threw his coffee in the sink, opened the refrigerator, cracked open a beer, and took in his slovenly apartment. He walked across the living room and into the bathroom, threw some water on his face, and stared at himself in the mirror. Then he walked into his bedroom and grabbed his dirty clothes basket, noticing its plastic material. Oil, he thought.

Out of the corner of his eye, something else caught his attention under his bed. A wrapper, something that would contain another petroleum byproduct. He picked it up, squinted, and made out bits and pieces of the words that billions of men across the planet have skimmed over before tossing them aside their beds. Shaft. Remove when finished. Pull out quickly. A latex condom wrapper, and it wasn't his, either. Someone had opened a condom in his bed lately, and he was positive it wasn't him.

"This isn't happening," he said, trying to process the situation. Then came that horrible sinking feeling when awareness chases away the initial numbness of shock. Brianna. She still had a key to his apartment. His heart raced, flooding his body with confusion and anger. Nostrils flared. Jaws clenched. Fists did, too. He was mad that she had cheated on him, and even madder that she had done it at his place while he was gone. Waves of anger clashed with confusion. He had already broken up with her and was happy she was gone, but now he was furious that he had been used and that she wanted him to know it.

"Unbelievable!" Street said. He threw the empty beer can across the floor. It smacked on his leather couch. Then he opened the refrigerator and grabbed another beer, cracked open the can, and slammed the door shut. He picked up his phone and stared at Brianna's profile picture, trying to identify the cropped-out man. Then he remembered the last night at the Grouchy Grouper, when she had texted his cousin Jenkins. He clenched his jaw again, then his fists, then realized he had no control over this situation. He exhaled and paced. Some calmness returned. So did a normal heartbeat.

He thought about waiting for when he had an even cooler head, but blew off that thought. Action was better than stewing and letting his thoughts and anger percolate into some nasty emotional brew. He dialed Brianna. A ring. A second ring. It went to voice mail. He was ready to unleash, but held back.

"Brianna. Street. Call me. Right now, and I mean right now. Just tell me it's not who I think it is." He cursed his cousin under his breath before he hung up, cursed him so she could hear him. Be passive-aggressive, he thought. Play her childish game.

CHAPTER

18

Street pulled into the office building the next morning and walked in. He
arrived at his desk, threw his bag on the floor, and turned on his computer.

"What the hell took you so long?" Street heard the question before
he even sat down. He said nothing and waited for his computer to boot up.

"So, how was it? Did the interview go well?" Brent asked.

"Went well. All written up and in your inbox."

"Did Domínguez hint at future deals with the government?"

"No. He said the company was done with Venezuela."

"Forever?"

"You got my email with the story notes, right?" Street could feel Brent
getting agitated. That made his mood lift a little.

"Well, did you even ask?"

"Of course, I asked," Street said. "Read the story and the transcribed notes."

He started typing in his username and password. He just gave Brent
his back. Look at that all day, Street thought. The computer booted up, and
Street went to his email. He saw some press releases he could use to fill up his
deals of the month covering tourism, aviation, real estate, new hires, ports,
and other industries in Florida.

"This deals-of-the-month thing is going to take a while," Street said.

He knew it would irk Brent, and he needed to irk someone, so he
started typing out stories sourced from press releases. He typed hard. Nothing

was more annoying than the sound of typing. To those who don't write for a living, it sounds aloof, alien, and conceited. To those who do write for a living, the sound of another person typing is the sound of someone being productive while you're not, bragging that they have work to do, while you sit back and do nothing. It didn't take long for Brent to get going.

"Well, what the hell did Domínguez say? Give me details," Brent said.

"He said they were leaving Venezuela," Street said.

He felt his stress level drop even more now, fully aware that his and Brent's bad moods were about to clash. The reality of the day had set in. There was nothing to dread anymore.

"Again, I sent you a copy of the interview via email. You saw and heard it all."

He kept typing up notes from the press releases in his inbox.

"Of course. I saw it," Brent said.

Street stared at the empty office in the corner. He stood. "Can I move in there? I'd be more productive."

"No," Brent said. "Back to Domínguez. Did he say anything about investments? I know you sent me the story, but refresh my memory anyway."

"Yes. He said there would be no more capital spending in the country because they're leaving. The numbers are coming."

"Did he say when they were leaving?"

"No exact date but soon. He also said he never met you at the San Diego oil conference."

"Your reporting is not good enough. You should have gotten a time frame, like the month they were planning on leaving."

"Brent, were you ever a reporter? People like you who springboard to editor without ever grinding it out in the pits as a reporter tend to bash journalists when press conferences or interviews don't go exactly as planned. Nothing goes exactly as planned, especially in this business."

Brent laughed. He leaned back in his office chair.

"Why don't you give reporting a try?" Street asked, standing to face Brent through the thin glass of his office window, willing to risk his career just to vent for the first time since working at *The Gateway*. "In fact, you go the next time. Go ahead and fire me and do everything yourself. Good luck hiring someone with my experience, with what you pay, or good luck hiring someone right out of college and can take on someone like Domínguez." Street sat back down. "Fucking fire me if you want." A calmness settled in over the office.

Brent stood up. He walked into the main room, pulled up a chair, and sat down across from Street.

"Well, at least you landed a good interview and story. It should run nice for our Latin American energy issue coming up. Great job."

Street frowned, a little confused by Brent's complete change of attitude but relieved at having vented. He even forgot about the condom wrapper for a second.

"So how did that digital recorder work out? Did it do the job?" Brent said.

"Sure. It was fine."

"Well, let's have it back."

"No problem."

Street rooted around in his bag and sought after the recorder. With each passing second, Brent became more irritated.

"Don't tell me you lost it," Brent said.

"No. I have it here somewhere," Street said. Apparently, he didn't. "I thought I had it. I listened to it yesterday. Look, if it's a problem, I'll buy another. It's not like we lost all the data on it. I only used it once and emailed you the interview. I was cleaning out my apartment yesterday and must have stashed it somewhere. Whatever, I'll handle it, or buy a new one if I have to."

Hundred dollars tops if he had lost it, and if it was lost, it was his responsibility. He'd man up to it and move on.

"Produce the one I gave you, or I'll dock your pay. I'll value that recorder at a cool grand," Brent said.

"That's funny," Street said, rooting through desk drawers.

"How could you lose something like that? Don't you know how important it is?" Brent asked.

"Apparently not," Street said.

"Let's just stop and try this again," Brent said. "I'm fucking serious, Street."

"Jesus, Brent. It's just a recorder. I'll find it or buy a new one. It can be replaced."

"No, it can't," Brent said. "I have some important voice notes saved on it. You see your interview and think that's the only item saved on the device since it's the only recording in its little file icon. There are three other files that have different recordings. You're costing me my business!"

Street looked around the office and frowned. "If it was that important, why didn't you back it up?"

"Just go get it."

"Why the urgency?"

"Because I have a call with Wallace, and I don't want you listening in while I get my ass chewed out about costs. Some information for that call is on that recorder. Now go! Please."

Street thought about Brianna cheating on him and then dwelled a bit on the health of *The Gateway*. If losing a voice recorder could disrupt company finances, things were really bad. Maybe running errands would be a good thing. Clear the mind.

"I'll bring it by tomorrow."

"Good," Brent said.

Street began packing his backpack to head out. *The Gateway* was going under sooner or later, especially if a digital recorder caused so much financial worry. Time to start searching for a job.

Street left the office in downtown Coral Gables a couple of blocks off Miracle Mile, the city's main artery, and headed home to Coconut Grove. He took the time to do a mini life evaluation. *The Gateway* wasn't working out career wise, so what else was out there? There was the freelance route. He knew he could make a living that way, but it took time to build up clients, which meant the money, prestige, and eventual job opportunities wouldn't be there for a while, probably not for a few years. Then a thought came to him. He picked up his cell phone and dialed. He dialed Venezuela.

"Patricia?" Street said, driving in Coconut Grove traffic.

"Street?" Patricia said. "Oh my God! Ian told me you got into some trouble in Petare."

"They thought I was someone else. Anyway, I wanted to ask you something."

"Uhm, okay," Patricia said. "How can I help you?"

"I want to look for a job right after I publish my story on your company. I want to take you up on your offer for help."

"Wow, Street. That's great! I'd be glad to help," she said.

"Thanks! I remember you said to reach out that night at El Techo," Street said, crossing US 1 at Grand Avenue. He came to a traffic light at nearby Douglas Avenue. To the right, million-dollar homes and luxury cottages hid under green tropical canopies. To his left, an African American community still reflected its Bahamian roots. He chose neither side and pulled into an open parallel parking spot at the corner of Grand and Douglas, stopping the car so he could talk safely.

"Look," he added. "*The Gateway* is fine, but I need something better. You might know people in Venezuela…"

"With crime out of hand and the economy in chaos, Street, not much hiring is going on around here, even for big risk-takers like you."

"I know that. But just keep it in the back of your mind. If you hear of anything in Venezuela or even here, think of me."

"Of course. In fact, I may even know of a few people in Miami. Let me think and get back to you on this," she said.

"Sounds good."

Street arrived at his apartment building a few minutes later, logged onto his computer, and began searching for jobs on his own. A few matched his experience. Midlevel editors across South Florida. Perhaps a job at a public relations firm or two. There were some calls for technical writers. He was ready to send out résumés fully aware of how little chance he had of finding a job that way. Relationships were more important than résumés. Still, sending out résumés over the web was better than doing nothing at all, and some did produce bites.

Not long ago, just before he took the job at *The Gateway*, Street had applied for an analyst position at a corporate security firm in downtown Miami. The Kesselman Group. It sounded like a great job: analyzing terrorism and crime in Latin America and elsewhere. Called for good writing skills. Cool topics too: murder, kidnapping, terrorist cells—the works. Even some travel. But no offers ever panned out.

The ad was up often, and on that particular day, the ad was running anew. Street loaded up a fresh résumé bound for the Kesselman Group with a cover letter he whipped up to one Roger Applewood, the contact whose name had been on the hiring ads for several years now.

Applewood's name came up in professional circles, and he and Street had many of the same friends. In fact, Street had met him several times going back to Street's college days, as the man hung out in bars with patrons much younger than he was, young ladies namely. On top of that, Applewood often carried on like a forty-something teenager, never taking anything seriously, though Street knew there was more than what met the eye since he worked at the Kesselman Group.

The worst they can say is no, he thought.

After uploading his résumé and cover letter, Street noticed the digital tape recorder nestled by the stapler right by his computer monitor, so he dialed Brent to tell him he had the recorder and would bring it the next morning.

"You found it?" Brent asked.

"Yes, I never lost it. I just misplaced it or whatever," Street said.

"Great news! Bring it by tomorrow and take the rest of the day off," Brent replied.

Street hung up. He picked up the recorder and checked out the number of digital files listed in the display. Just the one. He then fooled around with it and saw there were, in fact, different folders, many packed with multiple recordings. He picked one at random and pressed play. An interview with a prominent real estate executive talking to Brent. Several more contained similar interviews with South Florida aviation, maritime, legal, and other sources. They were all interviews conducted on an editorial level with Brent handling the interviews, likely before Street was hired. Some voice notes were on there as well. He thought about listening to all of them, but then blew off the idea when he stumbled back across his interview with Domínguez. He pressed play and listened to parts of it. That was it, the only one he recorded on his trip to Venezuela. He put it down. It was all there.

He stood up, stretched, and then checked his personal email account while standing. He did a search for Roger Applewood under contacts in various social media accounts, found him on one and saw he was online, so Street started a chat.

Roger Applewood. This is Street Brewer. I saw that you're hiring again, and I applied. Just wanted to reach out in person.

Hey, Street! How goes it?

Great!

Street noted Applewood's casual tone of voice.

Are you still hiring? I saw your ad on a job site and sent my résumé in.

Street knew he was repeating himself a little but pressed send anyway.

Yes, we're hiring. Just not you. LOL. JK. How's your job these days?

Did you just say 'JK' for "just kidding?"

You write like a teenage girl, Street thought.

I'm thankful just to have a job. It's rewarding, but I am looking for fresh challenges and greener pastures in which to broaden my horizons.

Street purposely wrote like a recent college grad trying to impress.

I'm not in HR. Cut the bullshit.

Street laughed.

In all seriousness, I need a new job. Got any room at Kesselman? Know anyone who is hiring?

Why not go to work on your own? Bet on yourself?

I thought that's what I was doing now. Betting on myself by applying to Kesselman.

Working on his own would be nice, but he needed the money, and he needed it now. He thought about the Everglades for a second, and then blew off the thought. That money was staying put.

Applewood must have known that Street was thinking, due to the length of the pause.

All journalism is headed toward outsourced reporting anyway. It's all freelance, dude. You need to take some risk and go out on your own and not trade your time for dollars making someone else rich.

I need money now. Dreams and aspirations can come later.

Everyone does. Just consider it. The days of big papers and big newsrooms are gone. They've been gone for a long time, and you know this. Even the niche publications are outsourcing more and more these days.

Like mine?

Nothing is quite like yours.

There was a pause and then Applewood began to type again.

How was Venezuela last week? How was your interview at that oil company? Patricia is a fine piece of ass, isn't she?

That's enough. And how did you know I was in Caracas?

We know a lot. We know you work at The Gateway, and we know you were in Venezuela recently. Just a couple of days ago. We keep tabs on all journalists.

Everybody knows I was in Caracas. I even mentioned it on my social media pages. I sent you my résumé anyway.

A pause.

Just got your résumé. I say work for yourself. Strongly recommend that. Anyway, you really want a full-time job?

Can I take a writing test? Write three summaries on country risk and basically do your reports for you for free?

Basically.

So, you admit it!

Street was happy he had some leverage on Applewood.

JK. All kidding aside, Street, we are hiring boys and girls with different skill sets, but first we're going to mainly focus on older candidates with accounting backgrounds looking for something neat to do in retirement.

Street thought for a second and then figured, what the hell. Who did Applewood work for anyway? Why was Kesselman so shadowy?

You mean you hire retiring spies.

Maybe, maybe not. LOL.

Maybe you're hiring active spies.

Street screwed off the cap of a water bottle and tossed the cap across his apartment. It bounced off the refrigerator and landed in his sink. Goal!

Getting warmer.

Half of these security consulting firms are covers anyway. Maybe yours is too. Do you work for the CIA?

No. You do.

CHAPTER

19

Street sat at his computer and stared at Applewood's words, assuming it was another of the man's adolescent jokes. He was about to type something back, a message to call Applewood out, but stopped. He stared at the monitor again.

So I work for the CIA? Is it possible? Typical thoughts rushed into his head, the most obvious questioning whether *The Gateway* was a dummy, a front company. Some dummies probably offered legitimate services alongside clandestine government work, but *The Gateway*? It couldn't be an active intelligence-gathering outfit. Street was the only journalist there, and he lived in the United States, after all, with limited presence abroad. Plus, he did the opposite of espionage—he collected information and shared it with the world as opposed to keeping it secret. So did Brent. Who did the spying? Wallace? That was a laugh. And Lord knows they weren't concealing or funneling any money there. If *The Gateway* was a front, it wasn't a good one. He needed to speak to Applewood in person. No time for chats or phone calls. Applewood was likely wrong, but then again, why was he keeping tabs on Street's trips? Something didn't add up. If Applewood wasn't going to hire him, he'd at least answer some questions.

Street sped his Jeep from Coconut Grove to downtown Miami along a straight shot of road that took about fifteen minutes with no traffic. He parked in a parking lot and bolted up Brickell Avenue, the lifeline of the city's financial district. Glass buildings that housed big law and financial firms, consular offices, and other entities that drove the local economy shot up into the sky.

After some pacing about and getting his senses, Street crossed Brickell Avenue and came to a large steel-and-glass building that looked similar to the one housing Worldwide Oil & Gas in Caracas only taller. He went to the security guard at the reception desk and asked for the Kesselman Group. It was near the top floor.

Street entered the elevator with several young women smelling of perfume, shampoo, and body lotions. Whiffs of coffee from several to-go cups made the sensory appeal even more pleasantly complex. Then a young man in his early twenties with a shaved head entered. He was on his way back to work from a cigarette break. So much for the sensory experience.

Street exited the elevator, found the door of the Kesselman Group, and opened it. A young receptionist sat behind a large desk. Candies and business cards lay neatly on the ledge. A sign reading First Impressions Specialist, identifying her position, sat on display as well. Cute, Street thought.

"Good morning," Street said.

The woman just stared at him with a blank expression.

"I'm here to see Roger Applewood."

"Do you have an appointment?" the woman asked, staring at her computer screen.

No eye contact. No greeting of any sort. No sincere smile. Street wasn't really sure what kind of first impression the Kesselman Group was trying to convey. "Just tell him Street Brewer is waiting for him."

The young woman looked at Street for another second, then picked up the telephone. Street heard a ring not too far away match the cadence of the phone in the First Impressions Specialist's earpiece. Applewood isn't that high up in the company if his cubicle is this close to the reception desk. He heard a mumble. A second later, Applewood appeared.

Applewood looked exactly as Street remembered him: short, pale, and redheaded. Neatly cropped hair. He was definitely athletic and looked like the wrestler or Eagle Scout that he probably was in high school. He was probably forty-five but looked much younger. Intense in seriousness and in humor, he still had a mischievous yet inclusive way about him, judging from his outstretched hand as he darted into the reception area.

"Street Brewer, finally we meet outside of the bar scene," Applewood said. "Let's go to a pub and get blitzed."

"For once, cut the BS," Street said, shaking his hand.

"Oh, come on. There's always time for BS for us. You're in media, and I'm in, well, whatever," Applewood said, staring at the First Impressions Specialist. Her eyes widened.

"You know what I'm talking about. Now let's get some coffee," Street said, grabbing Applewood by the shoulder, guiding him out the door. "Coffee will be your treat along with my early lunch."

A few minutes later, they were at a local bistro down on Brickell. Applewood took an outdoor seat.

"Go ahead and order coffee first. I buy, you fly. I'll take straight up black coffee," Applewood said, handing him a credit card.

Street walked off, totally at ease wearing chinos and a T-shirt despite the fact that Applewood had a dark-blue suit on. Street wasn't there to interview for a job anymore so why dress to impress? He ordered two black coffees and a ham-and-cheese empanada and went back.

He cut to the chase. "So, what's this CIA nonsense about? I work for a dummy company?"

Applewood laughed, crossed his legs, and sat back. "You don't work for a CIA dummy company, and neither do I. Your company, *The Gateway*, is legitimate. It's a niche business publication. It provides its readers with stories and news deemed important and of added value," Applewood said.

"I know what we do," Street said, then took a sip of his coffee and looked around him.

The place was about three-fourths occupied. Everyone there was on some sort of coffee break from work in the Brickell area. Two women in their late fifties in workout attire sat at the corner of the coffee shop, a small local outfit void of any brand names that held a concession with the landlord of one of Miami's tall glass structures.

"Good job," Applewood said, noticing Street staring at the older women. "They're the only ones who don't work around here. Keep noticing people and your surroundings. You're gonna need that skill."

Applewood took a sip of coffee and looked over Street's shoulder at the cars passing over Brickell Avenue.

"First of all, I'm not CIA. My firm, the Kesselman Group, provides corporate security and business intelligence services. We operate like an intelligence agency, in fact we are an intelligence agency, but we're private. All of our clients are entities or individuals that want to know what competitors or governments where they have interests are up to and how to keep their people and assets safe abroad. They often need background checks, forensic accounting, cyber threats—the works. You may, for example, have a client with spotless credit and a great reputation here in the States, but how can you tell if he's a crook—or worse—back home in Poland or wherever? That's what we do. We don't break the law; we just charge a lot and provide top services. Yes, many of our employees were CIA agents and operatives in the past, including myself, but today we are all retired or done with government work, and we're using our skills to help our clients succeed."

"Great, you're not a spook. Neither am I."

"You aren't, but you work for one. I suspect Brent Drum, your boss, is a mole, meaning he's still active in the agency but using *The Gateway* as a springboard to spy. Don't ask me how I know. We just know. People talk. And I'm sure you can tell he's not an editor. Did it ever occur to you he seemed like an outsider in this business? Has lots of information but doesn't think like you and your colleagues? Plus, word gets out. It always does, even in intelligence circles."

"I don't believe this for a second," Street said. "Brent is a moron. And if it were true, why are you telling me this?"

"Agreed that it's hard to take in. So why would I tell you?"

"Yes. Why?"

"Well, I just want to see how this plays out and learn from it, you know, spot industry trends. I'm in the intelligence business, after all. And maybe you can feed me info on how it works. Or maybe I can find a business opportunity in it. It's really no big deal."

"No big deal? It's illegal."

"Since when are you so squeaky-clean?" Applewood asked. "And relax. You are right in that it is no big deal. Let Brent collect his intelligence. He'll keep that secret. No spy is going to share secrets with you."

"Applewood," Street said. "If he's a spy sneaking into a legitimate business, then he's probably breaking the law. Either I get dragged into a legal mess, or I get killed. I can't believe I'm even entertaining this horseshit."

The two women snapped their heads in his direction. Street murmured an apology, slumped into his chair, and stared at Applewood.

"I can't really tell you much more," Applewood said.

"It's off the record, and besides, you were the one who brought it up. So keep talking or I'll tell everyone that job posting you have is just a tease and really designed to get job seekers to do your report writing for you."

Applewood smiled.

"Fine. Whatever. Me telling you is no skin off my nose," Applewood said. "Everyone knows intelligence agencies are present everywhere. They're secretive, and they're also business as usual for the most part. Bureaucratic and boring. It's not all waterboarding, black ops, assassinations, toppling governments and sabotaging economies, but rather, it's about building sources who know what's going on and taking care of those sources. Anyway, in your case, they're sneaking into your company without letting your firm know and are even sending you out to collect intelligence without your knowledge. That's what you do, Street, we're pretty sure. You mingle in Miami or travel and talk to people abroad and tell your boss about it. That's spying."

Street shook his head. "And how do you know this? Two seconds ago, you said not to worry about it, and now you're saying I am some kind of information mule abroad. If someone overseas caught onto it, I could be in serious trouble!"

"Hey," Applewood said, not appearing amused for the first time in the conversation. "We're an intelligence agency ourselves. We want to know what's going on in the field, legal or not. Technology, and the disruption it brings, makes some human intelligence spies a little scared, especially when they're under greater and greater pressure to produce results with little knowledge of the people and gadgets they're competing with in other agencies. In fact, why pay spies with MBAs money to collect info at embassy parties when drones, satellites, and God knows what else is out there can do likewise and in real time? Also, it doesn't cost much to spy on everyone's emails, phone calls, and Facebook chatter. Read the headlines."

Applewood took a sip of coffee, didn't look at Street, and went on.

"Human intelligence was different in the Cold War when threats to the US from defined sovereign entities like the Soviet Union were less opaque. We're still dealing with typical threats like foreign militaries and whackos, but we're also up against threats like terrorist cells here or abroad staffed with illiterate suicide bombers or teenage Chinese hackers or even other terrorist groups stacked up with state-of-the-art technology and hijacked US military hardware. It's always something. Don't get me wrong, human intelligence has its place, especially with people like you scooping up information in ignorant bliss, you know, asking questions as part of your daily work and telling your boss the answers to those questions and doing so at zero cost. Still, I want to find out all the reasons why spies like Brent are doing this. Are they just overworked? Is it purely for budgetary reasons? Are they scared of becoming obsolete, or—and this is what scares me—are they doing what they're doing for some other reason, maybe they have personal reasons?"

Applewood stared into his coffee cup. He took a sip and swallowed.

"You hit the nail on the head, Street. You're an information mule. With you, they have more manpower operating under the same budget. Plus, you work for the perfect company. A perfect company would be a small Miami-based business publication, such as yours, where someone has to travel abroad to write stories or to sell ads or whatever, and where travel takes that person to a dangerous place and in direct contact with people who matter. Or on the flip side, the company comes into contact with key foreign nationals here on US soil, especially here in Miami. And you are rock-solid thanks to plausible deniability."

Applewood paused to take another sip of coffee.

"There's no need for training. No need to teach you to lie to a local police officer or to even fool a lie detector test, because in your mind, you aren't lying!"

Street looked away at the mention of a lie detector test.

"Did I say something? Touch a nerve?" Applewood said, catching on to Street's growing unease. "Look, spies like you aren't sent to tackle the most sensitive of assignments, but you do serve a purpose. And most important of all, you do offer your handler leverage. Sprinkle a little technology in, it's not all analog of course, but enough to covertly pass information from human to human, and you have some value-added intelligence collection with zero additions to the payroll and company insurance policy."

Street closed his eyes. "This can't be happening."

"Is it such a foreign concept? Remember when US embassy officials in Bolivia asked expats there to keep an eye out for Cubans, be they doctors or whatever? It's the same thing. Who do you think the cultural or the press attaché in any embassy really is? So take yourself, going back and forth to Venezuela with open access to key assets down there, from top oil executives to pretty much anyone, and you're doing it in broad daylight. Everybody is sure you're just a reporter. Hell, they even see you drinking in bars and fully dismiss you as a threat. It's not all low-tech, either. What nobody sees are bugging devices you're carrying, and you don't even know it. Did your boss ever give you anything to carry down?"

Street thought about the digital voice recorder. He sighed.

"Yes," Street said. "A digital voice recorder. You know, to record interviews even though I can use my phone."

"Perfect!" Applewood said. He sipped his coffee again, calmly, as if they were talking about planning a fishing trip as opposed to criminal activities in espionage. "You did your job. You got your interviews and probably picked up some dropped info on that bugged recorder. In your eye, the recorder was legitimate. Everyone else thought so as well. And you probably willingly handed it over to anyone who asked."

Street thought about the police. They found it to be clean.

"Next question," Applewood said. "Next question you need to ask yourself is what other purpose did that voice recorder serve? In other words, what else was in it? Did anybody else touch it or use it?"

Street thought for a second and then nodded. "No."

"Think it over. Did anyone out of place even just catch a quick glimpse of it?"

"Well, an oil executive and his team saw it during an interview in Caracas."

"Good. That's a start, but they likely didn't use it to relay intelligence by voice. It probably has the capability to receive information, like a drop. Did anyone stare at it? In a public place?"

Street thought for a second. "Yes. There was this thin guy. Clicking a pen and staring at me. It happened twice. The first time I saw him was just after I interviewed the oil executive. He was in a plaza outside of a bar where I met an old friend. He showed up later in the bar and was clicking a pen again a second time. Staring at me."

Applewood smiled. A knowing smile, not obnoxious or accusatory. "It wasn't just a pen. It was something else. The CIA asset was dropping information, or sending it rather, from the pen to your recorder. Or maybe it was just a pen and he was clicking it to distract you while he dropped intel via his cell phone in his pocket. Or an associate not far from him made the drop while you wondered who that asshole with the pen was. Either way, congratulations. You just carried classified intelligence from the ground in Venezuela to the United States. You're a US spy. A good one probably, too!"

Street sighed. "And I don't get government benefits." Then he shook his head. "I don't know, Applewood. I'm still not buying it. Why couldn't he just go to the CIA himself? Why all this sneaking around?"

"His handler couldn't be there. So the asset was probably told you were a legitimate source. You were with people or in a crowd, so he was told to drop it that way. I don't know for sure. Maybe he knows you're a mule and doesn't care. The point is that it's all about leverage. More boots on the ground at no additional cost. Someone's probably breaking the law somewhere, so using you distances the real agents from their nefarious deeds," Applewood said.

He took another sip of coffee.

"Next question. Was there anyone down there in Venezuela who may have asked you questions or contacted you? Someone with years of experience and contacts all over? Add to that, anyone with financial problems who'd be likely to swap money for intelligence?"

Street swallowed, closed his eyes, remembering.

"So, are you here for much longer? Wife ever going to make you guys move back to London?"

"No, mate. We're not going to London."

"Why not? No interest?"

"No wife. We split."

"Sorry to hear that. What happened?"

"We just drifted. Most of my savings drifted with her. That's it."

"Ian Collins," Street said to Applewood. "My British journalist friend who's lived down there for ages. Just got divorced. He knows everyone who ran every business, occupied every ministerial post, and everyone who was elected to Congress. Cursed out the president a few years back. Took me to meet some government bigshot, though it never panned out."

"Damn! Ian's talking to people? I need that guy for the Kesselman Group! We'll pay him a hell of a lot better than Washington does. Someone's ass is going to get chewed out once I get back to the office for not knowing he's running around Caracas. If he's getting divorced, he's tight on cash. He's spying for somebody. Did your boy Ian act odd in any way?"

"We're just checking things out on a nice evening. We apologize. And we're just a little lost."

"Not a little lost, but very lost. You're not safe here. Out!"

"We went to look for an oil executive who hangs out in a coffee shop near a rough area of town. We left the subway, and Ian kept trying to light a cigarette. He dipped off the streets and into the cover of a small slum alleyway to escape the breeze and lit it. Then an old woman came and kicked us out. I think she was involved somehow."

"Maybe, maybe not. It's not possible to know for sure. Anything else happen?"

"We got arrested and sprung afterward. Cops thought we were…"

"Were what?"

"Drug runners. They even gave me a lie detector test."

"You were tested. It worked. That old lady was involved and so was Ian. Your boss, Brent, and his asset, Ian, worked it out to test you to see if you would crack under pressure and to see if the cops could dig up anything on you. You passed with flying colors. Not only did you spy on Venezuela, you also spied on US oil companies under the guise of a journalist. Good job."

"I feel played. And I'm a reporter, paid to uncover things like this. God, am I useless!"

"That's my motivation for telling you. You tell me details and methods of your spying and the intelligence you uncover, and I see if we find useful information for our private clients. See? I know who's involved and who your targets are. So, what did you pick up down there? I can pay you."

Street stared at Applewood. "Forget it. I want no part of this. I mean I gave up on the idea of privacy years ago. I didn't even ask if all my phones are bugged. But this is crazy."

"Right," Applewood said. "Anyway, I wouldn't worry. Nothing is going to happen to you, though I would try and get out of any traveling assignments, especially overseas. Stick around for a while. Don't go fleeing out of there and rustle up suspicions. It's not like they can keep on using you and then do away with you if, as they say in the movies, you know too much."

Street relaxed. "It's time I left anyway."

Applewood went on. "You should be fine, unless, of course, your handler is some deranged psychopath."

CHAPTER

20

B rent Drum sat at his desk chomping on an apple while looking at a
Google Street View image of the canal where he had drowned Olivia
Crawford. He scanned the news for missing persons or partially submerged
vehicles with bodies found in southwestern Florida. Nothing. Satisfied, he
closed the browser and glanced around the office. Street was nowhere to
be seen. He entered each individual office. Nobody. No Street Brewer, no
cleaning staff. Nobody walking down the hall. The neighboring office doors
were closed. Nobody anywhere. Brent closed the front door to the hallway
and then he shut his little office door. He was locked in nice and tight. Then
he picked up a cell phone from his desk drawer. A cheap unit he had just
purchased. He dialed and put it on speaker.

"Everything is working perfectly. I told you it would, Karen," Brent said.

The voice on the other end, a woman, Karen Whittaker, responded.
"Did Street get the information? All of it?" She had a neutral accent. She could
have come from anywhere in the United States.

"All of it," Brent said.

"Good," Karen said. "And this is the last time we speak on the phone
for a while. Buying cheap handsets is starting to cost me money. In fact, I'm
about five minutes away."

"Great! You're here already," Brent said. "Come to the office. We're all
alone." He hung up and stood. He walked into the main area and looked at
Street's empty desk. He took a seat and stared at Wallace's empty office and the

cramped layout room, which was overflowing with boxes of printed editions of *The Gateway*. A few minutes later, the sound of a moving doorknob broke Brent from a trance in the silent office. Karen Whittaker entered the room.

"Talk to me," she said. At five-foot-eight, one hundred and fifty pounds, Karen had a heavy yet solid and athletic build, shapely calf muscles, and long, silky blonde hair that glowed with health and nutrients. She had soft skin to match and crystal-blue eyes that still sparkled like those of a teenager, even at age thirty-seven. And perfect teeth.

"I told you sending in a mule would work," Brent said, sitting back down at Street's desk in the open room. "Our Russian friend down there dropped the information on the digital recorder. He dropped it off in the Plaza Altamira and even in the nearby El Techo bar, right in front of hundreds of people. The Venezuelan police, the US police, or even customs are light-years away from catching on, and most importantly, so are the FBI and the agency. The information is embedded in the tiny receiver hidden in the digital recorder that Street took with him. It's foolproof. I even tipped the police down there of possible smuggling and had Street arrested. They had to let him go. They found nothing. Not on him, not on the recorder, and not through a polygraph. He was perfect."

"I see," Karen said. She sat down and crossed her legs.

Brent took note of her silky-smooth skin. Then he caught her squinting eyes and taut mouth. Her rigid posture clued him in that she wasn't interested.

"Have you downloaded the intelligence?" she said.

"No. Not here. I'll do it at home, but I'm pretty sure I know what it is. We know Russia and Venezuela want to build a port. I suspect the drop deals with the Russians' take on the Venezuelan president and terms they want to attach to that base. The Russians don't trust Venezuela's loudmouth president. They want us to know that and will expect something in return. Pretty routine, so we'll give them routine stuff back. Give them what we have on some wackos who want to bomb Russian targets back closer to their home."

"Download everything and get it back to me by the usual channels," Karen said. "Is the voice recorder here?"

"It's safe. I'll do it outside of the office."

Karen stood and walked around the office. Perfume shot through the open room. She looked at Brent, who smiled. He leaned back in the seat, stretched out his arms, and crossed them behind his head, confident his armpits were crisp and dry.

"Talk about economies of scale and talk about leverage," Brent said. "While Street was spying on Venezuela and getting data from Russia, Olivia Crawford was spying on drug smugglers farther south. And because of her, we know that Manuel Rodríguez, definitely a threat to national security, is both making and moving his product across Central America with the help of government officials. And you know what that means? More cocaine headed north means more violence in Mexico and more problems along the border, including the Gulf states. Put that in your next briefing because that's bona fide intel. We needed them to do our work for us while we plan a little shipment of our own, a shipment that will be nicely tucked away from prying eyes."

"Give the Russians what you have on Manuel Rodríguez and any buddies he has in regional governments," Karen said, pacing around the office. She stopped and looked at various photos on the wall, pictures of Brent with various city politicians and local business executives. "Let them think he's directly supplying their corrupt embassy officials with the cocaine they're smuggling out of the region anyway."

"How great is it that Sebastián Ledezma told Olivia everything in broad daylight?" Brent said, his eyes following Karen like a good realtor gauging what a prospective buyer was noticing around an unfamiliar room. "I think he knows spies are all over him, you know, getting his copper export numbers to see how strong the Chinese really are. Human intelligence matters after all!"

Karen remained silent for a few seconds. She snapped her gaze away from the pictures on the wall and back to Brent. "We do matter. Good job so far."

"Good job? How about great job! You've got to admit that this little plan of ours is working. And trust me, it's going to get better. I think you're going to like this program. I call it the Placebo Agenda."

"The Placebo Agenda? I don't like unofficial nicknames attached to it. But whatever. We're almost done. Let's remember first that we're breaking the law, so I want you to be sure you aren't making any messes that can be traced back to us. Sooner or later, they will start asking you questions about Olivia over in Naples. Did we do a good job handling that? You handled her execution quickly and cleanly? You know our boss wants them all dead now."

"I did. We'll all disappear rich before anyone suspects a thing. And speaking of money, remember that the second phase of this program is just around the corner, the one with some lucrative shipments that make you and me and a select few very, very rich, and by that I mean wealthy enough to retire well before the New Year and forget our massive personal debts. I can finance my wife's second kitchen remodeling, overseas of course, and you can deal with whatever. Let's not forget, we both owe a loudmouthed Saudi royal hush money. I'm sorry he found out our identities when I was over there a while back, but since the head honcho took all his money in a shakedown of the rich, he's been pretty nasty about recouping his losses, which includes outing us. So let the CIA spend time and resources worrying about Manuel Rodríguez and copper flowing out of Chilean ports while we worry about getting rich."

"Just get rid of everyone as planned."

"The Spradlings are taken care of. The Tagle couple as well. Just those here in South Florida, and we are done with the first phase."

Karen turned to face him. "Can't believe we had to kill the wives."

"Yes," Brent said, rolling his eyes as if he had to remind her. "No loose ends, right? Wives become widows and started investigating. Paying off cops to look into things. Embassies get involved. We'll be fine. Trust me. Look, we're almost done with the killings. We've eliminated Olivia Crawford, the Tagles, and the Spradlings. There is Street next and then one more out there, a Molly Wells at Spartan Software, but we haven't used her in a while," Brent said.

Karen thought for a moment. Then conceded. "Okay. What about Wallace?" Karen asked.

"Ah, the owner of our little cover here! Let him live in ignorant bliss. No reason for him to find out he's got spies working for him."

"One last question," she said. "Do you suspect anyone is on to us? Have you received any phone calls? Are you being followed? Anything out of the ordinary?"

Brent tensed up. He thought about Olivia and her mystery caller. Cyra Harred, or whoever it was.

"Not a soul," Brent said.

"Are you sure?"

"Positive. Trust me, we're clean."

"Okay. I want this program closed within a matter of days. Then take the data the Russians dumped on that digital voice recorder and file it to me, and when the time is right, we go with phase two of the plan, and then we're done. Thanks," Karen said, leaving without saying goodbye.

Brent relaxed in the empty office but only for a second. He swung around in Street's chair, stood up, and entered his own office. He closed the door and looked out his window. The day was fading into night. Headlights and taillights told him that rush hour was still heavy in Coral Gables. He turned his back to the window, opened a desk drawer, and withdrew a GLOCK 19 and a large hunting knife. He placed both on his desk and stared at them.

"Cyra Harred, if you were FBI, we'd be detained by now," he said, touching the point with the tip of his finger. "So, then, who are you? Or better yet, who were you?" Brent pivoted in his chair. Then his cell phone rang again.

"Talk to me," a voice on the other end said in Spanish.

"Yes, sir," Brent said, answering in English. He stood up and left his office to pace in the main area. "We're on schedule. Ricardo is on schedule too." He hung up the phone, turned off his computer, and left.

A minute later, behind the door of the small office where *The Gateway* stashed its many boxes of back-issue magazines and office supplies, Street Brewer stepped out of the shadows. He stood in the middle of the office dazed and trying to process what he had just heard. Then reality hit him, and hit him hard.

"What the fuck! They're gonna kill me!" he said aloud, not caring if anyone outside the office heard him. "Fuck you, Applewood, letting me think I had nothing to worry about."

He dug into his pants pocket and withdrew a cell phone. He started dialing 9-1-1, inhaling and exhaling hard in an attempt to calm himself.

It didn't work.

The emergency operator answered. "9-1-1. What's your emergency?"

"Yes, my name is Street Brewer, and I..."

He looked back at Brent's office, then at the entrance door and out into the hall. Names shot through his head. His own name. Olivia Crawford. The Tagles, and lastly, the Spradlings. Names of people he knew and names of strangers, and they all had a few things in common, they were young, working hard to get ahead, and extremely fucked over. The emergency operator brought him back out of the clouds, though his racing heart threatened to send him up miles above earth when he should be grounded and thinking.

"Sir, your emergency?"

He was about to tell all, but he suddenly decided to hold back. "To tell you the truth, I am fine. My heart was racing but it's nothing."

"Shall I send an ambulance?"

"It's not necessary. I just took my blood pressure, and it's fine. Too much caffeine. Thank you." He hung up.

He assessed his situation. Calling the police may nab Brent for Olivia's death, but they'd be powerless to solve the murders in Venezuela, Pennie's especially. Plus, alerting the police now may give others involved enough wiggle room to escape. There were more out there. There was also talk of a phase two of this Placebo Agenda, something the local police would likely miss.

"Jesus!"

He walked around the office in dead silence, even his footsteps didn't make a sound. Then he reminded himself that he worked there and there was no reason to tiptoe around. He'd explain that he left something at the office or that he decided to catch up on some busy work if Brent came back.

Street focused on the last name he had heard mentioned. Ricardo. There was also talk of shipments. Was he smuggling? Cocaine? Heroin? The

CIA and drugs have a nice history. Money is involved too. Brent had just said so much to the blonde.

"It's got to be drugs," he said.

Everyone knew the Venezuelan military and political bigwigs were smuggling so much cocaine into the United States that it was easier to just ditch the carrier planes in some Central American river than use them again. Cash in pockets and some cash for the embattled government.

"But is it just drugs? Why would the US government help smuggle drugs to finance a government it's been trying to topple for years?" He looked up at the ceiling. "Don't be an idiot, Street. It's not the US government. It's these criminal rogue spies."

Street grabbed his ancient cassette recorder. He rewound the cassette back to the beginning and pressed record, not caring about erasing old interviews that may have been on it.

"Okay, so the CIA and somebody are up to something. There's this Ricardo. Not the same one from Worldwide Oil & Gas, is it? Are they together officially? Doesn't sound like it. Is this a systemic, organized deal? Or was this something concocted illegally? Fresh revenue for an embattled Venezuelan government? Doesn't seem like a sanctioned op," Street said, laughing, shaking his head. "Did I really just say a *sanctioned op*?

"You're a reporter, Street. Don't run to the cops yet. Find out everything and report it to the world."

Less than an hour later, Street was on his balcony overlooking Coconut Grove at night, taking large gulps from a glass of water. Then his phone rang. It was Patricia.

"Hello there," Street said, feeling truly at ease for the first time all day.

"Hi, Street," Patricia said.

She was outside in the streets of Caracas. He could hear cars passing. Loud buses and motorcycles rattled in the background, but her voice came in strong over the cacophony.

"What's new?"

"Just saving the world as usual," he answered.

He remembered her offer to find him other work, which was becoming an increasingly good idea. If he was going to bring Brent and his colleagues down, he'd need to be away from *The Gateway* eventually. He'd need to be working somewhere that would give him money to pay his bills but enough space for him to investigate Brent's agenda and then tell the story through as many media outlets as possible.

"Just considering my next career opportunities," Street said. He didn't want to come across as being too desperate, but at the same time he didn't want to seem too casual.

"Good. That's why I'm calling, Street. Call Matías Sánchez. He runs a consulting firm in Doral not far from you, a market research company mainly. A lot of advertising as well. He's a good friend of the family's and can point you in the right direction. He might even give you some work or even hire you. He's always looking to do something new. Got a pen?"

"I've got my sharp memory," Street said.

"Oh, that's right," Patricia said. "Well, take note, a mental one, that is, and call him now and tell him Patricia sent you."

She gave Street the number, which Street dialed a few seconds later.

"Hello," a man answered.

"Matías Sánchez? My name is Street Brewer. I'm a friend of Ana Patricia Osorio Harding's. How are you?"

"I'm fine, Street. Any friend of Patricia's is a friend of mine. How can I help?"

"I'm looking for work."

CHAPTER

21

The next morning, Brent Drum sat at his desk making notes for the day when an email hit his inbox. It was from Wallace Lockwood, owner of *The Gateway*.

"Great," Brent said aloud.

He knew Wallace let this magazine run on autopilot as long as it was profitable. Emails from Wallace aren't a good thing. We are profitable, aren't we? "At least I'm about to be," he said aloud. Brent clicked open the email with the subject line "In Miami." He read the message:

Brent. In Miami. Wife wanted to take a vacation. Plane departs Miami International Airport for the Caribbean this evening. Will make our way to St. Bart's. Wanted to have a video chat with you when I got back but will meet you in person to discuss our fate and the magazine. Just landed. Be there in about hour.

"Fuck!" Brent said.

He stood and paced and ran his hands over his head. Bet he's already pissed off, and he's not even off the plane! He hates it here, Brent thought. He sat back down. "Focus," he said.

He needed to remain at *The Gateway* and feared a visit from Wallace could jeopardize that. Could Wallace get rid of him? Replace him with someone younger and cheaper? Or worse, did this Cyra Harred contact him?

A surging fear tends to bring up other fears with it, and he thought of the mystery caller. He ran a new search on Cyra Harred, at least to distract his thoughts away from Wallace. Nothing came back. He checked internal police records across the country. Nothing fit the profile. Whoever it was wouldn't be a problem. But could she trace him to Olivia Crawford's demise? Still no item of her missing in the news, and in a short time he'd be rich and could retire from government work and disappear. All contact with Ricardo was done on untraceable phones or in person. Nobody had anything on him, so let this Cyra Harred come after him. She was probably some counterintelligence amateur who didn't know what she was doing anyway. And what is she going to do? Have him arrested and then admit to the world what was going on at the agency? If the FBI were onto him, Brent would have been arrested already. Brent knew that, and so did the mysterious Cyra. He was safe from law enforcement for now. Counterintelligence at the agency would be easy to deal with, especially when they were calling up Olivia and flat out telling her what they knew.

Idiots, Brent thought. He shook his head. This program will be over by the time they get to Street. Maybe he should be allowed to live, Brent thought. He didn't care what they might have on him. He'll be out of there in a matter of days, weeks at the most. He'll disappear so fast they'll never know what got to them, or however the goddamn cliché goes.

Brent then checked on the news in southwest Florida. Nothing yet on Olivia's disappearance. He was ready to cooperate with police under the cover of Ted Bullard. He had everything ready to go—where he was, his car with the flat tire at the office, and where he was afterward.

But first, there was Wallace. Brent knew that Wallace didn't like Miami very much and probably wished he was back at his office in Manhattan running his media business. Wallace was indeed annoyed before the plane even left LaGuardia Airport in New York. In fact, Wallace didn't like most cities in the United States. Not that he hated them, but he was just more annoyed with them. Most US cities either answered to New York City or competed with it, and Miami answered to it in Wallace's eyes. Go to Key Biscayne and look west across Biscayne Bay back to the city. What do you see? Miami branches of New York or foreign banks and law firms catering to people who lived someplace else. New York was where deals were born and where the markets were that saw real money change hands. Miami was mediocre at best, an also-ran, an appendage, a footnote to American business cities, and at its best, a weigh station for money generated elsewhere.

"At least we're not in the rust belt," Wallace said to his wife as they plodded through the airport.

Wallace was one of those guys who plodded. While everyone else in the airport walked at brisk paces on the shiny terminal floor with luggage in tow, Wallace looked like he was walking in three feet of pluff mud, wearing waders filled to the knees with heavy muck and seawater. By the time he and his wife—a well-dressed woman in her late fifties with flowing red hair that looked like it belonged to someone half her age—had soaked in the humidity and plopped down in the cab at the curb of Miami International Airport, Wallace was already past grouchy. When they did break free from the garage and were spit out in a tangled gnarl of lanes sprouting from the airport, the first thing he noticed on the sides of the highway were newly planted palm trees.

"Check out those trees. They were just planted," Wallace said, stroking his fine, very straight blond hair and later frowning at the sweat in his fingers.

His wife looked out the window, shrugged, took in a nice view of the Miami skyline, and then faced forward.

Wallace kept his gaze on the palms. Two-by-four boards were holding up the recently planted trees. The fronds were rigid and new, and the dirt around the bases appeared as if it had been just poured in by a truck. They didn't look like natural palms swaying in tropical trade winds, but rather like something hastily and messily erected on the side of the road by a careless work crew.

"This city always looks as if it just rolled off some cookie cutter a few minutes ago," Wallace said neither to his wife nor to the cab driver, but instead as if he were floating the idea aloud to anyone who would listen. The cab driver, who was a sixty-year-old Caribbean man who probably had little interest in South Florida urban planning, rolled his eyes.

"Where to again?" the driver asked him. "Address?"

"Downtown Coral Gables. It's nearby," Wallace said, giving the man the address on a piece of paper.

Before departing, Wallace had printed a map linking the office with the airport specifically for the cab driver. He did that every time he left New York City. It wasn't too hard to be prepared and organized. He was. Everyone else should be too.

Wallace guessed correctly that the cab driver was from some Caribbean island. What he didn't guess was that people from the Caribbean were not always as cheery as they appeared at the tourist resorts. If there was one thing Miami did do right, it was its ability to blow cultural stereotypes to pieces. The driver muttered something under his breath and drove away at a snail's pace.

"Is there a problem?" Wallace asked the driver, feeling a little better now that he had someone on whom to channel his annoyance, especially since that person was annoyed himself. The driver shook his head and turned up the radio. About three minutes later, the driver spoke.

"Why don't you have somebody pick you up if you are going just a couple of miles to the Gables? I could have been driving someone to South Beach now."

"Unbelievable," Wallace said aloud with an incredulous smile stretching across his face. "Let me get this straight. Are you complaining because I'm not going a long way and the fare will be lower?"

"I'm not complaining. I'm just pointing out that you could have had someone come and pick you up."

Wallace stared out the window. As they drove down LeJeune Road, he saw more recently planted palm trees standing at attention on the side of the curb. Far off to the east was the Miami skyline, which looked like it had doubled in size since he was here just a few years ago. Then he made eye contact with the driver in the rearview mirror.

"And this is a city that relies on hospitality for its economic well-being?" Wallace asked.

The cab driver just drove ahead, sulking.

Wallace had built Freedom Park Media from the ground up in New York City, where he was born and raised. After handling advertising sales at a midsize magazine covering courts on Long Island, Wallace found out how to make a buck in an industry notorious for making no bucks at all—print journalism. He commoditized his news outlets. Instead of treating them like the serious media companies they all aspired to be, he put a little effort in digitalizing platforms and more effort in rolling out events to midlevel executives. These were the executives who dreamed they were at the World Economic Forum in Davos conveying important messages to the world, when in reality they were in Miami hotel meeting rooms, telling their colleagues what they already knew. Do all that with as few employees wearing as many hats as possible—one earning well and the rest struggling (and who cares if they stay or go)—and then toss print versions of the product for free in select office building lobbies and other public places with some cheap ads to pay for it.

The Gateway was the perfect model for him. It was sleek, put out a good product, and it maintained editorial integrity. The issue for Wallace was Brent and his sales numbers.

When the last publisher had moved on, Brent walked in from out of the blue and aced the interview. He was hands down better than any other candidate. Brent had the right experience even if it wasn't local. His résumé said he was the publisher of a midmarket business publication in Oregon. Time spent at the wire in Belgium brought proficiency in Dutch, German, French, and some Spanish. While not too specific to Latin America, he knew the mechanics of international business and the local impacts of global economic events. Yet it was the interview that had really impressed Wallace, even surprised him a bit. It was as if Brent had hacked both his professional and personal emails, and was on the same wavelength for every project and business model at *The Gateway*. Take surveys. Ask the would-be disruptors at Davos to participate in surveys, which costs nothing, and then hold another profitable roundtable to talk about those surveys. Roundtables made the money. The magazine was window dressing.

In the end, Brent got the position despite his lack of Latin American experience, mainly because he would take the job for slightly less than the competitors. Add to that, most of the interviewees kept clamoring for more editorial staff, which made Brent even more appealing, since his pitch during the interview process was to cut people and overwork younger employees.

Yet despite his tendency to agree with Wallace on business strategies, Brent wasn't living up to his revenue deliverables lately, and that was a problem. Income was growing, but at a slower clip, and profits were falling, so it was time to pay a visit to Coral Gables.

After he got his wife booked into a hotel, Wallace arrived at *The Gateway* offices. Brent was busy at work, sitting back in his chair in gray suit pants, a dark-blue Ike Behar shirt, no tie, and sleeves rolled up. Wallace walked in and said nothing. Brent stood to greet Wallace with an ear-to-ear grin. Wallace wasn't impressed with imposing men. Threats and pleas and smooth talking never worked—live up to my numbers or live elsewhere.

"Welcome back to South Florida, Wallace," Brent said.

Wallace was even further dismayed that Brent didn't have any sweat stains under his armpits. He didn't even bother taking off his suit jacket. Wallace shook his hand, grunted, and sat in the chair in front of Brent.

"I guess you know why I'm in town," he said, pulling spreadsheets out of his briefcase, skipping any and all small talk. He handed a copy to Brent and began opening one for himself.

"Well, before we get into all that…" Brent said.

Wallace wasn't listening. To him, the numbers spoke for themselves in his business and everywhere else in life.

"Brent, you know and I know that the publishing industry is dead. Face it, Brent. You've done a good job, but I can't keep this publication afloat. Good content is only good if more and more people are dumping their data to sign up and read it, and since things aren't picking up, I'm going to have to pull the plug." Wallace chomped on some imaginary object as he stared at the spreadsheets.

Brent swallowed hard. Then he just stared at the large man in front of him. Wallace had on a dark-blue dress shirt, dark-green gabardine pants, and a large, beige linen blazer of some kind that was in style though disheveled.

"Wallace, I realize that things are tough, but I've got something that can change your mind. You've got to trust me on this one," Brent said.

"Look, I'm sorry, Brent, it's just not working out. I—"

"Well, at least hear me out. Can you do that? Just put the spreadsheet down and look at me," Brent said. A voilà moment was coming, and Brent knew that Wallace hated them.

Wallace sighed. He was annoyed but let the spreadsheet relax in his lap and looked up across the desk at Brent.

"Okay," Brent said. "You know how we run our publication, *The Gateway*. We focus only on Miami. Well, what if we could expand the model to include *The Gateway* Caracas? *The Gateway* São Paulo? *The Gateway* New York? *The Gateway* London? Then into Asia or across Europe? Imagine what it would be like if we could do in other cities what we do here."

"And what's that? Lose money in other markets and currencies? You know I tend to focus on community publications."

"Exactly! Expand the brand and still focus on different communities. We roll out fresh roundtables, crunch national economic indicators as they apply to cities and local labor markets, and we sell other products but on a community-specific basis. I think we need your business model but coverage outside of Miami. In fact, my reporter, Street, is getting a one-on-one interview with the president of Venezuela himself! That would drum up interest here and prep for a launch in Venezuela when things calm down."

"What?" Wallace looked up. Spreadsheets began to fall from his lap, though he scooped them up.

"Absolutely. We have a lot of Venezuelans living in South Florida. Face it, everybody wants to know what's going on with Venezuela, especially now that it's going from bad to worse with each passing day. It's important to Miami."

"For real?"

"For real. He'll talk to us since he doesn't trust mainstream media anywhere."

Wallace sighed. "That's a good interview, Brent, I'll give you that. But I just don't know. You really haven't turned this outfit around as much as you said you would, at least in terms of revenue. You've got the ads and the roundtables, and you have cut costs, but there's just no growth, which means my window to sell it is closing. Plus, I don't see online newsletters coming into my inbox like you said. No news on tourism in Miami, no news on fresh hiring in Miami. And when are these sponsored roundtables going to hit their new targets? Even whittled down to just a couple of people, you and this Street kid, the numbers just aren't there." Wallace glanced down at the spreadsheet. He frowned a bit. "I applaud the fact that you've got us a little better than breaking even, but we need more growth," Wallace added.

"What did we agree on for this fiscal year? Seven percent sales growth?" Brent asked. He had to keep *The Gateway* in operation. Phase two of the Placebo Agenda depended on it. "We came close. Be a little flexible and just stay open a little bit longer."

Wallace cringed at that comment. Flexible. He had been accused of paying too much attention to numbers in the past and not looking at the less tangible assumptions that should go into a business model. He sold one publication covering New York court and legal beats. He ditched it because the numbers weren't adding up. It took off just after he sold it. He still regretted that to this day.

Wallace stared at Brent, who seized on the silence.

"How about I double the seven percent sales growth rate in a year?" Brent said.

Wallace moved about uncomfortably. He didn't like being sold, and he knew that Brent was selling him.

"You won't be losing any money. What do you say? Just start with fourteen percent revenue growth in a year? Just imagine it?"

"I don't imagine much. And why are you so desperate to keep this going? You can find a better job than this. If you love it so much, just buy the company yourself."

Wallace looked blankly at Brent, who was thankful for a second that Wallace didn't read men. Just numbers.

"Nobody is going to buy it for the numbers you want. I'll start off holding more roundtables here so up-and-comers can pretend they're on record at major networks. Lord knows there are enough logistics and law firms that will sponsor them and give us some cash. I mean, they do add value. Plus, with Street's interview with the president of Venezuela, advertising money will come rolling in."

"I thought everyone in Miami hated that Venezuelan leader."

"True. But they want to know what he's up to." Brent thought he saw a nod. Wallace's wheels were racing in overdrive. Numbers here and there.

"We're paid up in full on our bills. I'm not asking for anything, not one cent. I just want to keep the business going," Brent said.

Wallace stared at his spreadsheets for over a minute. Then he sighed. "Fine. I'll give you one month to get revenue to seven percent growth, six months to grow ten percent, and twelve months to grow by fifteen percent, not fourteen percent. You've got three months to start bringing in more money. I don't care how you do it. Hold more roundtables, wow the advertisers with editorial content—whatever. And I want to see what that crazy Venezuelan president says, whatever his name is. That's a big interview, and it's the only reason I'm giving *The Gateway* one last chance." Wallace looked up from his numbers and stared at Brent. "I want to see a transcript of that interview in two weeks."

"You'll have it," Brent said.

Wallace shook Brent's hand and left.

CHAPTER

22

Wallace had left the office and probably wasn't even in the parking garage when Brent was on the phone dialing. He knew Karen wasn't going to be happy that *The Gateway* might be closing if the Venezuelan president wouldn't agree to an interview, but he needed to fill her in quickly. The phone began to ring. Get the bad news out quickly, Brent thought. Just get it over with. No sense in letting this little setback fester. Time for damage control.

"What's up?" Karen asked.

"Wallace is going to fold this magazine unless more money pours in, like, beginning right now, and we get an exclusive interview with the president of Venezuela." Brent just said it. He let it all out there.

Nothing but silence on the other end.

Brent felt better after getting it off his chest, until he heard Karen sigh. More long silences. The worst. Then he spoke.

"I'll need to boost overall revenue at an unreasonable clip. We could inflate the books. Or steal money from somewhere and pump it in, but I think Wallace would catch on. Telling him I need to raise money is no problem, but he wants milestones, and one of those is an immediate interview with the president of Venezuela."

"What? Did he suggest that or you?"

"I lied. I told him that Street already landed it. I need to buy some time to keep the company open. And the key takeaway here is that we're going to need that interview not only to keep *The Gateway* open, but more importantly, to finalize our little agenda. It kills two birds with one stone."

"Yes, you're right, Brent, but you told him Street already landed it? Wallace will get suspicious if it doesn't come soon enough!"

"We can arrange it. Easily in fact. We can get Street an interview with the president."

"Not immediately! He's in crisis now with a unifying opposition." Another pause. Then Karen spoke again. "How long do we have to arrange this interview? I can use my resources to get some face time, hopefully some time before November."

"Two weeks."

"Brent, you've said we're poised for the second phase of our agenda, you know, where we make a ton of money smuggling. Now you're saying we might have the rug pulled out from under our feet unless we snag an interview with a sitting president in an unreasonable period of time. These inconsistencies are making me very nervous, and I mean really fucking nervous. And you're right, we're not inflating the books. Wallace will spot that immediately."

Brent closed his eyes and clenched his jaws. "I don't even have time to fiddle with the books. I had to be in Naples to deal with Olivia, and with this Cyra Harred snooping around, our time is running short."

"We still need to report to our superiors, and eventually to policymakers, what all the Venezuelans are doing down there. Wait…"

"Yes?" Brent said.

"Who is Cyra Harred?"

Brent sighed. Full disclosure now. "Well, someone was calling Olivia Crawford and asking questions about me. She mentioned my aliases. Someone is onto us. I don't know who it is, but she's definitely agency though. They, well, she says she represents an investor at Cornbridge Capital and warned Olivia that I might not be who I say I am." The load was lifted off his chest. "Have you said anything? Has anyone overheard us? This might not be my fault. It could be yours."

Another silence. A long one. Brent could feel Karen balancing the need to process the problem and address it with the desire to lash out at him for his last comment.

"Somebody is on to us?" Karen asked.

Kudos, Karen, he thought. Stick to the problem at hand and solve it.

"Apparently," Brent said in a rather matter-of-fact voice. "It's all good. If she were FBI, we'd be questioned right now or even under arrest. Look, somebody suspects something. We don't know what, so let's just go with it. Everybody in our nook of the agency knows that Cornbridge is a CIA fund anyway, and some of the aliases I use in the Placebo Agenda are known to our superiors. We don't know what this Cyra Harred wants, and besides, we're out of here in days anyway. A couple of weeks, tops, now that Wallace has speeded things up for us."

"This has gone from bad to worse," Karen said. "How have you dealt with her?"

"I'm working on that."

"Brent, you have the capabilities to find out who she is and take her out."

"I know. I just wanted Olivia eliminated first, you know, unable to answer more questions from the mystery caller. I took care of that myself."

"Then have Ricardo deal with this caller. She probably doesn't know who he is. Like you said, she's definitely part of the agency, so we also need to find out who tipped her off. I don't need to tell you of the legal matters that could arise should anyone find out before we cash in on the final plan. So keep *The Gateway* up and running, stick to the plan, and then we disappear."

Brent remained quiet to see how Karen liked long silences on her end. Then it came to him.

"Well, there is hope. I'm pretty sure I can use our agency resources to help Street to land an interview with the president of Venezuela, possibly this week. It can be done if the US puts its muscle behind it. Plus, this Cyra Harred person will likely hold off to see what the Venezuelan president tells us anyway, if she's any good at prying into our affairs. In fact, maybe we can use Street to sniff her out somehow. And at the same time, maybe we can squeeze a roundtable out of it in a week or so and get our numbers. That will make Wallace happy. And I can't stress this enough, we need the Venezuelan government and this little media start-up for phase two of our plan. This interview is the key to it all."

"Yes, but Street will have to land it or think he landed it. We can't say we got you an interview with the president so go for it. We can help behind the scenes. But my concern is if Street has the time to land it quickly. I haven't tapped Street's phones yet. I don't have time to pour over his emails. We're stretched. Can we do an email interview with the president on such short notice?"

"No emails. Street would never agree to that, and people will want to hear his voice too. Anyway, he's the president of Venezuela and has proven time and time again that he'll abandon protocol and do whatever he pleases. He'll follow whatever schedule he wants. I think we can pull it off."

"Do it. And I'm not listening to another word." The phone slammed shut. Brent hung up and sat in silence.

"Well, that wasn't that bad," Brent said aloud. He let out a long exhale and left.

Ten minutes later, Street walked into the office. He turned on the lights and walked to his desk. He looked around and shrugged. I could be on film here, but who cares, he thought. He worked there. He picked up his desk phone and dialed Parker West.

"Hey, dude," he said after a few rings. "I'll be late for drinks tonight. I had to run by the office. Left my phone here. Don't worry. I will still be there." Put that on tape, he thought. He hung up, grabbed his phone from under a pile of papers on his desk, and took off. He stopped the phone from recording and then listened to Brent's conversations with Wallace and Karen. Cyra Harred, a name he knew. Olivia Crawford—a fate that Street could face soon. Now an interview with the Venezuelan president, one that they apparently needed for some reason on top of staying in business. Cornbridge Capital? That's where Domínguez keeps some of his money. Jesus does Domínguez know his fund is run by criminals? Is he a target too? Is he a placebo like the rest of them?

Street couldn't relax and didn't want to. That old dilemma of calling the police was dead. Now that Cornbridge Capital was involved and possibly more lives at risk in the US and South America, he'd have to blow off help from authorities and solve this himself. So he focused. He knew his cast of characters included CIA officers, agents and assets likely involved in smuggling, but sensed something was missing. Why did they need *The Gateway*, this little media start-up? Places to hide money like mystery hedge funds were obvious. But a small, barely surviving news outlet? Why did they need the start-up, and why did they need an interview with the president of Venezuela of all people to make it all happen? Yes, the magazine needed the interview to stay afloat, but there was something else. That interview served another purpose. Brent had just said it was part of his plans. Back to work. Find out.

CHAPTER

23

The next morning, Street arrived at the office very early, digital recorder in hand. He plopped down, said nothing to Brent, and turned on his computer. The big item on his to-do list was to land a one-on-one interview with the most embattled leader on earth, and he'd do it with an assassin looking over his shoulder. It was clear that Wallace was closing *The Gateway* unless Street interviewed the Venezuelan president in a matter of days, and that Brent needed the interview for his scheme. So until he landed that on-the-record dialogue and found out the extent of Brent's plans, Street would stay alive.

"Street, how about the opportunity of a lifetime?" Brent said, snapping Street back on guard in reality after a few moments of quiet. "And how about handing me my digital recorder?"

"You got it, boss." Street tossed Brent the recorder and noticed the much-anticipated wave of relief that shot across his face when he caught it. He put the recorder in his shirt pocket and looked across the office at Street.

"Hey, to follow up from your Worldwide Oil & Gas story, I had an idea," Brent said.

"Me too. I'm going to interview the president of Venezuela. Nice follow-up to our oil cahoots story."

No reaction from Brent.

Well played, Street thought. Good poker face. Eventually, Brent spoke up.

"Wow. That's exactly what I was going to suggest."

"We need more high-profile sources on record here. I'm going to get an interview with the president of Venezuela. I'm going to call him right now. We're going to do an interview and then golf this weekend at one of the Caracas country clubs. I'm sure he'll talk to me. Then we're gonna get high."

"Ha!" Brent laughed. Just one syllable. Like an affirmative in an Asian language.

Silence from Street.

Brent felt compelled to break the awkwardness.

"I thought he was going to close those golf courses down," Brent said.

"It was a joke. The president doesn't play golf or get high. Neither do I. Do they drug test here? This isn't some government job," Street said, letting that float out there for a few seconds.

Brent wasn't flinching at all. Let it go, Street thought. Don't let him know you're on to him.

"Besides," Street said, "The president wanted to close down the golf clubs to piss off the rich until he found out that many of his leftist cronies who suddenly came into power had become members. All of them. He's got bigger problems now, anyway." Street then remembered part of the conversation he had with Domínguez at Worldwide Oil & Gas.

"Listen, I have to run. Follow up with Patricia for anything you need from Ricardo," Domínguez said. He grabbed a stack of papers off the desk and frowned at a large envelope…

"Off to Texas?"

"Off to golf! Caracas Country Club. Gotta run! Got to talk about Venezuela's power structure on the green," Domínguez said.

"Well, they're not all cronies there. Domínguez plays golf there."

"Keep your friends close and your enemies closer," Brent said.

Street stared at Brent, entertaining the idea of bouncing ideas around with his would-be killer. "Why would Domínguez tell the press he's closing up shop in the country and then run off to play golf with the government he's going to leave holding wells that Venezuela just can't tap?"

"Who cares, Street," Brent said.

"I'm going to get an interview with the president of Venezuela and find out. Just help me line that up, Brent."

"I'll work the phones from my end. You do likewise."

"Good, because I'm on a roll," Street said. "I landed an interview with the head of Latin American operations at Worldwide Oil & Gas. Pretty sure I can land one with the president. Let's just say the powers that be want it to happen."

"What do you mean?" Brent asked. "What powers?"

"The celestial mechanics are at work for me. What did you think I meant?"

"Nothing," Brent said. "You really think you can pull it off?"

"Why not," Street said. "Worst thing that could happen is they say no. I'll contact Miraflores Presidential Palace in Caracas, the Venezuelan embassy in Washington, and the consulates here and in New York as well. The UN General Assembly is coming up, and it'd be a devil of a time if the president of Venezuela weren't there. In case you don't know, he tends to leave official meetings like that and mingle in the streets with normal people, so even if I don't get a one-on-one, there's still the possibility of shouting out a few questions. What kind of time frame are we looking at? I'll need at least a month to land this."

"I was thinking by next week."

"Of course," Street said. "No problem. Early a.m. on Friday, no problem. In fact, shouldn't I just go ahead and get the president of the United States to go with me and the three of us sit down and broker some kind of deal to end the disputes between these two countries while we're at it?"

Brent said nothing and just stared at Street as if he were asking him to get a quote from a public information officer at the Miami International Airport as opposed to getting an exclusive interview with the president of Venezuela in a week.

"Give it a shot. I have faith in you," Brent said. He walked off, closed his office door, and picked up the phone. Street could hear him talking to his wife about dinner plans.

Have faith in this, Street thought. He dialed the Venezuelan embassy in Washington, planning to attack this task on three fronts: make a request through the embassy, make a request through the Ministry of Communications in Venezuela through the office for foreign correspondents, and then make a request through the general press office at the Miraflores Presidential Palace. And with Brent's resources, this interview stood a good chance of happening.

He started off with the embassy. The media relations contact there was Brenda Montemayor. He dialed and waited for an answer.

I would have been a good spy, he thought. I need a code name. Double-0 Account Overdrawn, Agent Poor Credit, or something like that. The phone continued to ring. This is surreal. I'll never be able to watch spy shows or movies again.

Brenda answered. "Hello."

"Brenda. Street Brewer here. Remember me from Caracas?"

"Of course, Street. How are you? And where are you these days?"

"In Miami."

"Oh God! What are you doing there?" Brenda asked.

"I grew up here, Brenda. Not everyone here is a right-wing Cuban militant out to crush your glorious revolution. You should come here for a visit. We'll go check out a Marlins game. We'll have beers and Cuban food."

Brenda grunted and laughed at the same time. "What can I do for you?"

That was enough small talk for Brenda. All good PR people knew that no matter how nice and upstanding a reporter was, in the end, that reporter was never really your friend. Sooner or later, the tough questions come because sooner or later tough questions needed answering. Even in a church, mistakes get made, money gets lost, pedophiles arise in the pews, or property gets stolen, and the friendly journalist asks the otherwise pious priest who did it. Who do you suspect? Who do you point the finger of blame at?

"I'm calling to formally request an interview with the president. I can be there on a moment's notice."

"Okay. Well, you know the routine. I'll need—"

"You've had mine and everyone else's ongoing requests for presidential interviews for a while now. All my background information, topics I want to discuss, and dates I could do it are all the same." By practice, Street had requests sent out to interview most Latin American presidents.

"I do. Let's see," Brenda said.

He heard her typing.

"Just check your inbox," Street said. "There's only one Street Brewer."

Some time passed before Brenda exclaimed, "Aha! Here it is."

"It should be all there. Straightforward interview. He's been in power long enough to know what reporters are going to ask him," Street said.

"It's all here," she said. "I'll put in the request through the appropriate ministries and channels back in Caracas."

"I need to speak with him this week."

"What?"

Street hung up with Brenda. She couldn't arrange an interview that fast, not from Washington. He'd have to call Caracas himself. Within seconds, Street was dialing Carlos Smith, the head of press at Miraflores Presidential Palace. Despite an English last name, which probably made its way to Venezuela generations ago, Carlos didn't speak any English with the foreign press at all. Nor Spanish, Portuguese, French, or any other language it seemed. It seemed Carlos's only job was to tell people no and do it in as few words as possible.

The phone rang. Street heard a soft hello in Spanish.

"Carlos Smith! It's Street Brewer, remember me?"

Nothing.

"Street from the newswires? Years ago? The only gringo you don't hate? Got mad at me for pulling for the Americans in the World Cup? How are you?"

"Hi," Carlos said. It was barely a whisper, like something from a deathbed.

"So what's up?" Street asked.

Silence.

"Now that we've caught up and spent hours reminiscing, I'll cut to the chase so we can avoid more of this idle chitchat," Street said. "I'm calling to request an interview with the president. I can be there on a moment's notice, and I'd like to speak with him this week. Is the president in Venezuela or still on a trip?"

"Okay."

"Okay, you understand me? Or okay I got the interview?"

"Okay. I understand you."

"Any chance the president is traveling somewhere? I could meet him and do the interview there."

"No, he'll be in Venezuela."

"Phone interview?"

"I can ask."

"Well, I really need this to happen, so if he has any free time this week to squeeze me in, please let me know. And I realize there is no free time in any president's schedule," Street said.

"Okay," Carlos replied.

Street hung up without saying goodbye. Carlos wouldn't care. Street pictured him at his office in the press department in Venezuela. He was a devout socialist. He always managed to wear a pin of a little red star of some sort, a symbol that was probably anti-American in origin. Funny thing was that Carlos probably loathed the United States but was a nice, gentle person. He was a tall man of African descent, a sincere smile, and probably had zero blood pressure issues.

Street sat back in his chair. During his phone conversation, he had caught sight of Brent out of the corner of his eye getting ready to leave the office. A minute later, Brent was gone. Street sighed and relaxed, staring at his ancient cassette recorder.

"Alone at last."

There was something about a crowded office or house suddenly emptying out that Street found appealing, even more so than working in a place that was permanently vacant.

"See you and your crew in jail, Brent Drum. But you'll be on the world's front pages first," Street said, swiveling around in his chair to face the empty office behind him. His heart dropped into his stomach when he realized he was not alone. The buildings-and-grounds man was there, installing a new light bulb.

"Jeez, you scared the shit out of me," Street said, feeling his heartbeat slow to somewhat normal levels.

"I sorry," the man said in broken English, not looking at Street.

I gotta remember that quiet carpeting the next time I spy on Brent spying on me, Street thought, looking up at the man.

He began typing a formal email to Carlos Smith requesting the interview. He pressed send and checked his personal email. The buildings-and-grounds man had left, and Street enjoyed the solitude of an empty office for a little while longer. He looked at old copies of *The Gateway*'s printed editions and frowned. What a front page story all this will be one day, he thought. Then he left.

In a parking lot at a nearby strip mall, Brent sat in his parked car. He took the digital recorder out of his pocket and pressed play. He heard Street interviewing Domínguez. Then he pressed stop. He exited the car and walked to a nearby Latin American café and ordered a Cuban coffee and a ham-and-cheese empanada. He wolfed down both and then threw the medical-looking thimble of a coffee cup along with his napkins into the paper bag and crossed the parking lot, which was surrounded by a grocery store, oil-change shop, and pizza parlor. He took out his cell phone and dialed.

"Hi, Karen. Street brought the digital recorder back. I have it here. It's safe. It will never leave my possession. It has a nice drop on it."

"Good. When does Street get that interview? This interview kicks off the second phase, after all."

"Soon. I need to work my sources down there and then have him book the flight. But I'll deliver the Venezuelan-Russian port intelligence stashed on this device soon." He hung up.

Brent retrieved the digital recorder from his pocket and flipped open the battery cover door, ripped it off, and nestled it in his shirt pocket. He looked at the recorder and its now-exposed shiny golden batteries, then threw the device in the paper bag with the coffee cup and napkins, and tossed it all in a nearby dumpster.

He got in his car and pulled out of the parking lot, driving with one hand and patting the little battery door safely tucked away in his shirt pocket with the other.

"One down, one about to go down, and one more to go."

CHAPTER

24

That afternoon, with Street working to land an interview in Caracas, Brent effortlessly steered a new Porsche 911 through West Palm Beach traffic. It was as if he knew seconds ahead of time where the cars would be along Interstate 95. This one will move, this one will speed up, that one will stay put. He sped through traffic so fast that drivers never knew he had been there until he had passed, no matter how small the opening. No need for a tap of the brakes. No need for a honk of the horn. Definitely no wave of thanks to the drivers he just cut off. Not only did he drive fast, he also never got a ticket. Not ever. He was pushing one hundred miles per hour when he swerved across three lanes and made his exit off the interstate.

Brent liked Palm Beach County. Good place to retire if he wasn't going to be fleeing the country soon, he thought, slowing up to a red light on Palm Beach Gardens Drive. He raced through some more traffic and pulled into the parking lot of an off-white six-story office building complete with a small artificial lake in front that wouldn't garner much attention from anyone. Brent hopped out of the car and stared at his reflection in the car window. Like the building, he looked anonymous, like someone you'd see in a commercial for local legal services, tile supplies, or something—just an anonymous white guy. Blue eyes, shaved head with some stubble coming in, all run of the mill.

Except for his glasses. Today, he wore round tortoiseshell glasses. They looked okay but more like something a yuppie would wear in the eighties, he thought, staring into his reflection. He had parked way in the back of the building's lot. He wanted the car to have room to itself. Plus, he enjoyed the walk across the lot, much-needed exercise for his legs after the commute from Coral Gables. He locked the car doors.

A white Porsche. Should have bought a black one. The black ones have better lines, Brent thought. He looked one last time at his reflection in the window. "Perfect," he said aloud, trying to remember his alias's age. He could pass somewhere between thirty-six and fifty-five, and guessed today he was closer to the latter. Gotta remember my identities better, he thought. Haven't been here in a while. Haven't been here much at all lately really. That still doesn't mean now's the time to let up and get sloppy. Especially not now.

This particular office was home to Spartan Software, a fairly large maker of enterprise resource management programs that targeted industries of all sizes. While not at *The Gateway* and not under the cover of Ted Bullard at Cornbridge Capital, Brent Drum went by the alias of Beryl Phelps, a software marketing manager at Spartan Software.

Karen had asked her various government contacts to hack into the company's human resources systems as well as personal accounts of the hiring manager and, more importantly, the CEO to determine what they were looking for when they were bringing a marketing manager on board for the firm's prized software.

Afterward, she and Brent crafted a carefully constructed résumé that came with all the right names to get him into the company so they could use it as a spying platform. His résumé glowed for the hiring manager and the CEO. He had experience at the competition and in other industries with loads of expertise applicable to Spartan Software, including a completely made-up stint as a brand manager for a toy company's division in Eastern Europe and Russia. Stellar recommendations came from other past places of work that were actually CIA fronts managed under Karen's direction.

Brent landed the job, a contract position as an internal consultant, perfect in that he had access to the company and its employees but was distant enough to give him the freedom to work from home and travel. He was assigned to analyze markets and target customers at oil and gas concerns in Venezuela, copper mines, banks and retailers in Chile, and a host of industries in Brazil—energy, infrastructure developers, and agriculture concerns mainly. Gathering intelligence across the hemisphere allowed Brent to spend less and less time around the office, and when it came time to increase CIA manpower without adding to the government payroll, Molly Wells came aboard to work as his protégé.

Wells was a tough, intelligent yet down-to-earth woman, Brent thought from the onset. She volunteered in her community by helping sell Christmas trees at her church and by donating time and energy preparing meals in local homeless assistance centers. She also loved competitive sports, basketball and tennis especially, which instilled in her at an early age the ability to excel in both teams and on her own. She had won several big tennis matches in college before finishing her undergraduate studies in economics at the prestigious women's Barnard College in New York City and prior to beginning her MBA work at Stanford, where she specialized in international marketing and finished near the top of her class.

At Spartan, Wells's first task was to organize market research data surrounding the Latin American enterprise resource software market. Spartan ran offices in each Latin American country, all of which would commission their own market research data, such as the number of servers shipped in a country for a given year or the number of smartphones to be delivered based on focus groups and statistical modeling. In-country sales forecast data often contrasted research commissioned at the Latin American regional headquarters in West Palm Beach and even at the global headquarters in California. Multiple vendors selling multiple reports and data resulted in multiple—and often conflicting—takes on the health of global technology markets.

Disputes would arise between the West Palm Beach office and the subsidiary offices in-country as to who had correct numbers on computer and server demand. Or cell phone purchases. Or software upgrades. Or video game sales. Or gross domestic product growth forecasts. Or inflation. Unemployment. Durable goods. Whatever.

For Spartan, Wells, a contract worker like Brent, was the perfect candidate to clean up the mess. She pitched and won a budget to create a hemisphere-wide research purchasing unit, a procurement platform for data. The new centralized body served as a conduit that handled the flow of data. It didn't mean an employee couldn't get the reports that he or she wanted.

Data was still pretty much available on demand, though it came from one source, and that source was Wells. All about savings, and all about efficiency.

Brent recognized her potential and began to send her outside of Latin America to gain experience across company lines, expanding her talents to the Middle East, Eastern Europe, and Asia, where she provided consulting to Spartan employees and even public and private sector clients. Molly's streamlined process management saved the company millions upon millions, and Brent saw in her a most perfect placebo.

"I truly believe in intelligent design," Brent said to the security man, who shrugged him in.

Not only was Molly smart and often on the road, her warm smile and striking features helped win everyone over and willingly hand over intelligence, men especially. Her mother was half Brazilian and half Italian while her father was from the US state of Minnesota, which made for a stunning blonde woman with eyes the color of forget-me-nots.

That day, she was at the South Florida office. Brent had scheduled a meeting to ensure she would be in town. He crossed the perpetually waxed marble floor and the generic office furniture and whipped out his office ID card. A glass door buzzed, a receptionist smiled, and he headed to the sixth floor. Molly would be waiting at her cubicle.

"Molly," Brent said, reminding himself that he using the alias Beryl Phelps that day.

The greeting kiss dilemma was at hand. He knew people kissed women on the cheek as a greeting in South Florida due to the Latin American influence, but it could get awkward. An Anglo would greet a Latin woman with a kiss to show cultural awareness, while the Latin woman would extend a hand to the Anglo to do likewise, offsetting each other and resulting in a physical communication breakdown from the get-go. A mesh of cultures made saying hello complicated in this area of the state. Screw it, Brent thought. I'm going for the peck on the cheek. He did. She kissed him back.

"Beryl Phelps," she said. "Welcome back."

Good alias, Brent thought. Did he think of that one or did Karen?

"Great to be here," he said. "Who do I talk to about buying data? I need three different sets of conflicting numbers about computer shipments headed for my bathroom."

"We can handle that for you," Molly said. "I saw in my calendar that we have a meeting today. What can I do for you, Beryl?"

"A lot," he said. "Got your passport handy?"

CHAPTER

25

Street scanned Miami's western horizon. Thunderheads sprouted high into the sky. He pressed the gas pedal, and his Jeep responded, though lunchtime traffic might give the brewing storms time to catch his Jeep before he reached his destination. He took care of his car, though proper attention to the engine and auto parts would do little to shield him from a South Florida summer storm, especially when he was in a fine suit, silk tie, and a blue shirt. Blue. The worst color for moisture. Should have worn white.

He headed west along Bird Road in Coral Gables, one eye on the darkening horizon, one ear on his phone guiding him to Matías Sánchez's office. He threw an occasional glance at his suit coat, which rested a little dangerously on the edge of the passenger's seat, ready to fly off if an eddy of wind slipped beneath the fabric.

He studied the building storm at a red light before snaking his way northward into the City of Doral, a vibrant Miami-Dade County municipality. The clouds had hints of green, and the lightning hooked more frequently than normal, striking the ground hard and fast as if the skies were mining for something. Street hurried, dodging in and out of traffic. When the first drops of rain began to smack the window, he made it safely inside the offices of MSMarketing.

Matías Sánchez was a heavy-set man with short, neatly cropped blond hair and a ruddy complexion. His receptionist, Rosemary Martínez, welcomed Street to his office, which was located in the heart of Doral, home to the US Southern Command, the Federal Reserve Bank of Atlanta Miami Branch Office, lush golf courses, and a growing community of Venezuelan expats. Matías extended his hand to Street. Both men made eye contact and held a firm handshake.

"Have a seat, Mr. Brewer," Matías said. Rosemary said she'd be back with coffee and water. Matías leaned back at his desk, which looked more like a large wooden dining room table than a workspace. Sports memorabilia donned the office walls, complete with autographed pictures of baseball stars and snapshots of Matías fishing Florida waters and spending time around town with his children. His wife looked just like him, with blondish hair and pink skin. Nice smile. Street looked back at Matías, who was checking something out on his computer. "Give me two seconds," Matías said in a thick Venezuelan accent, staring down his nose at the computer screen, as if he were inspecting some fishy numbers or some other form of improper documentation.

"Take your time," Street said, feeling like he was buying a new car and had made it past sales and was now in the office of the finance guy, ready to negotiate. Matías made a few clicks on his computer and then gave Street his full attention. His eyes softened.

"So, I understand you are in the journalism business and want out," Matías said. Despite his thick Spanish accent, his English syntax was excellent.

"That's correct. No growth in it at all."

"Did Patricia tell you what we do?"

"Some," Street said.

"What did she tell you?"

"Well, not in these words exactly but you're a consulting firm trying to figure out your niche in a constantly shifting landscape. Consulting sprinkled in with computer-driven business intelligence along with technology advice in other areas, accounting in still other areas, and good old-fashioned marketing and advertising elsewhere."

Matías laughed. "That's more or less true. We're just like everyone else out there, stuck in the middle, trying to find that niche. Doesn't matter, though. Technology is killing once rock-solid protection barriers, and competitive landscapes are shifting so fast that a good niche today won't exist tomorrow. Still, there's always a need for a solid writer. I hate fucking writing in English or Spanish," Matías said.

The expletive took Street by surprise, but he laughed. "Looks like I'm your man," he said. "I can write in both languages. Plus, I'm a good reporter and a good writer. Some journalists scoop stories well and do bang-up reporting jobs but confuse the readers with their awful prose. Others write beautifully but are too afraid to pick up the phone to find something to write about."

"Good," Matías said. "Let's talk about a project I have. Do you know anything about corporate accounting?"

"Somewhat," Street said. "I can report on earnings, economics, and I can cover events, but if you want me to do some actual number crunching to the point where I'm restating financials or involved with financial engineering, then I'm not your guy."

"Of course," Matías said. "What I want to find out is where Miami fits into the US economy as well as in the global corporate world in terms of assets. Finding out how many companies have their headquarters based here is a good benchmark and can create value, but that's been done before. What I want to know is how many corporate assets may be here in Miami even if the corporate headquarters are far away."

"Wouldn't the chamber of commerce or the city or county have that data?" Street said.

"If they do, it will be spotty at best. So I'm looking to start from scratch, create a database and start selling this stuff," Matías said, returning his gaze to his computer monitor as if he were peering into a crystal ball.

Street glanced around the office again. Family fishing pictures stared back at him. Street took note of the boat, the *Knot Worrying*. Zero points for originality for whoever came up with that name. Matías went on, staring back at Street. "Since I'm looking to start from scratch, I figure a journalist would be a great place to start."

Street perked up. "To start?"

"Yes, you seem to have a good résumé. International business journalism skills. All the research and writing and little fear of numbers and even more important, little fear of picking up the telephone and cold-calling. So would you be interested? This would be a project?"

"Yes, but what exactly do you want me to do again? Compile of a list of all companies that have assets in Miami? Both companies headquartered here and those not headquartered here?"

"Exactly. Go through corporate balance sheets. Start with the Fortune 500 and then go through all those filed at the Securities and Exchange Commission. Go through the financials of companies no matter where they are, determine which of their assets are based in South Florida and then compute that fraction to the total of company assets. We'll create a database of South Florida and then compare it with other cities, and then we go global. Think about it. We could add some serious value here to publish."

Street went flush with disbelief. "Not all that material is just listed out in quarterly filings." Why not translate *War & Peace* into Sanskrit while we're at it, Street thought.

"Some of it is, and some of it will require phone work. I don't expect this any time soon, but I do expect a timetable from you in a couple of weeks as to when you might finish, like how many months it would take to complete once you do start. Does this sound like something that would interest you?"

Street said nothing. Never had he been tasked with anything so daunting, at least for one person to complete on a fixed timetable. He had seen some reports like these before. They provide great data points to show off at cocktail parties, but few people or companies would actually pay for them. Still, it was a challenge.

"So, you want to know assets by publicly traded companies, no matter where they are based in the world, broken down into this city?"

"Yes, and eventually private firms too. Lots of cold-calling there. Start building. Once we get that database built, we can crunch numbers and start analyzing data and writing stories. Will five thousand dollars a month work?"

Street stared at the man and said nothing. That was okay money but a Herculean task that would take years just to get off the ground. The short-term effect was good. It would give him a boost financially when the inevitable time came to leave *The Gateway* or to supplement himself while exposing Brent, but he'd be accepting a task that would ultimately fail.

"Is this a new position? You say it will start from scratch with a fresh hire, but have you tried to do this? Has anyone in your company started?"

"Nope. It would be just you. Seven thousand a month," the man said.

"What if the data is unobtainable? What if I get a fraction of what we're looking for? I am going to call companies who won't want to give out that information."

"Little by little," the man said. "Just start building."

"I don't know," Street said. "It sounds overwhelming."

"If it doesn't work out, we part ways, and I'll give you a solid recommendation and move onto other projects. I'm ready to get started today, but unfortunately, there is a catch. I need to go back to Venezuela to tie up a few loose ends before we can get started. Seven thousand a month is a good salary. You can always walk away from it. We're in September. Start date would be the first of December."

"No deal," Street said. "I can't wait that long."

The man stared at Street with a blend of resolve, patience, mistrust, and boredom, like an airport security worker succumbing to a bad mood. He sighed.

"You work at *The Gateway*, right? You get to write, but the pay is very bad," Matías said.

"That's right."

"Fine. Here is my final offer. Ten thousand a month. You'll have to pay taxes, of course. You'll be a contractor. You can start on the fifteenth of November, and even though I won't be here, you'll have time to go through the SEC websites and lists of South Florida corporations and begin identifying assets that are here. Then we'll really ramp up in December, when the timetable begins. Deal?"

Street stared at the *Knot Worrying*. Matías, his wife, and another young couple were aboard, smiling back at the camera. The captain or a mate snapped the pic, Street assumed. He looked at the young couple. They were only a few years older than Street, though they were light-years better off financially. It was something about their clothes, their relaxed smiles—smiles that knew the stress of work but were free from fears of economic uncertainty or even financial doom. He blew it off. Two months at *The Gateway* tops, and maybe he'd leave and start to smile the way they did, especially if Brent fled and failed to kill him off. And if it didn't work out here with Matías, he was a contractor, after all. Free to come and go as he pleased, and free to work on his story exposing Brent's agenda. And nothing was stopping him from adding other clients. He looked at the young, happy couple and then back at Matías.

"Deal," Street said.

Matías smiled and jumped up, extending his hand for Street to shake.

"I know it sounds daunting," Matías said. "And it will be at first. But once it snowballs, think of all the opportunities that will come out of it."

"Thank you, Matías. I do appreciate the opportunity. Talk to you in November," Street said. He left the office and walked into the humid Doral parking lot. The storm had passed, but the Jeep was soaking wet. It didn't bother him, though. Thanks to Patricia, Street now had a way out of *The Gateway* and its illegal activities.

The water in his Jeep from the earlier storm was pretty substantial, so he wiped the seat off with a towel and then decided to take a long drive to air-dry his car. He felt relaxed as well. Even if he failed in this new job, all he'd have to do would be to explain to a new recruiter what exactly the job entailed. Anyone with half a brain would realize achieving such a task would be extremely unlikely at least in terms of time and might even praise Street for trying. At least there was light at the end of the financial tunnel, which was a good thing. If he failed to expose Brent's smuggling scheme, Brent would probably flee the country before getting a chance to kill Street anyhow, especially if Street was wary.

Street made his way to US 1. Eventually, the sun wobbled up above as if the passing storm had bucked it off its back, though the roads were still wet thanks to a thick coating of humidity in the air. He sped up on the ramp that marked the end of US 1 and the beginning of I-95. Large buildings crested to the east under a purple sky, while the sun shone like molten gold and amber to the west, with many shades of cool blues above. Traffic was light, so Street thought he'd enjoy an afternoon drive. Growing hunger pains reminded him that his excursion would be lunch somewhere. Nothing back in Miami appealed to him, and neither did anything in Miami Beach or the rest of the county.

About half an hour later, he saw the exit to where he wanted to go. With his mind made up and resolution firm, he headed east and found himself at the Saluda Pig in Broward County, a charming ramshackle restaurant famous for its barbeque, fries, and lemonade. Street liked the shredded pork marinated in a vinegar-based sauce and later slow cooked with hickory wood. Carolina-style was the only way for him.

An old woman with gray hair and a hard, worn face, wearing a white T-shirt that bore the brand of the restaurant greeted Street with a smile to take his order—two sandwiches and fries. He opted for beer over his usual lemonade. Street ate in a silence broken by the gentle sway of the wind and a passing motorcycle or two mixed in with the occasional slam of a car door. His senses mellowed until the smell of flowery perfume entered the mix. Long, strong legs in very short shorts crossed next to him, and instinctively, he sat up straight and jutted his chest out. Blonde hair caught his eyes, though he forced himself not to stare.

She was a rarity, even for South Florida, whoever she was. She smiled at him and then looked away. The blonde ordered something from the older woman behind the counter, but Street missed what it was. He looked away. The young woman didn't seem interested in harmless flirting or conversation, so he left her alone. No sense in ogling. No need for one more creep in this world, South Florida especially.

He ate the first half of his first sandwich, sitting there quietly and taking in his surroundings. He looked up at the woman behind the counter and motioned for another drink.

"Your beer is three-fourths full," the older woman said. "I'll put one on ice anyway."

Street shook his head, and immediately the young blonde spoke up. "I think he means he wanted more water. From your angle, it looked like he was pointing to his beer."

Street nodded. "That's right, thanks," he said to the woman behind the counter. "And thanks," he said to the young blonde next to him.

"No worries. That's what I do for a living—sort out miscommunications. Sorry for giving you my shoulder earlier."

"You didn't at all," Street said.

"Yes, I did. Just a long day."

"I know the feeling," Street said. "My name is Street Brewer," he said and extended a hand. "It's nice to meet you."

"Molly Wells," the woman replied.

CHAPTER

26

After meeting with the Russian and international press to announce soft loans to improve food and consumer-product distribution channels in Venezuela, bolster power supply, and agree to look into future agreements, the Venezuelan technocrats were ready for some grunt work and to hammer out details of the deals.

Bernal let the president lead the way through the halls of the Ministry of Defense. The president walked fast, and Bernal did a good job staggering behind as best as his aging, battle-hardened body would allow him. The president glanced at the halls and offices.

"Our defense ministry should be bigger. Let's add on to it when we get back to Caracas," the president said to a nearby staffer.

They walked down more halls, conveniently emptied of government employees to give the Venezuelans privacy. Then they came to a small, quiet room. Russian President Sokolov was off attending to other affairs, and the media would be filing their stories from earlier press conferences. Attention fully diverted. All eyes were off the Venezuelans for now, and that put Bernal at ease somewhat. The president, Bernal, and a few aides took their seats at the large conference table and then a quiet came over the room. Bernal enjoyed the silence, the background sounds of air moving throughout the building, the hum of a car passing outside, the drop of a knuckle on a desk, calmness.

Then a man with bushy hair entered the room.

"Mr. President, I hope I didn't keep you waiting," he said in Russian and again in Spanish.

A mousy lady in a tight gray suit and hair in a bun translated into the president's ear. The Venezuelan president stood, as did everyone else, to shake the hand of this Russian. The Russian looked at Bernal, and both nodded.

"I guess it's time to discuss the more technical details surrounding the base, Mr. ...?" the president of Venezuela asked.

"Bogdanov. Peter Bogdanov."

The men shook hands.

"It would be my pleasure," the Russian man said.

He pressed the keyboard of a laptop computer that had been sitting on the desk. It sprang to life and shot a desktop image on a wider screen. Bogdanov muttered something to an assistant. The Venezuelans looked around. The assistant muttered something back. The Russian man, Bogdanov, then said in fluent Spanish, "I was just checking with my colleagues to see if this room were secure. No prying American eyes in here. Or Russian eyes and ears either. Pretty mundane conference room."

The mousy translator took her seat. She would be there if the president needed her.

The Russian man booted up a PowerPoint presentation and began. The first slide showed a map of Russia and accompanying illustrations of military expenditure figures.

"Gentleman, as you know, Russia has a strong and vibrant military history. We've played a pivotal role shaping the geopolitical world from the early twentieth century through today. Yet, as is the case with any country's military, weaknesses always exist. With Russia, as you know, warm-water ports in the past were hard to come by. Sure, we have an ice-free port in Murmansk and presence elsewhere, but it's time to increase our reach to deal with our dear old friends, the Americans, and feel at home in their own backyard."

Slides of ports, maps, and charts with military spending figures jumped across the screen as Bogdanov went through his PowerPoint presentation.

"That's where Venezuela comes in. We need friends with coastlines and friends who have a need to protect themselves. After all, if other countries in the region host foreign military and intelligence interests, why shouldn't

Venezuela do likewise and on a much bigger scale? We think La Orchila Island would be a good site, at least at first. Not a port in Sucre like the world is expecting but definitely a Russian military facility on Venezuelan soil, specifically one to house our aircraft such as Tu-160 Blackjack bombers. The port can follow and distract from the airbase."

"Doesn't matter. Just set up shop in my country," the Venezuelan president muttered. "Bombers, subs, ships, troops, whatever. I just need you here."

Both Bernal and Bogdanov raised their eyebrows, surprised at the apathy from the president over attention to military details.

"Can you feasibly establish a base in Venezuela to house Russian military activities in a very short time?" Bernal asked.

Bogdanov looked up.

Bernal eyed him and nodded. Just cut to the chase. No need for all these slides.

"Feasibly, yes," Bogdanov said.

"Good," the president of Venezuela chimed in. "Carry on with your speech, but be quick about it."

Bernal flinched.

"Before I go on," Bogdanov said. "You, Mr. President, you better do your part to stay in power. If you fall and we lose our Venezuelan assets, there will be hell to pay. There's no way we're ending up in litigation somewhere fighting your other creditors."

Bernal noticed Bogdanov was gauging to see how a sovereign leader would react to being chastised by a foreign technocrat. The Venezuelan president said nothing.

"Anyway," Bogdanov continued. "We're confident that won't happen. We'll send military advisors there to keep you in power if we have to."

"Don't worry about anything. We will stay in power, and the world will pay a little more attention to Venezuela," the president said.

"How can you be so sure?" Bogdanov asked. "Everyone will know light-years ahead when Venezuela and Russia are planning a base together. Even if we use existing infrastructure in La Orchila, people will find out eventually. It's good for Venezuela, but it's really good for Russia. This is a Russian story. And let's not forget melting Arctic ice caps. We can launch some pretty sophisticated submarines from our northern coasts if Venezuela doesn't work out. That could worry some Americans even more."

"You need Venezuela," the president said.

Bogdanov set the clicker down and paced in front of the Venezuelan delegation, blocking their view of his PowerPoint slides.

"We realize that establishing a military presence in Venezuela sends language to the US and its allies in the region. But seriously, no surprises will pop up for the Americans," Bogdanov said. "It's a military base with Russian planes flying in. It's not like you can build it in secret for long. Of course, we're considering a naval port, though we feel an air base on La Orchila should be our first priority."

The president of Venezuela laughed. "It doesn't matter. In fact, I want the word out ahead of time before their spies get the full details of all of our plans. I'll give interviews to the American media, big and small. The first unbiased, gringo reporter who asks for it gets an interview. I know we haven't agreed to all the concrete details, but we can always announce one of those deals under which we agree to look into something," the president said, motioning for a cell phone from Bernal to call his press people.

Bernal ignored him.

"Let's do it. Let's announce the details, not hide them," the president said.

"That's our call, Mr. President," Bogdanov said. "Remember who Venezuela works for."

The president stood.

Bernal saw that he needed to douse the fire before it could build.

"Mr. President, I think what the Russians are saying is that now is not the time for surprises, especially in matters of defense. Silence is golden."

"There won't be any surprises at all!" the president said, pacing the room in search of a window as if looking for a break in the ice that would give him air to breathe. He walked to one and stared outside.

Bernal looked at his boss and then stood.

"Excuse me, gentlemen," he said and then walked out of the room.

The president was losing it, he thought. This port was just a poorly crafted plan to keep Venezuela, and more importantly, its president, in the limelight. And now an air force base or some kind of forward outpost? It was time to ramp up spying on his own boss. He paced the halls a little surprised at the relaxed manner in which he walked. A young woman walked by, and he nodded at her cordially. She smiled back, not knowing that the foreign minister was making mental notes on who could help him find out what the head of state and government was really up to. A couple of names popped up. Then he chose two.

CHAPTER

27

"So, as the old question goes," Molly said. "What do you do for a living, Street Brewer?"

"I'm a reporter."

"Interesting," Molly said, raising one eyebrow and turning to face Street. Her food arrived. Same as Street's, except with slaw and imported beer.

"Have I ever seen or read your stuff?"

"I work at *The Gateway*," Street said. "It's a niche media company. I know it's not one of the majors, but it could grow and earn me some money."

Street gauged Molly's reaction. She seemed interested. Not floored, but interested.

"It's a business publication that, well…"

Street took a sip of beer.

"It's—"

"I get it," Molly said, adding "it's your job."

"What about you?" Street asked. "Where do you work?"

"Spartan Software, just north of here."

"I know it. What do you do there?"

A large couple sat down near them, bouncing the bench as they took their seats.

"Nothing as interesting as what you do. Market research mainly." Molly stood. "Shall we get a table with a little more privacy?"

"Sure," Street said.

They sat down at a table beside a screen window. The quiet afternoon noise seemed to insulate their conversation. "I'm going to be really cheesy right now," Street said. "You don't seem like someone who comes here a lot." "This is my cheat day," Molly said. "Plus, I'm traveling soon."

Street caught a glimpse of her strong legs, remembered something about how women are more intuitive than men and then assumed he got busted staring.

"Where to?" Street asked.

"Venezuela. On business. Down to meet the new man in enterprise software, a Mr. Ricardo something or the other. I forget his last name. Funny, maybe Beryl didn't give it to me."

Molly looked at her buzzing phone. An unknown number popped up. She screened it and turned off the phone.

"I was just there. I could show you a few things," Street said, taking note of the name Ricardo and the unknown caller on her phone.

"Really? I'm sure you could. Anyway, *The Gateway*. My colleague always has a copy on him, though I confess I'm not much into the news these days," Molly said. "I don't like politics, and pop culture is boring. I keep it at sports and weather."

"What kind of sports?"

"Tennis. And anything on the beach or in the water. Yourself?"

"Anything outside," Street said, looking over Molly's shoulder.

A middle-aged couple had entered, both wearing blue jeans and black T-shirts. Street looked back at Molly.

"Anything that gets me out of the office and away from my coworkers."

"I hear you there," Molly said, motioning for another beer. She pointed at Street's bottle as well and then shook her head. "Just bring us six of mine in an ice bucket."

The woman nodded.

The beers arrived while the middle-aged couple stared at copies of the paper menu.

Street took one of the beers, opened it with a bottle opener tied to the bucket's handle, part of the barbeque restaurant's rustic appeal, and took a pull. He looked back at Molly.

"I like my line of work, but let's face it, it's writing. It's all subjective in the end," Street said.

"Let me guess: long hours, very low pay, no benefits, no upward mobility, and no way to quantify if you did a good job writing or not?"

"You got it. Maybe it will lead to something different. I still believe skills are transferrable these days," Street said.

"Well, your situation is different than mine. I work for a software company in market research. I cleaned up the process, and you can measure my success by how much money we're saving due to increased efficiencies and best practices," Molly said, giggling and turning red, knowing what was coming next from Street.

"Don't give up your day job if you want to become a writer," Street said. She blushed even more. "Increased efficiencies and best practices," Street went on. "After these beers, we'll get around to some capacity building and secondary valuation formulation."

"Actually," Molly said, kicking his shin and making no effort to conceal her laughing. "Valuation formulation comes before capacity building. There's a lot of stakeholders you'll need to engage in between those two exercises."

"Wow," Street said. "Cheers to coming from two different sides of the communications jungle." He raised his bottle, and Molly happily toasted.

"I respect you for what you do," Molly said. "Too many people these days make it seem like they're rich and powerful, but they're not. They're all facades. People like you don't stay in low-salary positions for too long anyway, because you stay true to who you are. Besides, how long have you been where you are?"

"Too long," Street said.

They ate in silence for a while and then spoke for about an hour about common interests. After a lull in the conversation, Molly changed the conversation's course.

"So, are there many people in your office?"

"No," Street said. "We outsource a lot of work, but for the day-to-day it's just me and my boss, Brent Drum."

"Brent Drum," Molly said. "Interesting name. Just like yours."

"He's definitely more than he appears," Street said. "So, who do you work for?"

"Lots of bosses and a chain of managers, but mainly for a man named Beryl Phelps, who's always on the road. So have you always worked for small publications? You know if you start one up and sell it, you can make some money."

Molly's phone rang. Street saw unknown flash across the screen. He frowned. Wait a second, he thought. Something was off.

"Not always," he said, looking at her phone. "I was with a large newswire in Latin America. In Venezuela, mainly."

"What was your beat?"

"Financial news. Any news that moves markets, and in Venezuela's case, that's politics more than ever. We provided the news you see on the screens on the trading desks and on television as well. My news came with trading platforms, analytics, you know, the works."

"Sounds expensive. Traders and investment banks and brokerage houses must pay a lot for your news. Why not go back?"

"I would, but the wire service where I worked went under, and there haven't been any job openings at the competition in Latin America lately. People tend to hang on to those jobs, and when there are openings, they often fill them internally," Street said. He looked away.

"Well, in this day and age, you don't need to pay tons of money for a trading desk to get real-time news," Molly said. "Everything is real time now, including your publication. I'm assuming *The Gateway* makes good use of its website and social media accounts? If you don't, then God help you. Anyone you are quoting is tweeting away in open space anyway, forgoing the need to talk to a pesky reporter. Anyone can be journalist."

"Well, we're not dead quite yet," Street said. He thought about the office for a second. "We do act as a filter for our readers, a more independent source of information." Street thought of Brent and cringed at what he had just said.

"So what's to stop you from doing something cheaper than the big newswires? Something like going out on your own and working freelance?"

"Nothing, I guess," Street said, looking back at Molly.

She smiled at him.

"You may be on to something," Street said.

"Looks like you're thinking about something," Molly said. "Your boss must be lucky to have someone like you."

"I was thinking the same thing about you," Street said. The beer bottles clinked as they toasted.

After a few minutes of small talk, the woman behind the counter brought the check over to Molly for the extra beer. They split the tab.

"What was your last name again?" Street asked. "I missed it from the noise in the traffic."

"Wells," she said. "Molly Wells."

Street froze.

"Look, we're almost done with the killings. We've eliminated Olivia Crawford, the Tagles, and the Spradlings. There is Street next and then one more out there, a Molly Wells at Spartan Software, but we haven't used her in a while."

"Hey," Molly said. She snapped a finger. "Earth to Street. Are you still with me?"

Street came back. "Yeah, I'm here with you."

"Good to know," Molly said.

"I'm also here for you. Anyway, I have to run, but before I do, can I ask a quick favor?"

"Sure," Molly said.

"Don't be alone with your boss. Don't travel to Venezuela and stay away from Ricardo."

"What?"

"Just trust me," Street said, taking out his cell phone. He scrolled down, produced a picture of Phelps, and showed it to Molly.

"That's him, right?"

"What the fuck? How did you know? Are you some kind of a stalker?" She scooted far away from Street, shifting her body to size him up as well as keep her distance.

"No. Just trust me on this. I'll explain it all in a few days. I'm not a stalker. I'm actually a coworker."

"Excuse me?"

Street didn't want to freak her out and send her running. He didn't want to downplay the danger either.

"He's a scam artist. I'll let you know in a few days."

"Okay, you're scaring me," Molly said. She crossed her arms. "Or maybe you're a corporate spy. You show up here where I am, conveniently. Then you pull out of a picture of my boss. Are you some sort of corporate spy? You'd suck at it if you were."

"Not sure how to answer that, but definitely not, probably."

Molly stood up.

"You have to trust me. Like I said, I'm a reporter. And your boss is involved in some sort of scam. I did a story on your company a while back, and during follow-up research I found out your boss is up to something illegal," Street said with a twinge of guilt mixed with pride at his improved lying abilities. "Look, I didn't follow you here. Seriously, it's a coincidence."

"Then, coincidentally, why don't I call the police? Or the FBI?"

"That's a great idea!" Street said.

He thought about his plans to expose the agenda. Then again, this woman's life was in danger. He was done lying.

"Don't do it yet, though."

"Why not?" she asked, drawing her cell phone. "How about I just dial 9-1-1?"

Street sighed. He motioned for Molly to sit down. He studied her expression and saw that she was studying the body language of a man about to finally tell the truth about something. She sat down.

"I am a journalist, and I'm exposing something wrong here in South Florida. It involves your boss and mine. I heard my boss, well our boss, mention your name once."

"What?"

"Let's put it this way. You and I work for the same company."

"You mean you're doing work for Spartan?" Molly said, visibly confused and taken aback.

"No, we work for the same man."

"Are you some kind of identity thief? It doesn't matter. I'm out of here," Molly said.

Street scrambled to get his phone. Swiped across and dug up a video. "Look, it's the same man."

Molly stared at the phone, and her defensiveness morphed into curiosity. It was a video of Brent speaking at a roundtable, with a name tag at his seat clearly identifying him as Brent Drum. He even announced himself as Brent Drum.

"That's my boss, Brent Drum," Street said.

"That's Beryl Phelps, the man I report to."

"Want more proof?" Street said scrolling across his phone. "Check these out." He handed her the phone.

She took it and scrolled through several pictures. There were too many of Street and the man she knew as Beryl Phelps to keep her from doubting Street, who caught on to her racing thoughts.

"He's CIA, Molly. He's infiltrating legitimate companies and sending subordinates abroad to spy for him. Sometimes he plants devices on us. Sometimes he guides our business schedules so we meet with certain individuals, assets like they're called in the movies, and talk to them. We collect information that way without even knowing it," Street said, pausing to let Molly process.

"It gets worse. He wants to kill us and go on to some second phase of some agenda he's got going. I'm next," he said.

"I'm calling the police," Molly said.

"Don't," Street said. "At least not yet."

"Why not? Are you insane?"

"I need to find out everyone who's working with him first. And to bust them all, I need to let them continue working their plan. They don't know that I know. Don't worry. He won't be around you for long. I'm going to lure him away from you. Just don't be alone with him. Act busy and act normal but distance yourself," Street said.

Molly sat down. Stared at the table.

"How do you know all this? And how can he assume two identities in cities this close together. Someone will call him out."

"I've gotten pretty good at being a spy," he said. "And he never planned to keep these identities for very long."

"And after you lure him away? Then what?"

"We'll both be famous. Just stay away from him. Trust me, I've got this. I know you want to run from it all, and I know it's dangerous. But if you run, they'll suspect something, and they will find you."

Molly said nothing for about a minute. Then she cracked open another beer and took a sip. She cracked open a second bottle and handed it to Street.

CHAPTER

28

A day later, Street sat alone in the office, a little relieved that Molly knew to keep her guard up and not to call the police. He sat there letting his thoughts drift until the maintenance man came to work on the doorknob. He didn't make much noise, and Street knew he would be finished soon. Normally, it wouldn't have been such a big deal, but after putting a face on Molly Wells, having a maintenance man standing behind him was too much.

Street closed down all applications that had anything to do with work and checked his personal email. Nothing of note that day. He took off.

Not even a half an hour later, Street was seated at a Starbucks on Miracle Mile in downtown Coral Gables. Miracle Mile was at the heart of Coral Gables, and for Street, it got better and better with each year. About a mile long—as the name suggested—the street was lined with shops, cafés, bars, and restaurants. When one would close, another would pop up, much better than years ago when all it seemed to house were multiple bridal shops and other retail outlets that sold stuff that nobody needed, at least not on a regular basis.

Street powered up his personal laptop, a new one he had paid for in cash, clicked on his customized virtual private network software a friend had given him to mask himself online, at least for a little while, and went online. He avoided email, knowing it was bugged, checked his news sites to catch up on current events, and then moved on to sports and then the weather. He was just enjoying the sound of cars passing and the hot coffee running through his veins. He wondered who would win over his alertness, the sun with its sleeping and hypnotic effects or the caffeine in the coffee.

Then Street's phone rang, a new phone with a new line. Unknown, the caller ID displayed. "Screw it," he said.

"Hello," he answered.

"Street Brewer?" a female voice asked.

"You know it's me," Street said.

"Street Brewer? Do you know who this is?"

"Is this the same woman who was calling me at the Grouchy Grouper? You know Brent and friends can eavesdrop on this line sooner or later," Street said. He hung up. He stared at the phone. It buzzed. A text message arrived.

Yes. Same person. Nobody eavesdropping. You can't buy new phones or laptops without us finding out. You're alone now. But answer the phone away from everyone. Always assume the walls have ears.

The phone rang again. Street answered.

"Why answer? What are we not going to talk about?" he said, stepping away from his table to the sidewalk.

"It's time to talk."

"You talk, and I listen," Street said.

"Fine," the woman said. "My name is Cyra Harred. You need to quit your job immediately, get out of town and hide out. You're in great danger."

"No shit," Street said. "Didn't we go through this? Look, I'm not going anywhere."

"No, you look. I wasn't sure at first but after a little groundwork, I know I've got the right people. You're involved in something, and you don't know it."

"Rinse and repeat. Tell me something I don't know," Street said. "In fact, you're probably in on it."

"I'm serious. Your life depends on it. Listen, I didn't want to tell you over the phone but—"

"I'm a spy, I'll find out. I know more than you think." Street hung up.

A text message flashed across his phone.

Great! You figured it out, Street. But you don't know everything.

Then tell me everything.

By text? No way.

Why don't you meet me and tell me everything?

Fair enough. Where?

Someplace public. So do you work with Brent?

Better in person.

After a slight delay, Cyra replied.

I get it. No record of our conversation. Just give me something. In person.

Street wrote back immediately.

Can't wait that long.

Silence. He eyed his phone again and grew annoyed. He looked around at all the other customers quietly sipping coffee and banging away on computers and smartphones. Business as usual for most. He picked up the phone again and called Carlos Smith. If there was one thing he needed, it was to get out of town. The mystery caller had that right. In fact, let her listen to this call to the Venezuelan government. If she wanted him dead, she would have killed him. So let her follow him everywhere.

Jake waited for Carlos Smith to reply. The phone rang that dull sound that all calls abroad made. Instead of a crisp, well-defined ring typical of calls made inside the United States, the ring abroad sounded like a wet horn.

"Yes," Carlos answered.

"Hey, Carlos. Street Brewer here. Hope all is well with you."

"Yes," Carlos answered.

"Yes, it's Street Brewer again, yes. Just wanted to know when I can pencil in the president of Venezuela into my busy schedule." Street reclined in his chair and looked out across Coral Gables, bored and restless at the same time the way a child is after waiting for too long in the principal's office waiting room.

"This Friday," Carlos said. "Twelve noon. Sharp. Be here. You get a half an hour."

Street felt a rush of adrenaline flood every nook of his skull. For a second, he felt he knew what lottery winners went through, a rush of emotion fighting a rush of doubt, an eddy of mixed feelings of sheer joy and wondering if his senses were tricking him.

"Did I hear you correctly? I'm going to get the interview?" Both the CIA and I will be very happy, he thought. Maybe I won't get killed until afterward.

"Yes. The president is eager to speak with American media, an independent source. You called first, so you're up first. Plus, you're not Venezuelan with some kind of agenda." You're half-correct, Street thought.

"Thank you, Carlos! See you soon!" Street hung up.

A few hours later, Street was getting ready to go. He was in his apartment packing, checking and double-checking to make sure he had his passport and ticket information, gate number and voice recorder—he had bought one this time, and it would accompany his voice memo app on his phone as well as his old-school cassette recorder. He also contacted Molly Wells to let her know he would be in Caracas and to be extra suspicious but added that she needn't worry as he would be in Caracas and likely distracting Brent from Spartan Software. It was about five in the afternoon, and he heard footsteps at the door. He didn't bother to look up from his packing. He knew who was there.

Parker West and Turner Hickman walked in, opening the door while knocking at the same time. They entered and slammed the door behind them.

"Street Brewer!" Parker shouted.

Street was happy they were there. He opened the fridge and pulled out three Polish ales.

"So, you're off to Caracas?' Parker asked. "We got your text. You're interviewing the president of Venezuela? In person?"

"Yes, sir. Leaving tomorrow." Street walked from the kitchen into his living room as Parker and Turner made way to give him space. He went to an open piece of luggage and surveyed his clothes inside.

"How long will you be gone?" Parker asked.

"A couple of days. I'm making a trip out of it. Nothing on the jobs front, Parker?"

"Not much for me. Still getting out there and putting my best foot forward," Parker said.

"Aren't we all," Street said.

"Street, what are you going to talk to the president about?" Parker asked.

"This and that. Got any questions for him?"

"Tell him my grandmother wants to know when gasoline prices go back to a dollar or less."

"I can answer that one for you myself right now, but no problem. We'll see what he says. Turner, anything you need from the Venezuelan president?"

"Yes. Ask him what's it like having all that power and energy all around him," Turner said. "Does it ever go to his head?"

"Okay. That's kind of a broad brushstroke, but I'll ask him, especially when the nation isn't in a sweeping blackout," Street replied.

"He does have a lot of power," Parker chimed in.

"I know. Everyone knows that," Street said, then he slammed his beer bottle on the counter and stared at Turner and Parker.

"What?" they both asked in unison.

"Damn! You guys are onto something!"

"We are?" they both asked in unison again, as if they were part of a chorus in a Greek theater.

"It's all about power."

"Power?"

"What's the one thing the president needs to stay in power?" Street asked his friend.

"Jail those who want to take his power?" Turner asked.

"Yes, but someone will always come to challenge him."

"We get it," Parker said. "He needs higher oil prices if he wants to keep the military or anyone else in his corner for long."

"That's it," Street said.

266

CHAPTER

29

Street sat in the airplane looking out over the Caribbean. In a couple of hours he would be back in Caracas. Back in the cab and back in a hotel. This time at the Embassy Suites in El Rosal.

After unpacking in his spacious room on the sixteenth floor, Street settled down at the bar with a beer and watched the glass elevators shoot up and down the belly of the building. On the television, motorcycles zoomed about in a race probably somewhere not in Venezuela but more likely in the Middle East. People seated at several tables scattered about the restaurant glowed in candlelight. Couples sat and spoke quietly to each other. Businessmen and women strolled in and sat down and ordered drinks. A few stared at their phones in silence, the blue-white light from their screens highlighted their faces from the soft background of candlelight. In the corner, a man was setting up speakers, amps, and a synthesizer, while a woman set up microphones. Music would be on soon, but Street enjoyed the silence.

"Another beer?" the bartender asked.

He looked like many bartenders and waiters in Venezuela, middle-aged and clean-cut. He was professional and friendly, though he and most of his colleagues kept a distance from their patrons. Unlike in US bars, where a patron Street's age was on par socioeconomically with the bartender or waiter, in Venezuela's bars, the power distance was greater. The man, Street thought, could be brimming with anti-Americanism but kept it at bay and remained deferential and apolitical.

"Just one more. Thank you," Street replied. He drank his beer quietly, went upstairs, and went to bed.

A quick jaunt by car in Caracas can be rare, but it happened that day. Street left the safe reaches of El Rosal and headed west in surprisingly light traffic toward Miraflores Presidential Palace in the downtown area. An executive cab shuttled him down. Clean and well air-conditioned, the car zoomed heavily and with authority among the tattered buses and endless swarms of motorcycles in Caracas's normally clogged city streets.

Street liked the motorcycles. Couriers dressed in jeans, button-down shirts, and black helmets drove most of them, delivering packages and giving people rides to beat the traffic. Some, however, had a darker side. Days of riots in the past saw many swarming into wealthier neighborhoods and firing live rounds into protestors, even at the residential buildings above, polarizing the country further.

Street wondered why the driver didn't opt for the Cota Mil, a bypass expressway up along the foot of the Ávila that gave a nice view of the city below. But traffic was light along the main Libertador Highway. Street took in the sky from the cab. A prop airplane with the official Venezuelan flag descended into the small government-run airport back east near the hotel. The cab driver, who Street guessed rarely spoke to his passengers, broke the silence.

"They don't have neighborhoods like that where you're from, do they?"

Street stared at the back of the cab driver's head. He had a small cranium, largely bald save wisps of gray hair clinging to the back like fraying cobwebs. Street couldn't see his eyes, but his voice was strong and authoritative.

"Not really," Street answered.

"They're teeming with people. They want out—out of poverty," the man said.

"I realize that," Street said, staring up at the hills. Everyone does.

"You know the police won't even go up there," the driver said.

"I know." A silence passed. Both took in the hum of the car.

"You're a journalist," the cab driver said.

Street looked at the back of the driver's small orb of a head, which produced a voice from the other side that Street couldn't see. It was as if his head were a speaker of sorts, and all evidence of a face, such as eyes, a nose, and a mouth, remained fully concealed on the other side of the sphere.

"That's right."

"You're going to interview our president today," the driver continued.

"How did you know?"

"Well, not too many foreigners head toward this area of town except reporters, really. Most executives at multinational corporations here are Venezuelan or from elsewhere in Latin America, and even they are fleeing. And if you were going to interview a lawmaker, you would head to Congress. A government minister, you would most likely be interviewing the minister in charge of our finances or foreign affairs, and we've passed their offices. Since you've got a suit on, you're likely going to be interviewing someone and not going to a press conference at Miraflores, meaning if you were going to a press conference, then you would likely be based here and not staying at a hotel. You're going to the top, and there's only one person at the top there, and that's the president of Venezuela."

Street laughed and looked out the window. "Anything you want me to ask him?"

"Why not," the driver said. "Ask him how he plans to get people to care."

"To care?" Street stared at the back of the man's head. "I'm pretty sure people care."

"I mean to really care. The rich here think the people in the slums who support the president are either bought off or naively believe in his promises for a better tomorrow, but in reality, everyone is fleeing this place. Some of the rich recognize the fact that the poor here see the president as one of their own, truly acting in their well-being. But most of the rich seem to have written off the country. The poor, well, even though they've got a president who they can call their own, all they really seem to want is a perpetual door out of these slums, but they never take it."

"That's not always true," Street said.

"Yes, it is. This is my world, and it's true. Okay, some make it out, but many just want the opportunity to leave but never seem to do so when they have the chance. Many here are too beaten down to believe in a better tomorrow, so they just want immediate shots of cash to alleviate them from their current misery, all while having that perpetual door out of the slum and into a better life with a good job always open, you know, just out of sight. In the meantime, it's subsidized food, and that's when it's on the store shelves, and a string of lies and blame cast on invisible enemies. Ask him where he'll find that happy medium."

They rode in silence for a while.

"Maybe you're right," the man said, breaking the silence.

"I never said anything," Street replied.

"With nothing on the store shelves, people will be out protesting for his ouster, and his supporters will be out in the streets fighting back. It will get ugly. Not sure if that's caring or not, but you better get out of here and out soon."

A few minutes later, Street thanked the cab driver at the foot of Miraflores Palace, taking in his warning for his safety. He paid him the fare, including a tip, and took the blank receipt that he would fill in later for expenses. He made a point of not looking at the man's eyes, something he never did. He kept that voice to himself and the message it conveyed. A simple question. Are you really going to change the mindset of your country, and will you have time to do it? He'd need a lot of power to do that. He thought of Parker and Turner. Power. Did the president have enough?

Only minutes later, Street had gone through the security checks and everything else required to enter Miraflores. Like many presidential palaces, it was white, large, and full of named rooms and courtyards, only Venezuela's donned more tropical traits than its US and northern European counterparts. What did surprise Street was that the interview would take place in the Boyacá Room, one of the largest in the palace and home to major world political figures in the past. A chance of rain and a lack of cameramen from *The Gateway* cancelled a courtyard interview.

The president would be on time today. A door opened into the large stateroom, although Street knew it wasn't the president yet. You could just feel it when the door opened and a sitting president walks in. You can sense a surge of power before he or she enters, no matter how large or small the country. This time, the door opened at a quiet and slow pace, and in walked Carlos Smith.

Street stood and offered his hand to Carlos, tall and athletic as ever with a freshly shaved head and a wispy goatee. He smiled even less than he spoke although his large, moist eyes conveyed a sense of friendliness. Street always felt welcome around Carlos.

"Carlos Smith," Street said.

"Street," Carlos said. Carlos studied Street. Suit, nice digital tape recorder, and some notes and two pads of paper.

"You have half an hour. The president just asks that you stick with political and economic items. He doesn't want to raise any hackles. Don't ask him about his personal life."

It was the most Street had ever heard from Carlos. "I don't care about his personal life," Street said in response.

"Nobody does really," Carlos replied in perfect English.

"I know," Street repeated, then looked intently at Carlos. "I didn't know you spoke English?"

"Not everything is what it appears to be. Did you think I was a typical angry Latin American revolutionary, seething in some slum and spending day and night blaming all of my problems on the United States?"

"No, but I just assumed that you didn't speak English because you once told me you never traveled to the US or the UK."

"I said I never considered myself a tourist in the United States. I grew up there. My father taught economics there. Lander University in South Carolina. Small town. No Spanish around me at the time."

Street was stunned. Another thing wasn't what it seemed. Lander University. He had heard about it. Small college in a small town in South Carolina, a good school. He made a mental note to find out more about Carlos, but cast that thought aside when the doors swung open and men and women in suits raced forward. The president of Venezuela poured into the room.

"You," the president said, advancing toward Street, extending his hand. "I know you."

He gave Street a firm handshake. Hard eye contact.

"Yes, Mr. President. I used to live here in Venezuela years ago."

"Yes, we remember you. You know this country, unlike most of the media in the US. That's why you landed the interview. We don't expect to hear a lot of loaded questions and baseless horseshit like from those assholes in the opposition media. Well, welcome back. Where do you live now?"

"Back home in Miami."

The president released Street's hand. "Miami?" He shook his head. "What a place! Most of the people there hate me, but you don't look like you are from there originally. Anyway, please, over here."

Street had his picture taken by the president as is the formality with anyone granted an audience with a world leader, be it a new diplomat arriving in town to present credentials to a celebrated sports figure receiving official congratulations or a Hollywood actor off on some cause.

Silent waitstaff entered the room and served coffee. Then the interview began.

"So," Street started. "Oil. Every president of this country, yourself included, has been accused, for lack of a better term, of running a petrostate. Instead of solving fundamental problems with the economy, such as a lack of a formal labor market and creating productive, diversified sectors from either a capitalistic or socialist point of view, you throw oil money at people to stop them from complaining and fund bloated payrolls basically to buy votes. Debt builds, the currency weakens, and inflation rises, but in your case, hyperinflation is the worst in the world, and, let's face it, violence and chaos are out of hand, with many calling you not only the worst leader in Venezuela's history but at present, the worst on Earth. How do you respond to that?"

The president laughed. "Everyone demonizes me and accuses me of raping a Venezuela that was once an oasis of tranquility meticulously cared for by capitalist predecessors. You seem smart enough to know it was never the Garden of Eden everyone says it was before I took over. Let's be blunt, if things were so great, then how the hell was I ever elected? And by a landslide at that? But anyway, back to your question. Yes, Venezuela is dependent on oil. It's our chief export, and by far, our most important. We've got more reserves than anyone, and you know demand for oil is going to increase in the next few years before it eventually declines for good, which will be further out than people think. Sure, there will be slow periods along the way just like now, but China, India, and other rising powers will need it to develop in the long term, and let's face it, electric cars aren't as widespread as you think. It takes a while for these things to catch on. And refineries and petrochemical concerns will demand our crude as well. Also, the United States is still dependent on oil—your country is not going to stop consuming it anytime soon. Still, nothing lasts forever, so now to answer your question, yes, I am seeking to diversify. I have already sought to expand our farming capacity and am working on other projects as well, including tourism, once this crisis created by your country is behind us."

"What about more pressing issues? Your debt burden is high. Your shelves are empty. There's no more toilet paper or medicine. Violence is out of hand," Street said. "And tourism? For real?"

"All that's due to attacks from at home and abroad."

"Come on. We've heard this for years. The opposition and all your neighbors are ganging up on you, and they're even launching attacks to starve the people. Do you expect anyone to believe that?"

"They've withheld food in the past just to make me look bad. We'll work through all this, and after this crisis, businesses will do well here, just like many have done."

"What businesses? You've even seized farms from foreign companies and want to expand them for planting even though they aren't meant for crops. They're meant for cattle. In other words, your constituents, the poor who would ideally farm crops on these lands, cannot because it's just not doable due to floods. Plus, you've taken over all the major utilities, you've closed down media outlets, jailed opposition leaders, stacked the courts and rigged things so you'll never lose an election, all while blaming unnamed foreigners for the country's woes. Why would anyone want to invest here or do business here?"

"Oil"

"Again, that's all you got, and even that's risky here."

"Foreign investors are welcome here, and not only in the oil sector. Car companies, consumer products suppliers, and technology firms have done well—we love your smartphones, and other gadgets.

"Now let's be clear, private energy companies that used to control the oil fields here did invest money in Venezuela, but they never really pumped enough oil to really pump enough revenue back into the country's coffers. They operated on their own schedules, and their revenue streams weren't meant to help the poor when they needed it. We changed that. Today, Venezuela controls majority ownership stakes in many oil projects, yet did every foreign oil producer bail on us? No. How many foreign oil companies are still in the country today? Hmmm? Count them! One? Two? There are several oil companies operating here in Venezuela, including some from your very own country," the president replied.

"But for how long? You know better than anybody that with today's technology, it's easier to find, prospect, drill, and produce oil in ways never thought possible, in the US especially," Street said. "Plus, you have to admit that it's the big US, European, and other oil companies that have the efficiency and expertise to get the oil out of the ground in Venezuela, not the state-owned oil company due to its own lack of investment. Most of those foreign oil companies are gone, except for one or two. Plus, Middle East countries produce at cheaper costs than you do. And Texas? They are flooding the market with crude. Does anyone even need Venezuelan oil?"

"Good points. The world is awash in crude. And yes, bottlenecks lie in our capacity to refine and export our crude, which can be very heavy and may face unique economic challenges when it comes to production. But let's face it, and with billions of people coming out of poverty, there will always be a need for products derived from oil. Plus, refineries in the southern US are tweaked to burn Venezuelan crude. You still need us." The president crossed his arms.

"And you still need the United States." Street leaned forward.

The president paused. He uncrossed his arms and sat up straight. Fists planted firmly in his thighs, making him look like a powerful gorilla standing his ground. "Venezuela needs good business ties with the empire.

Everybody does. Firm oil prices benefit all, including parts of the US. Not sky-high prices, but firm prices."

Street stared at the president. Then he focused on a large portrait of the man who liberated Venezuela and a good chunk of the northern half of South America, Simón Bolívar. Bolívar seemed to stare back at the interview, seemingly disapproving of both the North American reporter and the large Venezuelan president.

"Mr. President, you've run up massive debts funding social programs that never led to improved productivity by giving oil away and making loans to other countries in the region that most say are designed to buy friends away from Washington. You're also stockpiling weapons while store shelves are short of basic goods all the time. Even beer is out of reach. So if oil prices do dip further, your debt burdens and foreign reserves may get dangerous with less oil money trickling in."

"Prices won't stay too low for very long. They won't soar, but they will stabilize soon."

Street smiled and shook his head. "How can you be sure? Have you seen the latest Chinese manufacturing indices? Have you seen the latest global supply numbers? Nobody can be sure."

"We're pretty sure. Sure, oil prices will go down at times, and we'll feel a pinch here and there, but prices will bounce back as well."

Street and the president went on and on. They covered more on Venezuela's oil reserves, relations with foreign countries, and, of course, relations with the United States.

"So," Street began, sensing the interview was hitting a plateau. Time to get anything out of him, especially on weapons. Nothing the president said so far was earth-shattering. Street wasn't sure why he agreed on such short notice to speak with an American reporter. "Would you say you are an enemy of the United States?"

"Definitely not," the president said, leaning back in his chair. He checked his watch.

"Would you say the United States sees Venezuela as an enemy?"

"I would say some in the government there do, especially by backing people who want to oust me from office, but the people don't. You know we've shipped heating oil at discount to poorer communities in the northeastern United States during winter."

"Yes, but that was a long time ago, and most argue that move was based on politics, and also it was convenient for you when oil prices were sky-high."

"Again, oil prices will go back up eventually."

"So to rephrase an earlier question, Venezuela has long been dependent on oil exports. What can you do differently? Your oil money is dwindling and your problems are mounting, and that's economists talking, not me. How do you respond to that?"

"Private companies are welcome in Venezuela, but they have to invest here on agreeable terms and make sure oil money trickles down to the people of this country," the president said, laughing. "And I know that I just said trickle down," he added.

"Just like in my country. To cut taxes or not cut taxes, to spend or not to spend. Your country is more polarized than the US. How do you get people to care? Can there ever be a happy medium between the opposition and your supporters? It looks like winner takes all from everywhere else in the world."

"I think there can be a happy medium, more than you would think. It'll take some time. I speak with local business leaders on the issue."

"Any you'd like to name?"

"Not on record. But mainly wealthy Venezuelans who back the opposition, executives and such."

"Okay. On top of social programs, where else will you spend?"

The president looked Street in the eye. "Infrastructure has to improve. We need new roads, highways, ports, and airports. And not just for us but for all of South America. Brazil needs ports on Venezuela's coast to boost its trade ties with the world, and we can help. Like I said earlier, we want to develop our tourism industry more. We've got incredible beaches here all along the southern Caribbean, which are free of hurricanes. But there're no roads leading to many of them, and their power and water supplies are too inadequate for real development. Obviously, manufacturing is on the list as well. We've got to improve there, and I am sure on your list of questions are our military outlays. We've been modernizing our equipment and diversifying away from the United States. If your country—"

"I'm not here representing the US government but rather *The Gateway*," Street cut in.

"I know that. Anyway, the United States doesn't want to sell arms to Venezuela or even to its allies in the region, which I can understand. Any country that has the best toys isn't going to want to share them. But Venezuela has to protect itself. Terrorists operate all across the world, and the threat of war is constant. Governments can't control conflict that much, but they do have some control as to where that conflict takes place."

Street thought of the Russian naval base he'd read about, the one the president announced not too long ago.

"So why the Russians? Why build a new port for them? I mean I know they control oil assets here, but wouldn't it make sense in Venezuela's case from a military point of view to focus on building rapid-response teams to deal with drug traffickers and terrorists crossing the border from Colombia, and build ports that focus on trade and even tourism over military matters?"

"We have those programs in place. We need to defend our coastline, one of the longest in the Caribbean. Plus, we need foreign investment, as you have so repeatedly pointed out. And the Americans have and will continue to try to topple my government and meddle in our country."

"Do you have evidence of that," Street said, leaning forward. "You've been saying things like that for years."

The president glanced at his watch, as if he were admiring it, not checking out the time.

Street tried to catch the brand of the timepiece. Looked like a Swiss Army watch, but he wasn't sure.

"Do you really think Americans are going to attack?"

"Their president won't rule it out."

"Why would they do that? It would mess up world oil markets and cause a quagmire in their own backyard. And why the Russians? Are you trying to provoke the United States, as some say by having that port you announced in Sucre State?"

"No. There's a business component as well. Russia needs more military presence, and it also wants to sell some of its military hardware, which Venezuela needs to buy. Besides, your government—"

"You mean the United States government."

"Yes, the United States doesn't want to help us modernize the equipment that Washington sold us in the past. So, it's a natural fit with the Russians."

"The Russians will help modernize your military?" Street paused, and the Venezuelan president remained quiet. "Anyway, will Russian ships be patrolling the Caribbean in greater numbers?"

"They're patrolling the Caribbean anyway. They'll just dock at the new complex, which could also house Venezuelan ships. Plus, it will create jobs as well, private sector jobs especially. Everyone says I'm out to get the private sector when in reality, I'm trying to help it. Case in point."

Street looked at his notes and talking points. This was good stuff, but not really new. Time to move on to something else. Just one more question on this topic, Street thought. A nothing question to wrap up the base. Ask anything.

"When will groundbreaking take place?"

"We'll announce a timeline soon. The port falls in line with the other construction projects, all part of our new power structure in the region," the president said, and then took a sip of his coffee.

"What other projects?" Street asked, peering up from his notes. "Military projects?"

"Well, you know, other projects. There's always something going on," the president said, not looking Street in the eye and taking another sip of coffee.

Street stared at the president. It didn't take a journalist's experience or police interrogation training to know the president spewed something out he shouldn't have or was dropping some sort of not-so-subtle hint. Time to find out.

"Are there other Russian activities in the country besides this port? An air base?"

"All in time. And we deal with everyone."

"Everyone? So I think I hear you. You've got new military suppliers on board who aren't from Russia, right?"

The president laughed. "We've got operations and suppliers everywhere. We're here, we're there. We're everywhere. Iran is even sending us materials to help repair our refinery on the Paraguaná peninsula."

Press staff and a few aides began to murmur in the back. One woman interrupted. "Perhaps we should take a break. Get some water."

"No need for that," the president said.

"You and Iran?"

"It's no secret. We need to repair our refinery there, and Iran is a natural partner to help us. We are both under sanctions from the United States, so Tehran is sending us materials on Mahan Airlines to restart the refinery. That's the extent of our relationship."

"Are you planning to develop other military projects? With Russia, Iran, or anyone else? Are you going to, let's say, set up missiles here in Venezuela?"

"When it comes to missiles, we'll have plenty of capabilities to take drug squads out."

"Are you going to develop a new military base with foreign partners near the Colombian border or even elsewhere?"

"No," the president said. "We're not going to build an outright base near Colombia, but you should be the first to know that we are considering installing intermediate-range missile technology on our borders to protect ourselves against narcotraffickers."

"Intermediate-range missiles? From where? The Middle East? North Korea?"

"That's classified."

"Not anymore. Won't you fear a response from Colombia? The United States?"

"They should encourage my decision. They accuse Venezuela of being too soft on guerrillas and drug lords or even smuggling drugs themselves, which is a lie."

"I was going to get there. Everyone says you let your military brass smuggle drugs out of your country to enrich themselves and stay loyal to you, even if their troops starve."

"Again, not true. I reject that."

"Fine," Street said. "So what kind of missiles?"

"Details are being worked out. I don't want to disclose those details, but they're intermediate-range missiles to take out enemies of both Venezuela and the United States."

"Are you thinking long-range missiles? Intercontinental? Are you going nuclear?"

"No nukes, yet."

"Not yet? So you won't rule out nukes."

"We will never rule out having nuclear weapons on our soil. Just none for now. Well, we will have Russian subs on our shores, so yes, we will be nuclear, in a sense. And when it comes to long-range missiles, we'll get there eventually," the president said, sitting up in his chair. "In fact, let me rephrase myself. Venezuela is going to put missiles on its border with Colombia and on the Caribbean coast. In the future, we'll have long-range missiles as well, possibly nuclear. Anyone who even thinks about messing with Venezuela will see its citizens, its men, women, and children wiped out, and their fertile valleys and plains will be nothing but a searing wasteland. Now, can I get any clearer than that?"

So he just hinted, and not so subtly so, at going nuclear. Nice, Street thought. Recreate the Cuban Missile Crisis. That worked out well. Anyway, he's crying out for attention. Let's just entertain him.

"Are the Russians involved in this, with these missiles?"

"Not with missiles but with the port. We'll do the missiles on our own. Maybe the Russians can help out, I don't know. And we're not going nuclear, for now, ourselves I mean. At least not yet. But we'll get there."

Unbelievable, Street thought. Is this guy doubling down on going nuclear?

"Okay, so let me get this straight. The Russians are helping you build a port, but they aren't giving you the missiles that are apparently on the way here. Correct?"

"Correct."

"Are you saying this to pump up oil prices? This is saber-rattling on steroids. Or is this a plan to deflect attention away from the protests, hyper-inflation, and chaos out there?"

"Nope," the president said.

"How much are you going to spend?"

"Don't have a figure."

"Are missiles already here?"

"No."

"There are no missiles here."

"Not yet."

Street saw Hernán Bernal, the foreign minister, standing under the portrait of Simón Bolívar. The elder statesman lowered his head and clenched his jaw. The man's hands were shaking. The president was dropping bombshells left and right, and in a messy fashion at that, without even consulting his most trusted advisors, including the most experienced and knowledgeable member of his government. That much was obvious to Street. Run with it, Street thought. Screw the time limit. The president is using this interview to threaten the Colombians and the United States, or something. Plus he needed to find out why this bombshell was necessary for Brent's plans. You can't be prepared for this. You always know news can blindside you at any moment, and that moment is right now. The best thing you can do is rely on your experience. Ask questions. Fire away. Start off with the money.

"What advice has your cabinet given on this? How much are you going to invest in these missile defense systems?"

"We're working that out."

"How far can they go?"

"Far."

"What do you mean *far*? To Bogotá? To Miami? Farther?"

"Anywhere danger threatens Venezuela."

"Any plans to develop homegrown nuclear technology?"

"None yet. Purely conventional, but of course we can never rule out enriching uranium right here."

Wow, Street thought. "Any infrastructure in place to do that?"

"Not yet."

"Of course not. Will it be Russian?"

"Who knows?"

"Who knows?"

"We'll see."

"What if Colombia puts up antimissile defense systems?" Street asked.

"Let them."

"How many missiles?"

"Enough. I don't know. I'll let my military advisors decide on that. But you can quote me on this, Venezuela is arming itself to the teeth and won't blink an eye at striking out at any threat—real or perceived."

Yeah, like that's going to happen, Street thought. He just told the press of his plans. Now there were no secrets. This guy was a liar, and not even a good one. Time to call his bluff. But what's he covering up? Street had no idea. He left the interview confused. An idiot in power invited a small-time reporter to his palace just to insult his intelligence.

Screw him, Street thought. He's in with Brent somehow. That he knew. The interviews were part of Brent's plans. This president was going down as well. Street promised himself that.

CHAPTER

30

Hernán Bernal quietly ducked out of the room, pretty sure he was suffering a minor heart attack, though he brushed it off. No time for cardiac arrest. Time for damage control, and he would need some help with that. Not only was the president shooting off at the mouth and dropping hints at things the cabinet, including himself, knew nothing about, but there was just something about this reporter that threw him off. Why not speak to a foreign correspondent based in Caracas? He would find out about the reporter first and then berate the president in private later.

Bernal walked down a quiet hall and pulled out a cell phone. A secure one nobody knew about. He dialed a number.

"It's Bernal. The president is firing away again. Shooting off at the mouth. Now he's talking about buying missiles and hinting at going nuclear to some American reporter who works at some news outfit no one has ever heard of."

The voice on the other end asked, "What's his name, this American?"

"Brewer. Street Brewer. The magazine is called *The Gateway*. There's something odd about this publication and about him. I don't know, I can't put my finger on it, but something doesn't add up. The president made good on his call to grant an interview to an informed and as unbiased American reporter as possible, but this one came in too quickly, and the president is going off script more than I have ever seen. He's gone beyond losing touch with his own people. He's lost touch with reality."

"Street Brewer. American. Probably thirty? Blondish hair. Tall?"

"That's him. You know him?"

"Yes. I detained him not too long ago on a tip he was a drug trafficker here in the country."

"I'm not surprised, Pérez. You always do good work, wherever you are. Just get me everything you know about what may or may not be going on and follow this Street kid. Get to Miami if you have to. Something doesn't seem right. Who tipped you off?"

"Foreign intelligence sources."

"Foreign intelligence sources? Not the police or the smugglers themselves looking to throw us a decoy? That doesn't add up at all. Follow him."

Bernal hung up. Pérez was his second source to spy on what his country was up to. The first one was already on the ground in the United States.

Street left Miraflores and checked his digital, phone and cassette recorders outside. He pressed the "Play" button on each device and heard the start of the interview. All voices came in loud and clear. Even his phone picked them up. Everything checked out okay.

He called Brent.

"I just got out of the interview. Ready for a briefing?" He smirked.

"Go on," Brent said.

"We got stuff on the navy base, and he told us he's going to set up missiles along the Colombian border. I'll transcribe my notes and file shortly."

Street avoided mention of the nuclear weapons. Don't give these corrupt spies everything right up front. Make them work for it.

Brent said nothing. Street could feel him processing the information, thinking about what he'd tell his superiors in northern Virginia.

"Brent, not to point out the glaringly obvious, but I don't think he was giving any more interviews to the press today. We're exclusive for now. I'm going to file now."

"Missiles? This is huge. Are you sure he said all this? We're not misinterpreting him?"

"We got it." And you know we do, Street mused. "He went back and forth. Repeated himself. He even said the US and Colombia should support the move in that it protects everyone from narcotraffickers and terrorists. He wasn't shy about giving the middle finger to everyone."

"Any timetable as to when they'll go nuclear?"

Street smiled. Brent had knowledge of the topic beforehand.

"I never said he was going nuclear," Street said.

"I meant did he say he was going nuclear."

"He hinted at it."

"Street, this is good stuff. Send your story. We'll blast an email and put a teaser on the site about the upcoming issue in a day or so. Good job." Street hung up.

He walked off, staring at the green trees just outside of Miraflores Presidential Palace. Pedestrians passed by. Ice cream vendors strolled over the concrete, pulling their chilled carts with them, ringing their bells. A few green trees softened the city's rough edges. He walked down the streets of downtown Caracas feeling safe as if he were in his backyard at home. He thought about what Applewood had told him about the agency's illegal spy-gathering regime. About spending the night in a Venezuelan interrogation room. He bought an ice cream sandwich from a vendor and was about to unwrap it when he caught site of a homeless man.

"Can I have that?" the man said.

Street shrugged and handed it to the man, a very tall figure who, despite being unwashed and homeless, had surprisingly noble facial features.

"Hey, thank you. Can I have twenty dollars?" the man asked in English.

"I'm impressed. Not with your English but your spine to ask for so much. Why not?" Street said. He handed the guy a crisp twenty-dollar bill.

"Thank you," the man said.

The twenty-dollar bill seemed to shine against the man's dirty hands, his dark, filthy clothing, and his long black beard and sun-dyed mop of hair that failed to conceal the face of a statesman from some bygone century. The bill's light extinguished when the man crumpled it in his hands and shoved it in his coat pocket, an old suit coat.

"You're welcome," Street said in slow English so the man would understand, and then he walked on.

"The president is lying," Street mumbled. But I've got nothing, he thought. First a port, then missiles along the border. This is just a ruse, and not even a good one. Street turned back to the homeless man. "A ruse for what?" he said to the man.

"Thank you," the homeless man shouted in Street's wake. "Thank, you!" the man repeated himself. He looked at Street one last time.

"You have the power to do everything! The power is all around you," the man said, this time in Spanish. He turned his back to Street and walked off.

Power. There it was again. Parker and Turner had planted the power thing in his head. The president was obviously on a power trip, and the down-on-his-luck gentleman reminded him again.

Power.

Venezuela had tons of oil, and, apparently, some smuggling revenue, but true power? True global power? Right now the country had none, really, just worldwide attention on its horrific economic and humanitarian mess, with crime and inflation rates pushing apocalyptic levels.

The president had the military in his camp, but for how long? The common soldier had it tough, just like the homeless man on the street. Unrest in the barracks could be dangerous. Sooner or later, he needed fresh income, yet the president was powerless when it came to pushing up global oil prices needed to pump in money, and many of the country's economic nightmares were concocted within his own government. He had no power at all, and stashing missiles in the country wouldn't do much. Slapping some nuclear warheads on the tips might help by inviting the world to enjoy the Cuban Missile Crisis 2.0, but everyone would see that coming. Something didn't add up, especially since Brent seemed to know what the president was saying ahead of time. This whole interview was a red herring, though one thing was for sure, the president needed higher oil prices. How could he do that on his own?

Street would find out. But he'd need help, and the only way to get help is to ask for it. Time to tap an old friend. Well, not that old, really. He was only about five years older than Street. Street drew out his phone and began to text.

How's it going? Long time.

Silence.

Anyone there?

Still silence. Then his phone came to life. Someone was replying.

Street Brewer?

Yes, it is. How's Venezuela?

You have to ask? Are you here in the country?

Yes, for a day or two. Up for a drink?

You should get out. It's going to get ugly here in days. Are you living in Miami?

Yes, along with half of Venezuela's middle class.

I want to bring them back.

I want to come back as well.

Lot going on here. The president's last election was his last sham. Time for a change, and any change here will be rough.

Change? Is there a coup coming?

Street's eyes were wide. To witness a coup d'état. Now that would be something.

I can't say. There are other ways.

Such as?

No answer from his friend, a young congressman.

Street took a break from his phone.

He remembered when he had met the man a few years ago. Covering a late-night session in the national assembly. Some vote on something that had dragged on. Street forgot what it was, but he did remember it running very late. Once the vote was cast and he filed his story from his office nearby, he began a short hike to the metro, which was still open. The problem was that there were too many unsavory elements out on the street that night. Obvious criminals, prostitutes of both sexes, drug addicts, and just some outright plain weirdos were coming alive while the creatures of the day had flown home to roost. With blond hair and blue eyes, Street didn't want to be out in the streets for long. So he walked faster.

He heard footsteps. Footsteps getting closer. Street picked up his pace even more, looking like a racewalker with the finish line almost in sight. He could feel eyes on him from everyone on the street, as the creatures of the night had caught sight of someone who didn't belong. It would be a matter of seconds before they'd find out he was a foreigner. Back to the footsteps. They were next to him now, not behind him.

"Quite a night, no?" the man asked.

Street turned. There walking next to him was another professional whom he had seen before. Some junior opposition lawmaker. Didn't even know his name.

"It's out of this world," Street replied, choosing to speak in as few words as possible so his accent wouldn't give him away.

The young lawmaker darted his head left and right, up and down, taking in the surroundings and their shadows. Street could see from his pace that he was uneasy too. Even those who ran the country were afraid of it these days. The man had caught up to Street to walk with him knowing there was safety in numbers.

"Metro is just around the corner," Street said.

"I know," the young lawmaker said. "I prefer it to driving."

The two men introduced themselves with few words and exchanged business cards. Street checked out the man's political party and the man checked out Street's media outlet. Eventually they made it to the subway, though they remained in contact over the years.

Street snapped back to reality and looked back at his phone. There was a new message from the young lawmaker.

Forget moving back here. In fact, fly out now. What little bit of food and medicine you can find will be gone; protests coming. Big ones. Violent ones.

I'm just in town for an interview. Leaving anyway. What do you mean there are other ways besides a coup?

Stay tuned. Who did you interview?

Your president.

Not my president. What did he say?

Hinted at bringing missiles into the country. All kinds of shit. Even nukes. It's a ruse or a smoke screen. Care to comment on it?

There was a pause, and then the congressman responded.

No comment. I'm too junior a lawmaker to comment. Plus the opposition is fragmented, but hopefully not for long. No way nuclear missiles will happen anyway.

How can you be sure?

I've got people everywhere scouring imports and exports, and I mean eyes and ears from Venezuela and abroad.

Street thought for a second. Sure, someone could sneak in missiles undetected, but moving them around, setting them up, and keeping them ready for action would involve more and more people, and the more involved, the better the likelihood that someone would talk and word would get out. Street went back to typing.

There's always somebody who can sneak them in and others to get them ready for war.

Sneak in missiles and keep them hush-hush? For real? He can try. I may be young and inexperienced, but I am opposition. We've got friends in the military and elsewhere who can keep an eye on such things. For now, I am sure there are no missiles.

Well keep at it, Street thought. Then he texted.

I'll be in touch. I'll give you stuff if you give me stuff.

Done deal.

Street tossed his phone on the bed when he got back to the Embassy Suites in El Rosal. He sat in his room feeling a little guilty that he would spend the night in such a fine place while the rest of the country suffered. He ordered room service and tipped the young man, who was sincerely appreciative.

"Thank you," he said. "You're one of our last guests. The hotel might close up shop until things get better. They say this place will go from awful to horrific." The young man left.

Closing down, Street thought. *The Gateway* and the Placebo Agenda were doing likewise, and it was time to save Molly Wells and whoever else needed saving before then. Then he thought of Pennie Spradling, who had jumped in front of a bus not far up the road and not too long ago either. They had been part of the CIA's agenda. That awful scheme, Street thought. What was so important that the CIA had to send in placebos in order to devote itself to its real plan? He knew a recently broke Saudi was onto them, so they had to make some money to hush him up, and whatever that get-rich scheme entailed, no loose ends could be left alive. Loose ends. If they were good, there shouldn't be any loose ends. Something happened.

Street shook his head and scrolled down his list of contacts. There was Pennie and Roland Spradlings' home phone number. Time to do some intelligence work of his own, and if it didn't pan out, at least he could pay condolences to whoever answered the phone. After all, he owed Pennie that much.

He dialed from a phone he had bought before he traveled. Someone answered. A woman.

"Mrs. Burnett?" Street asked, surprised he remembered Pennie's maiden name.

"Speaking," the voice came back void of any annoyance at an unknown caller, not seeming to care.

Street understood her numbness.

"This is Street Brewer. Do you remember me?"

"I remember you, Street. I remember you long before Roland," she said. "Glad at least you made it out of that country alive."

"I just want to let you know how sorry I am. I know words won't help much, but…"

"It helps, Street. Thank you. What can I do for you?"

Street paused. Now what? He didn't exactly have a plan. He didn't want to outright tell Pennie's grieving mom that her daughter and son-in-law were caught up in a murderous espionage plot. But he needed to bust Brent and save Molly Wells, and maybe Mrs. Burnett could help. Time to get the most out of her while not letting her catch on. I'm getting good at this spy racket, Street thought.

"I'm just calling to say I'm sorry. Also, I am a reporter in the end, so I want to find out what exactly happened. What—"

"What made her jump in front of a bus? Naked, in some unfamiliar area of Caracas? Your guess is as good as mine. Can we switch to video conferencing?"

In a couple of minutes, Street was looking Catherine Burnett in the eye. She had youthful, blonde hair, like her daughter's, though a little shorter. Big blue eyes that flared with a brief spark when she saw Street, though they went blank with grief when talk of Pennie returned.

"This doesn't seem like an express kidnapping. It's not random. Was Roland working on anything that may have created enemies?"

"It wasn't random. You're the first person I've heard say that," she said, her voice flat and apathetic. Her facial expression showed she could take no more sadness, anger, or confusion, and had therefore dumped all emotion out of her body, leaving her hollow, before she could refill her strength and drive.

Street paced about the hotel room, then looked out the window. A protest appeared to be organizing up the road, a peaceful march. Crowds with flags, banners and posters were gathering in the street.

"I don't think for a second that this double murder was random. They were targeted. But for the life of me, I can't figure out why," she said. "I've asked everyone in the hemisphere."

"Me neither. I'm guessing you got little help from the authorities there?"

"They say it was street crime and to just read the news about the country's violence. But suicide over street crime?"

"They're wrong," Street said.

"Tell me something I don't know."

"Was there anything out of the ordinary at work?" Street was asking questions to which he already had answers. "Any weird travel or assignments?"

"Pennie did notice he was traveling more."

"To where? Russia or someplace like that?"

"No. To the United States."

"That doesn't seem that altogether weird."

"No, but to Miami? It's not exactly an oil-and-gas industry hub."

"I see," Street said. "Forgive me if I sound rude, but—"

"Be rude. I'm sick of sympathy. I want action, and action isn't always nice," she said. Her eyes narrowed. "You knew Pennie better than I did, so speak your mind."

"Do you think Roland or Pennie were mixed up in narcotics, perhaps not knowing it?"

"I've thought about that. That idiot president down there needs every dime he can get, and smuggling drugs might inject some revenue into his coffers. But drugs? Roland?"

"It's possible," Street said.

"Not really sure what Roland could do. Launder money, I guess. He wouldn't know how to do that, though. And I seriously doubt he smuggled anything himself."

"What was he doing in Miami?"

"He came to visit us, of course. Most of the time here, he was fishing. We live in Coral Gables, you'll recall. As far as work is concerned, I don't know."

"No clue where he went? Anything odd?"

"Not really," she said.

Street looked out the window again. The protest was building, almost ready to advance. The crowd had converged and begun to assemble in order. He focused back on the conversation at hand.

"Why do you think he went to Miami? What was the purpose of his business trips?"

"Meetings, mainly."

"Why not Houston?"

"They did a lot of fishing trips here, for business purposes, I imagine. Miami is good for that, and it's close to Venezuela. I don't know, Street. I don't think the location of their meeting was an issue. All I want to know is who killed them and why. Don't you? You know you let Pennie get away. I'm sure you've gotten over her by now, but maybe if you solve all of this, you can put to rest whatever weakness was inside you that let her get away in the first place."

"That's what I'm trying to figure out." He thought of Pennie, and then quickly brought himself down from the clouds and back to reality. He looked at Catherine. He saw that she had waited patiently while Street had drifted into his memories before he refocused.

"I'm gonna take care of some personal issues and also bring a little justice into this messy situation," Street said. "I'm a reporter, after all."

Tensing lips and a slight eye roll let Street know she wasn't buying it or lacked faith that he would get anywhere, but then she focused. Maybe he was her last chance.

"What do you need from me?" she asked.

"Anything. An address where he went in Miami?"

"Can't help you there," she said.

"Pictures."

A quick flash returned to her eyes. "I do have a picture of him on a fishing trip while he was here with coworkers. It was our boat, after all."

"Send them to me."

A few seconds later Street was viewing them. There was Roland posing beside a large sailfish. A big smile, completely unaware he'd end up like the fish—dead and on display for his killers to see.

"That's nice, but it doesn't help. Anything else?"

"Well, I did book him an Uber while he was here. We were short on cars that day. Want the address?"

"Please," Street said.

A second later, he had it. He knew it well. It was the address to *The Gateway*. Give me something I don't know already, he thought. Clever of Brent to bring another placebo into the office when Street was out. But it didn't really help.

"Oh, and there's one more photo," she said. "Hang on . . ."

A few seconds later, Street was staring at Roland Spradling alongside a sailfish next to Brent Drum and a massive man with curly black hair and really short shorts. Behind them all, smiling at the camera, one hand on Roland's shoulder, stood another man with a stern expression on his face.

"Interesting," Street said.

"Problem? Or are you onto something? I think that hard-hearted, older man was the one who they hired to drive the boat."

"When I get to Miami, do you think I can check out the boat? It may be the scene of a pretty big crime."

"As you wish. But it rarely left Florida waters. Maybe once to Bimini, which is only forty miles away. Not sure how many kilos of drugs it ran."

CHAPTER

31

Cyra Harred soared up the Sabas Nieves hiking trail on the Ávila National Park overlooking Caracas. The worn earth beneath her feet and the green trees overhead flooded her senses with smells of nature and fertility lost in the chaos of the city. The climb wasn't overall that difficult, just steep and grueling at times. Still, it served as the perfect morning workout for many before heading off to the office.

Puffy white clouds passed over Caracas while Cyra ran up the trail, shooting past dozens of morning hikers huffing and puffing, shaking their heads at the energy in her legs. She enjoyed their reactions. In fact, she was fascinated by people, always had been. They woke up, downed some coffee, and then plodded through the day pushing papers and going through the motions for someone in power, be it a government, a company, or even a demanding spouse. And that was true everywhere, yet people still found something to make them happy, like a morning hike up a trail. Yep, she thought that morning, people were the same across the globe. No one community of people was cold and the other passionate. To think one ethnicity lacked the same range of emotions compared to another was ignorant in her eyes—emotion is universal; expression of it is cultural.

Cyra gripped five-pound weights. Five pounders were perfect for doing curls as she ran up. At thirty-four, Cyra was fitter than she had ever been. She was tall and muscular, with the big, shapely legs of an ice skater. Hard abs. The works. She had a bodybuilder's physique without crossing over into obsessive-compulsive muscular overkill.

About an hour later, after reaching the Sabas Nieves rest area, which was still low when it came to the height of the overall mountain, Cyra took in a quick view of Caracas, which seemed quiet and calm from a distance. A few stragglers were doing dips and pull-ups on nearby bars, while others were enjoying their rest at the ranger's station before heading back down to where the weekday grind would begin, that is, for those lucky enough to have work and income.

Cyra took a sip of water from a fountain and then turned right around and bolted down the hill, which was much easier. No resting at all. Good for the muscles over the knees. She pumped the five-pound weights as she passed people with mouths dropped open in disbelief. All the men turned their heads to check her out as she shot down the hill. A few women did as well. She hit the bottom of the mountain, which wasn't too far from the Plaza Altamira, and was home shortly afterward. She showered and was ready for work before seven in the morning.

A few hours later, she was walking down the hall of the US-Venezuelan Cultural Center, where she taught English classes as a cover for the CIA. The building looked like a learning center in any corner of the world, from a large public school to an older wing at an exclusive prep school in the US to a remote missionary in some far corner of the wilds of Africa. The bell rang, and she opened the door. Even though all the students were adults, there was still that childlike expression they all gave the teacher, even when wrinkles and gray hairs surrounded eager, peering eyes. A few stragglers came in and took their seats.

She went to the front of the room. "Good morning, class."

"Good morning Miss Williams," they all answered. For them, she was Lakshmi Williams, an English teacher originally from Georgetown, Guyana. She passed it off well, a trait she learned in life as well as in her career in the CIA. She could pull off any identity when need be, thanks to her long dark hair, golden caramel skin and especially her eyes. She had blue-green eyes that glowed like aquatic moons drifting in some cosmic ring. She could be from anywhere she wanted. In her career, she'd assumed the identity of a

Roman gypsy, an upper-class Italian twenty-something, and even a Pathan hooker once.

She sat on a stool before a small podium mounted on a desk. She set her books and stack of papers down, and looked at her class. Most were in their twenties and thirties. A couple in their forties and fifties. One man with bushy hair, a gentleman from Russia, who was sitting in the back, was probably in his mid-fifties and likely the oldest in his class. Cyra stared at the man briefly, the man she knew as Peter Bogdanov, though the class knew him as Max. He stared back at her, calmly, blinking slowly like a noble zoo animal. Time to begin her composition class, teaching on the one hand and handling a prized Russian asset on the other.

"Class, I'm very pleased with your writing skills. In the short story I assigned to you for reading, I asked you to figure out what the couple was talking about. All of the papers were well written, and almost everybody concluded what the man and woman were discussing."

She pulled out the stack of papers. "The author was a master. While he doesn't directly say what the couple is talking about, you can conclude from the words that the characters use what's going to happen. He's apparently prodding a reluctant girl to get an abortion at a time and place where abortions were illegal. The power of the story is the minimalism, and its subtlety. Only one name is mentioned in the story. The man is known only as the American, who coerces the young girl to do something she doesn't want to. Quite a powerful trait," she said, looking at Bogdanov, who continued to calmly stare back.

"Anyway, I have your papers. Kudos to those of you who caught on. You'll notice a sea of green ink. I don't use red ink to correct papers. When people use red ink, it looks like they are yelling at the writers. Don't worry if there are lots of corrections. It doesn't necessarily reflect on your ability to write in English, and some of my notes are suggestions as opposed to outright corrections. Everyone who writes needs an editor. It's often hard to catch your own mistakes or weak sentence structure." Cyra passed out the papers.

The students snatched them to see how they did, a rush that never goes away, from first grade to death. That stamp of approval. That gold star.

Cyra, aka Lakshmi Williams, went on, handing out the papers over the rising din of noise of students flipping pages to see commentary and errors.

"A friend of mine once worked at a large agricultural business magazine in the US, at what's known as a trade publication. They had a slew of editors—"

"A slew?" a student asked.

Cyra smiled. "They had many editors on staff to look for mistakes," she said, winking at the student who inquired as to the meaning of *slew*. "Fact-checking and editorial work aside, some three to five people viewed each and every story before they went to print. The owner, who never saw the copy until after it hit the newsstands, would show up at the editor-in-chief's office each month after publication finding a typo here and another tiny error there. So to fix the situation, the editor-in-chief came up with an idea: find someone who knows nothing about the subject matter, nothing about agribusiness or farming or anything at all about the industry, and have them take a quick glance at the copy at the very last stage, even after the editor-in-chief himself signs off on it. The idea being that someone knowing little to nothing about the agriculture industry would not get absorbed in the copy, and would therefore see the errors jumping off the page. The owner suggested his teenage daughter. She surely didn't know anything about agribusiness, or pretty much anything about business at all. Plus, she'd do it for free," Cyra continued, coming closer to the rear corner desk where Bogdanov was sitting.

"Well, the editor-in-chief handed the teenage girl the final drafts. The magazine complete with all the ads and all the artwork ready to go, the way it'd appear in print. He gave her a pen and told her to have at it. Go for it. Look for errors. We hope you find them, the editor would tell her. Surely enough, at the end of every month, she would find the tiniest of errors, normally a verb tense that could easily be overlooked or some misspelling that got past human eyes and the spell checker. Sometimes the autocorrect would put in the wrong word, like *overseas* when the word should have been *oversees*, or often, an extra space would pop up between words. Man and machine often see what they want to see. They fill in the gaps and overlook tiny little errors that can be fatal," she said, staring at Bogdanov. "But, our little teenage girl would always find a couple of errors, and it was because what she didn't know made her such a valuable asset," Cyra said as she reached Bogdanov.

She handed him his paper. He looked at it, in a much calmer manner compared to the other students, taking it from her almost gingerly, turning the pages slowly, the way a doctor does before entering a waiting room to see a patient.

"That said, we are going to try a new exercise today. We are going to edit a document." She walked back to the podium and grabbed another stack of papers. A neat pile, fresh off the printer.

"This is a copy of a story from my friend's agribusiness magazine from many years ago. It's about a Brazilian food giant expanding into the US. Anyway, copy edit this story. Look for errors, misspellings—whatever. Let's see if you can find anything and beat our fearless teenage daughter at her own game." She handed each a copy and off they went to work.

The room went quiet with soft background noises. Bangs of pens against the desks. The swoosh of legs being crossed. A murmur here and there. A soft clearing of the throat.

She knew there were two or three errors in there. Her friend told her where they were. One was obvious—a misspelled word that jumped out. She watched some of the students catch it and move on.

"Make notes if you want. Ask questions. The point here is to learn," Cyra said.

A few eyes darted up as she spoke. A pretty woman with golden blonde hair in her early to mid-twenties, wearing blue jeans and a nice white blouse kept her gaze on Cyra, a gaze of suspicion, competition, and admiration rolled into one, and then went back to work.

Bogdanov made a note and then closed his paper. When all were finished, Cyra collected the papers and put them in her bag.

"Now for some conversation," she said.

The class relaxed.

Cyra picked fun and playful conversation games for her class to complement her writing assignments and give the students a chance to speak as opposed to write all the time. Today they'd talk about the US holiday of Halloween and whether it was silly or not. Even Bogdanov perked up.

A few hours later, immediately after work and just before a CrossFit class followed by a heavy workout with weights at the gym in order to maintain her cover, Cyra rushed to her El Rosal apartment building right next to the Caracas Stock Exchange. A few posh hotels catering to business travelers and some office buildings under a green canopy sprinkled the area. She closed the blinds and took out the stack of edited agribusiness papers. She flipped through them and found Bogdanov's copy. He had caught all the errors. Then there was something heavy. At the bottom of his report was a small flash drive taped to the paper. She took it, slid it into her computer and read its contents. Then she erased all and threw the drive in her purse, where it would be safe until properly destroyed. Then she grabbed her phone and dialed.

"Hi. Cyra here," she said after a voice answered. "Our Russian asset came through. He told us the Venezuelan president doesn't care if the Russians build a naval port or, get this, an air base on La Orchila Island. What really threw Bogdanov a curveball was the president's indifference as to where the military base goes and on top of that, the urgency in which the president wants Russian presence. Bogdanov wants to work with us, meaning Washington and Moscow collaborate to find out what the president is hiding, and if Bogdanov senses Caracas is hiding something, then Caracas is definitely hiding something. He also stressed the president is so confident he'll stay in power that he said he'd start giving interviews to US media to talk about his military plans, something the Russians probably need to sign off on. He'll keep an eye on Street and dump some bogus intel on the young reporter that Brent will extract. Let me stress that Bogdanov is done with Brent. I told that bushy-haired Russian that Brent is killing these kids, and he was horrified. We've got the Russians on our side now."

She hung up.

CHAPTER

32

B ernal approached the president after Street left. There was always that
sense of relief once an interview wrapped up. When the reporter left, it
was time to think about how the story would play out. Time to think about
what the president had said, what he shouldn't have said, what questions were
loaded, and what messes were diverted.

"You can't fight moving water, but you can channel it," Bernal said.

"What?" the president said.

"Nothing. Good job today with that reporter. He'll get a good story.
Speaking of which," Bernal said, pausing and looking around. "Everybody
out. I'd like a moment alone with the president."

A few staffers hurried out making little sound. Bernal could sense them
breathing easier now and pulling out their cell phones and going about their
daily routines. The door closed.

"Is there something you want to tell me? Am I still part of this administration?" Bernal asked the president.

The president just stared at him.

"Why would you drop a bombshell like that?" Bernal asked.
"Announcing plans to stock up on missiles? Oh, and by the way, what missiles? Nothing is final. And what goddamn nukes?"

"Why not," the president shrugged. He walked by Bernal, bumping into
his shoulder. "Word will get out about any of our plans anyway. Hell, before

they crank up the trucks to haul the missiles down there, if we ever even get them, the whole world is going to know about our plans."

"Yes, but Mr. President, you can't just go around dropping bombs like that without consulting the right people, me especially. And hinting at nukes? I'm not even going to start on uranium. The Russians are not going to give it to you, and there's even less than a zero chance that they'll help you enrich any fuel sources. Nobody will. Iran doesn't even have it."

The president shrugged. "It will all be fine. The Russians benefit from high oil prices that will come from all this saber-rattling anyway. They have plenty of oil themselves."

"There are rules and protocols to this sort of thing, both written and unwritten. Not only does today's interview make you come across as a shoot-from-the-hip demagogue, but sooner or later, oil markets aren't going to roil on your words anymore, especially when some kid from a tiny publication calls you out."

The president began to pace.

"What do you care? You want us to remain some backwater country that nobody cares about forever? And don't fucking patronize me! You don't think I know that we're broke and in chaos? You don't think I know that we're dependent on that crap we drill out of the ground? Better to be controversial or even a loudmouth than a nobody."

"When was the last time you heard the American president mention your name?"

"What?"

"I said, when was the last time you heard the American president mention your name?"

"I don't know. Yesterday!"

"He hasn't publicly mentioned your name or acknowledged any of your rants lately! All he does is calmly support the opposition. Because of you, we are some backwater country."

The president paced around. Then he stopped. Glared at Bernal.

"He'll be mentioning my name soon enough. And let's remember who's the only one in the damn hemisphere that's standing up against the Americans right now. Me!" The president shouted. "Who used to be a rebel?

You. But that was decades ago. But who's in charge now? Me! Who got elected? Me! Who are scholars branding as the new kind of elected strongman for Latin America? Me! I'm in charge here, not you! You're just a goddamn nice guy who everybody says should be by my side but nobody really respects. In fact, before I came along, you were a nobody in Congress selling off our steel mills, aluminum plants, and other companies to appease your Washington masters. Now fall in line, do as you're told and do what's good for the cause!"

Bernal stared at the president. Got in his face. Nostrils flaring. Blood pressure soaring.

"Cause? What cause? We throw money at our problems and do a half-assed job of dealing with them later. Yes, I went along with Washington consensus but fought hard to make damn sure every last worker was going to be protected when the US was thriving and Russia was caving. You don't fucking believe in ideology, do you? There's no socialism versus capitalism anymore, at least as you see it. That's all just window dressing used on both sides, something to drum up support among what-have-you-done-for-me-lately voters, but you're just too fucking stupid to realize it. We're a petrostate, just as we've always been."

"I know that!" The president fired back. "That's what that gringo reporter was just saying. I'll tell you what else is true. When you're dead and buried, I'll still be running the show here, and everyone here and abroad is going to know who I am!"

"Running the show? Now just a goddamn moment—you're not running shit. You're just a figurehead, the winner of a popularity contest, and if the truth be told, Mr. President, you're an idiot who answers to other countries who set global prices, not us. You don't know the first thing about fiscal policy, monetary policy, foreign policy, or any policy. You're a fraud. You've forgotten your roots. You don't even know your own country."

"I know each and every person in Venezuela who either voted for me or wants me dead. I will take care of them all. And I'm a fraud? I'm the real thing! I'm a trained soldier!" the president countered.

"Have you even stared a US-trained Venezuelan soldier in your cross-hairs? Have you ever pulled the trigger not on a foreign enemy but on your own blood? Have you ever pulled the trigger on anyone, taken the life of another human being? I have, and I don't think you've got what it takes. You want what everyone else across the planet wants these days—instant gratification. No paying any dues. No hard skills. Just an entitled piece of crap like anyone else these days. Fuck you and your republic. The last memory the people will have of you is how hard you cried when the country forced you out of office."

Bernal stormed off. So did the president.

A few minutes later, the president was in his favorite office. Not his official office, just a stockroom in the government palace, a quiet closet packed with office supplies that he referred to as his true office, his private world. He liked being alone in the small, quiet room. Sort of like being in trouble as a kid. Once berated and sent to a room, all a kid had to do was think, let his imagination run wild, and enjoy the soft sounds of solitude with the wrath of punishment behind him. He drew a breath, relaxed, and calmed his nerves. Then the young brunette woman entered the room. She shut the door quietly behind her, and the president smiled.

"Time to get grilled again. This will be twice in one day. First by my political science professor, Bernal, and now by the folks who've really got my balls in a vice," he said.

"Another call?" she asked.

"Yes," the president said. He let out a long sigh. Then the young woman reached into the pockets of her tight white jeans and retrieved a cell phone, untraceable to the president. He looked at his watch. Five to four in the afternoon. It was early but close enough. For once, he wouldn't be late to a call.

"I'm in charge here," he whispered.

The woman dialed, and the president of Venezuela mumbled to himself again. "If things go wrong, I take the fall, not Hernán. It's my name out there. I'm the president. I run this place."

The young woman quietly put a finger on the president's lips and then put the phone on speaker and held it up for him to listen. A copper mesh covered the confines of the closet, turning the little room into his own private Faraday cage complete with other technologies that shielded him from prying eyes. US spy technology wouldn't be picking up the president's voice today. Nobody would. He'd keep quiet.

A couple of beeps chirped from the phone and a woman's voice in English said something.

The young brunette said something back.

"Who is on the call now?" the president said.

"There's the woman from Langley," the brunette said, burying the phone in her chest. "Try not to speak too close to the phone. Just in case they have technology we don't know about, which they probably do. We don't want them hearing your voice."

Another beep. One more person joined the conference call.

The president didn't catch the name of the woman from the Langley area, but it didn't matter. He knew who she was.

Then another voice chirped in, and the president knew this voice very well.

"Good afternoon, Mr. President," the gentleman said in native Spanish. "I'll translate for our friend in Langley."

The president nodded.

"Okay, *papi*," the woman said.

The president smirked and then shook his head.

"Are we alone? Secure lines?" the man's voice said in perfect English to the woman in Langley.

"Yes, it's just the three of us. These lines are clean. No drones listening in either. No wiretaps. No eavesdropping of any kind. I should know because I would be the one responsible for such a move."

"Good. I'll start off right now in Spanish. If you need help, just ask."

"Thanks, but I should be okay. Remember, I spent some time in the Peace Corps in Central America," the American woman in Langley said.

The president remained quiet. He understood the gist of what they were saying. Let's just get this over with, he thought.

"Well, Mr. President, you've managed to fuck up a perfectly good plan," the gentleman said. "Did I not make it clear to you that you were to wait until after the delivery to tell the press you are going to arm yourself to the teeth? My people were in that room for the interview. I know everything you said."

I'm in charge here, the president thought.

"And you in Langley, young lady," the gentleman said. "Did I not make it clear that I wanted all placebos dead and buried? Why is the president of Venezuela leaking information to a reporter who, by the way, happens to be a placebo? What in God's name is he doing in Venezuela, much less still alive? Should I send Ricardo to deal with you too?"

The young lady replied. "Sir, it's Karen. We needed Street to get the interview with the president to keep Brent entrenched at the magazine because it was threatening to fold. We need that magazine up and running to execute the second phase of the Placebo Agenda. Plus, there's the fact that Street is still soaking up intelligence each and every minute he's in the country. You never know what could fly in over the transom. Still, we are going to eliminate him."

"Brent still could have done the interview! I don't like it. I don't like it one goddamn bit!" the gentleman said. "A reporter breaks a story on missiles in Venezuela and then gets killed! Oh no, that won't attract unwanted attention! What the fuck kind of operation are you running up there? Make sure he dies while he's still in Venezuela. *The Gateway* can publish the story posthumously, and then we all move on to phase two."

Silence.

"And you, Mr. President," the gentleman resumed. "You better get with the fucking program, or I'll make your life a living hell, and you know I can. Make sure our deliveries are in order before you go spouting off like that. Goddamn Venezuelan government and the CIA can't do a fucking thing right! That's so typical of the public sector no matter where you go. Big corporations should be given free rein over the global economy, and everyone would benefit. Here's how this is going to play out. Like I said, the reporter is in Caracas now. He's going to die now. The only way he makes it back to the US involves his remains packed in a box. That should be easy in Venezuela, because the place is a crime-ridden shithole, but be sure to make his death believable. Just pay some glue-sniffing street child ten dollars to walk up to him and shoot him. Then we kill the street child and get our ten dollars back. Done. From here on out, here is what I want you to do. Grab a pen and paper because I want you both to write down verbatim what I am going to say. You two are so inefficient that, well, I can't even put it in words. So here's how this is going to work out."

Silence.

"Hello! Are you with me?"

"We hear you, Mr. Juan Vicente Domínguez," Karen said.

"Good. Now listen up!"

CHAPTER

33

The conversation ended and the brunette put the cell phone back into her pocket. She looked up at the president, who kept his head hung low. He reached into her jeans pocket and took the phone, dropped it on the floor, and stomped it. It shattered. He picked up the pieces and opened the door to his unofficial office.

He walked down the hall, staring at the walls of Venezuela's mightiest of buildings. Back in his real office. Bernal was gone. Nobody. A rare moment of solitude and white noise in the country's command center. He breathed out and felt his blood pressure fall, then tossed the bits and pieces of his phone in the trash. He thought about drones, satellites, and other technologies that may have picked up the conversation. Hopefully nobody had heard. That was the last phone call ever. Stupid on all parts.

Outside, pedestrians on sidewalks and buses in the street went about their way. So did life in the wealthy homes. So did life in the slums. He walked over to a window and looked across the city to the green swaths, where the rich seethed against him, and then to the slums, where the poor demanded he live up to his promises. He made a few mental notes, picked up the phone, and demanded a meeting.

"You can't please everyone," he said, heading to a conference room. "But at least I can do what's best for the country before they get rid of me. I know my own country," he said aloud, thinking of Bernal.

The man was right. He always was, and that's what annoyed the president so much. Time to make amends to him and to the people. Coup rumors were buzzing around town, even more than normal, and word was that a long-fragmented opposition was close to narrowing in on one person they'd back to oust him, one person who'd call out his years of sham elections, supreme court stacking, and quashing any person or institution that got in his way. Hopefully, this meeting would open the door to new policies that might not be so sexy but better for everyone in the long run. Higher oil prices would be around the corner one day, and he needed to start making plans to use that money to make life better for the suffering nation.

"That's how I stay in power," he thought aloud.

A few minutes later, staffers and aides entered the conference room. He didn't tell them what the meeting was about, but rather, he tossed a legal pad and pen to all who entered the room.

A woman sat down. "Do you need some paper?" the president asked.

"Uh, yes. That'd be great," she said, looking a little nervous and confused.

The president walked around the length of the large conference desk and then handed her a pad of paper in an almost fatherly manner.

The door opened, and a group of suits scurried in. An older man in a well-tailored suit followed. Organized and neat, the president's minister of public works and housing surveyed the room and made his way to his boss.

"Mr. President. Greetings," the minister said. A little uncomfortable.

"Samuel, sit down. Sorry for sending you here on short notice. But we need to act."

The minister sat down, staring at the legal pads. He looked around. There was no PowerPoint slide, no stacks of charts and government studies for whatever the president had in mind.

"Mr. President, is something wrong? Is there something new threatening our republic?"

"Nothing new," the president said. "In fact, it's something that has gone on for too long."

Venezuela's minister of public works and housing, Samuel Gómez, a stout man of about seventy and a career civil engineer, sat down.

"Let's get down to it," the president said. "Nothing new is threatening our little oil-rich country by the sea, but something old is, and that's poverty. This thing is something I have put on the back burner lately. One of the first things we need to do is tackle the problems with our slums. We need adequate housing if we're going to cut into crime and if we are going to improve the quality of life in this country. This takes priority over arms and over buying friendships abroad with discounted oil."

The president rolled up his sleeves and remained quiet for a few seconds, gathering his thoughts. Eyes blinked. People were waiting for him.

"One day I'll be out of office, who knows when. Time to leave some sort of legacy behind that wasn't mired in controversy." He looked across the table.

"You there!" he said to the young woman to whom he had offered paper earlier.

"Yes sir."

"Call the CEO over at that brewing and bottling giant he runs. What's his name? Ramírez or something. We need the private sector on this. They'll do anything to work with us, provided we get goods flowing into the country again."

Gasps.

"The CEO of the brewer? For sure? That guy? The country's biggest capitalist?" the young woman asked.

"That's him. Let's get him involved. How would he handle this? His workers never strike. Let's learn from him."

"You!" he said to a man of about twenty-two years of age.

"Sir!" he stood up. Snapped to attention.

"Relax, chief. This isn't the military. But I like it. Call the Colombian embassy and get a meeting. Let's make a long-term plan to develop our border. More neighborhoods and communities on the border mean more trade and fewer soldiers and guerrillas and cocaine labs. And while you're at it, get members of the US private sector involved. Hold off on the American government and stick with businesses for now. Let's take baby steps here. Just get like-minded American private organizations and not-for-profits involved."

"But won't that open the door for the CIA and others to send in more embedded spies?" the young man asked, wondering where this about-face in fundamental policy came from.

"Who cares what they might find out about this project. Besides, I'm looking for expertise. No matter how powerful and dominating Washington is, and no matter how whiny their big corporations are, the American people have always proven to be innovative and usually sensible, and I want Venezuela to be likewise. Now off you go, young man. The rest of us are going to spend the day drafting a three-month plan of attack, a six-month plan, and a year-long plan to build adequate housing with the oil money we have left here, even if that means cutting spending on other social programs and defense elsewhere. I realize this may seem sudden, but running a government means running something besides oil and foreign policy."

More gasps.

The housing minister stared at the president. He smiled and nodded his graying head. "It'd be my honor, Mr. President."

"Good. Okay. Our first order of business is zoning and feasibility. Where and how are we going to develop good housing. We'll get to financing and how we stay within the budget as we go along."

He took charge. He led with one eye on a window across the way, where protests were gathering, and one eye on his team.

The young woman confused earlier at the president's offer for scratch paper, quietly took out her cell phone and kept it hidden under the desk.

"All phones off," the president said.

"I know, I'm just texting my husband that I will be late."

"Go ahead," the president said. "In fact, everyone get what you need done now before we get down to business. This is a big change of heart for me, but let's face it, I won't be around forever, and everyone in my administration needs something for the country to remember us by. Something physical, like better housing and infrastructure, something worthwhile when we're all gone."

"Thank you, Mr. President," the woman said. She scrolled down until she found the name she needed: Hernán Bernal. She began to text a short but discreet message.

President calling meeting to revamp housing. Says for good of nation. Definitely a ruse. Be suspicious.

She turned her phone off and got back down to work.

CHAPTER

34

Street sat at his desk in his room in the Embassy Suites staring at the picture of Brent and the others in the fishing boat, especially the person who Catherine Burnett assumed to be the man her son-in-law paid as a fishing guide. Street stared at the man, Juan Vicente Domínguez, and wondered what the head of Worldwide Oil & Gas was doing in the Placebo Agenda. At least he could have smiled for the picture on the boat that day. Mrs. Burnett was right in that Domínguez was commandeering something. Just not the sportfishing yacht. Domínguez didn't know Brent the way he said he did. They weren't old friends. That would explain why he messed up the story about attending the conference in San Diego.

Street cast his racing thoughts aside and focused on writing up a final story on the interview. The president was very clear in that he wants missiles on his borders. Tons of them and with possible nukes too. Nukes in Venezuela. Smuggling. He stood up from the desk, paced into the bedroom and looked out the window. "Nukes in Venezuela," he said out loud and shook his head.

Street went back to his desk and ran through his notes one more time. He found it hard to decide which quotes to use from the president, since there were so many good ones.

He transcribed the entire conversation and then downloaded the recording onto his computer, which made him a little nervous, as if the interview would delete itself when moving from his recorder to the computer. He did the same thing with his phone. That made him nervous as well. Good thing he brought the old-school cassette recorder as a backup. Street successfully got the interview onto his laptop and sent copies to Brent and to his work and personal email addresses that he had just created on a public computer. He even uploaded a copy onto free cloud-technology software and saved another copy onto a flash drive. He also printed a copy in the hotel business office and snapped a picture of it with a cheap cell phone he had bought in Caracas. Getting a little paranoid, aren't you, Street, he thought. Another trick of the trade.

A few minutes later, Brent received the email and sent back a short reply that read, "Street, received the story. Just read it. Thanks."

Terse prose. No feedback. Great, Street thought. An interview with the president of Venezuela who says he's going to arm the continent like never before, and Brent acts as if he just read a story on a new bookkeeping technology application growing in popularity among the region's accountants. Then Street remembered who he was actually working for and dismissed any pushback. With the story filed, Street had the afternoon off. Enough of Brent. He had some time to kill in Venezuela. He thought of Patricia and called her up.

She answered.

An hour later, Street sat across from Patricia at an outdoor table at Touch Café in Las Mercedes. He was sipping coffee and wondering where the owner of the restaurant came up with that name while trying not to get lost in Patricia's long hair and striking eyes. He had told her that he was coming to Caracas for a couple of days—though he never said what for—and suggested they meet up. He was getting good at espionage, he thought. Keep the true nature of this mission quiet, but don't make your presence too shadowy. Still, he was keen on seeing her, and she had free time.

The waiter brought over their coffee, and Street enjoyed the pleasant sunshine. Despite its nightmarish economic collapse and human suffering, Caracas had great weather most of the time. Nice, he mused. Getting cynical. Was that another espionage trick of the trade or just something coming on naturally? He decided to turn negative thoughts into a conversation starter and hopefully move to something more positive.

"Nice weather you have here," he told Patricia, taking in the café's surroundings. "Is this place keeping regular hours?"

"Ah, yes, the weather. It's good," she said. "And, no. It will close soon."

So much for positive news, Street thought. He breathed in the cool air, sipped some coffee, and felt better.

"So," Patricia said. "What's going on with you and Matías Sánchez? We need to get you to that higher-paying job."

"He does have some work for me. It's a contract job, but it doesn't start until November."

"Well, at least you're leaving *The Gateway* for greener pastures," Patricia said. "There's light at the end of the tunnel."

"Seems that way," Street said. "Yes, and I have you to thank for that. Seriously, Patricia, thank you."

She smiled at him. "You can endure *The Gateway* for a little while longer. It's not like he's going to fire you. Then he'd have no news."

Street looked at Patricia. Then he threw it out there.

"What's your take on Juan Vicente Domínguez?"

She frowned and sipped her coffee. "What? He's my boss."

"Do you trust him?"

"What's all this about? Of course not. Nobody trusts anyone in this country. I like him because he leaves me alone and trusts me to do my job."

"He doesn't ask you to travel or do things that aren't in your job description?"

"Never. What's up with this?"

Street took in the sights and sounds of the city. Horns honked but in the distance. A small prop plane with an official government seal descended at the nearby airport. For a second amid chaos, life went on.

"It's nothing," Street said.

Patricia smiled. "Caracas will do that to you. So, what all did the president tell you?"

"How did you know I was here to interview the president?"

"Your boss, Brent Drum, contacted me about setting up a roundtable back in Miami. One on the fate of the energy sector after this administration has gone. He wanted to know if Worldwide Oil & Gas would sponsor it, which would keep the magazine afloat along with the interview with our president."

Keep that magazine afloat, Street thought. Back to Patricia.

"The president said that they're going to be armed to the teeth."

"For real?"

"Yep. He said, 'You can quote me on this, Venezuela is arming itself to the teeth and won't blink an eye at striking out at any threat—real or perceived.'"

"What kind of arms?"

"You'll have to read the interview."

"Who am I going to tell? Tell me." She put her hand on his forearm.

"I'll tell you. But first let's switch from coffee to something stronger. I'll tell you right after we publish excerpts from the interview online and right before I take you to dinner."

She laughed. "That was a good one. Smooth. I didn't know you had it in you. You're going to fit in well in this town, even though you seem like one of those sporty gringo guys, out in the woods, hunting, fishing, surfing and boating and all."

He looked at her hand. No ring.

"Well, I don't want to make you uncomfortable. So I'll let you buy me dinner, and then I'll tell you everything the president said. You buy and listen, and I'll shoot off at the mouth. Deal?"

She blushed. Looked down at her lap. Then back at him.

"You pay for the hotel. Just kidding," she said, but she kept her stare.

They both enjoyed the brief silence. Street looked down the Avenida Principal de Las Mercedes. Bells rang from ice cream vendors, and harried pedestrians walked to the nearby Chacaíto Metro station. Traffic began to thicken, though the afternoon rush hour was still an hour or two away. A couple of young lovers holding hands strolled by. A businessman shot by clamoring into a cell phone. An elderly couple tossed large pieces of bread to pigeons. A wiry man clicked a pen. He was studying Street, and he quickly averted his stare the millisecond Street made eye contact.

Street froze. Him again. "See that guy?" Street asked Patricia.

"Which guy?"

"That guy over there. About a hundred meters. By the fountain in the plaza. I've seen him before. He's clicking that pen and staring at us. I know who he is."

"What?" a visibly confused Patricia asked. "Everybody's staring at somebody in this city," Patricia said, craning her neck to see the man.

"I've seen him before. Same night when we were having drinks with Ian!" Street shouted. He eyed the pen. Dumping information on me again, Street thought. He quickly scanned his surroundings looking for possible accomplices, remembering that Applewood said the pen could be a diversion. Nobody. He focused back on the man. You're not getting away this time, Street thought.

"What pen? Street whatever it is, just let it go. You just got offered a job with a monthly salary of five figures!"

Street looked at Patricia. He threw down a handful of foreign currency on the table.

"That should cover the coffee. This is the second time he's done this. I can't explain it all now, but I'll call you in a few minutes." He gave her a quick kiss on the lips and took off.

"Street, wait! It's too dangerous. You don't chase out after people. Even in the United States you don't do that, much less in Caracas."

"I'll be fine!" Street said. "And if I get him to talk, he may save lives!"

Patricia watched him jog in a fast but relaxed pace across the street, dodging cars with relative ease. He reached the sidewalk and picked up the pace. Patricia noticed his posture turn a little rigid. His stuck his chest out, and his chin was high.

"Classic testosterone," she whispered. "And wise paranoia, especially in this city."

Street glanced back at Patricia. She was gone. The skinny man stood at a nearby corner, threw the pen on the ground, and then disappeared into the crowd.

CHAPTER

35

Street Brewer picked up his pace and dodged an ice cream vendor, who was ambling by and ringing a little bell attached to his cooler. He looked ahead. No skinny man. Street upped the pace to a slow jog, fast enough to move ahead but not too fast to draw attention from local police. He searched hard for the skinny man, who was wearing blue jeans and a green polo shirt just a few seconds ago.

"Why couldn't he have worn a bright-gold shirt," Street said aloud. He did a three-sixty-degree sweep of the wide Avenida Principal de Las Mercedes. Nothing. Then he saw a taxi speed away. A face staring back at him.

"Got him," Street said and headed for a nearby line of cabs. "I've always wanted to say this," he mumbled in English as he jumped in. "Follow that car," he said to the driver in Spanish.

The cab in front made its way to the main Autopista Francisco Fajardo and headed east, picking up the pace. Light traffic allowed for high speeds. To the right, the small La Carlota airport broke up the urban jungle for a bit with its green grassy fields bordering the runway. To the left, the lush Ávila jutted up into the heavens. Ahead of him to the east, sprawling across several hills, lay Petare.

"Back again," Street said, turning his attention to the driver. "Don't lose that cab. If you keep up with it, I'll hook you up."

"Fine. But there are parts to Petare where I won't go. You're on your own," the driver said.

"How about a tip in foreign currency?"

"It'll get you close enough to where you need to be. I don't think that cab we're chasing will go too far up the hill either. By the way, why are we chasing that cab?"

"I'm a US spy, that's a Russian spy, and we're doing some James Bond shit in your country."

"Nice," the driver said, gunning the engine. The sliver of wealth in Caracas disappeared behind Street as he headed east. Grayer and older apartment buildings rose, and shiny office buildings faded behind. Street kept his focus on the cab in front of him. It darted to and fro and pulled ahead. A face stared back at Street in the rear window. The man's head would snap around and address its driver and then stare back at Street. The cab driver ahead probably knew his wasn't an ordinary fare. Both drivers were probably freaking out, Street thought. Not too many foreigners hailed cabs these days in Caracas, and the very few who did never asked to chase other gringos out of the safe confines of the Chacao area of the city.

"So, what really brings you to this end of town? If you want drugs, I can give you my card and hook you up. Deliver it by cab. Plus, I know some great whorehouses around."

"Catch that cab, and then you'll find out."

A quick silence passed as the chase ensued.

"Seriously, tell me, boss, what brings you to Caracas?"

"Living the dream," Street answered blankly. He felt bad about saying that. So he added, "Work. I'm a reporter."

"What you cover?"

"Oil," Street answered.

"No oil in Petare," the cab driver responded.

Street laughed. "No. I cover the economy here. And that means oil."

"True, but you should return to the United States. Not that you're not welcome here, but life is better there."

"For some," Street said.

"Life is a dream there. There is no crime, no misery, everyone is happy, and the future gets brighter and brighter each day. Plus, you see stars like Bruce Willis and Madonna walking around," the driver said.

Street didn't know how to react to that. He didn't know if the guy still bought into an outdated version of the American dream or if he was being sarcastic. Hopefully the latter. He threw the thought into the back of his head, where he could chew on it for fun in the future.

The car drew closer to the impressionistic myriad of colors blending together that eventually gave way to a shantytown. Street was directly behind the cab now. The thin man was looking back at him. Glare from the sun on the window prevented Street from getting to know his face, but he could see from the shape of his head, denoted by thick gray hair, that he still had his man on the run. Suddenly, the thin man's cab jerked off the freeway and headed along a perimeter street to the edge of a steep incline east of Petare, where corrupt police had tried to shake down Street and Ian Collins.

Small, run-down retail stores pockmarked with soda or beer placards dotted the sides of the street. At a ninety-degree incline, the slums began their ascent. A few pedestrians hopped off minibuses that streamed into the narrow entrances into the neighborhoods. Swarms of motorcycles roared through the streets.

The cab in front of Street stopped, and the man ran out.

"Stop the car," Street said. "Right here is good."

"Here? Are you insane? You don't belong here," the driver said.

Street reached into his pocket and grabbed a handful of dollars. He didn't count but wanted to make sure he paid the cab driver well. He also made sure he had another wad of dollars left to get home quickly if need be.

"Enjoy," Street said, cramming some money in the cab driver's hand.

He ran into the slum, up where the thin man had gone. The thin man saw Street following him. He opened his mouth in disbelief and bolted up the narrow stairs into the La Bombilla section of the Petare area. No cops. Just armed street gangs high on geopolitical thuggery. Street knew assault rifles from Russia had made their way into neighborhoods like Petare and replaced cheap handguns. It didn't matter. Dead is dead no matter the bullet or power of the weapon.

Street brushed that thought aside and ran up the hill. The shadows of the houses enveloped him, dropping the temperature a few degrees. Inside the dwellings on both sides of him, stacked up way above, voices called out. Forks, broom handles, and other devices banged on the side of the houses, merging into a bolt of noise shooting up the hill at the speed of sound by design.

"I'm not with the police," Street said aloud in Spanish.

Women would pound on the windows, using the close proximity of the houses to alert one another of staged, large-scale police raids. The sound would shoot up the hill faster than a wildfire and give families time to warn their boys, innocent or not, that a roundup was on the way. When the police did enter via raid to arrest everyone, they were in full force and not on routine patrol.

Street ran faster and faster. His legs began to burn more and more with each passing step of the steep stairwell. Up ahead, he saw his target darting along.

"Hey, asshole!" Street said.

He raced harder and harder, his adrenaline wiping out any evidence of fatigue. Street began to close in on him.

"I'm talking to you," Street shouted out in English.

He thought about shutting up but then took a millisecond to realize that a foreigner running through the slum had already caught the attention of everyone there anyway.

"That's right. Run!" Street shouted in English.

Screw it. Let everyone know a gringo was chasing another gringo in their neighborhood. Curiosity could draw a crowd and slow the chase. Faces popped out through the windows, some wearing smiles of disbelief. Children peered through their windows and giggled. One old woman peeked out and shook her head. Now she had seen everything. Street thought about the old woman who had shooed Ian and him away. Maybe she's around. One who resembled her peered out of her door and also shook her head.

"Now every cop on this end of Caracas will be here," she mumbled and went back inside, slamming her door shut.

The thin man rounded a corner, and Street lost sight of him for a few seconds. All the sounds and smells of an unfamiliar neighborhood disappeared. Street focused. He noted the bars over windows, a mesh of power lines and outdated television antennae spiraling into the blue sky. He ran on.

Street rounded the corner. Then he froze. There were no old ladies, no couples walking. No kids playing. No ice cream vendors. Just gun barrels. Lots of them aimed right at him. Cold eyes behind them. Maybe fifteen men taking aim at Street, and not with rip-off handguns or something stolen from army barracks years ago. They were Kalashnikovs, one of the most recognized firearms around. Clean, polished, and new, pointing at him like bayonets.

During the split second it took Street to register the chase was up, he gauged his fear. He didn't know what scared him more, the weapons or the stare in the eyes behind the weapons. These guys were cold. Not jumpy or brash like typical teen gang members. Something was out of the ordinary. They had the backing of someone. Someone with authority. Even Street knew that, and he had no military training at all. Some were older, and some were younger. Most were well dressed, wearing ironed shirts and motorcycle riding gear. These were the armed government gangs that Street and the rest of the world had heard about. Pro-government *colectivos* ready to act as paramilitaries, called on by authorities to harass the public if needed.

He raised his hands.

"On your knees," a voice shot out.

Street didn't catch which one said it. He thought of a diplomatic way out. Nothing came to mind. Then just use a little humor to ease the situation.

"Men, let me tell you about Jesus," Street said in Spanish, dropping to his knees. "I have good news. You're all saved! The answers you seek, my sons, lie not in those gun barrels but in the Good Book and in my bank account. It's not too late to turn your lives around."

Silence.

He took note of the scenario. They were well positioned. Several stood in the alley taking aim. Some were in low-hanging balconies in the slum houses above. The rest were aiming at him from street-level doorways. No one was completely without cover, except for two blocking the alley. One emerged from the crowd with a fading print T-shirt of the city of Boston emblazoned across his chest. It looked like it ended up in Venezuela probably through a church charity in the United States. Another wore cutoff khaki pants with a Duck Head brand, which probably made their way to Venezuela via a church in the southeastern United States many years ago.

"Just chasing a thief," Street said in Spanish to the kid, who must have been a decade younger than him. "Sorry. I didn't see anything. I'm out of here. Later. Carry on. Good job, men. Thank you for your service."

Street stood up.

"You're not looking for a thief," Boston said. Street scanned the rest of the unit. Nothing but unblinking eyes and terse mouths, as if they communicated to themselves silently by jaw clenching. Noses twitched as well.

Silence passed, and for a second, Street lost a little patience.

"Fine, no thief. Whatever. I'm leaving."

"Back on your knees," Boston said. "Hands where we can see them. You know the routine from all those stupid movies Hollywood pumps out year after year."

Street stayed on his knees, hands in the air. He noted how there were no bystanders, even along the main road in the slum. Nobody else on the roofs. Nobody looking out windows. A hole in the slum's population. A few whispers broke the silence, but Street missed the words. He just knew the gang knew he wasn't police and that he didn't belong there. And whoever he was, he was dangerous because he could bring attention to their neighborhood.

Boston handed his rifle to a man who must have been twice his age. He stared at Street almost nose to nose. Street stared back at him.

"There was another gringo who ran up this road. Who is he?" Street asked.

Boston just stared at him. Resolve and disdain in his eyes.

"Don't worry about it. You have bigger problems right now. Ricardo? Should we get the tires?"

Chuckles arose. The young man in the Boston T-shirt looked back at a man who appeared from the crowd. He was likely pushing fifty. Curly black hair. Very curly. Despite his age, he had lustrous, youthful skin. He wore shorts. Short shorts, like something from an American gym class from the seventies. Big, hairless, and powerful legs, like a frog's. His T-shirt was faded yellow and fit poorly. He looked like sloppy nothingness, except for his eyes. No matter in what corner of the world, no matter in what slum, hard men held nothing but resolve in their eyes, no cares, no needless worries, not self-doubt, and above all else, no overthinking. If something didn't belong, if something didn't make sense, it was a threat and had to be eliminated.

Ricardo stepped forward. He nodded to the younger man who had just been in Street's face.

The younger man in the Boston T-shirt stared at Street and then shouted over his shoulder at the men backing him up.

"Get the tires. In his case, make it six or so. And the gasoline. Let's bring out the microwave," the man said. Laughs broke the breezeless slum air.

The leader said nothing, turned his back, and then disappeared behind a few men. Two ran off, and Street stayed on his knees. Frozen.

The microwave, he wondered.

Boston walked up and knelt down to make more direct eye contact with Street. Due to the angle of the steps, he seemed much taller.

"You're gonna cook today. If you were only in some Guantanamo cell being sliced up and interrogated, man you would be so lucky. Here, we're gonna do something a little different. A little messier."

There was no escape. Even with common thugs you could reason your way out. But not with these guys, especially the quiet ones. And the newness of the weapons. It was like they had arrived just yesterday.

"Gasoline, you dumbass American, is cheap here. You knew that. But you didn't know that it can also run a microwave. Ever heard of a microwave oven that runs on gasoline?"

"I'm not with the police, Venezuelan or foreign. I don't work for the government. I'm not a spy. Believe me. I've been through this shit before. I'm just a journalist who got lost chasing the wrong guy who most likely is spying on you. Let's go find him and throw him in the microwave, whatever it is. I'll light the match. Then I'll leave and never come back here again."

"Yeah, you're not coming back," the man said. "Or should I say, you're not going back. So get comfortable. Let's have some fun. Let's have a barbecue. Let's cook up a little something in the microwave."

Street could only imagine what the man meant by a microwave. He'd find out in minutes.

Two guys came around rolling tires. They set them down and raced back up the alleyway to get a few more. They were somewhat old tires, probably from a small city bus. The men moved with the silence and speed of a pit crew. One after the other. Then they came out with jugs of what Street could only assume was gasoline.

"Up," the kid said.

Street rose slowly to his feet. His hands in the air, gauging the dozen or so gang members.

Boston motioned for two others to follow him. They did. They wore jeans and generic polo shirts. In a second they had cleared Street's pockets of his wallet, passport, and hotel key card.

Street heard bouncing rubber and saw two more men rolling more tires down the stairwell. He looked up and saw a buzzard circling overhead. Symbolic, he thought.

"This way," Boston said.

They walked about ten feet up until the narrow road flattened out somewhat.

"Your hands. Put them up and together, as if you were going to dive into a pool."

"Go to hell," Street said.

Several clicks of rifles loading shut him up.

Street raised his hands. There were still at least six Kalashnikovs pointing at him. If he decided to turn around and run down the narrow stairway out into the city proper, he'd be dead. Even in a bad movie, nobody could miss such a shot.

"There's still got to be a way out of this," Street said.

"There isn't," Boston said in English. "Except for this. After we gave Roland Spradling the microwave, we cut off his head. Fucker just wouldn't die. The sight of his body freaked out his wife, Pennie, who bolted. Bitch flew down these stairs. Well, she didn't make it either. But she did have one last request. To show you this." Boston withdrew a dirty piece of paper. He held it up. "Well, Street Brewer, this was Pennie's last request and your last reading assignment."

Street stared at the paper and frowned, lowering his hands.

"Are you for real?"

"I am. Apparently, she wasn't. Makes no sense to me. Does it to you? She said if I showed it to you, it would save Venezuela. Doesn't really matter though. You and the country are both fucked."

Street stared at the paper. No message or anything. Just numbers. Lots of them. He read sixteen in total scrawled across the width of the paper. That was it.

"I don't get it," Street whispered to himself. The confusion took Street's mind off the looming microwave.

"She said it's all you need. Whatever that means. Anyway, it's too late now, at least here that is. In fact, take it with you to the afterlife."

Boston laughed, rolled up the paper, and tossed it into the tires free throw–style. The paper shimmied its way down to Street's feet and rested there.

"Goodbye my friend. This street is closed."

One of the guys threw two tires over his head. They dropped down over his shoulders to his feet and then his knees. Street smelled the rubber, and it reminded him of some lost memory of playing with a similar tire sometime in his youth.

Two more tires pulled at his hair as they dropped down to his waist and torso. Then a few more until he was up to his chest in tires. They gave him little support. He stood frozen, as if they weren't there at all. Eventually, he had tires up to his armpits.

"Relax for a second," Boston said.

Street rested his hands on the tires, feeling like he was about to jump in a pool and was using the tires as a flotation device of some sort. That thought quickly vanished. One of the guys took the remaining tires and laid them out in front of Street. He doused them in gasoline, and he ordered Street's hands back up in the air. From out of nowhere someone had taped Street's hands together. Then his mouth. Another tire. Then another. Then he couldn't see anymore. A slight breeze arrived and cooled the tips of his fingers above. Then someone capped the top off with a metal plate. Darkness.

"It's called a microwave," Boston said, his voice muffled from the outside of the tires. "Cops come here looking for a dead gringo and all they find is some overcooked meat. We put you in the tires, we light the tires, and then we'll get those tires to burn for a long, long time and cook you up all day."

"Fuck you!" Street screamed under the tape. He jerked to knock himself down and roll out of this mess. Let them shoot him.

"Trying to knock yourself out of this won't work. We've thought about that. We got guys who won't let the microwave budge."

Street could barely breathe. Moving was just as difficult. It was already hot, and all he could feel were how wide his eyes had stretched. Fear gripped him, and he panicked over the growing reality he could not escape torture and a slow, horrible death. His muted screams and attempts to jerk himself free were in vain. Hands and arms on the outside kept the tires in place. Still, he thrashed about, but the men on the outside prodded him back with quick jerks of the butts of their assault rifles and kept the microwave standing firm.

Laughter rose outside the microwave, while hyperventilation set in on the inside. Street told himself to relax, but soothing self-talk wasn't working.

"Don't pour any on the inside. You don't want him to die too quickly," he heard Boston circling the column of tires.

"Slow roast him. I'll bet all the dollars in his wallet that we can keep him alive for about twenty minutes before we cool him off and start this whole process all over again," the voice said. "Don't fuck it up! Jesus for the love of God, don't use all the gasoline at once!"

"I'm sorry," another voice said.

"*Eres un maldito idiota como Ricardo y el resto de esos coños,*" Boston said.

You're a fucking moron like Ricardo and the rest of those assholes, Street translated on the coattails of a last wisp of logic floating through his head.

"Did you hear me in there, fuck face?" Boston asked. You're gonna roast slow and hard. We're going to put out the flame just so we can keep you in there and let you suffer some more and then start it over again. Then when you're dead and in hell, you'll be going through this every second for eternity. So right now is as happy as you're going to get!"

Street heard nothing but footsteps and then silence. Then mumbling and then a collective uproar of laughter.

"Here we go!" a voice said.

The gang on the outside pushed the tires a little bit to make sure they were even. Street felt as if he were inside the belly of a large snake, and it was moving after eating him, relaxing to position itself in order to ensure proper digestion. Some muffles. Last-second adjustments to the tires, similar to the sounds made on an airplane before all of its doors slam shut and it starts to taxi away from the terminal.

Silence and then a collective whoa and the sound of high fives.

Immediately, the temperature shot up. Way up. The sweat on Street's forehead began to burn in his eyes. He was baking in a hell on the steps in Petare. He screamed and started to convulse. Involuntary movements. Pain. Sheer pain. Images of his childhood, of his parents' smiling faces, and one very clear image of Patricia raced through his mind while the last shreds of rational thought fled his mind, as if they were escaping with the heat.

He could sense the rising flames on the outside of the tires and began to faint. All he knew was that it wasn't as hot around his ankles. The rest of his body was beginning to boil. The glue on the tape around his mouth loosened in the heat and Street's pouring sweat. It was too much for any human brain to take. No amount of training could endure that. Jesus, this is finally it. His eyes rolled up.

Then he heard a voice.

Shouting.

"Do it now!"

He heard more voices and then a gunshot and muffled cries to calm down. Dizziness. Movement, a tipping movement. The tires began to peel away with the fall from being pushed over. Cool air blasted over him. A final stay of damnation sent from above.

After a second, when sight returned, he saw flaming tires bouncing down the narrow road. He looked up. Sunshine shot in its own blinding powers, exacerbating the sting from the sweat in his eyes. A wave of water fell from above and cooled him instantly. All tires were off him now, simmering on the side of the alley. Street didn't know how they removed them while on fire or who drenched him with water or, more importantly, who ordered the microwave turned off with a warning shot.

Tears still burned his eyes. He felt his skin and discovered he had been overcome with heat but had been spared from serious burns.

"Just let him go," a voice called out from a nearby slum house.

Street couldn't place a face with the voice.

"Good thing they didn't do it properly by putting the gasoline on the inside of the tires," the voice added. "Sometimes they give you a hose to breathe to prolong your torture."

Street darted his eyes about as sight began to return but still couldn't see all yet. He couldn't find the source of the voice. All he knew was that it came from inside one of the houses to his right. And the voice was in Spanish, but not Venezuelan. The accent was foreign.

"Escort him down. In fact, don't leave his side until you see him enter a cab," the voice said. Immediately, all men withdrew their weapons.

"Are you sure?" Boston shouted toward the voice. "I thought he was supposed to die here."

"I'm sure."

Boston rolled his eyes and spit. He shook his head, looking like a kid called in early from afternoon play to a dinner he didn't like. He nodded to two of his colleagues.

"Clean this place up," the man in the Boston T-shirt snapped, a little annoyed. Two guys, younger ones, grabbed Street and yanked him to his feet. They ripped the tape from his hands and mouth.

Another handed him his wallet.

"Give him all of his money back too" the voice said. "All of it."

Didn't I go through something like this recently, Street thought, finding a spring of humor in hell. The same ones from the gang who lit him on fire were now escorting him down the narrow stairway as if he were a visiting dignitary. As they got farther down, local residents started peeping out of their windows, but they remained silent. If anyone asked questions, they would say they never saw a thing.

Street began to cough and moved his head so he could cough over his shoulder. When he finished, he saw the house where the voice had come from that had saved him. The face behind the voice appeared. It was the thin man, the pen clicker, the man with the bushy hair standing in the doorway. Next to him, the quiet gang leader. The man with the enormous frog legs.

It only took minutes for Street to get back to the foot of Petare. He took a look behind him and the two were still there, watching him. Boston lifted his shirt and retrieved a handgun, typical of what a criminal his age should be carrying. He pointed it at Street, made a silent pop with his mouth, smiled, and lowered the pistol. A minute later Street was back in a cab.

Street stared at his escort from inside the car. The young man lowered his eyes and walked away. The adrenaline in Street's legs and body ebbed, while a heavy tiredness followed in its wake. He knew he hadn't just walked into one of the world's most dangerous slums and left it alive. He had just walked out of a stronghold of some type. One protecting some thin man who kept following Street every time he came to Caracas.

Street didn't remember hearing a thing when he boarded the plane and flew back to Miami. He sat in his seat, trying to take in information from the last few days. The Venezuelan president had told him he was arming the country. And then there was almost being burned alive.

"How did I end up here?" he mumbled.

"Right away, sir," the flight attendant said.

Street snapped his head back into reality. A moment later she was there with a cold beer. Street looked confused but not taken aback at all.

"Sir, did you not just say 'how about another beer?'"

Sure, he thought. One would be perfect. He just sat there and relaxed. He had a few hours away from everyone on Earth, time to reflect on his thoughts. Only one question managed to pop out of the flurry of cerebral activity and grab Street's attention. Why take the risk? Why not go to the police and be done with it? Cut your losses and live.

The flight attendant walked down the aisle and smiled at Street. She had silky blonde hair pulled up in a soft bun. Street thought of Molly Wells. Then he thought of Catherine Burnett. Telling the police wouldn't do her daughter and son-in-law any justice. It may get Brent arrested, but it wouldn't nab everyone in this horrific spying scheme.

He nodded off on the plane while planning his next moves to make sure nobody from the Placebo Agenda would make it out alive or without enjoying life in prison.

CHAPTER

36

Street entered *The Gateway* offices before sunrise. He didn't want to walk in after Brent had already arrived. He wanted to be there waiting for Brent and surprise the hell out of him. Then he could leave. He could not believe he had almost been burned alive, and he was sure Brent had ordered it. That was Street's execution.

Street thought about Brent with white knuckles, one hand gripping a pen as if it were a prison weapon. Why not rush in there and beat him to death when he arrives. He brushed that aside. Brent would be thrown off guard, and Street would have a little fun while saving Molly and sending spies to prison.

He sat down and booted his computer, took a sip of coffee, and then read the news. It kept his mind off his near-death experience, his pro bono espionage work for the US government, and images of Patricia's smile. He wanted to contact her, but he didn't want to seem shaken or even scared while on the phone. So he didn't. Back to the news to distract him. Even on a normal day, the mind needs a healthy distraction from time to time. Some say always focus on achieving goals, not on what releases worries, but paper shuffling has its merits.

It didn't work. Street ignored the news and began to wonder why the mysterious pen-clicking CIA asset returned to call off his execution. If he wasn't going to relax, he'd work on solving his attempted murder. Then he heard the key turn in the door and the clicking and pangs of locks unlocking. It was a terrible sound if you knew who it was.

Brent entered. His jaw dropped.

"Street!"

"Morning, Brent. I survived Caracas."

A wave of confusion swept across Brent's face, but he quickly shrugged it off.

Composure nicely regained, Street thought.

"Story is in your inbox. It's a good read. So hot off the press that it's on fire!" Street said.

Brent went into his office and left the door open. He went through some motions until he finally broke his own awkward silence.

"So, what do you have for me?" Brent asked.

"Again, check your inbox. You confirmed receipt of it," Street replied. "Not much really, just the ramblings of a madman threatening to take a burning Venezuela nuclear."

"Hang on," Brent interrupted him. The phone rang in Brent's office. He answered it and held the receiver in his chin, using both hands to type in passwords to log on to his computer.

"The story will run in the next issue," Brent told whoever was on the other line. "Yes, Wallace, it's a good interview."

Brent rolled his eyes, hung up, and glanced at his computer screen. Then he fuddled about his desk. Silence. Then Brent asked Street a question: "Is Bob still with the Canadians?"

"Who is Bob, and who are the Canadians?" Street asked, a surge of anger and annoyance mixing together like some unholy bile shooting up his esophagus. Vague questions always meant an argument was brewing, murder attempts notwithstanding. And this question was a vague one.

"Is Bob still with the Canadians?" Brent repeated, with an edge this time.

"No clue what you're talking about," Street said.

Brent's face turned red and then he shook his head, apparently in disgust.

"I sent you an email," Brent said, annoyance morphing into anger. "Don't you open and read your emails, or do you not do that anymore?"

"On occasion, when I have a burning interest," Street said.

He glanced at his inbox, enjoying seeing Brent's mood sour even further. Thousands upon thousands of emails were layered up going back through the year. Scores were sitting in there in bold type, emails read, reset as unread, and ready to be read again when, or if, needed.

"You're going to have to give me more details," Street said. "It would take a lifetime to find the email with the broad net you're casting, and I'm not sure my life will go that long."

"I don't know why I even pay you," Brent said.

"You basically don't. And yes, I can remember each and every email that pops into my inbox. Speaking of payment, you're late on my check again. I need my check for government work, which is going to burn me alive."

He was happy. Keeping Brent angry would keep Street focused more on solving crimes and less on being the victim of one.

"What?" Brent said. "What did you just say?"

"I'm out of here," Street said. "Taking the day off."

He stormed toward the door when all of a sudden he felt a hand on his shoulder pulling him back. Street turned and pushed Brent, who moved backward but recovered nicely.

"Don't fucking grab me," Street said.

"Just calm down. I meant Robert Adkins. From the Canadian consulate. He just called and reminded me that he wanted a copy of the story you wrote on him a while back. He's leaving and wants an extra copy. I can't remember when it ran, so I sent you an email not too long ago asking for the issue date," Brent said. "Take a couple of days off. Paid," he added in a matter-of-fact voice. "Just relax. You're needed here."

Take the office for yourself to sort out plan B of my botched assassination, Street thought.

"Just leave. Calm down. I'll take care of everything here. I'll transcribe the interview."

"You don't need to. The interview is already transcribed, and the story is written up with the angle I found to be the right one," Street said.

"You've been working hard, Street. You really have. Just take the rest of the week off. Go! Take off. Go grab a beer. Go to the beach. Get laid or something. By the way, how was Caracas? Did you get a chance to get out and unwind?"

"I got a chance to blow off some steam."

Street left the office door open and walked down the hall. It was empty. All the other tenants had their doors closed.

A half hour later, Street was on the beach, sipping a beer, and dialing Molly Wells on the phone. He updated her on what had happened to him, albeit in a heavily redacted version so she wouldn't freak out. He went to Caracas to conduct some interviews, though he omitted almost being burned alive. He sent her some fresh videos of Brent in the office to reconfirm that they shared the same boss though different aliases. He hung up and stared out over the ocean.

He made sure he stayed south of Fifth Street on Miami Beach. These four blocks still packed in the sleek high-rises and were home to some fine restaurants, but the sliver of beach was home to fewer tourists, the closest thing to a locals-only beach that this area of town saw.

That day the water was flat, typical of summer, so that meant no surfers would be out, and since it was a weekday, the crowd was thin. Street cracked open another beer and blew off any chance of getting in trouble. As long as he drank from a can, and not from a bottle, and as long as he picked up his trash, the police would leave him alone.

"Cheers!" he shouted to some low-flying seagulls that were hovering above him. "No food here. Do your intelligence work. Maybe you guys are working for the government and don't know it!"

An old man in running gear walked behind Street and stared at him, shook his head, and continued onward.

"Now everyone thinks I'm crazy. I don't care."

Street slouched a bit in his lounge chair and picked up his phone. No messages, no texts, no missed calls, no harassments or threats. Ten beers left in his small cooler and nothing but bright sun above.

He raised his open brew and toasted the low-flying gulls above anew. "Here's to the damn microwave!" The man in the running gear turned his head to face Street and then broke out in a sprint running south, picking up the pace.

Street thought about Patricia to ease his mind. He had managed to text her from the hotel but never properly said goodbye before flying out. She was a rare bird, a rarity that rises to the top on the shoulders of cheering fans, not on the backs of people, using them as steppingstones. He could awe at her beauty, talk politics or business with total security, and then go on a bike ride and enjoy a beer with her at an American football game. A total winner. If only she lived here in the United States. He brushed her out of his mind, grabbed his wallet, and marched west to the sand dunes. He left his chair and beer unattended in the sun. They'll be fine alone.

He cut across a small grassy park covered in palm trees just past the sand dunes, crossed Ocean Drive, ran up Second Street, and took a right on Collins Avenue. The absence of tall buildings allowed for abundant sunlight to drench the wide streets and warm up the gray concrete sidewalks and all the parked cars along the way. He walked down half a block on Collins and came to a Mini Mart, a hybrid between a US convenience store and a Latin American grocery market of sorts.

He walked in, and past the chicharrónes, beer, and sodas, he found some paper goods. There it was, a small spiral notebook. He also picked up a pencil. A young man behind the counter was talking in Spanish to an old man in front of the counter, who wasn't giving much space to Street or any others in line. Street eavesdropped. They were talking about produce in the store and when it was last unboxed. Not exactly the nefarious plots that some non-Spanish speakers assume their Latin American counterparts are conspiring. Finally, they finished their conversation, and Street paid and left.

Back at the beach, Street let the midday sun warm his face. He relaxed for a few minutes, then he rose and jogged down to the ocean. He dove in, taking in the warmth of the water. Even at its coldest, the ocean in Miami is always swimmable without a wetsuit. Street swam underwater and took in the sounds found beneath the surface of the ocean. A massaging quietness enveloped him, save the gentle hum from a passing wave that raced a few inches overhead. The wave drew him back to the shore and then released him quietly.

A minute later, Street was in his lounge chair, enjoying the comfortable combination of beer in his system and an increased heart rate from the swim. He took the spiral notebook and pencil from his bag and started writing: "Find Ricardo somehow. Find the pen clicker. Bust everyone." That was obvious, he thought. Then he tore up the paper and tossed it in a nearby trash receptacle. No need to take notes on the obvious. We're going low-tech here. Memories alone. Scan my email and phone all you want. Ransack my desk. He deleted the memo in his phone to contact Ricardo. Just try and burn me again, Brent. Keep trying.

He also made plans to check out the Spradlings' boat.

CHAPTER

37

With Street out of the office, Brent dialed Karen in Washington. He knew she was probably still a little miffed at his almost losing *The Gateway*, and any good news would be welcome. Bad news would not. Brent had both.

"Talk to me," Karen said after the first ring.

"First the good news. Street got the interview in Venezuela with the president, and it's going to sell us a lot of ads. The magazine lives! Plus it has everything we need for the agenda. The bad news is that he's still alive somehow. He either escaped or someone cut him loose, but that's okay. We can take care of him here. I never wanted him taken out in Venezuela anyway. Too much attention with a foreign journalist missing."

"Yes. Domínguez already chewed us out on that. Have you told Wallace he finished the interview?"

"Yes, I have," Brent said, relieved his boss wasn't too angry over the bad news.

"Good. It'll get him off your back. So what did our source in Venezuela drop on Street the first go around?"

"I've downloaded the information from the digital recorder I gave him as well as from the bug we put in his bag, and all of the information is there. It has the time frame, cost estimates, and financial planning for that large naval base on Sucre."

"Everybody knows that."

"Yes, but..." Brent said into the earpiece jammed between his jaw and shoulder.

"Go on."

"It looks here like Venezuela is also planning to build a nuclear reactor. To generate electricity."

Silence.

"Yeah," Brent said. "A nuclear power plant. That doesn't make sense."

"No, it doesn't. Why would Venezuela need a nuclear power plant? They can burn hydrocarbons to make electricity or put up dams along the Caroní River. In fact, there already are dams in southern Venezuela. Doesn't add up. It wouldn't even make a good cover for nuclear weapons."

"That's what we've got from the Russians. I'll give the Russians some stuff back."

"Has it crossed your mind that maybe the Russians are giving you bogus intel?" Karen said.

Brent remained silent.

"You're going to have to go down there yourself and find out what's going on. Talk to our bushy-headed friend in person. We're going analog here. No technology that can trace us. Again, you'll have to do this yourself. Street has served his purpose. Whatever you do with him now is up to you."

Brent leaned back in his desk chair and thought.

"Street will need to be taken out for real this time. I'll handle it," he said after a pause, speaking as if Street were an empty pizza box, and he had to decide whether he needed to toss it out now or if it could wait until the next day.

"What about Molly Wells? We need them both taken out this week."

"If I take Molly out, I can't kill Street yet." Brent looked out the window. "In spite of it all, I really can't be in two places at the same time, so we'll have to make Street immobile, and jail will do just that. Time dealing with the courts will keep him in town and out of the job market and away from his phone. Molly is farther away, so she should go first."

"Afterward, do you want him killed down there in Coral Gables?" Karen asked.

"In his home or in the Everglades. Not to sound like a bad television show, but I'm good at making it look like an accident."

"Do it," Karen said. "Maybe we can get his phone while he rots in a cell and sniff out this Cyra woman."

"Okay," Brent said. "I think I know just what to nab on Street."

"Maybe have him killed in jail?" Karen asked. "Pay someone to do it and then take that person out? I can help out if need be."

"Not a bad idea," Brent said. "I'll look into it."

"I have to tell you, Brent. I'm pleased at how well you've turned things around at *The Gateway*. Things go sideways, I get it. That happens with anything. But we're back on course to closing this thing. Keep up the good work."

Brent hung up the phone. He sat back in his desk chair and slouched. He propped his feet up on his desk.

"How can we treat Street to a night in county jail?"

CHAPTER

38

Street packed up his cooler, beach chair, and backpack, left South Beach, and headed west. About a half hour later after a short jaunt down I-95 and then South Bayshore Drive, he was at the marina in Coconut Grove and on the dock looking down at his Whitewater. He wanted a change of scenery, and Biscayne Bay was perfect.

A sailboat moved quietly northeast, gliding along the warm, shallow waters between Coconut Grove and Key Biscayne. Street watched it tack into the wind. A large sportfishing yacht with a soaring tuna tower broke through the no-wake zone after leaving the Coconut Grove marina, and sped up. It rose on plane and headed off. The distance tempered the noise of its engines, lowering them to a soft hum similar to a childhood memory of an air conditioning unit from some lost summer a long time ago.

Street hopped into his twenty-eight-foot Whitewater. He turned the key, started up the outboards, backed out slowly, and headed out through the channel. Small barrier islands once popular with homeless people gave away to a calm and open Biscayne Bay. Street pushed the throttle when he left the no-wake zone and lost all sound to the hum of the engines. He rode for a few minutes, and Key Biscayne grew larger on the horizon. Behind him, Miami grew smaller. To the north, the tall downtown skyscrapers jutted out of the bay's edge, and their proximity to the water gave them a metallic but soft appearance. To the west and stretching south, green trees and stately mansions held their own on the coasts of Coconut Grove and Coral Gables.

Now out of the no-wake zone, Street revved the engines and headed toward Stiltsville. A few minutes later, he had the colorful houses just off the bow of his boat. He throttled back to neutral and let the boat drift a bit.

An Etchells Class regatta was taking place a few miles closer to shore. This wasn't one of the larger sailing regattas typical of winter, as there were too few boats. It was likely some makeshift race among friends. He turned off the boat and decided to watch in silence, taking in the pointed sails moving along the horizon, crossing the starting line marked by two anchored boats with large race committee flags. One boat veered back from the pack, returned to the starting line, and did a three-sixty-degree turn. Then it headed back toward the fleet. It had crossed the starting line early, and the penalty for the guilty party was to head back, turn around, and start over. Not a clean start, but a start, nonetheless.

"A fresh start," Street said aloud. "Just what I need, even if I'm behind everyone else."

Street set the binoculars down in the console and sat on the transom, staring at the sails growing smaller on the horizon. He thought about his life and where he was headed. In the past, he wanted to find a way to make it in this America, the source of so many misguided dreams abroad. Now, he just wanted to survive. But would he get killed any day now? When would Brent and God knows who else try again? Soon, and he knew it. He couldn't be reactionary this time. Time to be proactive and take them out before they came for him.

He glanced at his phone. "Come on, tell me what I need to know."

Nothing. Then he looked off toward the horizon all around him. The city seemed calm from so far away. The Etchells sailboats moved quietly out toward the Atlantic, and the Stiltsville homes settled down into the soft sands beneath Biscayne Bay.

My phone isn't going to tell me what I need to know unless I ask for it. He texted his Venezuelan lawmaker friend.

What's up?

Street. Are you out of Venezuela?

Yes.

Good. It's going to get rough here.

How can it get worse?

People will soon fight for drinking water and pick trash for food.

So get rid of the president.

There was a brief pause, and then his lawmaker friend wrote back at length.

It's not that simple, Street. He has the military in his back pocket. Speaking of which, when you told me you interviewed him and he was going to load up on missiles, we all looked into it, including our spies in our own military. It's not happening. Nothing nuclear at all either. He used you just to distract the world from the country's misery, just like this port deal. Your interview was just a sham, just like his recent election. Doesn't matter. Any spike in oil prices that come from his rants won't last. Markets will shrug him off.

Street thought before writing back. On the one hand, it didn't matter. The president mentioned missiles, so he had a duty to report it. On the other hand, he didn't like being used.

Fine. Got anything for me?

Not really. I'll keep you posted.

Thanks for nothing. He checked his email and other messages. Nothing from Patricia. Nothing from Matías. Street threw the phone in his bag. Didn't even bother to worry that he might miss and chuck it over the side of the boat.

Then a thought entered his head, and he tried to chase it away. He knew if he uttered it, things would take a turn for the worse.

"Utter it," he said aloud, watching the sky go about its celestial business. "Don't be superstitious."

He paused, then stood up and faced the east.

"It can't get any worse than this!" he shouted over water, mainly out of sarcasm and less out of anger.

He laughed and then got behind the wheel of his boat, cranked the engines, and headed east, deeper into the Atlantic Ocean. It can't get any worse than this. He glanced back at his phone, which was peeking out from his bag. An app alert popped up. Not a typical news or email alert. This one came from an app he hadn't used all year. He grabbed the phone and stared at it, and his face muscles thawed from tense annoyance to loose relaxation before snapping back into a broad smile.

"Ha!" he shouted across the water, his mood lifting. "This is exactly what I needed."

He glanced back at the app on his phone and scrolled through a weather alert. Thousands of miles to the east, just off the coast of Africa, a low-pressure swirl of clouds was heading west across the Atlantic and beginning to organize.

CHAPTER

39

Street throttled the engines of the Whitewater and headed out toward the open Atlantic. A light chop allowed for air to shoot across the hull and send the boat on plane with ease. The closer to open ocean he drove, the saltier the air smelled. He veered southeast toward Soldier Key, a small island nestled between the heavily populated and super posh Key Biscayne and Elliot Key, a large, uninhabited island north of Key Largo.

The light chop gave way to rolling waves, though the heavy hull of the Whitewater sliced through with no problem at all. Ahead in the distance, a thirty-nine-foot cabin cruiser, most likely an Intrepid due to its unmistakable lines, floated in the distance. A police boat not far off, a Miami-Dade County craft, moved toward the luxurious Intrepid, its lights flashing. Street paid no attention to the lights, as cops frequently flashed their lights on the water. He gunned the engines and headed in the direction of the boat to check things out. As he grew closer, hands waved in the air. Street pointed the bow of the smaller Whitewater toward the cabin cruiser. He sped up quickly and throttled back just a few feet away from the other boat. The wake trailing the center console rushed under the now idle boat, acting as a buffer to stop the watercraft a foot or so from the apparently distressed boat. Street stared at the Intrepid. It was a beauty. Four three-hundred-horsepower engines. All of which were dead quiet.

"You guys need a hand?" Street said.

There were two men on the boat. Both middle-aged white men, both very tan and appeared comfortable on the water. One, a burly man with big forearms, had bushy curly hair and a thick beard, and the other, taller and thinner, had soft blond hair like a Scandinavian infant and a reddish moustache. Both permeated a good degree of education.

"That'd be great. The hot horn went off. Engines were overheating. Shut down to protect themselves," the taller one said. "If you could tow us to the marina, it'd be awesome."

"I got it." Street waved to the approaching police boat, who saw all was okay and sped off.

Street grabbed a line from beneath his bench seating and ran it through two cleats at the stern of his boat, one on the port and the other on the starboard. He pulled both ends over the rear transom and connected them with a square knot, the result being a secured loop of rope dangling over the rear of the transom.

"Throw me a line," Street said. The blond man did, and Street secured the man's line to the loop dangling over his transom via a bowline knot. The boats were now tied together.

"Ready?" Street said.

"We're ready," the burly man responded. Street throttled forward and then looked behind. The line from the distressed boat snapped tight as the bowline knot held firm to the loop Street had tied from his own line. The larger Intrepid jerked from side to side before moving steadily ahead in Street's wake.

Street maintained a slow speed, constantly turning his head to check on the men behind him in case they ran into trouble and needed Street to stop. The thin blond man remained on the bow of the large Intrepid, maintaining eye contact all the way. The burly man went below. A few boats dotted the horizon.

A Sea Tow boat drew near, with a small center console in tow. The Sea Tow driver, a squat man with a shaved head, stared at Street and nodded. The man may have been losing business with Street towing in the Intrepid, but the man seemed glad someone was helping a boat in distress.

The Miami-Dade Police boat appeared from out of nowhere anew, lining up between Street and the Sea Tow craft. The police boat was a gray inflatable but had a rigid hull with two outboard engines, unmistakable on the waters to most. The police officer waved at Street anew from inside a small cabin. Street waved back and gave a thumbs-up. All three boats then veered in different directions.

An hour later, Street was in the no-wake zone channel, coming in close to the marina where the men were headed. Luckily for him, it was the same marina where he kept his Whitewater. Street let go of the steering wheel and untied the line on the cleats. He held the end of the line with one hand and grabbed the steering wheel with the other. He pointed the bow to the marina and its accompanying restaurant, typical of the southeastern United States, with its nautical ramshackle appeal coupled with not-so-ramshackle prices. Street came close to the outer docks and hooked hard to the starboard. The boat in tow followed suit, building speed as Street made the sharp turn. Street released the line towing the boat. The large Intrepid, moving on its own accord, had gained enough speed to coast into a nearby slip.

"Thanks," both men yelled in unison.

"You bet," Street said, wheeling back around to check on the distressed vessel. It was now safe in port. The burly man waved over a dockhand. Street heard him say they didn't need assistance but he would be up shortly to pay the landing fees to keep the boat safe overnight.

"You saved us big time. Do you know how much a tow would cost?" the blond man asked.

"I can only guess," Street said.

"How about lunch to say thanks?" the burly man asked, looking over his shoulder while following the dockhand to his office.

"Sounds good," Street said.

"Great," the burly man replied. "Dock up there," he added, pointing to a nearby slip, and he walked away.

"One more thing," the blond man said. "Can you help us unload?"

"No problem," Street said.

Not long after lunch, Street navigated the Whitewater through the canals in Gables Estates, a neighborhood so posh that Street shuddered to think what the owners of all the multimillion-dollar mansions paid in taxes. He had texted Catherine Burnett earlier and asked if he could check out the boat from the photographs. She said she might not be there when he arrived but to feel free to board the large custom-made sportfishing yacht. And there it was, a stunning eighty-foot Rybovich, the very same one from the photo Catherine had sent over. Beautiful lines, gorgeous teak deck, and a total price probably well north of God knows how many millions of dollars. Roland couldn't afford this boat, considering where he was in his career, Street thought. Pennie Spradling, though, came from old money. Serious money.

He docked his Whitewater and hopped up onto dry land. He took in the sites of one of South Florida's most desired neighborhoods, home to world-class athletes, business leaders, and the upper echelons of North American and other societies.

Some house staff from next door caught wind of him as he walked along the dock. They stared at him suspiciously, frowning and crinkling their noses out of curiosity, not because Street looked out of place, but because they had never seen him before.

He checked out the Mediterranean mansion that was home to Catherine Burnett. Easily north of $15 million. Probably surpassing $20 million, and with enough space to dock such a fine boat with uninterrupted access to Biscayne Bay and the Atlantic Ocean. Must be nice, he mused. Things from childhood and adolescence often seem smaller when revisited in adulthood, Street thought, but not the Spradling estate.

He looked over at his suspicious audience. "It's okay. Ms. Catherine told me to check out the boat," he said in Spanish. "I'm probably going to buy it today anyway, but I wanted to have a peek at it by myself before all the brokers and whatnot take me out on a sea trial. I always steal a moment alone with big yachts before I take delivery, you know, to see if we are one." They rolled their eyes and walked away.

He boarded the boat. The warmth of the teak deck beneath his bare feet brought his head out of the clouds and back to reality. He would never be able to afford a boat like that, and he had work to do. Still he stole a moment to imagine how smoothly the boat would run, especially with its wooden hull, probably crafted of some fine mahogany. No vibrations or noise, and all impacts nicely absorbed compared to its fiberglass or closed-cell-foam rivals. Inside was just as he expected. Tasteful furniture, teak interior, and luxury oozing out of the boat's four staterooms. He looked at the photo on his phone. Same one. Roland Spradling and the murderous Placebo Agenda directors offshore. Fishing offshore. What was the big deal about that?

"Like what you see?" a voice called in.

Street snapped his head to the stern.

Catherine Burnett, mother of Pennie Spradling and mother-in-law to Roland Spradling, stood in the aft deck. She entered, checking out the interior of the fine boat, though not as impressed as Street. She viewed it neither disapprovingly nor with reverent affection—it was not a costly burden though not a source of wonderful family memories either. Just another possession. Street just stared at her. She was even more striking in person. Youthful, confident, and poised, even amid her time of grief, which brought on endless questions that might never find answers. Street imagined Pennie maintaining her own grace and poise during her horrific final hours on earth.

"Mrs. Burnett. I'm sorry..."

"I know, Street. I just came to see if you needed anything. Something tells me you know more about what's going on than you are letting on, and that's okay," she said, walking to the galley. She opened the refrigerator and grabbed two beers, opened them both and handed Street one.

"Mrs. Burnett..."

"Call me Catherine."

"Catherine. I will do what it takes to find out what I can. I don't know why they were murdered or who did it."

"You know something," she said, walking from the galley to take a seat in the main salon. She moved with self-assurance, forcing Street to get out of her way, as if she walked with an invisible force field, then she sat on the large L-shaped sofa and set her beer down on the teak coffee table. Street took one of the three stools at the nearby bar and plopped down.

"If you knew enough then this whole awful, awful, awful thing would have been solved or prevented. But you do know more than me or the police. So tell me what you do know."

Street hesitated. If he told her, he'd risk coming across as delusional and paranoid. Then he looked at her, and he knew she was reading his mind and his processing outcomes.

"Street, don't worry about what people think about you. Don't worry about how crazy the thoughts and theories in your mind may seem to others. If you want to help, then tell me. Not that I can do anything, but I can be a sounding board for you," she said, staring out the window. "And let's no longer ignore the massive elephant in the room. You and Pennie dated, though she left you. If you weren't so hard on yourself all the time one day and then overcompensating to make up for whatever twenty-something insecurity you had going on the next day, maybe you would have been more successful, and Pennie would be alive and happy with you today."

Street took in what she said. He knew his past with Pennie would come up. And it did, and surprisingly, it wasn't that painful.

But he focused on the task at hand and decided to trust Catherine Burnett. "Roland's bosses are actually CIA operatives. They're illegally working in legitimate companies getting their employees to do their spying for them. How do I know? Because his bosses are my bosses. They get us to do their espionage for them while they've got something else planned, something that will make them rich. That's where I'm lost, though it looks like drug smuggling. Maybe weapons shipped into Venezuela. Either way, I've hit a dead end."

Catherine's face was flat, as if she had been told a campfire story everyone had heard for generations. Then she shrugged. "I wouldn't put it past them. Nothing surprises me. They picked you for your journalism skills, but Roland for his accounting skills? Something's missing there. Why did they kill him? And why my Pennie?"

"I'm working on that. Anyway, I would run to the police, but I want to tell the world what's going on, you know, break this story and nab all involved."

"Be a hero? Sounds risky."

"It is. I'm finally taking a chance in my life."

"Betting on your full potential, are you?" she asked.

"I'm working on that too."

"Well, have a look around the boat. If Venezuela wants to smuggle cocaine into the US, it's going to need a million boats like this to give that country the money it needs right now. Nothing has changed since Roland used it last. Kind of a shame. We've had it for a while and didn't use it that much. We charted it a lot so people could enjoy it and keep the cobwebs from gathering, but it rarely left international waters. Maybe as far as Bimini tops, and that's not even fifty miles away. You can check the engine hours if you want. Here are all receipts regarding maintenance."

Catherine handed him a large accordion folder, stood up and set her untouched beer on the table. She motioned for Street to finish it after his.

"Good luck, Street. If you need anything from me, just ask." She took one last look around the boat. "Roland loved this boat. He loved offshore fishing more than anything else, except for Pennie. He was a good man, Street, and so are you."

She pulled her phone out of her pocket and stared at it for a couple of seconds.

"Maybe this will help," she said, sending him a new text. And then she left.

Street stared at the new photo on his phone. It really wasn't that much different from the others she had sent him before. Roland and crew fishing and enjoying life. He shrugged and shoved his phone in his pocket and then got to work.

He rummaged through the master and guest staterooms, all the heads, and everywhere else he could think of where he might find something, anything. Anything that would provide clues to the deaths of Pennie, Roland, or anyone else. But nothing jumped out as suspicious. He checked bait freezers, drink coolers, tackle boxes and storage, ice machines, storage compartments, more gear boxes, and even the engine room, where he scanned both diesel engines up and down like a police officer searching for fingerprints. The latest computer software showed the engines had but a few hours in use each. Everything looked great. There was no way this boat had ventured too far away.

He walked up to the salon and out onto the rear deck. He scanned the tuna tower and the entire bridge. Opened every box and cooler above. Knocked on every square inch for secret compartments. Nothing. This is going nowhere, he thought. This boat never smuggled drugs. Nothing out of the ordinary here.

He walked back inside and into the crew stateroom, which he had overlooked. There was a closet hidden behind a small raft designed to be pulled by waterskiing ropes from a boat. He moved the raft, opened the door, and looked in. Dismay. No pounds of cocaine or caches of weapons. Just fishing rods, or rather, cases to hold fishing poles. The rods themselves were gone, probably safe and dry in a garage or rec room inside. Just ten fly-fishing rod cases, long cylinders with screw tops. He was about to slam the door shut but stopped and took a second look inside.

His dismay was short-lived, chased away by mounting curiosity. Fly-fishing rods were normally used in shallow backwater flats around South Florida. A little interesting to find them in an offshore boat but not entirely out of the realm of possibility, as some have mastered the art of fly-fishing in the open ocean. But ten? Street grabbed one and shook it. It was empty. He shrugged and grabbed another. He opened the top. Same thing. Nothing inside, save some grit and grime, which he thought was weird. They all were like that. Who would own a fine boat like this and not care for their fishing equipment?

He walked back to the stern, grabbed his phone, and stared again at the picture Catherine Burnett had just sent of Roland, Brent, and company.

Something caught his eye. "Busted," he said aloud. He smiled and shook his head. Busted big-time, Brent.

He remembered the accordion file full of receipts, and he ran back to the stateroom, grabbed it, and started rooting inside. Boats required lots of work, let alone one this size, and the sheer volume of paper inside the accordion folder illustrated the amount of money and time that had gone into the large yacht. He shuffled through the papers and eventually found what he was looking for. Maintenance work on the engines. Lots of dollars jumped off the receipts. Lots of dollars. And lots of time had passed since anything major took place on those engines as well. All the receipts revealed that work was completed several years ago. He went back to the engine room, checked the engine hours, and took in the cleanliness. Then he stared again at the photo.

I'm one step closer to you, Brent, he thought. Just not there yet. Or am I? Then one last thing hit him.

"Numbers! Jesus," he said aloud.

He thought about Boston and Pennie's message for him before she took her own life. He remembered them.

"What are you trying to tell me, Pennie?" he asked aloud. Just a random sequence of digits? No. She wouldn't do that. That would make no sense. She knew Street would remember the numbers, each and every one of them. Memories. The past. That was what Pennie wanted Street to tap. His unparalleled ability to recall things. That much was clear.

He searched his memory bank of Pennie, and images of his late teens and early twenties rushed to the surface. Going out on the town in South Beach while home from break in college. Boating in the sun in December while his college buddies up north froze. Fond memories indeed. But fond memories wouldn't bring Pennie back, and they wouldn't save Molly Wells either. Focus on the numbers. He ran through them in his head. Nothing. Nothing at all. Sixteen numbers. Or was it sixteen numbers?

"Moron!" Street shouted at himself in the large yacht. "Heaven forbid some of those numbers might be two digits. Idiot!"

He grabbed the fly-fishing rod cases, ran back into the stateroom, and finished his beer and the one Catherine had left on the galley table. He tossed both empty bottles into the trash, ran onto the dock, threw the rod cases aboard, hopped into his boat, and cranked up the engines.

"Thank you, Pennie," he said, revving up the outboards as open water lay ahead and the tranquil Gables Estates grew thin on the horizon. "I hope you and Roland rest in peace. There is no pain anymore," he said, throttling the engines. "But those who did this to you are going to feel some pain, no matter how far up the power ladder they may be," Street said over the sound of his outboards. "I can promise you that."

A half hour later he was drifting in Biscayne Bay. He killed the engines and stared at the horizon. The wind blew onshore, and some cloud cover to the west allowed the skies to darken a little quicker than normal. The waters of the Atlantic were taking on richer blues as the sun chugged westward.

Street took some time to think. Patricia was safe, and so was Molly. He could protect them. Pennie was another story. She was gone. But her message to Street was alive and well. This was no time for overanalyzing, yet there was still time for this one last trip down memory lane.

He gunned the engines and headed east away from the eastern reaches of Biscayne Bay and out toward the open Atlantic. On the horizon, a cast-iron lighthouse began to take shape. The Whitewater made it to plane, and the bow lowered, thus allowing cool winds to shoot across the entire boat. The horizon was wide open and free of other boats for a mile, which made thinking and driving at the same time an easy task. Street kept his eyes on the beacon, on the Fowey Rocks Lighthouse standing firm on the edge of the bay as it had since the late nineteenth century.

He accelerated, both engines willingly responded and roared behind him, as if they were part of a team rallying him on. As he got closer to the lighthouse, Street slowed to a near idle. He looked around. Nothing but blue skies and calm, blue waters. He was about seven miles south of Key Biscayne, and it seemed like he had the entire Atlantic to himself. A true rarity. He took a trip back down memory lane.

Street knew that Pennie would have remembered that he had a photographic memory. Hers was pretty good too. Good enough to write down some numbers from her past while naked and staring down the barrels of several guns. He remembered the numbers she had written. They weren't random. And there weren't sixteen numbers. There were eight: Twenty-five, thirty-five, twenty-two, zero-five, eighty, zero-five, fifty-five, and twenty-two.

After adjusting for current and wind and drifting for a few moments, Street pressed a button on the console, and the windlass at the tip of the bow released the anchor. A few more moments and a few yards of drifting later, the anchor caught and the line went taught. The boat ceased to move.

Memory lane.

Street looked that the GPS monitor on the console. His exact location was 25°35'22.05" North, 80°05'55.22" West. He was exactly where Pennie had told him to go. He took one last look around him. Nobody. He pulled off his shirt, stood on the transom, and dove into the water.

CHAPTER

40

The president of Venezuela sat behind his desk. Bernal stood beside him. They both stared at the door, not saying a word to each other. Whoever they were waiting for couldn't get there fast enough to break the ice. But the door was still closed. Eventually, Bernal spoke first.

"I'm sorry if I overstepped my bounds. I was out of line and disrespectful," he said. "You've won elections year after year, and I'm here to support you."

"You were right. I need to tone it down a bit. Apology accepted. And I apologize to you. Now, onto business."

Finally, the door opened and the president's next guest was announced, Russia's Ambassador to Venezuela, Yuri Reoutt. The diplomat entered. Tall and a little fair, with thick, red hair cut short, neatly cropped military-style, just long enough to pass as civilian. Gray, pin-stripe suit. Crisp white shirt with just enough sleeve peeking over the cuff. He had a long red nose, though, Bernal thought.

He knew the man never missed a social function, especially a cocktail party. Yuri had his driver discreetly drop him off at several preferred bars from time to time when out and about. Lunch was starting earlier and earlier these days, Bernal had observed, but the man never missed a beat.

The president of Venezuela and Reoutt shook hands. They then sat down in two distinguished chairs and began small talk in front of a few invited photographers, engaging in cross-legged, good-natured chuckling with a blend of folksy smiles and occasional I-see-your-point eye contact. No reporters were there, just photographers. Then all were ushered out in what was really left to be truly closed-door talks.

The ambassador leaned in. "I just denied extended arms deals to the press. It's amazing who talks to these people."

"Good," Bernal said. "No more surprises."

The president of Venezuela nodded; his lips sealed perfectly shut.

"We finally get new facilities for our military in the region, and you get the investment in your infrastructure and some arms for, well, for whatever you see fit," Reoutt said. "Who knows? There are wonderful beaches along the Caribbean coast here, and now that you'll have more access roads, developers will put up hotels and bring in the tourists to hundreds and hundreds of new Caribbean destinations."

"Why are warm-water ports still so important to Moscow anyway?" Bernal asked. "I could understand if this were the Cold War, and I do see the strategic importance, but why the urgency?"

Reoutt smiled. "We might not need to sneak around Norwegian fleets like in the past, but there's always a need to sneak arms around the world to our friends, especially under the eyes of arms embargos like the one we've got in Syria now. Come on, Hernán. You know why we back those guys much to the chagrin of the Americans."

"Yes, I know," Bernal said.

"A little conflict is always good for business and oil prices," Reoutt said with a smile. A hiccup sputtered out of his mouth. "We export more of that stuff than you do now."

Bernal shook his head but smiled.

"What can I tell my superiors in Moscow?" Reoutt asked.

Bernal spoke first, before the president could utter a word.

"The project will be financed by Russia along with Venezuela in conjunction with private companies in Venezuela and elsewhere. We could get a little help from abroad if need be. Most likely, Brazil will want to put up money just to develop infrastructure related to the base such as highways in order to get their bulk commodities out of their country and onto the high seas at nearby Venezuelan ports, even if it's outside of their borders. It's going to take a long time for them to deal with their crappy roads and creaky bridges, so they'll jump at the chance to finance new ports and roads on their neighbor's shores to get around their own bottlenecks, which will help with your base. So make one of those 'everyone in the region wins' statements. We do not anticipate assistance from multilateral lending institutions or foreign banks. In other words, the US will have a tougher time sending in moles delivering money from the Inter-American Development Bank. This is our deal."

Reoutt took in the information. Stroked his chin and stared at the table, as if someone were informing him of something important albeit a little more trivial, such as swings in wheat prices.

"The entire area will handle both container and bulk commodity shipping concerns, with ample room for military ships," Bernal went on. "Let's be clear. Your base will be far away from other shipping operations, and it will come complete with a munitions depot, barracks, and ample room for an airstrip and all the necessary functions you want. Submarines are welcome. Of course, La Orchila comes first. That stays silent."

They all smiled. Then the president jumped in.

"We need towns outside of Caracas. Your naval base is going to create jobs and help move people out of these slums and into more dignified housing."

Reoutt perked up. "We're going to make a ton of money. Oil prices will stay as high as we need them to be. Venezuela, an OPEC giant, and Russia, a non-OPEC giant, can flex our muscle to the world's markets. We can hold war games. We can move a carrier closer to Cuba. We can welcome ships from anywhere that irks the US. But first the mundane stuff. Assault rifles and other hardware. We'll ship them in and help distribute them to your military—"

"We'll handle that. Just get them here." The president cut him off. He stood, walked to a nearby window, and gazed out.

An amused Bernal shook his head. The president looked like a bad actor trying to strike a pose like that of a statesman.

"I've waited for this all of my life," the president said. "For so long, even my mentor in Cuba couldn't pull this off, a dream come true."

The smile on Bernal's amused face vanished.

Reoutt continued. "Venezuela will host a naval fleet fully armed with nuclear warheads, just a stone's throw away from the US coast. Nuclear bombers on La Orchila as well. And that's just the beginning."

Shortly afterward, Reoutt left, and the Venezuelan president and Bernal sat quietly in the room digesting the fairly routine meeting. Bernal spoke first.

"Didn't mean to cut you off, but I have more experience with these diplomats, especially this guy, and I need you calm these days. Still, you may not be the ultimate statesman, but you are a leader, and a good one, and more importantly, a strong one. A strong one that normally pays attention to policy details."

The president shrugged it off. "Doesn't matter. Deal with him. I'm taking steps to improve our housing policies. I'm going to ask Colombian and even American civil engineers and other experts to help me out with that."

"Good olive branch," Bernal said. "There's just one problem, Mr. President. Even if the Russians do bring their nuclear warheads here, they still aren't the property of Venezuela. Technically, we're still not armed. I know everyone wants to be in the nuclear club, but it takes an awful lot to get hold of uranium and then enrich it to weapons-grade capacity. You have to install centrifuges and employ technology we don't have, and spies will catch on if we try. It takes time and manpower to enrich enough uranium to declare yourself at having achieved weapons-grade levels. The Americans will find out. Still, I think having their presence on our coasts and islands will ultimately serve our goal to let the Americans know they don't run the show as much as they did in Latin America and elsewhere. But telling Reoutt that your dream has come true? Mr. President, do you have other plans that I don't know about?"

The president shook his head. "No, Hernán. Of course not."

The president walked away. He walked down the hall, and in a minute, the young brunette woman found him. The president nodded, and the woman dialed a clean cell phone. "Operation Firefly is a go," she said.

CHAPTER

41

Street adjusted his eyes to the salty depths, kicking hard toward the sea floor. The water was about twelve feet deep, well-lit, soft and greenish-blue. Down he swam. It didn't take him long to approach the sandy bottom. Although the water was shallow, there was enough depth for pressure to build around his head. He pinched his nose and exhaled to adjust. His sinuses were sealed off like a plane ready for takeoff. The external noises of the water went silent due to the change in pressure in his nasal cavities, and he focused on his surroundings.

The marine floor was like everything else in South Florida—flat. Though it wasn't without its own personality, with stretches of bright underwater sand here, some clumps of vegetation there, and some coral rocks over there. Good diving spots were a fair distance away, and so was the nearest boater that afternoon.

He turned around a few times, mainly to enjoy being underwater, then he got back quickly to the task at hand. After some sharp forty-five-degree scans, he found exactly what he was looking for. An old lobster trap. It was not tethered to a rope and a surface buoy, rather, it appeared to be abandoned in the shallow waters not far from the drop-off to a much deeper part of the Atlantic Ocean. Nobody would ever find it. Just like Street had left it.

When they were students, he and Pennie had set it there years ago to make an artificial fish reef. They had some PVC pipes and some buckets in there as well, hoping coral would take it all over and create a habitat for fish. Fortunately, waves of guilt had come over them. They didn't know what they were doing, as such a task was best left for marine biologists, so they returned to clean up. They got all the plastic, though they had forgotten to return for the trap.

It was still there. Pennie had remembered, and she wanted to make sure Street would remember it as well. He grabbed it and smiled into the vast expanse of ocean. It had enough weight in it to secure itself in the water but not too much weight to make it immobile. He gave it a couple of yanks with his feet on the bay's floor, and it broke free.

He began to kick upward with the lobster trap in tow. He pumped hard, legs flailing but in rhythm, which gave him the appearance of a fishing lure of sorts churning through the waters, though there were no signs of marine life anywhere around him save the seagrasses. Street looked up and saw the base of his boat darkening the surface. Up he swam, his head fixed toward the hull of the boat. It's manufactured curves and right angles gave it an out-of-place appearance on the water.

Street broke the water's surface, grabbled ahold of the ladder of the aft swim deck, and made his way aboard. With one hand on the transom, he hoisted the slimy-yet-sturdy lobster trap in the air and then gently onto a towel on the floor of the boat. He stood over it like a winning fighter catching his breath over a fallen enemy, and then he scanned the horizon. Far away, a large white motor yacht strutting with confidence moved slowly northward.

He turned his attention back to the lobster trap and flipped open the little door. He looked inside. No lobsters, of course. Just some stones to keep it from moving. He reached deep within the trap in a manner similar to a child rooting around the base of a cereal box in search for a secret surprise. Nothing. Just rocks, mud, and seaweed.

"Great," he said aloud.

He frowned and pushed the trap and towel to the starboard aft of the boat as if it were a gear bag that was in the way. He was about to tie it off but determined that there were enough stones inside to keep it from sliding around when the boat got moving.

Why did Pennie want him to remember it? Was this a message from beyond the grave to keep the bay clean? Practice a little environmental sustainability while exposing murderous spies? The lobster trap was a dead end.

"Gee thanks, Pennie. Duly noted. I'll get a sailboat next and ditch this gas-guzzling center console."

He sat on the transom bench and looked back into the water, down to where the lobster trap had spent a decade resting in a marine prairie. Something's not right, he thought. There was something else down there.

He walked quickly to the bow of the boat and lifted the top of a storage locker. It was empty. Of course, he thought. That's what you get for cleaning things up and staying organized. That's what you get for properly stowing your equipment back on dry land where it should be. He hopped behind the console, cranked up the engines, and headed ashore.

Almost two hours later, he was back at the same waypoint, back where Pennie had told him to go. Everything he'd need was on board this time, including a mask, snorkel, and diving fins. And a scuba tank. And equally as important, he had a diving flashlight. The sun had set, racing westward, as if it were urgently needed elsewhere in the world, leaving the East Coast to settle into darkness. The water was darkening fast, losing the deep-blue hues typical of lower-angle sunlight.

Street killed the engines and took in the last ribbon of light to the west behind the city, which glowed like a strip of lava that was quickly cooling and losing its luster. The water below was as dark as ink, revealing nothing below its surface, unlike the way it had earlier in the day with its inviting blue and green shades. He quickly slipped on his gear, tossed a dive buoy overboard, and then he jumped over the side of the boat. He was back in the water.

Down he swam but with greater confidence, knowing he didn't have to go back and forth to the surface for air. In seconds, he was at the floor again, checking out his surroundings. The diving GPS around his wrist let him know his proximity to the boat and to Pennie's waypoint. Now start searching, he thought. But for what? He swam around looking for fish. There were none. Nothing to accompany him on his nighttime swim. Focus, Street thought. Why did Pennie send you here? He swam back to where he had found the lobster trap. Nothing. A few yards here and a few yards there. Still nothing. Jesus. A little help, Pennie. Then a wave of guilt washed over him. He felt badly about getting annoyed with her because he couldn't find whatever clue she had stashed out in the water. So he swam around, peering into the darkness while checking the small GPS monitor on his wrist to keep his bearings.

It was now fully dark. He looked around for sharks. None appeared from out of the darkness seeking food in his flashlight beam. He thought of the alligator back in the Everglades. It was miles away. So was any other sign of life.

He swam, scouring the sea floor until he decided to increase the scope of his search area. It didn't take long until he caught sight of something—something that reflected back to him in his light. Something yellow and bright shot up from the mud. It was shiny, definitely painted and definitely not natural. Street swam closer to it, circling it, getting a bird's-eye view of it, as if he had unearthed some lost archaeological treasure and was surveying the best place to begin work. It only took a few seconds for him to discover that it was a discarded tackle box, something that may have slipped over any boat on its way to and from South Florida's many popular fishing spots.

Street approached it headfirst and waved a layer of silt away, quickly finding a handle. Fragments of sand swirled like snowflakes in a blizzard around the box as he unearthed it. He yanked it, and after a few tugs it moved with surprising ease. He could feel the contents inside rattle around in response to the quick jerk. He held it up in front of him, and examined it with his dive light. It was fairly new, judging from the lack of nicks and scrapes and the brightness of its paint. He turned it around to gauge what may be inside but with some care so as not to break anything, as if he were appraising some piece of art or a rare book. More rattling inside. He shook it, confident now that it wasn't in the water long enough to come apart. Whatever was inside was probably wet but not yet decayed. Then he turned it upside down. Across the bottom, written in large black letters that contrasted sharply against the yellow paint, was the word *Spradling*. He had found what Pennie had sent him to find. Let's get this back to the boat, he thought.

He looked up to begin his ascent. The last rays of sunlight were long extinguished, which reduced visibility to absolute nothingness. Even closed eyes revealed more images, though anything caught in the beam of light came in clearly, colorfully, and with detail. He shined the light around him. Patches of sand and sea flora were below him, some stray fish swimming with the incoming tide darted above him, some floating seagrass, a lost baseball cap drifting in the water, a large tiger shark.

Street froze.

The shark was not just large but massive, and Street wondered how long it had been circling him before he realized the fish was even around. He kept it locked in his flashlight beam, guessing it was about twelve feet long. Street paid close attention to the tigerlike markings covering its body, feeling both mesmerized and panicked at the same time. The stripes were clear and well-defined, which let Street know the fish was young and healthy. The shark seemed to glance at Street out of the corner of its eye, like a prison-yard shot caller sizing up a new inmate. Whatever the case, the shark was letting Street know it was around and that it was the boss in these waters.

Street remained motionless, keeping the fish in his light. The shark, in response, seemed only happy to relish in the limelight, circling around and wavering closer to let him see what he was up against. Street noticed how slowly the fish swam, which let him know this showdown was not going to end soon. He sighed in his regulator, realizing there was no slapping this animal on the tail and chasing it away.

After a minute, Street broke his stare from the fish and looked at the tackle box in his other hand. It was closed tight, the clasp shut and the handle tight in this fist. He relaxed his grip and shook the box, while the tiger shark and the entire Atlantic Ocean seemed to ignore him. The fish just swam.

Fine, Street thought. You win. This is your show, and I'm out of here. He turned off his flashlight and darkness covered him totally. It was so dark that his balance was off. The fish was there, and Street knew that it could see and sense things infinitely better than he could. He turned on the light on his wrist GPS and checked the direction of his boat. Slowly he swam, paying close attention to his legs, wondering if he would feel pain from a bite or if it would be an attack so massive that he would go from normal to numb to dead in a millisecond.

He figured the boat was a few meters away, and he stopped swimming, opting to drift for a few seconds in the water probably midway between the bottom and the surface. He turned the light back on and caught sight of the tiger shark. It circled him anew. Then its fins stopped. It ceased swimming and slowed to a drift, looking like a plane that had idled its engine and begun to glide to slow its momentum. Then it jerked hard and fast, rushing straight toward him. The tail exploded left and then right, and the fish shot at him as if propelled by something beyond muscle. Its mouth opened. Teeth revealed themselves, with the back rows leaning forward, eager to jump to the front of the line and get in the game.

Contact.

Street blinked, not breathing at all. He felt the impact on his chest and saw the predator's eyes roll back in that primordial blend of necessity and bliss that comes from taking a bite of something to quell hunger. The impact was hard and knocked him back a couple of feet.

But that was it.

His eyes opened at the sight of a tail in front of his mask, a tail that was swimming away. Street looked down at his torso. No bites, no blood. The fish had just pushed him, again letting this strange creature with bubbles, tubes and a metallic tank know who topped the food chain and who was a guest. Duly noted and respected. Street kept his eyes on the tail and watched the fish swim off into the darkness. A fish out of water yet deep in hot water, he thought. Then he was alone again.

A few minutes later, he climbed aboard his boat, shed his tank and scuba gear, and caught his breath. He blew snot and saltwater from his nose and reached over to wash his hands in the warm Atlantic. Relaxed now, he stared at the tackle box, which was viewable in the console lights.

He opened it. There were a few fishing lures but mainly hooks, several large sinkers, some line, and even some wire cutters. There was also a small tube of sunblock for lips. He wondered for a second if he had the right tackle box. He turned it over and written across the bottom, the name *Spradling* was still there in large black letters. Great. Pennie asked me from the grave to clean up the bay bottom as well as her garage. Lost tackle box found. Success. Street dismissed any thoughts of sarcasm. Surely Pennie wanted him to find more than just a tackle box.

42

Not long after he had docked his boat and changed clothes, he was savoring a beer and a fresh snapper sandwich at the Grouchy Grouper, ruminating over the contents of the tackle box with an occasional glance up to a Marlins game on the bar television set to keep him company. Back to his phone. No missed calls. No pings on social media. He ordered a diet cola for the road and checked some weather apps. There was still something swirling out in the Atlantic, yet it remained far away.

He paid his tab and left. The warm South Florida air wrapped around him and scrubbed off the stale conditioned air from the bar. A little life flowed through his veins, and he was off. He decided to walk a little. Get a little exercise before turning on the television and catching up on the tropical weather update before going to bed back at home.

As he walked, he checked his phone, and he saw that the National Hurricane Center had hiked the chance of the system turning into a storm in forty-eight hours to 40 percent from 20 percent. He put his phone away and then caught sight of a small convenience store, just a block away across Grand Avenue, and decided to go in. A bell alerted the cashier that a customer had entered, though the young man paid no attention to it. A blast of cold air hit Street. Back to an artificial atmosphere. Street bought a bottled energy drink. He paid cash and turned to walk out.

A few Miami police officers entered. Big guys with smooth, shaved heads. Blue uniforms. Tattoos and bulked-up hairless arms. Dispatcher voices cackled through their radios.

"Evening," Street said to one who was walking in as Street was leaving.

The officer stared at Street and said nothing. Mean, accusatory eye contact was all.

Street headed back to his Jeep, which was parked on the street.

He hopped in, cranked up the engine, and began to head home. A sea of blue and white lights behind him let him know instantly a good night's sleep in his own bed was a long way off.

Police lights. A quick blast of a siren. Street killed the engine and waited for the officer to approach. He did. Another heavily tattooed skin-headed law enforcement officer from the convenience store walked over. Then another.

"Evening, officer. What seems to be the problem?" After a shake-down with the Venezuelan police, this stop should be as routine as it gets, he thought.

"License and registration," the officer said in a surprisingly soft tone for such a menacing-looking man.

Street handed it to him and sat there, a little curious about being pulled over. He noticed the other officer who snubbed his greeting earlier in the convenience store doorway was on the scene as well.

The police officer checked his papers.

"Mr. Brewer, the reason I'm pulling you over is for a broken taillight."

"Broken taillight?" Street asked, concern brewing.

"Please step out of the car," the officer said.

Street did. Both walked around and saw the taillight was out.

"How much have you had to drink this evening," the police officer said.

"Three beers in a period of almost two hours," Street responded.

The officer nodded.

Street began reciting the alphabet backward in his mind to prepare for a field sobriety test. He checked his shoes. Good thing he wore running shoes and not flip-flops. He'll need the support and balance for the physical portion of the sobriety test. He was ready to consent and just be done with it. He would pass the test easily.

"Officer, I am not intoxicated."

"You're not under arrest. I'll just ask you to undergo a field sobriety test to assess your impairment. I can smell alcohol on your breath."

"Whatever." Street followed the flashlight with his eyes with no problem. Standing on one leg after boating was a bit of a challenge. It didn't matter. Just blow, record small amounts of alcohol, and I'll be on my way, Street thought.

"Mind if I check your vehicle?" the backup police officer from the convenience store asked.

"No problem," Street said.

"Anything you want to tell me about first?"

"No," Street said. He stared ahead down the road. A few onlookers watched, including a blonde woman, heavy but athletic. Beautiful skin and lustrous hair. She walked away and looked over her shoulder. She smirked at him and turned the corner. He knew who she was. His concern grew at not only seeing Karen Whittaker, but making eye contact with her as well.

"Mr. Brewer, are you prescribed any tranquilizers?" the police officer said.

"No," Street said, his unease building even more.

"Why did you lie to me?" the officer said, holding up a big bag of marijuana and a bag of what Street guessed were prescription benzodiazepines. Lots of them. The officer set it on the back of the car alongside a small envelope of rolling papers. There was enough marijuana to get him on distribution charges, not just simple possession. Possession of the pills without a prescription would be another charge. He was off to jail. No doubt Brent wanted him locked up, at least for a night. A record and pending court issues would keep him in Miami and out of the job market. It was so obvious. Worst of all, Molly Wells had no eyes on the ground watching out for her.

Was it his time for termination? Again? Would someone be waiting for him in county jail? I will survive this, Street thought.

CHAPTER

43

Street found himself handcuffed in a small entryway made of cyclone fencing as he entered county jail, casting aside all hope of finding a new job now. His deal with Matías would likely end, too.

Three guards appeared as if they were some sort of defensive line and not the first faces of jail intake. Large men with relaxed faces decked out in thick, green jackets approached Street slowly. Only a few feet inside the facility, the guards lined Street up with other inmates, backs to the wall. Mugshot time.

When Street's name was called, he stood, still cuffed, and was told to stare at a small digital camera lens. He knew what was coming because it was cliché: a front shot and then a side shot. There were even pictures of other inmates hanging up to show people the dos and don'ts of posing for a mug-shot. The dos looked upright and stared directly in the camera. The don'ts slouched, cocked their head, and gave attitude. Street went along with the dos, as this pic would surely be on the arrests page of local news and mug-shot sites within hours. He saw his picture on a monitor and felt surprised. It wasn't half as bad as he thought it was going to be. One young man in his mid-twenties, covered in tattoos and likely Latin American based on the language of the ink on his arms, waited calmly, looking neither like the dos nor the don'ts. He wasn't focused on the rest of the jail intake procedures, but rather stood there fixated on Street, unflinching and with some sort of resolve. Street blew him off.

After his picture was taken, a guard uncuffed Street and took him toward a small, filthy bathroom. The walls were a faded blue, the paint was peeling, and the lack of adequate lighting gave it an aura of a haunted hospital. A slab of piss-stained cardboard lay beneath the toilet and inside, an African American man was taking off his clothes. In a few seconds, the man was out and Street was told to go in.

"Strip down," one of the guards said.

Street did.

"Lift up your balls," the guard said.

Street did, although the guard really didn't seem to pay attention. Street peered over the guard's shoulders. More inmates lined up. The Latin kid in his twenties with the heavily tattooed arms was next in line, staring at Street.

"Turn around and squat," the guard said.

Street did, realizing the guard was checking to see if he had smuggled something up his ass. A mini bottle would have been nice, Street thought. This is just great. If he were going to jail, he at least should get a laugh out of it, especially under such ridiculous circumstances.

The guard then told Street to open his mouth.

Street did, but the guard barely noticed. Street wondered if the man even cared or if Street came across as so unthreatening and so out of place that the guard knew he was incapable of smuggling anything. Eventually, Street had all his clothes back on save his belt, which the guards whisked away with his wallet and keys.

The guards escorted him to a cell with the door wide open. There were a few inmates in there, all in street clothes. No orange jumpsuits in his cell. He sat down and stared out at the hall. He noticed the smell of sweat, urine and garbage drifting about the place, coming and going in waves of various intensity as if something awful was being prepared in some unholy kitchen nearby.

Street blew off his right to a phone call, and not long afterward, he was escorted to a much more crowded and dimly lit cell, and the door was closed. All the other inmates had on street clothes, and Street saw that those wearing orange county jail jumpsuits were kept in separate cells. He didn't know why, but he felt safer as a result.

He stood for a few moments after the jailer shut the door and tried to size up the other inmates without making too much eye contact. There were a few homeless, some drug addicts, and surprisingly, there were a few people like himself, branded white, middle-class at the least, and not affiliated with any gangs.

A bench ran along all the walls, yet there was no room to sit, so Street sat down on the hard floor. A few people slept and were using their shoes as pillows. Street did likewise. One Latin guy, the same one from when he was processed earlier, stood and looked down at everyone. He made eye contact with Street and held it. Then he looked away.

It took a few moments before the conversation resumed among the inmates. One other thing registered with him now, and it was the reason why the guards all wore thick jackets. It was freezing in there. Street ignored the temperature and focused on his cellmates. Two preppy white guys in their mid-twenties were sitting on a narrow bench attached to the wall above Street. A similar looking young man in faded red shorts that appeared more fitting for a country club than jail sat opposite them. The cliché of a question for Street came immediately.

"What are you in for?" one of the white guys seated above Street asked. They looked identical, khaki pants and white Oxford shirts. It was coincidental, because they didn't know each other. One had wavy brown hair and the other had slick black hair and glasses.

"Possession with intent to distribute," Street said, hoping they would leave it at that.

"What a dick cop," a voice arose from somewhere. "They pull you over on a traffic stop and find it?"

"Something like that," Street said. He stared at the two preppy guys. "What about you two? What's your story?"

"Driving with a suspended license," the guy with the slick black hair said.

The guy with the wavy brown hair rolled his eyes and said, "Boating under the influence. I was out on the bay with women out of my league just a few hours ago. Police boarded me to make sure we had sufficient number of life vests, smelled my breath and got me." The young man shook his head and laughed. "Man, not just a few hours ago, I was on the water hanging out with absolute angels."

"Now look who you're hanging out with," said the heavily tattooed Latin guy, with one eye on Street. The cell exploded in laughter. Street held the young man's gaze, not backing down for a second.

It didn't take long for all eyes to drift to the third preppy white guy, sitting uneasily across from the other two, and his broken-in red shorts and a white polo. He looked like something out of the Hamptons. A young African American in a sleeveless undershirt broke the ice.

"Yo, dude? Why you here?"

The kid squirmed. He was a bit younger than the other two, maybe twenty-two tops.

"It was a misunderstanding," he mumbled.

"It's all a misunderstanding, niggah. Come on," sleeveless shirt said.

The kid squirmed and then let it out. "Dining and dashing."

The whole cell burst into laughter anew. Even Street, who was trying to finally sleep through the ordeal, let out a deep laugh.

"Dine and dash? Man, you a trip," sleeveless shirt said. He stared at Street. "You really are a trip, and so is this motherfucker, Street Brewer."

Surprisingly, Street didn't freeze in fear. He remained calm and stared back at him. This could be Brent's man. He eyed the kid who called his name and then looked away, realizing that physically reacting to his name would not only reveal to the kid who Street Brewer was, but, more importantly, how responsive he'd be. The man had played his cards too soon and had let Street know he was Brent's man on the inside, Street thought, surprised by his calmness and alertness to such details.

Dine and dash blushed and then laughed, distracting Street a bit.

"We were at South Beach having dinner at this diner when my friend said, 'Let's go.' When we were outside and I asked him if he needed money to pay for my share of the check, he said that we should just keep walking. Before I knew it, the police had us."

The laughter subsided, and eventually Street drifted off into a light, dreamless sleep for a few moments, surprised he was able to nap even for a short while with a potential assassin in the cell. He sat upright and swore he'd stay awake.

A few hours later, a guard came and called out the names of about half of those in the cell, including Street's.

The tattooed guy mumbled, "Pretty soon, we'll be upstairs after a quick health review."

A few guys had said that earlier, leaving Street wondering what was upstairs. Hell, he figured he would ask.

"What's upstairs?"

"Beds. And it's not as cold," the guy mumbled. "Watch that shit-talking kid in the wifebeater shirt. He's Brent's eyes and ears tonight. And he may not be alone."

"Who the fuck is he, and who the fuck are you?" Street said.

"Not now. I'll tell you later. Walls have ears," the kid said.

Eventually, Street and the rest were directed to the enchanting upstairs. An elevator took them up, and they were unshackled and released into a large room with several bunks. Unlike the blue rooms down below, this one was green. It didn't smell as bad, and the temperature wasn't close to freezing. Truly, they were lapping in luxury now.

Early morning light crept in through some narrow windows. The "beds" were flimsy mattresses that looked like discarded pieces of Styrofoam wrapped up in packing tape. Men were asleep in bunks, some using mattresses as covers. A few were asleep on the floor. One guy had three of the flimsy mattresses, and Street asked him for one. He gave it to him, and Street lay down on the floor comfortable for the first time since being arrested. But he wouldn't sleep. His tattooed friend plopped down next to him. So did the young African American kid.

"Yo, dude," the latter said. Street stared at him. "What the fuck you lookin' at? I will fuck your shit up, niggah."

"Fuck off," Street told him back.

The kid then reached for something in his pocket.

Street had seen enough movies and television shows to know what it was, some kind of makeshift weapon, though a bit surprised he had it in this very early stage of incarceration. He stood. The kid stood up, his tall height catching Street off guard. Murmurs from the other cellmates grew in anticipation of a fight.

"Don't do it. The guards will get you," the voice of a homeless man shot out.

"Do it, Street," the tattooed kid said. "Do it before the guards get here."

Street punched, and he punched hard, landing a clean hook across the kid's chin. So clean that his hand didn't even get hurt. No broken or sprained fingers or wrist.

"Damn, niggah!" the kid shouted. He fell back, and his makeshift weapon, a nail wrapped in tape, shot up in the air. Street kicked the kid harder, surprised at the young man's size. He was tall, and he definitely had a reach advantage over Street. So Street kicked and hit him a few more times, anything to prevent him from getting up and using his reach advantage. The kid threw a punch back though it didn't land. Street swore he could make out a smirk on the young man's face.

The tattooed guy immediately grabbed the weapon and kicked it under the feet of some inmates sitting with their backs to the wall. Then he pulled Street from out of the fight and jumped on the kid, covered his mouth, and whispered something in his ear. All Street could make out were the words 'gone too far.'

Murmurs erupted into shouts, but the tattooed kid quickly stood and motioned for silence. All were quiet by the time the guards came by. Sleeveless sat back in the corner, looking defeated but not really seeming to care. The tattooed guy motioned to him to be quiet. Some time passed, and the tension eased in the cell.

"Just do as I say. The quicker you get out of here, the better. When you leave here in a few hours, walk around the building. Enjoy a hot dog at that stand on the side facing the hospital, and wait for further instructions," the man said.

"What?" Street said back.

"You heard me. Now shut up."

"Who are you?"

"I got your back. Now shut up. Don't draw suspicion."

Not long afterward, after some brief arraignments and similar procedures for the weary group of petty criminals, Street and many others were free and roaming the streets. He stopped and thought about walking home in the sunshine, even though home was miles away. But he didn't want to be out in public alone, so he ordered a ride share on his phone.

"Great," he said aloud, watching Miami pass by him. He had a criminal record now, which would take time to clear. Then he thought about his new friends from county jail and took a couple of laps around the bustling jailhouse. People were coming and going. Hot dog vendors were selling their products around the old building. Hot dogs. On the side facing the hospital. He had forgotten.

He headed that way, and a car turned the corner with a glowing ride share brand in the windshield, and Street motioned it over, not caring if it was the one he had called. The make and model of the vehicle were similar enough. It pulled over. A hand emerged from the window, motioning Street to walk around the corner. Street nodded and began to move, pretty sure the ride share was the contact his jailhouse friend had wanted him to meet.

He turned the corner. The car was behind him, and the driver indicated to Street to keep walking. A large parking lot lay ahead. Street understood and walked toward the lot, most of which was hidden under a highway overpass. When the car came around, Street walked straight up to the front passenger door. Then the front passenger window rolled down. A face peered out. A skinny face with energetic eyes. Green energetic eyes. Street froze.

"I told you I would keep an eye on you, and why didn't you get a hot dog?" a voice shot out. It was Pérez, from the Venezuelan intelligence police.

"Pérez? What are you doing here?" Street stared at the driver, his tattooed friend from jail. In the rear seat was the young African American man from the cell as well, the man he had assumed to be his assigned killer and jailhouse fight opponent.

"Following you. These two were here to protect you. Their fight and kicking of that makeshift knife would have flushed out any of Brent's goons who may have tried to take you out. No one came forward, or maybe they were too scared to take the bait after you punched our dear friend across the jaw."

Street glared at the tattooed Latin American man and the young inner city youth in the back seat. They both smiled back at him, warm sincere smiles like that of a teacher proud of a child that received his first gold star in first grade.

"You make a shitty actor," Street said to the African American.

"Agreed," the tattooed Latin American said. "He overplayed the part. Though he took the punch very well, did he not? He's a professional boxer, so you weren't really going to hurt him, though your punch surprised him."

"Not bad at all, Street," the young African American said. "With a little conditioning, some coaching and discipline, you might have a boxing future weighing in at, I'd say—"

"Very nice job, indeed," his tattooed colleague interrupted. "Fortunately for you, there was no one from Brent's camp in there, or, like Pérez said, our little fight would have coaxed them to make a move, especially with a discarded shiv on the floor. Then we could have gotten ahold of the would-be killer and learned more about what all is going on."

"We tried," the African American man said with a smile.

"Look," Street said, feeling an eddy of anger roil in his gut and then shoot up his chest. "If using racial stereotypes—"

"Anyway," Pérez interrupted. "I have a little delivery." He handed Street a flash drive. "Take this. You didn't see me or my two friends here. Neither did the FBI. You're going to be fine from now on if you trust me, even though I'm spying both on you and for you."

"What? Wait, what?"

"Lean over. Always assume that there are lip readers everywhere, maybe."

"What is it?" Street repeated, not trusting Pérez and still shaking off the disbelief he was speaking with him right there in Miami after just getting released from county jail. "And bullshit. There are no lip readers around."

"A little souvenir from Russia. Just check it out. And this time, don't give it to your boss."

Street never left anything behind in Venezuela. And he certainly didn't have a flash drive. In fact, he rarely used them, preferring cloud technology for several years now. He looked at it with skepticism. For all he knew, Pérez was an enemy of the United States, Venezuela, and himself.

"Oh, and here. For your troubles," Pérez said, extending his hand out of the car. He shoved a wad of bills in Street's hand. They felt good, new and folded neatly. Street caught a glimpse of several hundred-dollar bills, a wad about three inches thick.

"What do you mean, Russia?"

"Recognize this guy?" Pérez held out his phone. A picture was on the screen of Pérez's phone. Street knew the face immediately. From the bar with Patricia and Ian. From the microwave. A thin man. The CIA's pen clicker.

"Yes."

"Remember when you almost got torched alive in Petare? A voice? That was this guy. I don't know his name, but he's my new frenemy now after finding me and giving me this stack of money and some data. Both are for you. Not sure how he knew you were in jail, but he does his job well."

Street didn't even think about counting it and was about to throw it back.

"Before you throw it back," Pérez said, his thin, wiry neck leaning out of the car like some wading bird. "Before you throw it back, know that the money comes from government sources. Your government, not the Venezuelan government. Consider it as severance pay for your work in the public sector. It's already taxed. Don't forget that flash drive in your hand, and one more thing. Lean in close, I don't want everyone to hear."

Street leaned in. Then he saw lightning. A flash. Some pain. A split second later, he was on the concrete, looking up at the parked car. Pérez was laughing at him. He had thrown one of his quick punches across Street's chin. Fast enough to jar him but easy enough to be harmless and relatively damage-free.

"I told you I'd keep an eye on you! I'll be watching you. Okay? I've got your back. We've both been played. Remember when I said we should work together? We are now." The car sped off.

Street didn't want to know who saw him getting punched in the face in front of the county jail, which was very close to Jackson Memorial Hospital and a mountain range of other medical buildings. He thought of the tiger shark and its warning shove in the dark waters of Biscayne Bay. Neither the shark nor Pérez were his friends, but they weren't enemies either. He eventually caught a ride share home. Exhausted, he would sleep first and then deal with his legal and espionage matters later.

But first, he turned on the television. The low-pressure system off Africa had become better organized and was rapidly strengthening into a storm. The weatherman said it could turn into a tropical depression at any minute.

By the time Street fell asleep, Tropical Storm Granville was churning west. A ridge of high pressure over the Atlantic parked north of the strengthening cyclone, giving it no room to move northward the slightest bit. It was as if the storm was moving along the teeth of gear bits, with only one direction on its path, and that direction was west.

When he woke up very late the next morning, the storm had become Hurricane Granville and was fueling itself off the warm waters of the Atlantic Ocean. The high pressure to the north strengthened, blocking any northward movement, and in weather laboratories all over the world, complex computer models were in full agreement that the storm had only one place to go. And that was east toward South Florida. Warnings were likely soon, and for Street, they couldn't come soon enough.

Street spent lunchtime cooking some bacon and eggs. He ate quietly and stared at the wad of bills and the flash drive across the table, as if they were other people, strangers sharing a table in a crowded restaurant. He took another bite and pushed his plate aside. He grabbed the flash drive and popped it in his computer. One file. A video. He pressed play.

There was the pen clicker.

"Street. I don't know you. The CIA doesn't want me to know much about you at all, but trust me, they know everything about you, which you already know. I saved you from being burned alive because it was the right thing to do. Brent and his team are going down, and only you can prevent a horrible thing from happening. Go look under your kitchen sink." He started laughing as if he were engaged in some fraternity prank. That was it. The video ended and deleted itself. Street walked over to his kitchen sink, kneeled down, and opened the door. Nestled in a neatly lined group of cleaning products was a cell phone, and on the back was a sticky note, and on it were the handwritten words 'dial me.'

Alice in Wonderland nonsense, he thought. He turned the sticky note over. There was a phone number. A seven-digit number with a Miami-Dade area code.

He dialed. A voice answered. "Street, meet me at that public boardwalk on Biscayne Bay just behind Peacock Park in Coconut Grove. Just off the field, right next to that public baseball diamond." The man hung up.

Minutes later, Street was there on a small boardwalk that overlooked a slew of sailboats moored into protected waters behind small, green barrier islands. Two minutes later, a man walked up eating from a bag of potato chips, sipping from a large fountain cola. Street knew him in an instant—the pen-clicking man from Plaza Altamira—which seemed like decades ago after a night in jail.

"Street? My name is Peter Bogdanov." He didn't offer his hand. Neither did Street. "Just relax and listen. I work with the Russian government. Within the Ministry of Defense as far as you know. You don't trust me. Good. Do I work for the Foreign Intelligence Service? Does it matter what answer I give? To the point, you remember back in Venezuela, when I was shadowing you that night you met Ian Collins in the bar? I was dropping information into the voice recorder that your boss, Brent Drum, or whatever his name is, gave you. It was bugged. I was keeping the Americans informed of our plans in Venezuela to a degree—just like the Americans do with us. We know what the Americans are up to, they know what we are up to, and more importantly, we both want to keep each other in the loop regarding what the Venezuelans are up to. Yes, we need that idiot in power to stay down there, but personally, I couldn't give a shit. He goes, we lose our oil assets, which frankly, will be cheap in a decade or two. Still, we need the US when it comes to dealing with Venezuela to make sure the country isn't going to make things more complicated, especially when that president has had too much coffee and opens his mouth. Believe it or not, we do have common enemies, like drug traffickers. Look at it this way. Cops in your country have a tougher time dealing with small and unstable street gangs more often than they do with the larger Crips and Bloods. Two small gangs fighting each other one week can ally and battle someone else the next. That's the case with smaller but unstable outfits like Venezuela. They often pose more threats to global security than the big, established gangs like the United States or Russia, just because it's harder to gauge their loyalty."

A young couple walked down the boardwalk. They paused to take in the view and strolled on.

Bogdanov continued. "Am I a double agent? No. Am I a CIA asset? No way. The information I pass on to the Americans is always approved by my team. Did I know certain CIA officers were using you as a spy like a mule? At first, I did not. Did I care about the legal and ethical ramifications of such practices when I did find out? No. That's the Americans' business. I drop off information on you, and you do your freelance intel gathering and deliver it to Brent. Things got messy, however, when I found out Brent was killing his placebos, as he calls them, and when I suspected Russia may be exposed to some horrific spying scheme out of the US, I wanted nothing to do with that. So I'm getting involved to stop it. Appreciate the irony?"

Street shook his head and stared across the bay.

"A woman named Cyra Harred with the CIA has been tracking all this at the request of her boss. She reached out to me and let me know what's going on. We gave each other stuff along the way," Bogdanov said.

"Her boss? Someone knows about this? Give me her number. I've got a few things to say to her and her boss. She's called me by the way."

"She was gauging how much you knew about this agenda without trying to come across too obviously, and I'll be blunt here, she was also trying to see how effective it was and the extent of all the intel you were digging up."

"I'm going to come across very obviously to her. Who's her boss?" Street asked.

"I don't know who he is, but he is high up in the agency. Nobody knows how, but he found out about it and wants this program finished. No FBI exposure. Take care of it internally. You were supposed to die in Venezuela. I think you know what I am talking about. That was me who yanked you out of the microwave, and you know that. I gotta tell you, those guys were even due to come down and take you out when you were at the restaurant, but you ran right up into their lair unarmed! I was impressed and a little spooked. As it turns out, the man I use to smuggle arms into the country is also working with Brent and the Americans," Bogdanov said. "His name is Ricardo, and I don't need to tell you he's dangerous."

Street stared ahead toward the sailboats.

Bogdanov went on. "Anyway, I was up in the slums delivering Kalashnikovs as instructed."

"Who instructed you?" Street asked.

"It doesn't matter. It's a shame many of them didn't go to the military but to pro-government gangs, but anyway, that's where I come in. Taking care of the dirty part to arm urban militias so the Venezuelan military officially has no knowledge of it. Fine. Whatever. I do my job. I make the delivery, but I'm not killing Americans, especially not with brutal and stupid gang members. I want no part of Brent's agenda."

"Look, Bogdanov. I saw you in Caracas. I chased you into Petare. Did you want me to chase you? You led me in there, so you could kill me, just like I am going to do to you and everyone else here in about two minutes unless you start making sense. I'll call the FBI on all of you."

"I was actually approaching you to have this conversation, when I saw that young lady join you. I tried to back out, but I got sloppy, and you saw me. But as it turns out, I saved your ass. Anyway, I was keeping the CIA informed of our plans to build a base. But then things spooked Moscow. For one, Cyra told me about this Placebo Agenda crap. A hedge fund woman disappeared in Fort Myers, Florida. Another female, some software star, is about to die as well. It's all so horrible. But, and not to sound cold here, but the problem is that, technically, this could involve us, and I can't have that. I don't want the Americans tying us in with the killing of their citizens. You can imagine how messy this can get. Anyway, you did your job. You came to the country, you asked questions and scooped up some nice intelligence. The president corroborated to the press—you, basically—and to the CIA everything that he has told us. No amount of technology can replace that. But something is not adding up. I think that the base is a ruse, meaning the president is even keeping us in the dark about something, which could be a fatal mistake for him, and we fucking mean it."

"How do you guys communicate? You and the CIA?"

"I take English lessons in Venezuela. Cyra is working under a nonofficial cover as an English teacher there."

"Again, who is her boss telling her this stuff? The one who found out about this Placebo Agenda thing?"

"I don't know much about him. His name is Roman. I do know he was a Navy SEAL or Special Activities Division. A skilled assassin. Astute businessman. Harvard undergrad in economics. MBA as well. The works. That résumé may be too good to be true, but he's a genuine leader and always under the radar no matter what profile he assumes. I don't know how he discovered Brent's scheme, but he did. Maybe with technology, maybe someone tipped him off, I don't know. I do know he's one of those scary-smart guys from somewhere in the US."

"So, you say this port and whatever else Russia is working on down there is a ruse?"

"Sort of. We need military presence in the Caribbean, and Venezuela is a good place for it. It won't help us move goods in and out of Russia, but we can hide stuff there, and it will give us a place to set up a military post in the region and keep our navy mobile. Plus, we can keep a good eye on you and our friends in Cuba and in Caracas. And full disclosure, we might set up an air base in the Caribbean on La Orchila Island. Brent doesn't even know that. I dumped bogus intel on this supposed port, by the way. Bogus stuff on a nuclear power reactor as well. While we're at it, have Brent or the Venezuelans mentioned our plans to you? Has anyone said anything? Maybe let something slip? You're involved in global policymaking now," Bogdanov said.

"Not anymore." Street stepped back and looked out at the bay. Sailboats that were normally moored near the barrier islands had begun to thin out due to the approaching storm. Street gave his mind a break from processing Bogdanov's info to think of where the sailboats may have fled, likely up local canals or way south in the Florida Keys out of harm's way.

"Street, this is beyond you now. I know you're going to get angry when I say this, but you need to stop thinking about yourself and just let everything go. I think there's another angle to Brent's plan, and it goes beyond using mules to collect intelligence. There's a second phase, one that double-crosses the Venezuelans. I can feel it. I don't know what it is. Russia can use Venezuela for whatever purposes it sees fit. Venezuela is ours. But that idiot in Miraflores better fucking not even think about using Russia in some kind of agenda of its own. There will be hell to pay. Help me out. Let's brainstorm. That's why I even told you about La Orchila. I just gave you highly classified Russian intelligence. Work with me."

Street paced the dock and stared at the sailboats. It was still a calm summer day.

"I am also here to tell you Roman is going to slip some more evidence in your apartment under your sink as we speak. This meeting got you out of the house for that as well," Bogdanov said. "The CIA wouldn't trust me to deliver it. I don't know what's in it, but I can help you. Even if you reject my help, you need to put an end to this."

Street shook his head and felt annoyed.

Bogdanov went on speaking as calmly as ever. "Cyra's boss isn't the only one with serious military training, Street. The only one without military or formal espionage training in this whole mess is you. Help me out. You work with Brent. Is he up to something? I have a feeling it's financial, and it benefits a select few."

"You want me to spy on the CIA, and on top of that spy on some rogue agent who is a lunatic who is out to kill me? Add to that working with you would be spying for the Russian government and probably for Venezuela as well. That's treason on multidimensional levels. Are you out of your mind?"

"No. I want you to save the world."

"I've had enough. I wanted to expose this whole thing, but this is too much." Street began to walk away.

"You know something. Either you'll find out what Brent is up to, or he gets to you and takes you out. I strongly suspect he has more agents in his program, likely someone in Langley. Is there someone he's talking to? Maybe someone who shows up at the office at weird hours?"

"I'll take my chances."

"It's too late. You're involved now, Street, and you can calm this thing down. There are no sides here. There are no good guys and bad guys here, well, except for Brent and crew. But it's largely murky, it's gray, you know.

Pérez gave you some money. Why did we pay you? To get you on the right side, and there's plenty more where that came from. Use it. Buy yourself a gun. They're coming for you. Work with me here, and maybe I can help. You don't want to be part of Brent's agenda and neither does Moscow, which is where I'm headed. What do I tell them?"

"I can't buy a gun. I just got out of jail and a storm is coming."

"Then take my gun," Bogdanov said. He retrieved a handgun and extended it to Street. "Take it and hole up in a hotel for the storm. Get away, but just for a couple of days, but by all means stay in contact with me."

"There's no way I'm doing that. Keep your gun. Things are bad, and you want me to hole up in a hotel with a gun and just think about things? Do you want me to go insane, like you already are?"

"Well, you have to do something."

"There's a hurricane coming. I need to board my parents' house up. They are away helping my cousin."

"Stop with the monotone accent shit, Street. Let me help you. If Brent doesn't come for you, one of his thugs will. You know something, something that can end all this mess. Don't bury your head in the sand and ignore what's going on. Let's talk. We can end this."

"There's a hurricane coming, and it may buy me some time," Street said.

"Hurricane or not, you're no match for what's stalking you."

"Not everything that stalks me ends up killing me."

"You've got my phone number. Call me if you change your mind," Bogdanov said. "In the meantime, just know that you've got rogue CIA agents, elements from the Venezuelan government, thugs working in big oil companies, and God knows what else who all want you dead."

"They can get fucked," Street said. He walked off.

CHAPTER

44

Street checked under his sink. Sure enough, there was a small shaving kit that wasn't his. He opened it and found a few flash drives. He grabbed one and looked at it as if he had been panning for gold at some tourist trap and suddenly came up with a really big nugget. He walked across his room and jammed it into his computer. Eventually, he found a video. It showed Brent and Karen discussing the Placebo Agenda and plans to murder their agents. It was the same conversation he had recorded himself. He withdrew the flash drive, put it back into the shaving kit, and then he stopped. There were four drives in the kit. He took two out and put them back under the sink and put the remaining two in the shaving kit and then shoved it into his backpack. And then he went back to monitoring the storm.

He and pretty much everyone else watching television from West Palm Beach to the Upper Keys had heard it before. A hurricane watch was in effect, which meant a storm could strike within two days. But judging from the plainly obvious hints the National Hurricane Center was putting in advisories on its website, full-blown warnings were coming very soon.

For Street, Hurricane Granville was a welcome relief. It took this espionage mess off his shoulders for a brief moment and gave him time to think. Even murderers and deranged spies had to board up and plan for rough weather. Plus, it could keep Brent focusing more on his home and less on Molly Wells. So first, there was the family house to board up, but before that, Street felt like he himself was too boarded up. He picked up the phone and dialed.

"Hi, Street," Patricia answered. "Are you ready for the storm?"

"Just boarding up my house," Street said. "I'm a little behind, I guess."

"You okay?" she said. "You sound stressed."

"Well." He sighed.

He had a lot on his mind and needed to vent, but he knew he couldn't tell a soul about the Placebo Agenda. So he picked the least dirty shirt from his emotional laundry basket and decided to air it out.

"I got arrested. Marijuana and prescription pills. I don't use that stuff. I think my ex, Brianna, left the stuff in my car." Street felt relieved that he had told someone about it. He didn't bother telling her it was planted by rogue government agents and that it really wasn't Brianna's. He knew it was to keep him in Miami, keep him from leaving town so they could kill him. He'd spare her some details.

"Wait, what? Marijuana? Brianna? I thought you broke up?"

"We did. I was just having dinner alone," Street said. "The cops pulled me over and found weed and pills in my Jeep. I don't know how it all got in there."

"Where did this happen?"

"In the Grove."

"What time?"

"Early. Why?"

"More reliable witnesses around," she said. "Why did the police pull you over?"

"Cracked taillight. Another surprise. To tell you the truth, there's a lot of weird shit going on, especially at work. Someone wants me in jail."

"You're right, something isn't adding up. I think you're not telling me everything, though."

"That's most of it," Street said.

He was spinning the event now, and spinning to a woman whose career was spinning corporate messages to the press, telling her the truth but withholding lots of info. He was definitely diving deeper into the world of espionage.

"Street, I believe you and support you. This, whatever it is, will blow over."

"I know, but something doesn't—"

"You're damn right it doesn't add up. Someone had you thrown in jail. Are you working on any stories that may piss off the wrong people?"

"No."

"Work hard and get to the bottom of it. I'm here if you need me."

"I'll work this out after the storm," he said, staring at the tackle box he had yanked out of the water. He opened it. Nothing new inside. No clues or sources of inspiration.

"You'll do what's best," Patricia said. "Look, Street. Whatever it is, generally the answer is right in front of you."

"I'll talk to you later, Patricia." He hung up.

Street relaxed at the thought of having a little breathing room until the hurricane passed, though his levity didn't last. He had Bogdanov and Pérez to worry about. What were they doing in the United States? And what did they think he knew and could put a stop to anyway? Everybody knew everything anyway, but somehow, everyone assumed Street knew more. Nothing made sense, especially now he was a more seasoned US spy and, more recently, a potential recruit for the Russians and Venezuelans. Plus, he was worried about Molly. Get to work, he thought. Clear your brain.

Street arrived at his parents' Coconut Grove home and walked outside by the pool house, taking in the sunlight. The sky was clear and blue, and the sun was shining uninterrupted. He knew the winds would pick up, and then thicker clouds would roll overhead in outer feeder bands. Once those digital green and blue arms showed up on the radar screens across South Florida's television sets and exploded into yellow and red, the time to prepare would be coming to an end and the time to hunker down would begin. Since his parents were out of town, he'd prep the house for storm himself.

Street began by boarding up the second floor. He set up a ladder and started with the shutters already attached to the windows. They were easy—all he needed to do to secure them was screw a flat bar on top of them. It was like in old western movies when the bad guys rode into town, and nervous folk peered out and closed the shutters. He used plywood to board up the windows that didn't come with their own shutters and made a mental note to buy impact glass once the storm season had passed.

While the weather was still clam, Street took notice of the passing breeze from his ladder. The wind was still soft but moving in a single direction as if hypnotized; the breeze was not light and variable, ambling toward multiple points on the horizon, typical of a hot September day, but was making its long trek to the eye of the storm. Hurricane Granville was far away, but it was already making its presence known well in advance of its arrival.

After he boarded all the bedroom and bathroom windows, he went on to secure a few doors and a few larger windows and then the entire downstairs. Pretty soon, the entire house was secure and stocked with plenty of water, sports drinks, colas, and beer in the fridge and in a cooler that would keep cold for days on end.

Street circled the house sipping water to make sure he had left anything outside like patio furniture that would blow away. Satisfied, he looked around to see if his neighbors needed any help. He paid little attention to the white Porsche cruising up the road. The driver kept his eyes fixed on Street.

CHAPTER

45

"Your last day on earth will be a stormy one," the driver said, under the cover of the tinted windows. Street turned for a second and looked at the Porsche, right into the eyes of the driver, even though he couldn't see him due to the glare from the tinted window. The car sped up to avoid suspicion, but the driver kept his gaze on Street as he drove off.

"There's our boy," the driver, Brent Drum, said to a passenger next to him, before turning the corner and leaving Street to himself. "We'll see him soon, won't we?"

The passenger said nothing.

Brent went on. "I think we could stab him. Slit his throat and make it look like a robbery during the storm. Police would blame it on looters, and we can plant evidence to support it."

The passenger still said nothing and stared out the window.

"An overdose always works. After all, you helped throw him in jail for that possession charge. Good thinking too."

The passenger remained silent.

"Here are my thoughts," Brent said, speaking to his silent passenger and aloud in general. "We will, well to be more accurate, you will wait for the eye of the storm when the winds die down and jump in before the police mobilize, like the good looters do. The power will be out and his house has no alarms or security cameras. In and out. Smash and grab, kill him and go. Got it? Or do you like the overdose plan? You're the expert."

The assassin said nothing.

Brent sped up and made his way out of Coconut Grove's canopied streets and onto to US 1. He headed back in the direction of *The Gateway*, looked at his passenger, and nodded.

"Not to sound like a cliché, but he knows too much, just like all of our placebos. In fact, find out what he knows and then dispose of him. I will take care of Molly Wells. I am behind schedule on her."

His passenger, eyes fixed out of the window, remained silent.

"Need I remind you that you've been breaking the law too, you know," Brent said. "You're just as involved as I am in this Placebo Agenda. You know what to do. You've been working for the CIA for a good while now. You're a solid career intelligence professional who stands heads and shoulders above your colleagues. Find out what he knows and then kill him, or maybe something will happen to you. Do you know what I mean? Something seriously awful could happen to your family and you."

Next to him, Ana Patricia Osorio Harding stared ahead and said nothing. She uncrossed her arms, stared at Brent, and clenched her teeth.

"Am I clear on what your assignment is?" Brent asked.

Patricia sighed. "You're the boss."

CHAPTER

46

"Ricardo. That's still my alias for this little project going forward, even in the United States," the large man mumbled to Boston. He barely moved his lips when he spoke. He smoked a cigarette and looked across the wilds of a slum near the 23 de Enero neighborhood in western Caracas.

"Slums are the same no matter where in the world they are," Ricardo said in English to Boston as well as to his mute, captive disciples.

"I guess," Boston said in English right back at him. "So do we stick with English from now on?"

"Yes. I can't understand your Venezuelan slum language," Ricardo said, looking back out the window. "Slums are only tough for the weak, like that American kid and some of you here. To me, they're just dirty, like all of you here. Good hiding places, though. That's how it goes in cities like this one."

"Damascus, Cairo, Los Angeles, Karachi," Boston said.

"Wherever there's poverty, I thrive," Ricardo said.

"We thrive."

"Not everyone," Ricardo said back. He looked up at the blue sky and across the city. Green hills from far away gave the city a hint of a pastoral feel, something from a past storybook lost in memory a long time ago.

"We need to do a little housecleaning," Ricardo said.

"Yes, we do," said Boston. "It's time."

Ricardo threw the cigarette out of the window and watched the flickering butt bounce its way to its destiny. He turned to face the inside of the slum house. It was bare bones: modest furniture, ramshackle electrical wiring, complete with a light bulb suspended over a table by a thin wire, although all appliances were new. Dark corners and small, shadowy alcoves made for rooms, giving the place a jailhouse effect. Ricardo made sure the entire slum house was scrubbed clean. A television with antennae kept the room flooded with the news. The Venezuelan president was on, rambling on about a new housing project that would bring poor people out of the slums and into a better life.

"You better hope oil prices rise and stay high to fund that," Ricardo said, looking at the television.

He glanced down at a nautical map of South Florida's waters. Several men in the house watched him quietly but on edge. Like hungry cats waiting for a meal, they waited for their next orders. Ricardo took notice of their eagerness and scanned a stack of Kalashnikovs arranged in neat rows in one of the little corner rooms. They sat alongside empty gasoline cans.

"We should have killed that American man," Ricardo said.

Two young men blinked emptily. Boston motioned for them to stand up.

Ricardo rolled his eyes, put down his map, and walked over to the window. "This apartment is unclean, just like this situation. I am going to make it clean, Mr. Street Brewer."

Ricardo turned and faced Boston and the men behind him. He walked over, grabbed a pack of cigarettes from one of the men's shirt pocket, took one, lit it, and put the pack back in the man's shirt pocket.

"Street knows who I am. He saw me here and left alive after we almost charred him in that microwave. Heard my name called out. Even before that, Juan Vicente told that Patricia girl to contact Ricardo, which was me all along. I was supposed to be some guy in finance, apparently to arrange numbers for the kid's story. That way the real guys in finance don't start a relationship with Street. I guarantee you, Street is connecting the dots and is on to us. We should have killed him back then, but that goddamn Russian said it could get messy."

Ricardo looked down at the burned tires. "Stack those up in that bedroom over there," Ricardo told the men behind Boston.

They did so. Dutifully.

"How many guns did we have on that American? Back in Petare?"

"Between ten and twenty," one of the dutiful ones said. There were four men behind Boston, two stacking burned tires, two staring up at Ricardo.

"How many Kalashnikovs were there in total?"

"I don't know. Several thousand. They're being distributed among the neighborhoods to carefully chosen paramilitaries as we speak," Boston said.

"Good," Ricardo said, stroking his chin, surveying the living area. A few leftover Kalashnikovs lay neatly in the room.

"Time to get going," Boston said.

Ricardo looked at the two men organizing the burned tires and the two others waiting for their next orders. The men organizing the tires finished their task and stood attentively, facing Ricardo, all eager for work.

Ricardo nodded to Boston. "Help them organize the last of the cache. Take the rifles to those paramilitary whackos up the hill, and then we're finally done. Leave two rifles behind." Ricardo motioned to the two in the corner and then to the layers of polished Kalashnikovs resting on the wall. Boston pointed to the rifles, mumbled something, and nodded up the hill. The waiting men began loading the guns into boxes. They headed out, leaving Ricardo and Boston.

"All right," Ricardo said. "Do you have passports?"

"Yes," Boston said.

"What country?"

"Peru for them, and USA for us."

"Good. Do you know the routine when we land in Miami?"

"Yes. Are you going to do to Street what you did to that couple in the bedroom here?"

"I will if his assigned assassin doesn't come through," Ricardo said. "Get out of here. I'll make sure this place is clean, take care of the men when they come back, and then meet you in Miami." He paused. "Miami!"

Boston left, and Ricardo made sure the tires from Street's microwave were properly stacked alongside the remaining two Kalashnikovs in the corner. He found a row of Peruvian passports, the ones for the others hauling weapons up the hill.

Ricardo picked up a can of gasoline and walked to the center of the slum house. He stood there alone in the room and lit another cigarette. Background sounds settled in with the absence of humanity. A dog barked amid some distant chuckles of women climbing the alleyway steps. Just outside the window, a white kite soared against a deep-blue sky. A moment later, the four men returned.

"Where's the money?" Ricardo asked.

"Here," one of the followers replied.

He handed Ricardo a large envelope. Ricardo took it, sat down, and then peered into it with a degree of boredom, as if he were expecting the contents of a bowl of soup he ordered in a restaurant and not money from an illegal arms deal.

"You know officially, these rifles are meant for the military," Ricardo said, assessing his audience. "Unofficially, they're for you. Go force your political agenda on this slum. You better hurry, a coup is always around the corner."

The men looked at Ricardo, blinking in quick succession and nodding in agreement.

"Too bad Venezuela has a plant now to build these kinds of guns today," Ricardo said, counting the money, his cigarette dangling from his big lips, making him appear like a large grouper sucking in a small baitfish. He shoved the envelope into his pants pockets. Good thing he never told the gang the weapons were supposed to be free of charge and instead lied, telling them that Caracas was giving them rifles at a deep discount.

"Still, Venezuela doesn't want to arm the paramilitaries with guns made at home." Ricardo laughed and glanced around the room. The four young men stood quietly. Mouths shut tight. Eyes continuing to blink. Sighing occasionally. Ricardo walked to the refrigerator, grabbed a malt drink and walked back across the room.

"Jesus, don't you guys speak English?"

Nothing but blank stares.

"Don't understand me? How about this?"

He grabbed a Kalashnikov leaning against the table and shot all four men with quick blasts. Their eyes jolted wide in surprise before they rolled up dead in milliseconds. Their bodies fell with thuds as the ringing in Ricardo's ears faded. He wiped the rifle clean and kicked over the gasoline can. The fuel raced across the cool concrete floor like urine spreading across some back-alley corner. It pooled along the edges of the dead men, enveloping them slowly. Blood mixed with the gasoline like ink dropped into an aquarium. Ricardo picked up another can and sprinkled gasoline up along the walls. He walked outside with the gasoline cans, envelope, and passports jutting out of his pants and into his gut. No large crowds gathered to question the blast of gunfire, though a child walked up the hill. The young boy of about ten years of age stopped and looked up at Ricardo.

"Who did you kill?" the kid asked.

Ricardo stared at the kid. He said nothing but pointed up, up to the top of the hill.

"Man, give me a smoke!" the kid said.

Ricardo snapped his finger and pointed up the hill.

"Fuck you," the kid said, shaking his head and marching up the steps, looking back at Ricardo. He shook his head one last time and disappeared around the corner.

Ricardo walked down the stairs, pouring gasoline here and there along the ramshackle walls. He came to the corner and threw his cigarette down on the soaked stairway. Beginning with a puff, flames exploded and raced up the hill, soaring high into the sky, charring everything up the slum, engulfing houses. Snaps and crackles of popping wood and electrical lines broke through the roaring flames. Screams of men, women, and children shot through the wall of fire as well. Their cries didn't last long. Power lines fell, rickety roofs, walls, and television antennae collapsed as the fire raced to the top.

Ricardo walked down, moving in the direction opposite to the flames. People popped out of their houses below and stared at the inferno above. Shrieks of horror deafened Ricardo, who skipped down the hill with a smirk on his face.

"There's your smoke, kid," he whispered into the scream of approaching fire sirens.

Seconds later, Ricardo stood at the edge of the slum and threw the passports set aside for the dutiful ones into the street, careful not to let them burn. "Crazy Peruvians running around here burning shit. Let the police find them," he mumbled and disappeared into the city streets.

A few hours later, Ricardo landed in Miami. He walked through the airport, listening to the different Spanish accents. He handed his US passport to a suspicious customs official, who stared at a rather long Indian name. Anil was his name for the next five minutes, and the last name had too many letters for him to pronounce properly. The customs official, a young man with bright-red hair and very light skin, stared at Ricardo.

"Where are you coming from?"

"Caracas."

"What were you down there for?"

"Pleasure."

"Pleasure?"

"My family, originally from Trinidad and Tobago, ended up in Caracas and found a home. No matter where they are, I find pleasure in their company," Ricardo said.

The man stamped Ricardo's US passport. Minutes later, Ricardo caught a cab and hopped in. He gave the driver an address, lit up a cigarette, and paid no attention to the No Smoking sign. The cab driver stared at him, and when Ricardo met his stare in the rearview mirror, the driver looked down, put the car in gear, and drove away.

CHAPTER
47

B rent Drum left the office of *The Gateway* and strolled through downtown Coral Gables. He withdrew a fresh prepaid cell phone from his pocket and dialed his superior Karen Whittaker in the Washington, DC area.

She answered quickly. "This better be good," she said.

He assessed his surroundings. He wasn't being followed and no one could hear him.

"Patricia is going to spend a little time with Street, eliminate him once and for all, and then we're done and on to the money-making phase."

Brent looked over his shoulder. The streets of Coral Gables were busy, as if the entire Atlantic were as calm as glass.

"We got a storm headed our way, and it's not going to veer off. So while law enforcement scrambles to organize gasoline lines and battle looters, we'll have the perfect window to take care of our placebos. No messes to deal with when the eye hits."

"Just handle it. Is the interview ready to publish?"

"We got it. It goes public with the click of a button. Life goes on at *The Gateway.*"

"And now the second phase?"

"The Venezuelans are in for a surprise. They don't know what they've gotten themselves into when it comes to imports and exports."

Karen said nothing for a few long seconds.

"Good. Did you pay Ricardo?"

"Ten million dollars straight from Cornbridge Capital. Too bad the firm lost its star in Olivia. She was good. Really good. Do we have other hedge funds out there, should the need for some fresh capital arise?"

"More than you'll ever know," Karen said. She hesitated. "I get this nagging feeling that Street suspects more than we know."

"Maybe he does. It doesn't matter."

"Let's just close this chapter on American intelligence collecting. I will talk to you after the storm," Karen said. She hung up.

Less than two minutes after she hung up with Brent, Karen threw the cell phone away in a city wastebasket not far from a Starbucks. She found her car, a small Ford Fiesta, got in, started it and headed in the direction of Langley, Virginia.

Scores of officers and agents reported to her directly or indirectly from US embassies, other embassies, and from other covers. She even worked with some in station chief positions, others in nonofficial cover interests, and all everyone else saw was a nice, strong, thirty-something woman driving in traffic. She sipped her latte as she drove on I-495 and headed out of Silver Spring. It was a big loop around DC. Very nice. Trees and hills. She pushed forward, thinking about the many towns along her way to work and what most Americans would think about them. Chevy Chase: the actor. Bethesda: rich people and medical services.

She pulled into a small office complex in the city of McLean, a nice little property for agents who needed cover even from CIA headquarters. She parked and entered the building of Glenwood Consulting, her cover. After a short trip up the elevator to the sixth floor, she was at her desk. Safe and secure.

She checked her day's schedule. Morning and afternoon briefings. Reports on activities in Latin America. Preparing more and more PowerPoint slides and getting superiors ready for a report due to the US House of Representatives Permanent Select Committee on Intelligence. Basic stuff. She had a slew of data. Assets across the region confirmed that Manuel Rodríguez, a major producer of coca paste and now into refining, was shipping operations back northward into Central America to feed Mexican distributors for the US market. Government officials across the region were helping him. Karen picked up a legitimate phone to call Brent for a few last-minute details when her superior, Roman Decker, approached.

"Hi Karen, how are the PowerPoints coming?"

"Good morning, Roman! They're fine. Just putting the finishing touches on them now."

Roman, a man in his late forties with neat brown hair and a summer tan, appeared to be a mild-mannered everyman from the Midwest. He looked like a financial planner or a wills and estates lawyer, showing zero hints of the military experience that jumped off his highly classified and arguably nonexistent résumé.

"Great. Want to grab a cup of coffee? I need to get out of here and unwind before diving into a pile of data bound for Capitol Hill," said Roman.

"Sure."

"We'll take your car," Roman said. "You drive."

A few minutes later, they were in line at a nearby Starbucks. Black coffee for Roman. Salted caramel hot chocolate and a croissant for Karen. Roman paid while Karen waited in the car. A few seconds later, they were driving. After a while, Roman spoke up.

"Karen, you've been an exceptional addition to our team. When you were recruited many years back just after undergrad, I knew you were going to be a star. You were born for this industry. Today over this coffee break, I'd like to talk about your future."

"Thank you," Karen said. She looked over at Roman.

"Let's talk about that and how we prep for Congress out in the open air before the day heats up. Let's check out Rock Creek Park."

Karen drove the car under the park's canopy. Trees still rich with summer foliage blocked the sun.

"I've always liked it here. So relaxing," Roman said, sending a text on his phone.

"It is. Some woman got kidnapped here not too long ago. They never caught the guy, but they found her." Karen glanced at Roman. "Amazing how people can get away with things. Even murder."

"Not all secrets come to light. But some do. Anyway, pull over and relax."

Karen parked the car, and Roman handed her the croissant. She unwrapped it, took a bite, and swallowed. She sighed and took a sip of hot chocolate.

Roman broke the brief silence. "I would never do anything like that," he said, staring ahead of him as if the car were still in motion.

"Murder? Jesus, Roman, I know. Good Lord," Karen stared at him. "Have a sense of humor."

"No, I mean I would never do anything like what you've been doing." She stopped chewing. "What are you talking about?"

"What I meant to say is that I would never do anything like what you and Brent have been doing, you know? Using American citizens as intelligence guinea pigs and then killing them," Roman said.

Karen froze for just a second.

Roman caught her guilty reaction, and she knew he had caught it, but she protested anyway.

"I'm sorry." Her croissant-filled hand dropped to her lap. "What?"

Both Roman and even Karen herself were impressed with her recovery and resumption into character, feigning utter disbelief.

"Karen, where did you go wrong? And why do this?"

"Do what?"

"You know what. Actually, there's no reason to work out your planned reaction to this."

"Reaction to what? Have you lost your mind? Or is this a drill of some sort? I have not ordered anyone to be eliminated."

"Oh really? Have a peek." He held up his phone and made sure Karen saw the screen. "You're pretty easy to bug."

"Sir, it's Karen. We needed him to get the interview with the president to keep Brent entrenched at the magazine because it was threatening to fold. We need that magazine up and running to execute the second phase of the Placebo Agenda. Plus, there's the fact that Street is still soaking up intelligence each and

every minute he's in the country. You never know what could fly in over the transom. Still, we are going to eliminate him."

Karen's other hand dropped. As did her jaw and her eyes.

"Want to hear more? This award-winning clip of Brent?" Roman said. He pressed play.

"Look, we're almost done with the killings. We've eliminated Olivia Crawford, the Tagles, and the Spradlings. There is Street next and then one more out there, a Molly Wells at Spartan Software, but we haven't used her in a while."

"On a positive note, I'm not going to the police with this, though Street will get a copy of this video if he doesn't already have it. On a negative note, negative for you at least, I crammed so much cyanide in your croissant and hot chocolate that you'll be dead in minutes. Don't worry. You won't be alone. Brent and the rest of your team are right behind you."

Roman sighed. He looked at his watch again and let the second hand run for a few seconds. Then he looked over at the driver's seat. Karen was dead.

"Rock Creek Park. You and I have been using your trees and cover for this sort of thing for too long," Roman said.

He turned the ignition off and made a note to have the correct coroner handle the examination and come up with an appropriate cause of death that would wash with police and family. He removed Karen's seatbelt and let her body fall flat in his lap, her head in his crotch. He then slid out of the passenger-side door and stood in the quiet of the woods. After about ten minutes of cleaning up fingerprints and other trace evidence, which didn't matter because Karen had driven him in this car several times, he pushed the vehicle down a hill. Metal banged against trees. Birds soared into the air upon the car's impact with a large oak. Then it was quiet.

Roman walked to the parking lot of the Carter Barron Amphitheatre. He called a cab, careful to avoid a ride share, and was back in the office shortly afterward.

CHAPTER

48

Patricia sat in a room at the Ritz-Carlton in Coconut Grove, a couple of blocks away from Street's apartment, after Brent had dropped her off the day before. She stared out the window in the one-bedroom suite and took in the early morning sunshine. She shook her head in disbelief and then looked down at her cell phone. A SIG Sauer firearm lay next to it alongside a knife. Pills as well. Brent had left the door wide open for her. Just get it done, he had told her, and make it look like a break-in or an accidental overdose. Patricia shook her head again. It was time to go kill Street. She stared at her tools, at the gun, at the knife and the pills. It was as if she were playing some twisted version of the game Clue. This isn't happening, she thought. It's not going to happen, she told herself again.

"God, please get me out of this. Or give me the resources to help me get myself out of this," she whispered. And just then the phone rang. She didn't recognize the number, though it was local to South Florida. She answered.

"Hello?"

"Ana Patricia Osorio Harding?"

"Who is this?"

"You don't have to kill Street. Actually, if you do it, then you'll be killed. Meet me at the Mayfair Hotel in the Grove in ten minutes."

"Who is this?"

"Cyra Harred."

"Who are you? Who is this?"

"I'm counterintelligence. I'm about to put an end to this placebo thing."

Cyra let that sit there.

"Am I under arrest, or will I be eliminated?"

"No. You can help me end this and have it all behind you."

"Excuse me? Are you admitting that you're counterintelligence?"

"You and I both know this is no ordinary quagmire."

Silence from Patricia.

"Look, I'll make it simple. Go about your mission from Brent and die. Do nothing and die. I'll kill you either way. Or work with me to end this mess."

Ten minutes later, Patricia was there. The hotel was not far at all. She entered the lobby of the luxurious property. A large, incredibly athletic woman approached her. Strong legs. Graceful steps.

"Patricia? I'm Cyra."

They shook hands and sized each other up.

"Let's take a walk somewhere to talk," Cyra said.

"I pick the place. I walk alone. I will meet you there. I'm not going with you. I will call you when I'm there."

"You got it," Cyra said.

A few minutes later, they were sitting together at a popular corner café that enjoyed a steady flow of customers at all hours. That morning it was packed. Everyone wanted to be outside before the hurricane hit. Despite the crowd, there were a few tables available with plenty of space for some discreet conversation.

"This place is good. Neutral territory. We'll blend in," Cyra said. She looked at Patricia. "You know how this goes."

"Talk to me," Patricia said after the hostess left. "I need to know what you and any other counterintelligence agents have on me."

"How did you get mixed up in this, Patricia?"

"I knew Brent was asking those around him, like colleagues and casual acquaintances, what they knew about events in general. At first, we subtly peppered reporters, media bosses, public relations executives, oil executives, politicians, teachers, scientists, and pretty much anyone else to actually report to us what's going on, or where they saw threats to US national security. Like at a cocktail party, for example. I'd casually bring up Cuba. I'd say I thought I noticed more Cubans running around town and ask others if they had seen anything similar. Many did, so I took note and tracked their movements. Pretty simple trick of the trade, and those telling me had no idea I was an operative planted in Worldwide Oil & Gas. It really started off simple like that, and then it just got out of hand when Brent got hired at real companies and used employees to spy for him on a more active basis."

"Why didn't you report it to the agency?"

"At first, I didn't know how serious it was, and a real operative in some company added more value than just an asset. I also kept Street employed at *The Gateway* by arranging a job with Matías—you know him. He is a good career operative. I did similar things with the Tagles and the Spradlings, which in the end made me an accomplice. But I didn't find out until very recently that Brent was killing off his placebos," Patricia said. She looked down. "I found out when I got my orders to kill Street. Kill Street, or my parents and ex-husband die in Venezuela, where it will be easy to carry out and cover up."

Cyra processed Patricia's story for a moment. Then she moved on.

"A woman named Olivia Crawford from a Cornbridge Capital hedge fund in Naples is dead, and a woman named Molly Wells, a software marketing whiz, may soon follow suit. Do you know anything about them?"

"No," Patricia said. Her jaw dropped and she looked away. Then she quickly composed herself. "When it came to Florida, all I had to do was distract Street and not much else."

"Go on," Cyra said.

"I first suspected things were getting out of control when I arranged for Street and my asset, Ian Collins, to meet some finance whiz at the state-owned oil company, who grew up poor and maintained his roots in Petare, to see what he knows about Venezuelan oil production and whether it may be declining. We wanted to know how healthy Venezuela's cash cow really is. That part was easy. We just dared Street to leave the safe part of the city. Any man will take a dare like that when goaded by a woman."

"Especially one that looks like you," Cyra said.

"Whatever. Anyway, as it turns out, the finance exec was not around, so Ian went ahead with the second part of the plan that night, which was a test to see how foolproof Street's performance would hold up under interrogation. Ian directed Street into a nearby slum, and another one of my assets, a local elderly woman originally from Guyana who keeps an eye on the neighborhood, informed Ian of the setup and that Venezuelan intelligence agents were on the way via coded language. That's where it ended, at least for me. Killing Street? That was something I couldn't fathom. Brent let me know if I don't play along and end this program, then I could be wiped out along with my family. I think Domínguez is in on this too. Worldwide Oil & Gas agreed with the agency to allow one of us to infiltrate the company. That would be me in the nonofficial cover. We get a platform to spy, and they get some free intelligence and don't have to pay the salary of the position that the agent occupies. In this case, it's corporate communications and media relations. I was the perfect fit. Anyway, one of the benefits of having a government agent embedded in a private company is the ability for the government to spy on that company as well. Domínguez wants oil prices to rise, as higher oil prices are good for his top and bottom lines. I know he and the Venezuelan government are up to something. Something weird with someone named Ricardo. There were several calls to a mysterious hedge fund in Naples—the one you just mentioned—Cornbridge Capital."

Patricia crossed her legs and gazed across the street. Another packed café bustled in the sun.

"Juan Vicente Domínguez," Cyra said. "I think it's safe to say that he and the Venezuelan government are up to something too. They all want high oil prices, and I think this Russian military project is just some kind of distraction or something with another hidden agenda attached. I just get the feeling as well."

She took a sip of coffee and looked Patricia in the eye.

"My Russian contact on the ground in Venezuela has the same feeling. He even thinks the Venezuelan government will be pushed out of the deal and that something else is going on, that there is something personal behind all of this. My contact is as sharp as they come."

"You mean that thin man?" Patricia asked. "Street chased him into a dangerous part of town. Is his name Peter Bogdanov? I know who he is, more or less. I may have seen him out a couple of times on the Caracas cocktail circuit."

"That's him," Cyra said. "He told me at the English school where I've been working under a cover that he's been sending intel to Brent. Normal stuff. Russians and the Americans sharing information on Venezuela and its president. But he grew suspicious eventually."

"There are others in on this deal, whatever it is," Patricia said. "There's this Ricardo guy, basically an office gopher at Worldwide Oil & Gas, who handles a lot of information. He's never around. Domínguez brought him up during Street's interview because he didn't want Street in touch with actual Worldwide employees. I get the sense Ricardo is there for some other reason. Do you know him? Is he one of yours? Is he even one of us?"

"No," Cyra said.

"Are you going to have me arrested? Hand us over to the FBI?" Patricia asked.

"No," Cyra said in a matter-of-fact way. "You can either cooperate with me and end this program or die with Brent."

"I'll cooperate."

"Tell me more about Ricardo."

"Well," Patricia said. "He's very large and stocky. Massive legs and enormous arms, like two large hams. Curly hair. Very curly. I think he's an errand boy for Domínguez, there to handle off-the-radar stuff."

"Does he look like this?" Cyra said, holding up her phone.

"That's him."

"Bogdanov never disappoints," Cyra said.

"Anyway, I don't know to what degree the Venezuelan government is involved. I really don't. I just suspect it. You just can't tell with the president, especially one who says he's going to slap up long-range rockets along the Colombian border and arm the country to the teeth. Everything he says is so over-the-top that it's hard to know when to take him seriously," Patricia said.

"It's obvious that he wants the world to focus on those missiles while he smuggles nukes into the country. That or a shitload of drugs out of it. But let's focus on what we need to know," Cyra said. "We do know that the government is busy making noise about a Russian port on the Caribbean coast. Something

doesn't add up here, especially when it comes to Big Oil, meaning your boss."
Cyra said. "Why Domínguez? Anything you'd like to share?"

"I don't know anything," Patricia said.

"You sure? You do remember what I said earlier?"

"I'm telling the truth," Patricia said. She looked at Cyra. Looked hard.

"Okay, I tell you what. Hang out with Street and see what he knows.
Let's get all the details we can, and then we'll confess to him, and I mean
everything. Don't worry about Brent. When this hurricane hits, Brent Drum
will cease to exist, and I mean that."

A wave of relief came over Patricia's face.

CHAPTER

49

S treet blew off Bogdanov and made sure he had not overlooked the last touches of boarding up his parents' house. A half hour later, he was sipping from a bottle of ice-cold water when his phone rang. Unknown. Why not, he thought. He answered.

"Hello," he said.

"Street! It's Patricia. I'm in Miami. Where are you?"

"Hey! I'm at home, boarding up. Where in Miami are you?"

"Gables Estates," she said.

"Gables Estates? That's awesome! Who all will be at your hurricane party? Miami Heat basketball players? Famed surgeons? Hedge fund whiz kids? Exiled Latin American leaders?"

"Ha, ha," Patricia said. "I was in Texas on business and popped in to visit family members. I was supposed to fly back tomorrow, but judging from the news, I think the airport is probably going to be closed."

"Well, come on over. I'm by myself getting the house boarded up. Then I'm going to pull the boat out of the water. Better yet, let's take the boat for a spin for a little while before I yank it. Up for a swim?"

"A swim? Sure. But a boat ride before a hurricane?"

"The winds aren't here yet. It's still calm. I have to pull it out of the water anyway. You do swim, right?"

"I swim well. Sure, I'll be there."

"Okay. Meet me at Dinner Key Marina in twenty minutes."

Street ran inside and showered. Put on deodorant and sunscreen. Ten minutes later, he locked the front door of his parents' house, hopped in his Jeep, and headed to the marina. He waited for her at the front of the docks. Street saw her arrive in a large, weathered white Ford Expedition. A little banged and scratched up but with brand-new sailing stickers on it, mainly stickers advertising regattas around the United States.

Patricia waved from the driver's window and parked. She walked over slowly, wearing a white beach sarong and a large, white sun hat, big sunglasses, and an incredible smile.

A man with his wife and three small children watched her cross the parking lot—it was the same man who had been eyeing Brianna just days earlier. The man's wife, probably in her mid-thirties, looked at her husband in amusement and laughed when the man saw the smile was meant for Street and not him. Street chuckled as well. The couple had seen Street boating with two gorgeous women in a matter of days. What did they think? That Street had women all over him? That he was some carefree ladies' man? Appearances, he thought. If they thought that, they were way off.

"Let's go, Jackie O. I've got plenty of beer, colas, bottled water, and turkey sandwiches in my cooler. Let's get out of here."

He looked back at her car and the regatta stickers.

"I didn't know you sailed," he said.

"I'm not great, but I get out there when I can," she said.

Street punched in the combination to an electronic gate that opened to docks that welcomed everything from little fishing skiffs to massive yachts at the end. Midway through, they came to his Whitewater. Street took off his flip-flops, climbed down a small ladder, and stood on the transom of the boat. He reached up and grabbed the cooler off the docks and jumped in, nimble like a cat. He set the cooler down and offered his hand up to Patricia to help her down. She handed him her bag, took his hand, and boarded the boat.

"I've got the lines. Just sit back and enjoy the sun while it lasts," Street said.

He cranked up the engines and left them in neutral. He undid the spring line, then the stern lines, and then the bow lines. The boat drifted gently into the bumpers alongside the dock pilings. Then Street pushed off, turned the outboards in gear, and headed out of the slip. He navigated through the channel, snaking through small spoil islands and moored sailboats that were likely going to ride out the storm.

"Those spoil islands were going to be used by Pan Am back in the mid-twentieth century, when planes took off on the water," Street said.

"Cool," Patricia said. "I've actually sailed around these islands before, though it's been a while."

Street pushed through the channel for several hundred yards, taking in the breeze. Then he hammered the throttle down and headed east on plane. A surprisingly large number of boats were out on the water that day. Street pushed the boat past Stiltsville and headed east into the open Atlantic. He drove until Miami shrank into a small strip of land and then disappeared. In the distance, the Gulf Stream, a warm water current that moderates climates in Iceland and the UK, began to kick up. Street killed the engines.

"Beer?" he asked.

"Sure," Patricia said.

Street drew two bottles from a cooler in the back of the boat. He cracked them open and handed her one. He also opened a bag of potato chips, took one, and set the bag on the console next to the steering wheel after offering Patricia some. She declined.

"So what happened the last time I saw you? You chased some guy in the street," Patricia asked.

"Oh, that guy. He's nobody."

"So why did you chase him?"

"Because I thought he was threatening us. I've seen him around. In fact, he was there that night at El Techo. False alarm, I guess. So anyway, what brings you to Miami again?"

"Spending time with family after a big meeting in Texas," Patricia said. "Wanted a little vacation. Guess I should have remembered to check the weather first."

She removed her cover. Small bikini. Black. Street took notice.

"Here with your husband?"

"No. He's in Venezuela. We're sort of apart now and are starting our divorce, remember?"

"Of course I remember. Just checking. Sorry to hear about the divorce."

"No you're not," she said.

"How's Domínguez?"

"He's not the reason we separated."

"So why did you separate?"

"My husband has permanent potential. I'm tired of watching him make plans for life but never have the courage to follow through. I mean, it's sort of sad to see someone handed the keys to the kingdom in Venezuela and do nothing with them. He can get a good-paying job just through family contacts but doesn't seem to want one. I can't live like that. So how's work?" Patricia changed the subject. "What all did you get done in Venezuela, by the way?" She arched her back and stretched out in the sun. "You know more about what's going on in the country than I do."

Street checked the Garmin navigator system. He pressed the "Man Overboard" button, giving him a GPS location of the boat at the time a person falls off. It was also a good tool to test the power of currents. Right as he pressed the button, he grabbed a potato chip and tossed it overboard. It raced away from the boat as if it had velocity on its own. The current was strong that day, Street took note. He looked at Patricia, smiled, took a sip of beer, and glanced back at the Garmin. A second had passed; the spot where he had pushed the "Man Overboard" button was several yards south of him.

"Quite a current we've got going on," Street said.

"Which way is it headed?"

"It's headed southeast. The energy of the storm is surging ahead."

Street let the boat drift in the Atlantic Ocean. Waves roiled on the horizon of the open ocean, looking like fins of giant fish cutting the surface in an angry feeding frenzy.

"It sure is getting rough out there," Patricia said.

"Storm surge. It comes in ahead of the weather. I remember when I was a kid, before a big hurricane hit years ago, the night skies were clear, the stars were out, and the winds were calm several hours before the storm hit, though a nearby canal was several feet above normal and racing in."

"Pretty scary."

"We'll stay close to shore," Street said. "Cheers," Street toasted Patricia and sat on the transom next to her.

"You know, Street, I thought it was pretty stupid to chase after that man like that. You could have been kidnapped, if not killed."

"I know. It was a little brash. I guess I'm the opposite of your husband. Ex-husband, that is."

"In more ways than you'll ever know."

Street looked at Patricia. Her hair fell across her shoulders in the summer breeze. He tried not to smell her shampooed locks and suntan lotion, but he did after a wisp of wind caressed him with her scents.

"Did I ever tell you what went through my head when I first met you before the Domínguez interview?" Street said.

"No," she said, in a weak voice. Patricia leaned forward and parted her lips for a kiss.

Street stood up, took her hand, and brought her to her feet.

"Do you really want to know?" he asked, his own voice a little weak. He leaned in and kissed her. She leaned into him and kissed him back.

"I've been waiting for that since I first saw you," he said.

"Me too," she said. "So what went through your head when you saw me?" she asked.

Street put his arms around her waist.

"Before that, there's just one thing," Street said, stepping back. "Close your eyes."

"What's this?" Patricia said, giggling. "Are we on a doomed ocean liner?"

"Just close your eyes."

"Okay," she said.

"Now give me both of your hands."

"They're yours. I'm yours," she whispered.

"Walk forward to the bow." Street led her. "Take your top off," he said.

"Why don't you do it for me?"

He released one hand and took off her top with the other.

"Don't stop there," she said.

"I want to see you take the bottom off."

"You want to see me naked?" she asked, opening her eyes.

"Yes. And do more than just see you naked."

"Okay."

She rolled her eyes, smiled, and then closed them again. She untied one small knot on one hip. The knot on the other hip held as the free end cascaded gently down her thigh, like a curtain opening that would reveal something magical. Then she untied the bikini knot on her other hip. The black bikini sailed to the boat deck, landing without a sound. She kept her eyes closed but her mouth open wide in a smile.

"God, it's been a while," she said. Street stared at her. Her breathing picked up in the breeze and in the small wind chop lapping on the side of the boat. Then he realized after a couple of seconds had passed that he was barely breathing himself.

"Come here," Street said.

"Okay."

He took her hand. "Just one more step, and I want you to see something."

She stood in the bow of the boat.

"One more step, and then you can open your eyes and look toward the horizon, but not until I tell you to."

She took a step.

"Are your eyes still closed?" Street held her from behind, his face caressed by her long, brown hair.

"Yes they are."

"Good."

Then Street gently tossed her overboard. A small splash broke the silence in the open water. Street walked back to the console, cranked up the engines, and pressed the "Man Overboard" button anew on his GPS to get a fresh reading.

"Looks like I beat you at your own game, Case Officer Patricia, or whatever the hell your name is. Enjoy your front-row seats to Hurricane Granville."

Patricia bobbed in the water, fighting off both confusion and saltwater in her eyes. She pulled the hair out of her face and squinted up at Street.

"Are you insane? Get me out of here!" she screamed in the open water, drifting away from the boat.

"I'll give you a fighting chance," Street said, tossing a small orange life jacket over to her. "If you survive, I'll tell you how I figured you out. Later," he said.

He backed the boat in reverse against the current, distancing himself from Patricia even farther, and then sped away. Patricia's flailing hands grew smaller in the water.

CHAPTER

50

Brent Drum sped up on I-95 toward Palm Beach County. He rubbed his hands over his freshly shaven head. He took it down a little close and glanced in the rearview mirror. He was Beryl Phelps again, and he was in character, back from a trip to see how Molly Wells was doing. He pulled the Porsche into the parking lot of the office building, and then a wave of panic came over him. The storm. The office would be closing, if it wasn't closed already. Let's just get what we can out of Molly, he thought. Get her data, cram into the next briefing, blame the hurricane for rushed reporting, and then get rid of her, even on the property of Spartan Software if need be.

The parking lot was sparse but not empty. A few stragglers were coming in and out of the building. Storm warnings didn't stop those wanting to get out of the house to do some busy work at the office, especially since the worst of the hurricane would stay to the south. And they didn't stop Brent Drum from becoming Beryl Phelps strolling effortlessly into a still-open office building. He walked past the guard and went up the elevator. He crossed the large room of cubicles. Blonde hair. Stunning crossed legs.

"Molly!" Brent said.

"Hello, Beryl," Molly replied, standing to attention, darting her eyes around.

"How was your recent trip?"

"It was great. I have so much to tell you."

"Great," Brent said. "Let's take a walk."

"Let's not. I'll tell you here before I leave in five minutes."

Street killed the engines and drifted in the silence. Somewhere in the Atlantic, Patricia was alone and naked, swimming in the face of a powerful hurricane. She was probably trying to remain calm and figure out a way to survive the ordeal. Street looked at the Garmin GPS monitor and tracked her location. She was drifting to the south. Not far away. He waited one minute, then throttled the engines and headed back to her.

Then he turned the boat around and headed away from her.

"Damn it!" he screamed.

On the one hand, she was perfect, and he knew she was as crazy for him as he was for her. On the other hand, she was a spy and had betrayed him. She was part of Brent's agenda. If there were a third hand, he thought, it would be that she was alone and naked in the water. That was no way to treat her. Maybe she got coerced into this scheme all along.

"Damn it!" he repeated.

He cranked the boat engines and drove around in circles. He wondered if he should go get her or let her die before she killed him. He went through the motions. Her car was parked at the marina, and security cameras would have evidence of her boarding his boat. What would he say? She's a spy who was trying to kill me after I served her purpose, so I eliminated her in some sort of preemptive assassination? Wouldn't work.

Maybe she fell overboard? He tried to find her and couldn't. Could still be messy. He drove the boat north, parallel to the coast. Back and forth his mind ran. And the longer he thought, the more his feelings for her trumped his distrust and fear. Plus, if he was going to unravel this mess somehow, he'd need to know more, and she would be the perfect source.

It was time for trust in both an institution trying to kill him, and in a woman from that institution who was trying to love him.

It was time to go pick her up and let her know how he had blown her cover. He turned the boat around, checked his GPS, and eventually, he saw arms waving—and the bright-orange life vest he had tossed over for her, the one he had also tagged with a GPS device. He pulled up closer to her, reached over, and yanked her in by the life jacket. She jumped into the boat and got her balance, water dripping down her legs onto the deck. She stood firm and got her bearings. Then she clocked him. A perfect punch right across the chin, the so-called Fu Manchu line. Street absorbed it well.

"What the fuck!" she screamed.

"I pressed the "Man Overboard" device. You weren't in too much danger, especially considering there's a GPS transponder in that life jacket. There's some current, but I knew where you were all along," Street said, smiling, checking to see if there was any blood on his lip, surprised at the force behind her punch. "Do you know how cute you look when you're angry, especially when flailing in the Atlantic Ocean just before the onset of a nasty hurricane?"

"You sick—"

"Just shut up. You were in some danger. True. But not as much as you thought, and not nearly as much danger as you put me in. Besides, you're here to kill me, right?"

Patricia sighed. She stood not caring at all if Street saw her naked, though her exhausted posture conveyed far less sex appeal than when she was sitting on the transom, back arched and barely breathing a little while earlier. She saw Street checking her out, grabbed a towel, covered herself, and sat back down on the transom.

"How did you know?" Patricia said.

Street looked at her and threw her another towel. She took it and covered herself up more, as if she were some war-weary refugee concealing herself in a shawl.

"The SUV parked up at the marina gave you away. Nice paint job from black to white. Pretty clever to sprinkle in some dents and scratches, but don't you remember? I have a photographic memory. That license plate was the same one on the black car that was spying on me when I was out in the Everglades, the one that did a three-point turn and almost fell off the road and into the sinkhole. That was you driving that day, and let me go out on a limb and guess that Brent was riding shotgun. If you had taken a different car, I might not have guessed right away but still would have gotten suspicious. Nice job telling me a little while ago that you used to sail around here. But did you forget that you get seasick? You told me that when I called asking for Ricardo and his data."

Patricia crossed her arms and looked down at her lap.

"Please tell me they taught you better than that to conceal guilty body language," Street said.

Patricia said nothing. She just shook her head.

"Anyway, want more clues? During my interview with Domínguez, you met me with a smartphone but during the meeting, you snuck out with a cheap cell phone. Pretty weird. Also, remember when I called you and asked for help finding a new job? You told me that there was no reason a smart and hardworking person such as myself should be slaving away at a small outfit like that with no hope of ownership in it. How did you know I didn't own a sliver? Weird word choice, too. No hope. Just an odd thing to bring up in conversation—like you were planting some idea in my head. You also said at lunch in Las Mercedes after I interviewed the president that Brent wanted to know if Worldwide Oil & Gas would sponsor a roundtable, which would keep the magazine afloat along with the interview with the Venezuelan leader. How did you know it was going under? How did you know the magazine needed that interview to stay, as you put it, afloat? Then, after putting all these fucked-up pieces together, I figured you put me in touch with Matías to chase bogus job interviews to keep me at *The Gateway*, so I couldn't leave. Matías is a spy, and his company is a cover, right? He made me an offer but delayed the start. That'd keep me with Brent for a few more weeks. You knew how much that offer was, and I never even told you. You should not have told me at lunch in Las Mercedes that I got an offer with—and I quote—a monthly salary of five figures. There were a couple of other things as well. You and Ian seemed to be hiding something at El Techo that night. Plus, in the slum, an old woman who shooed us away said Ian and I should see more in our own countries, as in countries plural. How did she know he's from the UK and I'm from the US? I figured you were using me and Ian. Plus, you kept peppering me with soft questions and looking so hot that night, asking me about Russian assault rifles and coast guard intel on smuggling. And remember during my interview with Domínguez when I asked for Ricardo's contact info? You said you didn't remember *which* Ricardo. After, when I called, the operator said there was nobody named Ricardo at Worldwide. Speaking of Ricardo, he tried to burn me alive, by the way. I figured that since the microwave didn't kill me, you were plan B, C, D, or whatever."

Patricia sighed and kept her head down.

Street went on. "So I figured I'd pitch you over the side of my boat before you did the same to me. But I came back, because deep down inside, you wanted me to find out. You yourself told me the answer I'm looking for is right in front of me."

Patricia shook her head. "I can't believe it's come to this. You're right. I was involved in this Placebo Agenda program, but I was never going to harm you."

"I know," Street said. I know it now, he thought.

She stood and cast off the towel Street had handed her. Then she took the first towel and removed it. She snapped it in the air to dry it off, not caring if Street saw her with nothing on. She noticed Street's back arch and his chest jut out, but she felt perfectly at ease around him.

"The Placebo Agenda," Street said, shaking his head. "That is the stupidest sounding thing I've ever heard of. Anything that absurd is bound to collapse. I'll make sure of it." Street walked back to the console and looked for Patricia's bikini and sarong.

"I can't believe it's spiraled out of control like this," she said, sitting back on the transom and taking in some sun. She threw both towels on a small sitting bench in front of the console and sighed. "Yes, Brent's boss, Karen, is also my senior and got me involved. At first we did our jobs, you know, asking people what they know, just like I did with you at El Techo. It was all innocent enough. But it got carried away."

"Patricia, you know better. You're a smart woman." Street stared at her body.

"If I blow the whistle on Brent, I could lose my job and definitely worse," she said, taking her bikini and sarong. "Or something could happen to me or, God forbid, my husband."

"Your soon-to-be ex-husband."

"Right. Plus, I had no idea Brent was killing people."

She stood and noticed other boats several hundred yards away. She could hear one blasting music, and she put her clothes back on.

Street felt a swell of disappointment mixed with a sigh of relief that he could breathe normally again.

"Who all has he killed?" Street asked, making eye contact a little easier now.

"Sources in the agency who are on to him say he killed a hedge fund employee in Naples, and we are trying to save a marketing manager at a place called Spartan Software up in Broward. Two couples in Venezuela are dead."

"What are their names?"

"I don't know that."

"Yes, you do," he said. "The placebo in Naples was Olivia Crawford, and the one in Palm Beach County is Molly Wells. The Spradlings and Tagles disappeared in Caracas. Molly will be safe because I'm way ahead of the curve."

Patricia looked up at Street. "How do you know?"

"Don't worry about it. But if we are going to trust each other then we need to keep the secrets and lies to a minimum. Who is your source who's on to Brent?"

"Her name is Cyra Harred. She contacted me in Caracas. She's here in Miami."

"She's contacted me too. How does she know?" Street asked, hoping to find out who Cyra's boss was and how he unearthed the agenda in the first place.

"Her boss just knows. I don't know who he is."

"Let's find this Cyra. I want to talk to her. For my sake and for Molly Wells's sake. I've already warned her that her boss is not who he says he is. Let's just keep Brent around us and not around her."

"Fine. And Street, I just want to say that I could never kill you. And also, I just want to say that…"

"Go ahead," Street said.

He sat down next to her on the transom. She arched her back in the sunlight, crossed her legs, and stared into his eyes. No acting this time, Street guessed. Just trust her in spite of it all.

"I just want to say that…"

She put one hand on his knee and grabbed his hand with her other, guiding him to her leg.

He leaned in, feeling her soft breaths float from her mouth into his. Her skin was smooth, warm, and dry in the late-summer sun.

"I want to say—"

She was interrupted by a siren blast. A very loud blast.

Just a few yards away, a Miami-Dade Police boat was ordering a nearly overcrowded center console to kill their engines. Someone, one of the many college-aged kids on the boat, was likely to be ticketed for having too many passengers and not enough life preservers onboard. None of the kids seemed to care, as long as the music was loud.

"Let's get out of here," Street said. He gunned the boat and headed to port.

On the horizon, the first feeder bands from Hurricane Granville roared across the open Atlantic, and with the eastern Bahamas in their crosshairs, they moved closer to South Florida.

After yanking the boat out of the water, towing it safely to ride out the storm inside his parents' very large garage, he dropped Patricia off for an urgent meeting with Cyra and to update Brent with a bogus report on her plans to eliminate Street.

Street woke up the next day before dawn to finish preparing for the storm, which was now showing up on the eastern fringes of local weather radar screens. He double-checked the boat and all the doors and windows in the large house, confident it's sturdy construction made of coral rock and Dade County pine could withstand the approaching hurricane as it had for a century.

By midmorning, he was sitting across the table from Patricia at the Grouchy Grouper. The bar had open two hours before noon to get as much business as possible before the storm hit, and both were enjoying an early lunch consisting of multiple sodas and fresh snapper sandwiches. Patricia looked out the window and around the bar. It didn't take long for the place to fill up with people taking a break from securing their houses and getting ready for a party before being boarded up in their houses for a day at least. Most were drinking beer outside the bar on the sidewalk via a small to-go window.

"This noise is great," Patricia said. "Perfect for a quick covert talk. I approve. Also know this. I was never going to hurt you. I wasn't going to go through with it. I can't stress that enough, and I think you know."

Street looked out the bar window. Then he looked into her eyes and shook his head.

"I know," he said. Then after a pause, he said, "What's up with my evil-genius friend, Ian Collins?"

Patricia hesitated, and Street saw she was gathering her thoughts.

"No filters and no spin, Patricia. Remember what I said about trust."

Patricia shrugged. "Ian Collins is one of my assets. I pay him when needed, and he keeps me informed about what's going on in Venezuela because he's one of the best reporters I've ever seen and speaks to everyone, a true doer in every sense of the word. And like you, he's a journalist, and he doesn't raise red flags when asking questions because he's so visible. I'm pretty sure everyone knows Ian is a reporter. He's the best there is. He couldn't do anything else."

Street shrugged. That was probably true. Ian was the best.

"So Ian is involved? He better be okay."

"He's fine, and he is not involved in this agenda. I just told him to encourage you to go to Petare to see if you would chase that source. Remember that old lady, the one that shooed you guys out of her neighborhood? She's an asset of mine as well, which you've probably figured out. She speaks native English, you know. I guess you wouldn't know. She's from Guyana and knows what's going on in eastern Caracas and back along the porous resource-rich border."

"Ian told her that 'we're just a little lost,' and so we left," Street said.

"Ian was letting her know that he made his delivery with you right around the corner and that it was time to tip off the authorities that you may be drug smugglers. We didn't know the local police were going to try and shake you down first. That actually worked in our favor, and it also gave us a little more time to tip off Pérez that you may be smuggling drugs out of the slum, which was kind of stupid on our part anyway, since a smuggler would likely hole up on Margarita Island."

"It wasn't all bad," Street said. "Do you work with Pérez? He's pretty much Venezuelan intelligence, right?"

"No, I don't work with or against him, but, yes, you're correct. He is Venezuelan intelligence. A little less civilian in nature than the CIA as their security needs are different."

"What all do you know about that pen-clicking man? Remember that guy? In the plaza before you, Ian, and I were at El Techo? The same man I chased into the slum?"

"You know who he is. Someone Brent sent to spy on you as part of his own agenda. He's one of Cyra's contacts as well," Patricia said.

"Fair enough. And where is this Cyra?"

Just then, the crowd parted, and a large and very toned woman walked through the throngs knowing that everyone would get out of her way, and they did. Every man in the bar checked her out as she walked by.

"You could set this beer on that ass, and the bottle won't fall," a ruddy blond man in a Miami Dolphins jersey said. Cyra made eye contact with the man. His red cheeks grew even redder, and he looked down. She found her way to Patricia and Street.

"So you're the famous Street Brewer. Recognize my voice from the phone? My superior will be glad we have you safe and sound," Cyra said, extending her hand to Street.

After a few seconds, Street took her hand. He motioned for her to sit. The two just sized each other up.

About fifteen seconds passed, and Street finally spoke. "So you're Cyra, the crank caller. Glad to know our intelligence agencies act like children to gather info. For all I know, you're lying to me now."

"The US government is sorry for what has happened to you," Cyra said.

"Are you authorized to make a statement like that? Can we go public?" Street said. "Cut the bullshit."

"Street, all we can ask is that you don't go to the FBI," Cyra said. "We want to cover this up. That's right, I said it. We are blatantly trying to cover this up, at least for now. Go public with it later, but not yet. We'll take care of you, somehow."

Cyra looked at Patricia.

"You can try," Street said.

Patricia said nothing.

"Street," Cyra said. "This is a bad thing, but we can all make it right—you, me, and Patricia. Plus we will find a way to make it up to you, even pay you. We have the resources. You want to move out of that old apartment building and do a little better than that underpaying typical Miami job, right?"

"Maybe Matías can hire me," Street said.

"Street—" Patricia started to say, but Cyra interrupted her.

"Thank God Patricia couldn't take you out, but I'm definitely taking Brent out. Full disclosure here. I know you're with the media and even have the power to go public and also the freedom to go to the police. For all I know, you're recording this now. But just hold off, because I need to know the full extent of this agenda, so I'll tell you everything in hopes you'll help me. Then we'll make it up to you somehow."

Cyra looked at Patricia again and then at Street's wallet on the table.

"We caught on to Brent and tried to warn others in danger, which eventually tipped Brent off."

"How did you find this out?" Patricia asked.

"Like I said, my boss suspected it and asked me to look into it."

"And how did superspy find out? What's his name?" Street asked, knowing full well his name was Roman.

"His name is John Smith," Cyra replied.

"Funny," Street said.

He sighed and stared out the window for a few seconds. Some college-aged girls walked in with some younger guys who looked like they never finished high school. Young white men with sun-bleached dreadlocks, faded tattoos and trimmed beards that seemed to be the color of their own skin.

"I'm not going to listen to any more of this. How do I know you aren't here to off me right now?"

"You don't," Patricia said. "And I don't blame you."

"Street," Cyra said. "She's right, you don't. But let's just try and save future lives. We'll make it up to you somehow."

Cyra glared at Patricia, who said nothing.

Street kept looking out the window. The streets of Coconut Grove teemed with pedestrians checking out locally owned clothing stores, cafés, bicycle shops, and more exotic venues like body piercers and tobacco shops. All were boarded up, yet most still kept their front doors ajar for some last-minute business, earning a few dollars and giving people something to do before the storm hit.

"There's one more out there," Patricia spoke up. "A woman named Molly Wells. At Spartan Software up in Palm Beach County. She's due for termination."

Street shook his head. "Keep Brent away from her, and she'll live. It's that simple. I warned her that her boss, Brent but with another alias, is bad news. Didn't tell her everything. That would really scare her." Street was a little irked at himself for cooperating.

"Great. You figured that out as well. But you're not telling us everything," Cyra said.

"Well, all you need to know now is that keeping him in Miami will keep him away from her. Then you kill him and be done with this mess. You have my solemn intention that I won't print any of this right now."

Patricia laughed out loud. Clapped her hands and crossed her legs. "Solemn intention. Classic!"

Cyra stared at her.

Patricia's smile imploded into a tight swallow but quickly bloomed back into a childish grimace. She looked at Street, and then her smile broke out again. "I don't blame him for telling us to get lost."

Street shook his head. "All right," he said with a long sigh. "Let's do this if it will save Molly's life, and we're doing it my way. Give me your phone, Patricia."

Patricia handed it to him.

Street dialed Brent, who answered after the second ring.

"Patricia. Is it done? Talk to me."

"Yeah, it's done. You're done, Brent," Street said. "I prepped my house and boat for the hurricane, and now I'm off to tattle. I figure the FBI may be especially interested in your placebo program. I'll talk to my reporter buddies as well."

"Street," Brent said. "What a pleasant surprise. What are you going to tell the FBI? Are you going to walk in there and make some outrageous accusation that CIA agents have infiltrated your company? What can you prove? Nice to see you overcompensating for being such a coward your whole life."

"Maybe you're right about that," Street said. "And maybe it'll be that simple. I'll tell the police, or they can read about it in print nationwide, of course after I pop off a copy on *The Gateway* website. I have to be exclusive with my own story, you know."

"Street, you've gone crazy, chief. What evidence do you have?"

"Patricia's sworn testimony for one." Street said, winking at Patricia. "I also have my greatest hits recordings of two chirping idiots in my office talking about your agenda. This won't turn out like it did with my colleagues. I figure you might choose a different method than the one you used to take out Olivia Crawford in Naples or the one you're about to unsuccessfully use with Molly Wells. They'll find the trace evidence linking you to Olivia, and I can guarantee you one thing, no amount of military or intelligence training in the world is going to protect you from the upstanding young men in prison."

Brent remained quiet.

"I know you personally killed Olivia Crawford. I have audio evidence to prove it. You're sloppier than you think."

"You do, huh?" Brent said.

"Yup. Nice job, by the way." Street winked at the two women.

Brent was quiet for a few seconds, then said, "You think you're safe right now?"

"Yep."

Street heard a blip in his ear.

"Did you hear that?" Brent said.

Street looked at the phone. There was a new text message.

"It's a text from a little birdie in your area. A big birdie actually. Do you think Patricia and whoever that woman is with you right now, Cyra Harred probably, can really help you? The Grouchy Grouper may be crowded, and there may be a storm on the way, but I can guarantee you one thing, Street Brewer, you won't survive this night, and you will die a painful death. Nice crisp T-shirt by the way, and tell Cyra she looks great. Nice legs! I might even offer to buy her a beer and set the glass down on that ass and it won't fall, just like the little red-faced man in the Dolphins jersey suggested," Brent said.

Street hung up. He heard his own phone beep and frowned at it. A text. He opened it and saw a picture of himself, Patricia, and Cyra seated at the Grouchy Grouper. Patricia's phone had received the same. He stood up quickly, and Cyra and Patricia recoiled in surprise. He looked at where the picture had probably been taken, judging from the angle. Nothing but college girls and their scruffy boyfriends. He scanned the room, and even the bartenders stopped to see if there was a problem brewing in their corner pub.

"He's on to us. Let's get out of here," Street said. "We were successful. Tipping off Brent moves him on to us and away from Molly or anyone else who may be involved."

"You're crazy," Cyra said. "I can't believe I let you do that."

"I like it, though," Patricia added.

"Well," Street said. "If you're serious about closing down this agenda, then we do need to take out Brent and whoever else is in on the agenda, today more than ever."

"I agree," Cyra said. "But this is best left up to the professionals, Street. Not you."

"Who? Roman?" Street said. "Is he here? And are you going to do it? Right now?"

Cyra just looked at Street. She pursed her lips and left with Street and Patricia.

Across the bar, in the corner by the small kitchen, hidden by throngs of bar patrons, Ricardo watched Street over a soda. Street motioned to a gorgeous, athletic, dark-haired bartender in a tight, black shirt that accentuated strong, heavily tattooed arms, for the tab. Street squinted in the direction of the man, who was also concealed in part by a thin man wearing a Boston T-shirt. The bartender took Street's money, thanked him. Street stared at the kid and walked away.

CHAPTER

51

Street Brewer hopped into his Jeep. Patricia sat in the front, Cyra in the back. Street cranked up the engine and grabbed his cell phone. He dialed. "Yo," he said.

Cyra and Patricia stared at him. All they could hear were crackles of a voice coming from Street's phone. Indiscernible.

"Not much," Street said, still in park.

He took note of Cyra and Patricia eavesdropping and revved the engine. Both women rolled their eyes. Patricia seemed at ease, ready to go along with anyone who'd end the agenda. Cyra was noticeably tense.

"Listen, I need a little help. Meet me out in the Everglades. You know where."

Patricia and Cyra strained to eavesdrop anew, and then Street gunned the Jeep down the small one-way strip of street and turned right onto Main Highway, where a patch of traffic slowed his progress.

"Look, I found the condom in my room. You've had your eye on Brianna, and only you would be so stupid as to do something like that in my apartment. Be there, or I will find you. In fact, I know where you are right now." Street hung up.

"What was that all about?" Patricia asked.

Cyra leaned over.

"Not much," Street said.

"Not much? That was juicy!" Patricia said.

Street looked over at her. She turned her head but held her smile. She had a little dirt on Street after all. Nothing she could use but good to know anyway.

Then Cyra spoke up. "Street, nobody can know about this. I'll eliminate whoever you spoke with on the phone if it means protecting national security."

"How do I know you're not going to kill me?"

"You have no proof. But you know that's not going to happen," Cyra said, looking over at Patricia. "Besides, the world needs a squeaky-clean boy like you."

"You got that right, Cyra, or whatever your name is," Street said, speeding along Main Highway. "Relax, this person doesn't know what we're up to and won't ever know. He's going to help us, but he thinks we're up to something totally different, something you two don't even know about. I'm getting good at this."

Then he slowed up and looked in the rearview mirror. No traffic behind him, and nobody following him from the Grouchy Grouper. Up ahead at the end of a strip of commerce along Main Highway, Street saw a familiar pair of crossed legs at a Mediterranean café. Brianna sat sipping a Chardonnay next to some woman. Street recognized her but had forgotten her name. Next to Brianna, a tall, thin man sat with all-one-length brown hair. His big hazel eyes widened when he saw Street. He was a handsome man, though he had a gaunt face, and dry skin. The man appeared tired, as if he had been up for days, which was probably the case.

Street pulled up in front of the outdoor table. "Been partying too hard, Jenkins?" he asked, parking the car on the street and then standing up on the running board so he could see over the Jeep. "Shouldn't you be home? Did the courts allow you to venture this far south while out on pretrial release? Ladies, this is Jenkins, my cousin. If you ever want to party and stay up for three days on end, this is your guy. And as always by his side is his loving companion, the virtuous and noble Brianna."

"That's enough, Street," Jenkins said, surprised that Street had just showed up, let alone with two women he had never seen before. He just stared at them, processing, both hands in his front pockets.

Street stared at Brianna and then shook his head.

Patricia stared at Street for a second, studying him.

"You're no angel, Street," Jenkins said. "Do these women know what you do to make ends meet? How much you've got stashed—"

"They will. Anyway, it looks like you traded down, and I traded up," Street said.

"Hi, Street," Brianna said weakly.

Street remained silent. Didn't even look at her.

"Listen, Jenkins. DUIs are the lowest priority for cops right now. They are too busy getting ready for this storm. I need you to meet me in the Everglades. I need your help. Be there as quickly as possible. Be there or go with the public attorney. Oh, and Brianna, I'm the one who earns the money, not Jenkins. Whatever money he throws around comes from me and my private account in the Everglades."

She frowned, a mixture of anger and confusion.

"Just know that." Street sped off.

He looked in his rearview mirror. Both Cyra and Patricia were looking back at Brianna and Jenkins, and Street wondered if they were putting faces, voices and mannerisms to the names of his ex-girlfriend and cousin, who until now were just individuals in their notes and files, names and faces on a bulletin board of assets and liabilities or people they had followed casually as part of the espionage practices.

"We'll need Jenkins later," Street said. "Don't worry—again, he doesn't know a thing, and nor will he know. He'll stay clueless. In fact, he'll be our placebo for the afternoon and mine for life once this mission is over."

"Did you just tell him to meet us in the Everglades?" Cyra asked.

"Yes."

"Street, we aren't going to the Everglades," Patricia said.

"If you want to end all this, you will. Trust me. It's all you can do."

Street drove along Main Highway. Coconut Grove's cafés, shops, and bars gave way to a thick green canopy of tropical foliage like some kind of tunnel, which cooled the pavement and gave majestic houses some cover. Traffic was light, and Street pushed ahead with ease. He hung a right on Hardee Road and veered into Coral Gables. A few turns later, Street jolted northbound on US 1.

"Where exactly are we going?" Cyra asked, a little annoyed. "Street, you better realize that national security comes first. I will do what I have to in order to make sure life goes on. This agenda will die, but I swear it will do so silently."

"National security isn't gonna mean shit in a hurricane, a major one at that. You want to close down this agenda? Then first we go to my office, *The Gateway*. Well, technically speaking it's my office and yours and Patricia's too. It actually belongs to all the US taxpayers in a way, since we do intelligence work. I just need to get some personal things out of there. And if Brent and pals show up—and they will soon—you are more than welcome to take them out."

"I'll take you out as well if you get in my way."

Street ignored her and headed north along US 1. A few minutes later, he was in downtown Coral Gables and parked on the street in front of *The Gateway*. Unlike any other time, there were plenty of parking spaces.

"Watch the car. I'll be right back. I have to get my evidence," Street said, eyeing Cyra. "Keep an eye out for Brent. There's a good chance we're being followed, so you may get your man after all."

"Street, you're not in charge here," Cyra said.

"You want Brent and company gone? By all means kill them, but we need to flush them out away from the city and into the Everglades. And then we keep them out there."

Street walked off and ran up into the office building.

Patricia saw that Cyra was processing Street's plan. Maybe the Everglades is a better place to eliminate rogue agents, after all. Cyra noticed Patricia was staring at her, so she stared back.

"You like him, don't you?"

Patricia looked down at her lap.

"I guess my body language gives that away. He's not your typical upper-class elite with a house in the posh Gables Estates section of the city. But there's something about him, something so different than my husband, who inherited the world but never used it."

"Well, maybe when this is over, you two can get together and have a normal life, or as normal of a life as possible. But first, we need to find out what all Brent knows, and then we kill them all. Got it?"

"Got it. What's your take on Street?"

"Street? Probably very intelligent but never knew what he wanted to do in life, professionally that is," Cyra said.

"We're not recruiting him. What do you *think* about him?"

"He's not my type."

Patricia chuckled. "What is your type? NFL quarterback? Global soccer star?"

Cyra smiled and looked into Patricia's eyes.

"Someone like you, a little petite brunette but who flaunts it a little more and gets a little pouty."

Patricia blushed. "Oh, I see."

Cyra shook her head, smiled, and glanced at the office building. "Here comes our boy," She said.

Street came running out. He threw a few backpacks and duffel bags in the back and started the car.

"Let's go to the Everglades."

CHAPTER

52

Brent Drum stood in the parking lot at Spartan Software and snapped his phone shut. Street Brewer wasn't going to get the best of him. He was going to take care of this himself. He made his way into the building and stormed across the sixth floor between the cubicles. He got to Molly's desk. No Molly. It was empty, save a sticky note on her computer monitor that read, "Beryl, I had a flight to catch. Talk after the storm." A text on his phone reiterated her message.

"Fuck," Brent muttered, his teeth clenched. He bolted out of the office building and then broke into a sprint to his car. He plopped in the Porsche and sped away. He meandered west for a while. On the passenger seat, a leather messenger bag rested quietly. He stared at it while at a red light and then moved on. It had seemed to stare back at him.

He drove for about half an hour, pushing into the far western reaches of Palm Beach County, and then he pulled a small plastic trash bag from the messenger bag. Inside was a fifth of vodka and more than enough fentanyl to kill Molly Wells, enough to make it look like a most unfortunate and tragic accident. He drove into a small strip mall, parked the car, and dumped the opioids and the bottle of premium vodka into a garbage receptacle.

"Molly Wells, I'll have Ricardo deal with you later. Street Brewer takes priority now."

A little over an hour later, Brent was back in Miami-Dade County. He shot off I-95 and whipped into Coconut Grove in a matter of moments, this time in a Mercedes-Benz. Outside of the Grouchy Grouper, he laid on the horn. Pedestrians snapped their heads in annoyance at the loud blasts of noise. Brent tried to peer into the bar's tinted windows but couldn't see through the darkness. Throngs of cigarette smokers who had popped outside to light up between beers blocked his view even more. He sent a text, and Ricardo was out in a matter of seconds. The large man hopped into the rear seat behind Brent, who sat impatiently in front.

Boston left the bar as well, nodded to Brent, and walked off in the direction of a small parking lot at the corner of the narrow one-way street. A few yards ahead, a driver waited at a no-left-turn stop sign with her left blinker on. The road was too narrow for Brent to make a U-turn. He was stuck with Ricardo in the back seat and a group of smokers outside of the bar beside him. He took out a cell phone and dialed. The phone rang.

"Hello," a man answered.

"You here?"

"Yes," the man answered. Both hung up.

"Great," Brent said. "Domínguez is here in Miami. Let's get this done."

CHAPTER

53

Street sped down the Tamiami Trail, pushing west toward the Everglades. Cyra and Patricia rode in silence, entranced by the hum of the engine, the wind in their hair, and the stretch of businesses sprawling out over western Miami-Dade County. The strip malls gave way to melaleuca trees and saw grass. They were now in the eastern fringes of the Florida Everglades and its neighboring pine forests and cypress swamps.

They shot past a county-run shooting range and the large Miccosukee casino. Pumps regulating the flow of water streaming down from the southern rim of Lake Okeechobee and an occasional sign advertising airboat rides and alligator wrestling dotted an otherwise rural highway.

Street pulled off on a nondescript road and headed deeper into the mysterious ecosystem. Large suburban neighborhood homes gave way to smaller quirky houses as he headed west on Loop Road, which pushed ahead into a thick, tropical canopy. Street killed the engine and let the snap of silence bring Cyra and Patricia back to life. A warm gust of wind packed with the scents of earth, water, and foliage blew over them, much different from city sea breezes.

"What's in the Everglades?" Cyra asked.

"Just hang on," Street said.

He took out his phone and began texting. Gotta talk to my Venezuelan caucus. He typed out a text:

You there?

His lawmaker buddy was quick to reply.

I am here, Street. Have you seen the news? For once the opposition might not be so fractioned that we can actually oust this guy.

He still has the military. Keeps them rich with drug-smuggling funds. Everyone knows that.

We'll see, Street. Hey, are you still reeling from your interview?

Not really. I don't think I was the only one who was played. The rest of the world was.

What are you talking about?

Stay tuned...

"Street, there's a storm coming," Cyra said. "If you don't drive, I will."

"Don't worry about it. We'll be back well before the storm hits. It takes longer than you think before the brunt of it gets close," Street said. "Anyway, we've got Brent chasing us because he knows that I'm on to him, which will hopefully throw all of you in jail. Turns out, I want him to chase us and even catch up to us."

"What?" Patricia and Cyra said in unison.

"We can defend ourselves better than Molly. So just follow my lead. We also need to address the issue over who Frog Legs is with the short shorts. Ricardo or whatever. So back to comparing notes. Patricia, you work for CIA as a mole planted inside the oil company. Anything else irregular going on? I can tell you from my end what's irregular. The president tells me in an interview the country is going to load up on missiles along the Colombian border, which is stupid. There's no need for that. Anyone can jump back and forth across that border unseen, and a quick response team can cross into Colombia to take out drug guerrillas and smugglers much better than long-range missiles. If Venezuela really wanted intercontinental ballistic missiles, it would stock them up on the Paraguaná peninsula, and maybe they'd nuke the US. But I don't think the Russians want to go that route. They want their presence known, but they don't want a repeat of the Cuban Missile Crisis with their local partner being a crazy idiot who doesn't know how the game of foreign policy is played. So anyway, I chase down that pen-clicking guy, a Russian, Bogdanov, into the slums. A gang almost burns me alive." Patricia's jaw dropped at that last comment. Cyra looked away. Street studied their reactions and then just shrugged. "But some of them aren't from Venezuela, including this Ricardo. I don't know where they are from."

"Cubans maybe?" Cyra asked. "Interesting, Peter didn't fill me in on this one."

"Maybe he was about to," Street said. "Anyway, I don't think they were Cubans. Most were Venezuelan, but a few sprinkled in there were not from the region. Just before I was about to be slow cooked, I heard one of the Venezuelan gang members say in Spanish, 'You're a fucking moron like Ricardo and the rest of those assholes.' Rest of them. The word choice he used in Spanish suggested the Venezuelans were dealing with foreigners, most likely non-Spanish speakers. One was Russian. Who was the other? The noble and upstanding Ricardo! Obviously an alias."

Street looked in the rearview mirror past the two women toward the road behind him.

"There was always our friend Ricardo at the oil company that had access to financials."

"Yes, him," Patricia said. "He was more of a courier type than a finance guy, at least at Worldwide Oil & Gas. You know how Latin America is. Lots of couriers. He was probably told to deliver the info. He doesn't manage company finances. I think Domínguez probably wanted a courier to get you the data instead of opening up contact with our CFO and let you build a reporter-source relationship, which is legitimate on his part. Anyway, I did see Ricardo once. He looked like any other courier. Big and burly. But his Spanish seemed native, though he didn't speak much."

Cyra was staring out the window. Street took notice. Her mind was thousands of miles away.

"Anyway," Patricia went on. "There was something odd about him. I said hello to him in the office once, and he said nothing. He just stared at me through these dead eyes under his thick curly hair."

"That's him. That's the one who was there when they tried to burn me," Street said. "A voice shouted out to stop. Bogdanov. This guy is a good spy. Does his homework. He speaks with the Venezuelans, the Americans, and whoever else is in the country. He's doing his job. He's not our friend, and he's not supposed to be. But he's not our enemy, either, and he's not going to let things get out of control. Anything else to add?"

Street made eye contact with Cyra. She said nothing.

"Cyra, when I say anything else, I am specifically talking to you," Street said.

Cyra remained fixated on the Everglades.

"Great," Street said.

He looked in the rearview mirror and cranked the engine. They rode in silence for about thirty seconds until Cyra sighed and told Street to stop the car. They were deep into Loop Road now.

"There is something to add," she said. "About Ricardo."

A mile or two away from the Grouchy Grouper, Ricardo told Brent to pull over at a gas station. Brent complied. "This won't take long," Ricardo said.

Brent squirmed. The gas lines were dwindling, and the tank was largely full, though the weather was going to go south quickly. Still, he relented, and Ricardo slammed the door and headed inside for the gas station's Mini Mart.

Inside the very cool, small grocery store, Ricardo bought bottled water and a carton of Marlboro Red cigarettes. He ambled through the aisles to see if anything worth an impulse buy would catch his eye. Nothing but seriously processed snacks. He was about to grab a small jar of peanut butter when his cell phone rang. He answered.

"I'm here in Miami. My role is more or less done. Soon I'll be on my way."

He watched a family pull up in a large white Ford Expedition with a center console boat in tow.

"On my way to where, I have no idea yet."

Three kids sprang from the car and raced into the Mini Mart. Their mom, from what Ricardo could gauge was an upper-middle-class woman in her mid-thirties in white shorts and beach attire, followed the children in. The husband, probably around forty, had filled the car and boat up with fuel and then parked on the side so as not to hog up the gasoline pumps. The kids ran around the Mini Mart, stocking up on candy. Their mom snagged a few batteries and whatever bottled water was left on the shelves. One child stared at Ricardo. Ricardo stared back at the children and the parents as if they were items for sale themselves. Then he remembered his phone call.

"Brent will have the money. I'll finish up here and then fly home. I'll get there somehow," Ricardo said in his phone, keeping an eye on the family. The father stared at Ricardo. He studied the large man for a second, and then he focused on the noise of his family at the register. He paid, rounded everyone up, and pulled out into traffic, heading west.

"What language was that big man speaking? It wasn't Spanish," one of his children asked.

"Yeah, what language was it then, Mr. Linguistics Expert?" the wife asked. "Was it Portuguese?"

"No," the man said. "That was Farsi."

54

"Ricardo is Iranian, though Tehran wants nothing to do with him anymore," Cyra said, still staring out blankly across the Everglades.

Street looked through the rearview mirror, and Patricia turned to face Cyra.

"We knew some Iranians were meeting with the Venezuelans to discuss setting up missiles on the Paraguaná peninsula," Cyra said.

"What?" Patricia interrupted? "There are no—"

"Let her finish," Street said. "I know how this ends, even if you don't. Cyra doesn't know either. But go on, Cyra."

Cyra stared at Street and then continued.

"As I was saying, to discuss setting up missiles nicely shuffled out of the global spotlight."

"Go on, Cyra," Street said.

"If the US or Israel attacks Iran, Venezuela attacks the US, or can always threaten to attack when it needs to beat its chest and pump up oil prices by stoking war cries. In the end, however, Caracas and Tehran scrapped the plan. It was too hard to sneak infrastructure out of the Middle East and into South America. There were plans to say both countries were going to build a nuclear power plant made from Iranian materials and basically sneak military equipment in with it, but that would have drawn red flags. Venezuela is rich in both oil and hydroelectric water resources, so doing anything regarding nuclear energy together would have raised suspicions. Plus the timing wasn't right. Tehran didn't want too much heat at the moment, especially when cutting a nuclear deal with Washington and the rest of the world a few years back, according to my superiors at least. It didn't need the world looking out for uranium in every corner of either Iran or in Venezuela, even if the uranium wasn't weapons grade. Still, the Iranians didn't leave Venezuela. They stuck around."

"Great, but what are Iranians doing in Petare of all places?" Patricia asked.

"My Russian counterpart, Bogdanov, outsourced some of his work to the Iranians. He used them to help move Kalashnikovs from Russia into Venezuela. They are about to manufacture Kalashnikovs in Venezuela now, if the plant isn't running by now, but this batch bound for paramilitaries in the slums were from Russia. I don't know why. Maybe Caracas could claim they were smuggled in if word got out the government was arming gangs with military equipment. Venezuelan-made rifles would leave less wiggle room. Anyway, the Venezuelans insisted the arms deal go down in Petare and well below the radar. Bogdanov hung out there for a while. He told me the lead Iranian guy, a big burly man that fits the description of your Ricardo, was contracted by the Venezuelan government to help distribute the Kalashnikovs to Venezuelan gangs in the slums. That way, the guns get into the gangs' hands, the president has armed loyal militias in the slums, and the Venezuelan military isn't responsible for moving those guns, and technically, neither are the Russians."

"And the Iranians then wash their hands of the monstrous Ricardo by leaving him in South America. That's pretty solid planning," Patricia said.

"But wait," Street said. "There's more, isn't there Cyra?"

Cyra hesitated and looked down.

"My mother is from the Old Country, from Iran," she said, pausing to stare at both Street and Patricia in what seemed like evenly timed intervals. "He's an affront to all things good and decent in my family's country, something you never see in western media. I want nothing more than to take this monster out. So I may be CIA, but I want one of us to destroy that walking atrocity for the good of the Iranian people."

"Okay," Patricia said. "Announcing a Russian base distracts US intelligence from what's really going on. Iran and Venezuela secretly discuss setting up a missile base on the Paraguaná peninsula but then scrap the project. They'd get caught and have to live with economic sanctions from Washington. But why are the Iranians helping smuggle arms into Venezuelans slums? Why can't Bogdanov just do it himself. Something still doesn't make sense."

"Yes it does," Street said. "It all makes perfect sense. Ricardo is a smuggler, and rifles aren't the only contraband he's smuggling."

CHAPTER

55

Hernán Bernal shuffled through the halls of the Venezuelan presidential palace. Everyone knew to get out of his way just by the expression on his face. He moved quicker than normal despite being in pain. His skin wasn't the only thing scarred from fighting battles his whole life. His bones were creaking like aging railroad bridges. But he pressed on.

He bolted outside of the presidential palace and walked through the busy streets of Caracas. Pedestrians heading to and from work in the cool-but-tropical morning largely ignored him. A few stared at him, recognizing him as someone they should know, but brushed him off. For most young Venezuelans, and there were a lot of them, only one face symbolized power and decision-making in the country, and, fortunately for Bernal, that wasn't him. He bought some popcorn from a street vendor and sat down on a bench in a small plaza that looked like it could have been anywhere. He ate the popcorn kernel by kernel, enjoying the afternoon sun. Then his phone rang.

"What's going on, Pérez?" Bernal said.

"I've been tracking Street and crew in Miami," Pérez said from a secure wireless phone in Miami. "Fortunately for us, South Florida is packed with Venezuelans, and they can help me out without knowing which governments I serve. I've got police trying to follow Street now. He's making a run for the Everglades, but with this storm, it's hard for them to properly tag him. That's a bad thing because he knows something."

"Do your best. Tell me what he knows and doesn't know," Bernal said.

"The same thing we don't know. What our president is up to. Iranians are still in town moving shit around, according to very local chatter."

"I knew it. Something's going on, and I suspect Big Oil and US agents are behind this shit. There's a hurricane about to hit up that way. I know you support the opposition, but let's work together. Find out what Mr. Brewer and any moron in South Florida knows, and find out what else we're smuggling into Venezuela from God knows where. Infiltrate wherever you need to infiltrate. I've hired a freelance agent there. He's a good gringo boy and can help you. So that makes two spies I have on the ground. In the meantime, I'll put the president's feet to the fire. I have a feeling I'm out of the loop on something, and that idiot is in on it. Something nuclear and some need to speak to some journalist from some publication nobody has ever heard of. Follow him, and I'll follow the president, and we'll find out what's being smuggled into this country."

Fifteen minutes later Hernán Bernal slammed his way into the president of Venezuela's office. The president was hunched over, staring blankly at his desk. A nervous secretary was staring at the nation's leader. Protocol shattered. The president motioned to her that Bernal was welcome. She closed the door.

Bernal looked around. Newspapers and other files grew in neat stacks on the president's desk and blocked out half of his massive frame. The president was drawing red circles over an article in an opposition newspaper. Bernal watched him read, thinking the president was trying to come off as an academic of some type. The president put the red pen down and picked up a blue one. He drew another circle. He squinted at Bernal with a look in his eye as if the two were going to compete in a boxing match. So much for academia, Bernal thought.

"I'm reading the opposition press. Red circles are for lies and blues are for the truth. As it turns out, they don't lie about everything," the president said.

"Mr. President, we need to talk. And this talk isn't going to be a pleasant one," Bernal said.

"What's on your mind, Hernán?"

"I wanted to ask the same of you. What's going on here? I'm hearing from my sources dialed into the Americans and the Russians that there are Iranians crawling around Petare nowadays, long after we scrapped a plan to set up an Iranian missile base on the Paraguaná peninsula, which, by the way, was the right move. To stay relevant, we need to remain a thorn in the side of the US, not an outright threat. Plus, do we even know if the Iranians have enriched uranium to the point of calling it weapons grade? Global intelligence sources say they were close but never had it."

"Whatever," the president said. "Anything to keep oil prices high."

"And a Russian base will do that?"

"Nope."

"I'm not here on a personal visit, Mr. President. I'm here to tell you that I'll resign right now and take half the cabinet members that matter and half the military out with me if you don't let me know what's going on. That'll surely get your oil prices spiking. It will also get your ass kicked out of office by a coup that I may or may not endorse unless you tell me right now what in God's name you are up to. Need I remind you that loyalty in the Venezuelan military rank and file is thin at best."

The president stood up and looked out a window. He took a deep breath, sighed, and lowered his gaze. Almost a minute passed.

Bernal saw a defeated man. Nothing like a series of high-level resignations to bruise a leader's strength. He let the president dwell on that and digest the threat. Bernal then studied the red and blue circles on the newspapers scattered across the president's desk. The story was on housing policies. Nothing to do with the US.

"It was called Operation Firefly," the president said. "Nobody knew about it. I kept my entire inner circles in the dark, save two or three people, and they were not part of my administration. Anyway, it went like this," the president said, walking back to his desk. He plopped down in his chair. "We developed and then scrapped plans to set up a base in Paraguaná peninsula with Iranian missiles and its uranium that the whole world knows about and went conventional with a Russian base. I thought naval. The Russians want an airbase. Whatever. Anyway, you can see where I am heading. With the world focused on Russia, we sneak Iranian uranium into Venezuela, have the

US find out when the time is right, and let oil prices surge. Nothing stokes oil prices like conflict."

"I know how war and saber-rattling move markets," Bernal said. "Don't patronize me."

"Just bear with me," the president said. "Anyway, you get the picture. With the threat of war in the hemisphere, oil prices rise, we win, oil companies win, everybody wins. That's what our people really need. Yes, we fucked up with our economy, but higher oil prices, not some short-term bump but a good, sustained rally could give us exactly what we need to get out of this mess. You said I don't know my own people, but in reality, I'm trying to help them, opposition included, and if that means keeping you and everyone out of the loop to ensure a shock factor then so be it."

"Shit," Bernal said looking away, pacing the room. He stopped, stroked his chin, and turned to face the president. "If our oil company wins, then US and European oil companies win. An unholy alliance. I don't like them, but sometimes they're necessary. That's why you asked me to be foreign minister to distract everyone, including myself. Tell me more. Tell me everything, Mr. President. Who's involved in this deal?"

"Anyway, we were going to sneak the uranium and the missiles in. We stash the uranium in Petare or in 23 de Enero or somewhere. UN weapons inspectors would never venture in there. Hell, neither will our own police. It's really not hard to hide it there before shuffling it into the Paraguaná peninsula after prying eyes there get distracted and focus on Russia. Add to that, we've got armed gangs stocked with fresh Kalashnikovs to keep everyone away anyhow. Inevitably, the Americans caught on to our plans. They always do. I think the Russians are now helping them. It infuriates me that superpowers prioritize each other over their smaller allies, even if the superpowers hate each other. They don't care what goes on in Venezuela. Russians just want to know what Americans are doing in here and vice versa."

"That's how it always works, Mr. President. If you keep trying to act like a superpower, you will fail. Back to the issue at hand. The Russian Bogdanov probably tipped off the Americans on the rifles and the uranium. It wasn't out of malice, Mr. President. He was just doing his job. He didn't sell Russian secrets to Washington. He told the Americans what he knows, and they probably told him what they know. Everyone spies on everyone. Don't take out the enemy all the way because you may need to use that enemy to get back at someone else down the road, Mr. President. It's how the game works. But back to the point. Are there nukes from other countries here in Venezuela that I don't know about? You hinted at going nuclear and were anything but subtle about it. If not from Russia or North Korean, is there uranium from the Iran nuclear program here in Venezuela?"

"I don't know," the president said. "The only thing I do know is that we've been double-crossed."

CHAPTER

56

Juan Vicente Domínguez stared at the Atlantic Ocean from the Ritz-Carlton hotel on Key Biscayne. It seemed like he had the vast expanse of water to himself. Hard to believe a hurricane was on the way. He sipped a cup of American black coffee. Not the expensive stuff. Just a cup he bought at a gas station nearby. Despite all his money and all of his power, he still held on to some of the simple tastes he acquired when he was younger and struggling. Black coffee. He picked it up when he was a young engineer studying in Tulsa years ago. Big cups of American-style black coffee. Convenient. Did the trick.

He withdrew a cell phone from his pocket and dialed. It rang once.

"Talk to me, Brent. Storm is coming, and I'm going to have to evacuate soon. Cell phones might not work, so where do we stand?"

"I've got Ricardo. We're en route to the office. Street got away, but we can get him. Even so, at this point, it doesn't really matter. Phase two is ready and will be done before the storm hits."

"We'll see about that. See you at *The Gateway* soon with two friends."

Moments later, Domínguez shot across the Rickenbacker Causeway over Biscayne Bay and headed west to the mainland in a new Lexus LS 600h L he had bought two days ago. With a hurricane barreling down on South Florida, traffic was light. He looked off to the right, and the shining Miami skyline—a steel-and-glass testament to a blend of hard work, luck, risk-taking, ingenuity, and recklessness—stood defiant before the storm. A shiny ribbon of wealth and power that served as a thin shell, concealing a county packed with all walks of life from a hemisphere working hard just to make ends meet. He smiled at the buildings and headed their way. In a matter of minutes, he was driving toward Coral Gables with two more passengers.

Domínguez tapped on the door of *The Gateway*, Brent opened the door, and the oil executive entered, a wave of surprise shooting across his face.

"I know what's on your mind, Domínguez. Everyone reacts that way," Brent said.

"This is it? This tiny office space produces news?"

"This is all the space *The Gateway* needs," Brent said.

"Interesting," Domínguez said. "Next time I give an interview to someone, I want to be damn sure it's for real and not some glorified blog like this outfit. Anyway, I guess it's fine for a cover that you need. Maybe a little bigger so you could blend in a little more, but this works."

"Great," Brent said. "You know my job better than I do. Whatever. Who's with you?"

"Ah," Domínguez said. "This is Pablo and Pérez. They're part of my company's security detail. They'll be my eyes and ears every second I'm not around during this operation and will help you take out Street."

Two men stepped forward. One was a short, stout man largely of African descent. The other was tall and thin. He had very dark skin and short wiry brown hair. Green eyes. They stood behind Domínguez quietly. Brent and Ricardo nodded to both.

"Which one's Pérez, and which one is Pablo?" Brent asked.

"The thin man with the green eyes is Pérez and this other man is Pablo," Domínguez said. "Let's get to work."

"Right," Brent said.

"Okay," Domínguez said. "Get Cornbridge on the line and those trading desks open. Let's get ready to go seriously long on oil. How's the upload of the Venezuelan interview, the one where we let it drop on *The Gateway*'s website that Venezuela may go nuclear?"

"We're good to go in about two seconds," Brent said.

"Double-crossed?" Bernal asked. "I'm speechless. How does one double-cross a sitting president without anyone else finding out about it?"

The president slumped in his desk and stared at Bernal.

"I always hated smarter nice guys like you. I'm the leader, the alpha, the top dog. Not some pencil-neck like you," the president said.

"Jesus, would you get off yourself! This pencil-neck has seen more military action in a day than you've seen in your whole life. Back to the point," Bernal said. "I know it's hard, but you need to tell me what's going on. Don't take your frustrations out on me."

"You're right. I should have never mistaken your good and calm nature for weakness. Now I'm the one that's fucked," the president said.

"For God's sake, just tell me what's going on, and we'll fix it. If you remain open and honest with me, I'll continue to support you unless you've done something that can be construed as genocidal or maniacal. Have you? Have I pledged allegiance to some crazed despot?"

"No."

"Then go on."

"The Russian naval base was a ruse at first, well sort of," the president said. "It will help us out and them, and it will create jobs. It's a win for everyone except the US, but as you said, we're still playing host to the Russians. We don't have our own nuclear capability or much input on when to launch. So I mulled the feasibility of setting up a nuclear launching pad with uranium from Iran on the Paraguaná peninsula. Conventional missiles could strike targets only a few hundred kilometers in Colombia, while nukes could reach US shores. The whole idea was, if Iran is attacked by the US or Israel, they'd have a place to fire back in this hemisphere. Not only that, Iran was going to pick up the tab to build the base, the barracks, the silos, watchtowers—everything. The base would also include weaponry to counter air attacks from the US, if need be. Word got out in intelligence circles in the Middle East that something was up, unclear as to who but something, so we scrapped the plan, especially with Iran trying to cement a deal with Washington. You knew about this as well—everyone did. Every NATO member would have spies crawling all over us if they found out we secretly shipped in Iranian nukes. But," the president paused, shaking his head and looking down. "We didn't exactly terminate the plan. We just put it on hold."

"Just stop there," Bernal said, annoyed. "This was before I was foreign minister, but everyone knows Iran has yet to enrich uranium to weapons grade. They don't have it. Every spy and journalist on the planet has been checking up on that one. There's no enriched uranium in Iran."

"You're right," the president said. "Well, sort of right."

"What?"

"They did it. The Iranians enriched uranium to weapons-grade levels, and I welcomed it here secretly and behind your back.

"What?"

"They pulled it off. And then they stashed it here the second after they enriched it to weapons-grade levels. It was perfect, all part of my plan to play a role in deciding not how to end conflict, but rather control where conflict takes place. My plan for Venezuela to be something—a global power. And you know that lovely effect that global crises can have on oil prices."

"Who helped you do this? I keep my eyes and ears wide open throughout this administration. I would have known if anyone in this administration was up to something."

"That's why I kept it out of the administration."

"Who is in your unholy alliance?"

"Just ask yourself who else wants oil prices to stay high."

"Big Oil," Bernal said. "You and Domínguez."

"He helped me live up to my promise to make Venezuela a true power. A nuclear power."

Bernal said nothing.

"Then he stabbed me in the back," the president said. "I didn't see what hit me. That's what this was all about! He has some other plan, some agenda that I didn't even see coming, the full extent of it at least. I was so busy looking out for the country and thinking of others that I got blindsided."

"I believe you got blindsided, but too busy thinking of everyone else? Do you expect me or anyone, besides yourself, to believe that?"

The president looked down.

"You've lost it," Bernal said.

"I said let's get to work, meaning get that interview up," Domínguez said, looking at Ricardo, or whatever his name really was. "Then I'll make a last-minute check on the markets and we get out of here before the storm hits.

"Markets?" Ricardo asked.

"Yes, markets. Jesus, if you want something done right, you need to bully people around yourself or buy them off yourself. What's good for my company's stock price is good for the economy and not some bureaucrat's stupid ideas and self-serving rules and regulations."

"What are you talking about?" Ricardo asked.

"We gave Tehran a simple task—get the uranium out of Iran and into Venezuela. There, we slap it onto a missile, and Venezuela officially becomes a nuclear entity with its centrifuges buried under Iran. A new, bold, and multilateral path to join the nuclear club. That way, oil prices go up, meaning Venezuela wins, and my company wins, and eventually human intelligence at the CIA wins," he said, turning to face Brent. "When the time comes for Langley to miraculously discover those nukes, while that idiot in Miraflores Presidential Palace isn't looking, you boys can call him out for stashing such a horrific concoction and come across as heroes in the UN. Meanwhile the global diplomacy community will stand flabbergasted, saying, 'Wow, nukes in Venezuela! Slap me in the face and call me silly!'" Domínguez said, approaching a smiling Brent. "Of course, you won't be at the agency anymore, but who cares? You'll be rich. Plan B."

"How the hell do I win?" Ricardo asked.

"You have to ask? Domínguez said. "Iran wins with higher oil prices as well and keeps the enriched uranium it denied it had. Even though it's outside its borders, it's still Iran's. We all win." Domínguez looked at Ricardo. "You seriously have to ask?"

"That's good for Iran," Ricardo said. "But will it be good for me?"

"It's too bad Tehran wants nothing to do with you, but we'll take care of you."

"Right," Brent said. He jumped up and slapped Ricardo on the shoulder. Ricardo said nothing. Didn't even move. "You made this happen, Ricardo, thanks to your smuggling expertise. When the word does get out, Washington will pressure Venezuela to open up its hiding places and let inspectors in to find the nukes," Brent said with a mischievous smile, like a teenager about to unveil his first joint to his friends. "Inspectors would be insane to venture into parts of Caracas where you do business, dear Ricardo. No one will find anything thanks to you."

Ricardo shrugged.

Brent caught on to his unease and walked to the small, clustered office room, the one he kept off-limits to Street.

"Let's finally launch phase two now," he said. "Let me just boot up the computer in here, and we're good to go."

Ricardo and Domínguez watched Brent disappear into the small office that was too cluttered for use. The sounds of paper shuffling grew louder. Packages moving around. The sounds of cardboard box lids ripping up echoed across the office. Sounds of boxes tossed against the wall followed suit. Pens, paper clips, and highlighters flew from the small alcove. So did a small pencil sharpener and a string of obscenities.

"Is there a fucking problem?" Domínguez said. "Is the computer up and running? Or did someone steal it."

Brent shook his head, confusion, and panic merging into anger.

"Street Brewer dies!"

CHAPTER

57

"Great. Ricardo is a smuggler," Patricia said. "I get it. He moves stuff into Venezuela from his bosses in Iran and probably cocaine out of the country."

"Drugs don't play a role here," Street said, pulling the Jeep off Loop Road onto a narrow shoulder made wide enough for parking. "Ricardo really doesn't work for anyone. He's a contractor. His primary job was never to arm Venezuelan gangs—that was actually some screwed-up cover, another diversion. His real job was to smuggle Iran's weapons-grade uranium into Venezuela. The materials Tehran denied it had all along. He did it. That was the easy part. He may have delivered it along with a shipment of materials from Iran to repair a refinery." Street hopped out of his Jeep. "But, as it always does, the plot thickens and grows ever-complicated." Street unzipped a bag in the rear of his Jeep, squinted at the sky, and pulled out foul-weather gear.

"What are you talking about?" both women said.

"This," Street said, opening another bag.

He set a bright-yellow tackle box next to his raincoat and some fishing tackle, namely sinkers, on top of the coat.

"Are we going fishing? Why are you weighing down that coat with fishing sinkers?" Cyra asked.

Both women followed Street to the back of his Jeep.

"It's not fishing gear—it's weapons-grade uranium from Iran, right here in Miami," Street said.

He watched Cyra's jaw drop. Patricia's eyes grew wide as well.

"It's encased of course. Fully enriched and right here in the United States of America. Ready for use."

Both women remained frozen. Street watched them process the information.

"Uranium? For a dirty bomb?" Patricia asked.

Street opened a bag wide enough for the two women to see what appeared to be more fishing sinkers and what looked like garden stones. Lots of them.

"Again, weapons grade," Street said. "Not for a dirty bomb but enriched for a real bomb."

Both women stood speechless for another spell.

Street broke the silence again. He needed them to focus.

"Yep. Uranium. Enriched in Iran and warehoused in the United States, right here in South Florida! Smuggled in as fishing gear and also tucked away in fly-fishing rod holders and tackle boxes," he said, feeling like a game show announcer telling contestants what they had just won. "When I said 'wait, there's more,' this is what I meant. Surprised?"

A door opened in a nearby house, and a man peered out with a wary gaze at Street and the two women. Street nodded to him, knowing full well he was drawing suspicion among Miami-Dade County's most suspicious residents out in the Everglades, especially with a hurricane bearing down. Many out that way were armed as well.

Patricia looked at Street and smiled. "The answer was right in front of us."

"Let's get out of here," Street said, smiling back at Patricia.

He drove deeper into the woods, eventually finding what he was searching for, a shoulder on the road that was wide enough for parking. Underneath was a small bridge with four large culverts open wide to let water pass through. After Street parked, he jumped out of the Jeep, again startling Patricia and Cyra for a split second, and watched the deeper water cutting through the hammocks below.

After about five minutes of digesting the information, Patricia spoke up.

"Uranium from Iran? Weapons grade? Here in the US?"

After another few moments of taking it all in, she focused.

"I guess it's pretty smart: hostile nukes are hidden on US soil and not in Venezuela, where the president wants everyone to think they are," she said.

Another long pause.

"Are we safe here?" Patricia asked.

"Yes, but not for long," Street said. "Brent definitely has a bug on this Jeep. Once he finds out that I took his loot, you can be damned sure he and his entire crew will come here to get it back, hurricane or no hurricane." He walked around and peered over at the water from the other side of the bridge.

Patricia shook her head, staring at Street's back. "I'm still in shock."

Street turned around. "In shock? You guys are both CIA. You should know this." He looked up at the sky. Gray clouds rushed overhead. More of Hurricane Granville's first feeder bands, those whips of wind and rain that herald the arrival of a monster, would be here in a matter of hours.

"We don't," Cyra said.

Street sighed. "I guess it takes the private sector and not government agents to do things right. That's where I come in. Domínguez would be proud."

He laughed. Patricia and Cyra did not.

"The president makes these baffling statements to me in an interview. He says that they are going to arm themselves to the teeth and hints at going nuclear. I took it as an obvious ruse. Everyone knows Venezuela wants to compete with the US on the global stage and be more than just a thorn in its side. But it needs power to do that, not just money but power. He has money, meaning he has oil. But he spends too much money and runs off at the mouth and dilutes his power. The best he can hope for are shots of cash when oil prices rise for reasons outside of Venezuela, like surging economies elsewhere or saber-rattling in the Middle East. Financial security is one thing, but power is another. To be truly powerful, he'll need not only cash, but the ability to control his cash flow."

"Power to control global oil prices," Patricia said. "The power to hit the US economy when he wants to."

"You got it. The president was so outspoken, even by his standards, and so adamant that it was obvious he was hiding something. Meanwhile, everyone is tracking arms shipments, and intelligence agents such as yourselves are working overtime to monitor who might be moving things into Venezuela and cocaine out of the country. What you overlooked is the true currency behind this whole thing," Street said. "Uranium he has some control over and not on a Russian military base."

He rooted through the open bag. Inside were several more concrete tubes not much larger than cans of tennis balls. In fact, tennis ball brand logos and packaging covered some of the tubes, which were concrete as well. A pretty good disguise unless someone picked one up and saw how much heavier they were than actual tennis balls. More big fishing sinkers in the form of pellets and rocks resembling garden stones were nestled in there as well.

"Don't worry. It's all properly encased. Your hair isn't going to fall out. It's not too hard to smuggle into the United States really. Bring it in on a plane or ship, even better—on a large sportfishing boat. Pennie Spradling's mother sent me a picture of Roland along with Brent and his friends fishing on their boat, supposedly just off Miami." Street held up his phone so they could see the picture.

Both women stared at the picture with curious frowns.

"That could be anywhere," Cyra said.

"Anywhere but around here. Look in the background. You can see in the picture a small hill," Street said. "It's too large to be in Florida and even Bimini. Domínguez, Brent, and even Ricardo aren't from around here. They don't know just how flat South Florida is. Bimini's highest point isn't even that tall. I recognized it myself and knew right away it was the Los Roques island chain, just off the coast from Caracas. It's the hill on Gran Roque. So they took this boat down to Venezuela, scooped up the uranium underneath the clueless Venezuelan president's nose, and headed back. I checked every square inch of the boat. The problem for them was they did too good a job covering their tracks. It had very few engine hours on it, way too few to travel thirteen hundred miles to the Venezuelan coast and back. So they did their run, and then they slapped new engines on the boat to conceal hours spent out on the water. According to Pennie's mom's paperwork on that yacht, the last time it had serious engine work was years ago."

Street gave them another few minutes to soak up what he was telling them.

"Anyway, Roland Spradling caught on to the Placebo Agenda somehow. Did you call him up to warn him, Cyra, like you did with me? Start getting him to question his line of work?"

Cyra looked at Street, giving nothing away. No blinking eyes, no muscle twitches of the jaw—nothing. Whether she had or not, that secret was going to the grave.

"Well," Street went on. "In any event, Roland found out, must have told Pennie, and Pennie, thankfully, tossed a tackle box overboard with some of these pellets in it at a spot where she could remember. In the end, it was her way to talk to me from the grave. Throwing that tackle box overboard was her last act as a free woman before she was rounded up and whisked to Caracas, where they figured it would be much easier to kill them. In that tackle box was just the tip of the iceberg. Take a good look—pounds and pounds and more pounds of weapons-grade uranium. To validate my hunch, I had a friend of mine who works at the nuclear power plant down the road verify this stuff. Definitely nuclear. Take it back south to Venezuela where you can slap it on a warhead and aim for the USA, or just keep it in South Florida. Blow up the goddam place. Who knows?"

"Who knows? Street, this is serious." Patricia said. She picked up a tube, dropping some of the pellets in her hands due to its weight. "And your friend who verified it will be detained. Cyra will make sure he's off the streets and not saying a word about any of this stuff. Who is he?"

"A fellow boater. He has a nice Intrepid boat. I towed him in recently. Anyway, the uranium is all here. Thank you for playing, and don't forget your parting gifts stashed in fly-fishing rod containers, tennis ball cans, and, of course, these lovely garden stones," Street said.

"This isn't funny, Street," Cyra said, then threw a glare back at Patricia. "You should have known this, Patricia. In fact, how do I know you're not involved somehow with Brent even now, Patricia?"

"You don't," Street said. "Anyway, there's more to this story."

"Go on," Cyra said.

"The Venezuelan leader seeks out partners in this deal, Big Oil naturally, but he makes the mistake of trusting Big Oil too much by letting them act as the project manager so the government can distance itself. That manager would be your boss, Patricia. Anyway, Domínguez gets tired of the volatile Venezuelan president drawing too much attention to himself, and add to that, he sees a profitable side deal in this whole thing. He needs a partner in that side deal. Enter the CIA, the perfect third party to handle double-crossing and kicking the weak link out of this greedy troika. Domínguez and Brent steal the stuff and stash it in the US. Venezuela loses its power, Iran loses its uranium, and as is usually the case, the CIA wins, well not the agency but a few rogue agents. These guys, feeling the sting of seeing human intelligence disrupted by technology, seize the nukes and then shout to the world, 'Look what we caught Venezuela with. And Iran helped them do it. Hooray for human intelligence!' Everyone will rally behind the US in the face of Venezuela and Iran for whatever cause. Too bad they needed money to blackmail a Saudi to keep their covers safe. But greed is what ultimately got the better of them."

"How's that?" Cyra asked.

"It dawned on me when I was having barbeque and beers with a pretty young thing in Broward County that we placebos were helping you out in more ways than one."

"What are you talking about?" Cyra asked.

"The placebos were not just chosen for their skills. They were chosen for where they worked. We've got a hedge fund and a news service. Coincidence? Not at all. The president leaks his bombshell to the newspaper, and when the news goes public, oil prices shoot up and the hedge fund trades on it, making some major money. Domínguez and Brent get rich. So why not leak it to the press in general? Why speak to *The Gateway*?"

"We give up, Street," Patricia said. "And what pretty young thing in Broward County?"

"Molly Wells. She told me that anyone can be a journalist now thanks to social media, websites, and everything else, and it all made sense. *The Gateway* publishes the president hinting at going nuclear. That was my job, and the key here is *The Gateway*, a nobody in the media world, really. Why not speak to a major media? Because with a smaller outfit, there would be a lag between when the story breaks and when the world finds out about it. If a major media outlet did that interview, it would have gone global that instant."

Both women stared at Street. Cyra nodded. "I think I see where you're going," she said. "Go on."

"Okay," Street said. "Right when the news breaks at *The Gateway* and before the big media powerhouses eventually find out and pick up the story and run with it themselves and move markets, there's the lag, maybe a few hours or even a day, when the story is out there but no one really knows what's going on. In other words, there's a time lag where not too many people in the general public have read the story except for *The Gateway*'s handful of readers. During that window, Cornbridge Capital—Brent's other business—just happens to stumble on the story and place trades on oil before the broader market gets wind of it and bets that geopolitical concerns will firm up crude prices, all under Domínguez's direction, of course. He and his company benefit as well."

Street let the two women digest the news. Do some head-scratching and chin-stroking.

"What role did the Tagles play in this second phase?" Cyra asked.

"Not sure." Street said. "Maybe nothing. All placebos had to die."

"Deborah was an asset," Patricia said, after a pause. "She did lots of translating work as well as in-house English teaching at the national oil company and most likely some other jobs requiring native English-speaking capabilities. It looks like she found out about the incoming shipment of materials to upgrade refineries as well. Expats meet up all the time, and she and Pennie, who undoubtedly were friends, put it all together. The husbands, in this case, may have been extras. It doesn't really matter now. When they say 'no loose ends' they mean that everyone dies. I fell for it. I was too busy focusing on what was stashed in Venezuela, and not here."

Cyra sighed. "No, Patricia. You did fine. Good work, both of you."

"Thank you," Street replied.

He took out his cell phone, snapped a pic of the uranium.

"I'm snapping a photo for myself and for a good friend," Street said.

He took a few more pics and looked at Cyra. This will be one messy report to file to her boss, he thought.

"In fact let's all snap some pics. Group selfie with the uranium?" Street said, laughing, snapping a pic.

"Street," Patricia said.

"It was a joke. I will delete it."

He scrolled down and mumbled something about deleting that and other photos in earshot of Patricia and Cyra, but in reality, he began to type out a message, secretly glad he found the one sliver of road wide enough that would allow for just enough signal to send out a text. He reached out to his lawmaker friend.

Are you there? If so, we have in our possession what your president hinted at. Just sent you a pic!

Are you for real?

He pulled it off. I have to run now. I will send you details. Hurricane is about to hit.

Okay. Hurricane there, shit storm is hitting here. Word is Bernal has abandoned the president. Prez might step down and flee.

Stay tuned. Gotta run.

"Okay," Cyra said, taking a deep breath. "What are we going to do?"

"We're going back into town and eliminate everyone involved," Patricia said. "We'll take out every last one of them and then get this to the appropriate authorities."

"Oh good," Street said. "Let's just go and start shooting people in a hurricane. You guys aren't military. You're intelligence agents. Spooks, maybe, but murderers, no. Maybe you are, who knows? But you're no match for Frog Legs."

"Frog Legs?" Patricia asked.

"That abomination who wore short shorts up in Petare."

"Ricardo," Patricia said.

"He's a sociopath," Street said. "I looked into his eyes back in Petare. This man has no conscience, a vacuum instead of a soul."

"You don't know the half of it," Cyra said.

"Let's hear it," Street said. "All of it. Who is he exactly?"

She sighed. "He's a monster, so much that Tehran has disowned him. He has military training and also quite a criminal past. When moderates were pushed out of power a while ago in Iran, much to the favor of the ruling clerics then, many opposition members were systematically jailed for no reason at all. Inside prison, guards encouraged inmates to rape, brutalize, and kill targeted prisoners. Our Ricardo, in there for several violent crimes, found it a natural fit. Inside Iran's prisons, Ricardo took on a leadership role, impressing the guards with his blends of rape and torture. Once he was freed, and somehow resumed his position in the military, he ordered and even performed many torture activities in the outside world, targeting men, women, and children. It didn't take long for him to end up in Syria, where his model thrived, spooking even ISIS and catching the eye of some unsavory CIA people—take a guess who.

"Still, I don't think Brent and Domínguez knew what they were getting into when they brought Ricardo into this weapons theft gig. Tehran used him to move the uranium in, and since he was in the neighborhood, Russia used him to deliver some Kalashnikovs. Now that all is said and done, the Iranians were set to get rid of him, probably hoping he'd die in a Venezuelan slum. Even the hardliners hate him, though he lived. Bogdanov informed me through one of our covert meetings that took place in broad daylight at the English school. He was the one dealing with Ricardo when sneaking Russian assault rifles into the slums but got a little spooked when he got to know him, especially when he started to suspect Iranian uranium was headed to Venezuela without going through Moscow channels first. It makes sense now. He told me the Venezuelans would lose on this one, that they were out. And to top it all off, he wasn't even born in Iran. He is Iranian, but he grew up in Argentina."

"I knew he wasn't Venezuelan. Anyway, to hell with him and everyone else," Street said. "They're in my backyard now, and when I mean my backyard, I'm not talking about the city, I'm talking about out here. Plus, we've got the material with us. They lost, we won."

"Yes, Street, but they're going to come and get it back," Cyra said. "You said the car was bugged."

"Yep."

"They'll find you. They'll find your parents and anyone close to you. Ricardo will do God knows what. It won't be pretty."

"Well, I'm just going to have to outsmart them and then kill them all," Street said. "That's why we are out here in the Everglades. You just said we were going to eliminate them, right? I'll do it for you out here."

"You? You mean you are going to do this?" Patricia asked. "Street, they did their background information on you. You're a nice guy. You can't kill anyone. You're a squeaky-clean, small-time reporter who missed his shot at making it at the news wires. And I know why."

"Oh yeah?" Street said.

"Yeah," Patricia said. "You were fired, you weren't let go due to bank-ruptcy—that was what you told the world. Your company was still in business for many months after you were cut. I don't even think they had filed for bankruptcy protection yet. You know what happened to him, Cyra?"

"Confirm what I may or may not know," Cyra said.

"Street here got a good scoop about some vehicle recalls from an automobile company's Caracas-based executive in an expat bar one night. The executive was drunk and spilled the beans to Street. Recalls not just in Venezuela but in many countries, including here in the US. Street told his superior, Ian, who told his boss, some midlevel regional editor, who got the bright idea to make a trade in the stock market with Street's intel before the story published. Street wouldn't go along with it, fearing it would be illegal insider trading, so his workmates let him go. No witnesses, so to speak. Of course, they attributed his firing to downsizing. Too afraid to take risks, right Street? You probably wouldn't have gotten caught. Your coworkers got away with it. Since then you've taken the path of least resistance, in terms of your career that is. With that chip on your shoulder, you were ripe for recruitment into Brent's scheme."

"Bravo," Street said. "We're taking big risks right now, if you haven't noticed. This show's not over yet."

Patricia thought for a minute. "You're right, Street."

"I don't know," Cyra said. "Brent liked you because you know your way around Venezuela, and you're pretty aggressive when it comes to getting a story. You're no idiot, but you're out of your league here. We'll handle it. Let's drive out of here and deal with them."

Street ignored them. He studied the cypress trees, which were swaying in unison with the wind. He looked up. A gray cloud raced in. It was much lower than the thickening ceiling above, breaking ranks like some scout pushing ahead of an advancing army of ghosts. The cloud seemed to catch sight of the Jeep, honed in on Street, Cyra, and Patricia and screamed down at them. Out of nowhere, a gust of wind shot in and chased away hot and wet air. Swarms of raindrops, much smaller than those from typical summer storms, pelted everything in sight. Street ran around to where the uranium was stashed in the back of the Jeep and pulled out a soft top from underneath and began to install it over the roll bars. After several minutes, Patricia and Cyra were dry inside.

"Sooner or later, these feeder bands will give way to hurricane-force winds and rip this soft top right up and eventually toss the car and kill us," Patricia said.

"That's not going to happen. Not here," Street said, looking around the corner. He stood in the middle of Loop Road as if it were his driveway. He walked in the direction they had come from. Cyra and Patricia stared at his back.

"Perfect timing," Street shouted back toward the two women.

A ten-year-old Ford Explorer rounded a curve and meandered down Loop Road. It stopped a few yards in front of Street. Its lights flashed on and off. Street waved and pointed around the curve in the road, indicating for it to park. The Ford inched forward and made its way to the Jeep.

Street stood on the road and let the rain from the storm's feeder band whip him around. A flash of dull-green lightning lit up the belly of the racing clouds. It wasn't a crisp, blue hook of lightning typical of summer thunderstorms but something else, something sadder and less festive, almost condemned. Cypress trees began to jerk in the wind, while palm trees whipped like car wash brushes revved up into overdrive, ready to fly off the handle and wreak havoc. Minutes later, it was calmer and the feeder band raced westward, signaling the imminent arrival of a meteorological monster. Street gave another thumbs-up to the Ford Explorer. It sat there.

"Don't be shy. The storm's not here yet. I know what you're doing in there," he shouted to the truck.

It inched forward again, as if the car itself seemed to hear him.

Cyra and Patricia looked at each other. Patricia shrugged.

The car pulled alongside the Jeep and then ahead to where some shoulder was available. Then the driver turned it off. The driver's-side door opened, and Jenkins emerged, appearing confused amid the rapidly deteriorating weather. He tried to light a cigarette, despite the lingering winds from the recent feeder band. Amazingly, he managed to light it. He walked around the Jeep and stood in front of Street, exhaling hard. The smoke flew out of his mouth into the winds like exhaust exiting a spacecraft. He looked bleary-eyed and sluggish.

Street shook his head, walked over to the driver's side door of the Ford, and leaned in. Cyra and Patricia just watched him. Jenkins stared back at them, wondering who they were. He rolled his eyes, then shook his head.

Street emerged with a bottle of vodka about half-full and set it down on the hood, dove back into the car, and quickly retrieved another. The second one was still sealed. Street set it next to the opened bottle. He stared at Jenkins, like a patrolman expecting answers from the driver before slapping the cuffs on. Gusts of wind rattling the bottles made Jenkins visibly nervous.

"Take a drink, Jenkins," Street said, handing the already opened bottle to Jenkins, who took a chug as if he were gulping down a sports drink instead of a distilled spirit.

"Take two more," Street said. Jenkins did, eyeing Street in an obvious state of confusion. Then a third chug, a long pull.

Street then grabbed both bottles and walked to his Jeep. He rooted around under the seat and withdrew some duct tape. He taped both bottles together, grabbed a backpack, and ran off into the nearby cypress hammock. All three shrugged, but soon he was back.

"All right, Jenkins. I'll give you your booze back, provided we do this quickly. You know and I know how bad off you are going to be when alcohol withdrawal kicks in. So now that you are properly motivated, let's take a walk."

"A walk? What are we doing?" Cyra asked.

"You'll see," Jenkins said weakly. They walked over to the culverts. Street jumped off the side of the road and into the water with a large splash. The water rushed out of the culverts and flowed along with determined energy as the storm approached.

"Remember this place, Patricia? When you were in the black SUV the last time I was here, evaluating me for spying work? Remember, I was with my friends—"

"Parker West and Turner Hickman. Yes, that was me. I remember. What were you guys doing down there?"

"I was winning a bet with an alligator," Street said, squinting into all four culverts. No alligators in there today, he thought. This whole place is going to wash out soon, so let's do this.

"Alligators?" Patricia said, looking around. "And what are we going to do?"

"Stash the uranium and do some banking transactions," Street said.

"Let's get this over with," Jenkins said. Then it dawned on him. "Uranium?"

"Just go with it, Jenkins," Street said. "You're not going to remember any of this anyway," he mumbled.

Jenkins shrugged and walked to his Ford Explorer and came back quickly with a backpack. Soft, green, no-tear material. Fine stitching with new straps whipping around in the wind. A water bottle nestled in a mesh pocket. It remained firmly in place as Jenkins secured the bag onto his shoulders. Street eyed the bottle and safely concluded it wasn't water but blew it off.

"Okay," Street said. He jogged back to his parked Jeep and quickly loaded himself and Jenkins up with more bags—heavier and loaded-down bags. "Let's take this stroll. We can finish what we need to do here long before they get here."

"Excuse me," Patricia said. "Are you sure stashing it here is a good idea? There's a major hurricane on the way, not to mention a rogue intelligence agent and an Iranian nutjob financed by a megalomaniac oil executive out to get back the goods that we took from them. What are we going to do when the storm hits? Find a place to camp, ride out the storm, and hope they don't find us?"

"Maybe," Street said. "Let's go. If you guys want to tag along, you can. Or you can just sit here and wait for them and explain to them why their stuff is gone." Street counted four broomsticks from the back of his Jeep, kept one and handed one to Cyra, one to Jenkins, and one to Patricia. He threw them some gloves to protect their hands as well.

"For panthers, snakes, crocodiles, and ankle sprains," Street said as he grabbed some empty duffel bags and threw them over his shoulders on top of the heavy bags. Then he headed off into the Everglades.

Street and Jenkins trudged heavily under the weight of their bags. Patricia and Cyra followed. Street looked back at the culverts. All four were as clean as whistles, with the rushing water scrubbing them clear of debris. The flow of rising water caught them all as they entered the deeper part of a creek, knocking them all off-balance. All four gave up on walking and swam across the narrow creek. They then came to solid footing under the cover of cypress trees where the water was shallower, and they renewed their trek.

"Hold the broomstick out in front of you," Street said. "Use it as a cane here in the swamp. Jab the ground to make sure you have solid footing. Out in the open prairie, do the same. Sometimes the prairie will see knee-deep water, and sometimes we'll be over soft mud. If we cut through larger chunks of saw grass, hold the broomstick ahead of you as if it were handlebars. Keep it parallel over the ground. Walk forward. Let the broomstick push the saw grass down. The gloves will protect your hands. We'll be in the safety of another large hammock within moments."

They were. It didn't take long, and a few minor cuts later, they stood in knee-deep water surrounded by towering cypress trees. The wind continued to pick up, and the thick gray underbelly of clouds racing above seemed to grow closer. Still, they could stand with relative ease, save a blast of wind here and there.

Cyra, Patricia, and Jenkins looked up at the canopy. Street looked ahead and then proceeded to move through a small rivulet of water that made for a clearly defined path.

"Use the broomstick to keep your footing. There are roots and rocks and all kinds of things beneath the surface that can blow an ankle. Keep an eye out for rattlesnakes, water moccasins, coral snakes, pythons, panthers, bears, alligators, crocodiles, rabid raccoons, and anything else, including angry otters. With the storm pushing the water this hard, you're likely to see some. Good chance that at least one of us will be bitten by something today. Decent chance one of us will get really sick or die today from a bite, and not a bullet from Brent and company," Street said.

"Otters?" Patricia said.

Cyra smiled, amused that Street was having fun with their lack of experience in the Everglades, playing on their fears.

Jenkins looked up and down with wide eyes.

Street glanced up at the towering cypress trees and then down at the underbrush of the hammock, which had calmed down once the feeder band had passed. The rivulet of water, the path, continued ahead.

"Concentrate on holding that stick. Take a pull of your water if you want," Street said. Jenkins snapped the bottle out of the backpack's side pocket. He took a sip, not a pull.

"This way," Street said, and took a left on the watery path. Then a right. Then another left over the swampy ground. They got to the edge of the hammock and proceeded to slog across open prairie with very shallow grass. Bald cypress trees, very small and scraggly at best, popped up out of the grassy, watery expanse.

"I like it better out here than in the swampy hammocks," Jenkins said.

"How so? You mean you like it exposed? One clean shot, and you're dead," Street said, staring at his cousin.

"Where are we going?" Cyra asked, eyes rolling at both Street and Jenkins, her stress subsiding into annoyance.

"To make withdrawals and a deposit or two," Street said. "We'll need a good chunk of my money before we get out of here to buy things when the hurricane knocks out the power, some for my boat, and some to hit the road, if we need to."

"Money?" Patricia said.

"You'll see," Jenkins said.

After about five minutes, they were way out in the middle of the famous river of grass. Nothing was around them, save for a few cypress trees. Clouds raced above. Another feeder band appeared ready to whip them hard when Street stopped. He examined the ground and then pulled a small camping shovel from his bag. He struck it hard against the rocky bottom just inches beneath the surface of the water and grass. And he struck it again.

"I don't think there's too much soil in there," Patricia said.

"I've always wondered where you did this," Jenkins said. "Do you get here by remembering the GPS coordinates?"

"Nope," Street said. "It's all in my head."

"What's all in your head?" Patricia asked.

"This," Street said.

He stopped digging and pried a large rock from the ground. He bent his knees, went in low, and lifted it up. It was about four feet wide. He tossed it aside, and it landed with a heavy splash. Then he dropped to his knees and jammed an arm deep into the dark, cool water. His entire arm was submerged. He looked up at Patricia, Cyra, and Jenkins and winked at them. Up he came, as if he were operating on hydraulics. Unlike going in, his arm wasn't empty coming out. A big bag was firmly gripped in his hand. It was a nondescript green tote bag with thick, tar-like mud and water dripping down its sides. Street opened it. Inside was a large airtight bag. He cut it open, and immediately the smell wafted over them all.

"The Caribbean's finest marijuana. Just for you, Jenkins. I stashed it here not long ago when I was out with my friends Parker and Turner, sloshing around here in the Everglades. They never saw a thing. Amazing what people fail to see when they are scared to death of being bitten by snakes."

Patricia's jaw dropped.

Cyra stared at Street with narrow eyes. Then she looked at Patricia, and her eyes narrowed even more.

"Nobody knows this backcountry better than me, and there's more around here from our suppliers, one of whom works at the power plant I was telling you about, just another underpaid, overeducated stiff deep in debt trying to make ends meet in South Florida. I towed them and their beauty of an Intrepid the other day. Several times, actually. It's amazing what people fail to see when you are unloading a boat on a dock and breaking the law in clear daylight, right Patricia and Cyra? I'm getting good at this. Or should I say, I've been good at this for longer than you thought."

Street glanced up at Patricia, his playful smile vanishing. "Look, I'm not a drug dealer. I'm just a middleman, stashing pot here in the Everglades just to make my financial ends meet. Salaries in this town just don't cut it. This gig was a short-term gig, anyway. Wildfires in California created a market for imported weed, so chalk it up to a changing climate. But that's all over. This stuff is basically legal here now, anyway," Street said.

Patricia clenched her jaws, and then she shrugged, surprise giving way to confusion. "But we gave you a lie detector."

"Yes, and I passed. Technically, I was telling the truth when I said I don't smuggle drugs into the country. The drugs are already in the country when I take delivery, most of the time. Just a couple of miles offshore or even on the docks. I hold them here and then pass them off to my chief logistics coordinator," Street said motioning to Jenkins. "Give me one of those heavy bags."

Jenkins handed one to Street.

"You should have known this, Patricia," Cyra said. "You didn't do your homework."

Street put an end to any conflict between the two women.

"There was no way she could have known. It wasn't permanent. I never even wanted to do this, and it was just a few one-shot deals. I just needed money to live in my own city in the US. Money for living expenses and new boat engines. Anyway, I feel bad about it, but let's move forward and be done with all of this, smuggling included. Fortunately, my skills are going to help us with your current predicament."

Street turned to Jenkins. "Can we get this sordid business over with?"

Jenkins opened up his backpack. Pulled out what looked like a brick. It was a sealed bag. Everyone knew what it was within a moment.

"Here's the money. Thanks for storing the product," Jenkins said, adding "and without me and this little business, you wouldn't have shiny new boat engines or even your own apartment. You'd need to find a roommate. A little gratitude is in order."

Street ignored Jenkins and grabbed the brick.

"Hand me another one of your heavy bags, one that Brent and friends are freaking out about. Let me lighten your load," Street said.

Jenkins gave him another bag.

Street married the concrete pellets and stones into one bag, stashed Jenkins's money in the same bag and buried it. He used the same rock to cover it.

"I like to leave a few chunks of change behind out here, especially at this spot. It's safer than a bank—no prying eyes from regulators. Plus it keeps Jenkins from spending too much. Let's get any remaining weed out of here," Street said. "Follow me."

They walked on. The dull gray sky darkened, and the underbelly of the clouds grew closer to the earth. Trees jerked in the wind like skeletons summoned awake to engage in some unholy dance. Patricia was appraising Street, who led the group in the open air. The nearest cypress hammock was just under a mile away. They were exposed.

Patricia broke the silence. "So, you aren't so squeaky-clean? Or are you overcompensating for overthinking and playing it too safe in the past?"

"A little. Or you could say that I'm doing what I have to do. I don't get greedy, and I stick with pot, and pot only. I do have my scruples and won't have anything at all to do with the hard stuff. I don't need that on my conscience, and no, I don't smoke weed either. You can appreciate the irony. Jenkins here handles the distribution, the dealing and occasional usage. I just handle delivery and keep some money out here for safekeeping."

Cyra smiled. "Looks like you guys didn't do your homework so much, did you, Patricia?" Cyra stared at Street. "Another surprise. You busted this uranium smuggling ring, and you've managed to smuggle pot without getting busted. Bravo, Street."

"Yes, good job, Street, and no, I didn't recruit Street. The surprise is on Brent," Patricia said. "So is this the only reason you live humbly but own a boat in perfect condition?"

"Pretty much," Street said. "Let's take a break. I need to pee."

"And stash something when we're not looking?" Patricia shouted.

Street threw all the bags at Patricia's feet. "Come with me and observe."

"We'll keep an eye on you from here, thank you."

A few minutes later, he led the group for several yards and gazed around in the late-afternoon grayness. They were far out in the Everglades with no cell phone reception. Street stopped near the edge of a small hammock, took his shovel, and struck down again. Within a moment, he retrieved another bag and tossed it to Jenkins. He looked up. Patricia, Cyra, and Jenkins were watching him. He motioned for Jenkins to hand him all of his remaining bags. One was very heavy, brimming with power and might. The others were extremely light. Street married the contents all into one bag and buried it. He slung the remaining bags over his shoulder.

"The uranium is safe. So are a couple of dollars for safekeeping." He threw some puffed up bags that weren't very heavy to Jenkins. "Take the weed." Then he stared at the eastern horizon.

"Street," Patricia said. "Can we speed this process up? We're gonna get killed."

"Killed?" Street eyed her with a bit of a crooked smile. "Haven't you figured out that I'm full of surprises out here? I don't need a gun. I've got Mother Nature on my side. And they'll never find their loot. That ought to buy us some time."

"Just hurry. And how do you remember where you stash this?" Patricia asked. "There're no big trees around with markers on them, no signs of any sort. No big rocks, at least none you can see. You haven't used a GPS at all, and I'm not getting any cell phone reception out here. Anything you put down to indicate where your buried bags are will wash away."

"I have a good memory," Street said. "And don't worry. We'll be finished in minutes."

"Bullshit. No one can remember a fixed spot under a changing landscape. It's impossible," Cyra said.

"He's been doing this for a while. Never fails," Jenkins said. "By the way, how much do you have buried here?"

"In total, including what's come and gone?" Street said. "We've stashed just shy of two million dollars in product out here," Street said. "A total value of one million, eight hundred thousand dollars, to be more or less exact. I've moved several dozen bales in the Everglades. Of course, that money is not ours, but good chunks of our commissions are, and they have been safe out here."

"That's great," Patricia said. "But shouldn't we get out of here? A hurricane is barreling down, and we're exposed. We'll get struck by lightning."

"You're not even phased by the amount of money? Wow," Cyra said, staring at Patricia. "Just wow."

"Ladies, there's not much lightning in hurricanes. That's the least of your worries anyway. Besides, I've got places to ride out the storm if we need them."

Cyra shook her head. Save for a few cypress trees, the area was flat. A vast prairie under several inches of water. The Florida Everglades. The river of grass.

Street looked around and then headed west. Patricia, Cyra, and Jenkins followed. He stopped periodically and glanced across the waterlogged prairie. Hammocks jutted up in the distance. Street cut east, then west again, backtracking only slightly. Cyra, Patricia, and Jenkins watched him, trying to figure out his system. Street anticipated what they were thinking.

"Don't try and use your GPS coordinates to mark these hiding places. Your phones won't work out here, and I'm not giving you enough time to ping a location if they were. Plus, I don't use the same spots more than once anyway."

"How is that possible?" Patricia said.

Street said nothing and zigzagged for several more moments, keeping his eyes on the horizon as opposed to the ground. The wind was gaining enough speed to make walking more difficult. Small drops of rain pelted them, and Street knew the stage of on-again, off-again feeder bands was over, and more sustained winds and rain were arriving. Fortunately, the storm was a slow-moving system, which gave him a little more time. Unfortunately, once it did hit, the slow-moving storm would spend more time overhead.

Street trekked through the river of grass and then suddenly stopped and stared at the ground. He grabbed his shovel and struck the earth. Seconds later, out came another bag of pot. A half hour of more zigzagging, more bags emerged from the ground, both big ones and little ones. By then, Patricia, Cyra, and Jenkins knew which bags had money and which bags had pot. Street had pulled so much by then that everyone was hauling a couple of bags. "Now we're really loaded," Street said.

"Let's be sure we get all the pot bags, or as much as possible. It can't stay here but for a couple of days tops," Jenkins said, already carrying a few himself to help Street. "And my vodka."

"I guess we have enough money out here to meet my reserve requirements. If there is any weed leftover, I'll get it after the storm. Let's get out of here," Street said.

"That's the first good idea I've heard all day," Cyra said, staring at Jenkins's water bottle.

"Can I please have a sip of water?" Cyra asked.

"No," both Street and Jenkins said in unison.

About twenty minutes later, they were back at Street's Jeep.

"Give me all the pot bags you got," Street said to Jenkins. "I need to make sure they're secure and stay dry."

Jenkins shrugged and handed them over to Street.

Street took them and set them down in the back of his Jeep alongside the moneybags. He grabbed some large rocks from out of the Everglades and fastened them to the bags to weigh them down, eyeing Jenkins as he worked.

"Guess you didn't expect to see me with women like these two when this little transaction went down," Street said.

"Nope. Way better than Brianna," Jenkins said. He looked up at Street, and added, "Oh and by the way, I just ran into her in the Grove today. I didn't invite her. There's nothing going on."

"I see," Street said.

"You do believe me," Jenkins said.

"I believe there's nothing serious going on between you and Brianna. You're the flavor of the month," Street said, staring at Patricia, who was rinsing mud off her feet with a water bottle alongside Cyra.

"Really?" Jenkins said.

"I'm not into Brianna anymore, so whatever," Street said. "But you and Brianna in my apartment? Your cousin, the son of the man who is working for free to keep you from doing jail time? Do you have any respect for me at all?"

Jenkins stared at the ground.

"Jenkins?"

"Yes?"

Nobody saw the punch fly right across Jenkins's jaw. The slap of bone pounding on flesh echoed across the road like the crack of a whip in the mounting winds. Jenkins's eyes rolled up, then his body went limp and fell down like a sandcastle besieged by incoming waves. He coughed and spit. Blood sprayed out of his mouth as he lay on the gravely road.

"Street, are you insane?" Patricia said. "This isn't the time to be fighting among ourselves. We need to act as a team. Brent, Domínguez, and that lunatic will be here shortly, and so will the hurricane."

"It's just a respect thing," Street said. "Anyway, we're almost finished, but I'm staying out here. There is still more uranium. It was too heavy to carry in one trek. I'll take care of it now. They'll come for it."

Street gave Jenkins a hand and pulled him up to his feet. Jenkins stood briefly but fell to one knee.

"Wait, you're for real?" Patricia said. "You're staying out here? In a storm?"

"You heard me. I need Brent's whole crew out here too. They'll all come."

After a few seconds of shocked silence and shaking heads, Patricia and Cyra went to check on Jenkins. Street watched them. Both women had their backs to Street. While Jenkins was regaining his senses, Street went to his Jeep, came back with several of the bags, and set them out on the road.

"Jenkins doesn't belong out here. He's not part of this team, and I want him out of this business. Now he's going to leave. Jenkins, take your weed and some of the cash. Our program is over. I've done enough for the both of us, and this is where it ends. Get out of here now, and forget anything you may have heard about people following us here. You're exhausted, and all of this will be a blackout. Go to my parents' place and toss these bags in the pool. These bags are airtight, and I fastened rocks to them so they'll sink safely to the bottom. The storm will throw palm fronds and enough mud and debris in there that nothing will be visible after an inch below the surface. It will be safe in the pool and not in some parking lot of your hotel or whoever you hang out with down here. Do you understand me? Now is not the time to move this stuff."

Jenkins stood, a little shaky on his feet but growing stronger and a little more coherent.

"I got it, Street," he said, unable to make eye contact with his cousin. "Look, Street, I'm sorry about—"

"Jenkins, just go stash this weed in my parents' pool. Here is a key to the house." Street tossed Jenkins a key chain. "After you ditch the weed into the pool, clear out the beer from my fridge, take it to your hotel or wherever you go when you are down here, and wait for further instructions. Here's some traveling money."

Jenkins stared at Street in disbelief, a wad of cash in his hands.

"Compliments of the Venezuelan government. Don't spend it all at once. And remember, drink all that beer. Hang on. I'll get your vodka." I need all of this to be a blackout, Street thought. He trotted off in the woods and came back with one of Jenkins's bottles of vodka, the half-full one. "I'm keeping one for myself out here as a souvenir."

"When can I head up north with the last of our weed?" Jenkins asked.

"Obviously not today. I'll let you know when the time comes. Just take your weed bags and stay put. I can't have you getting arrested either. After all, my dad is giving you free legal work. He doesn't need to lose money to give you more. Just toss all the bags into the pool. I'm taking my cut with me, though I will leave some money and pot out here that we can come back for after the storm passes. Now drive off, not the way we came but push forward until you are on Alligator Alley. It's quicker that way."

Street threw another loaded-down bag at Jenkins, who caught it, stared at it, and walked to his Ford Explorer. He opened the door and threw the heavy bags into the passenger and back seats and more toward the rear. He stared at Street with moist, apologetic eyes, got into the car, put it in gear, and headed off. The sound of tires on gravel began to fade into the building wind and rain.

Street looked at the clouds. It must be blowing at about forty-five knots and picking up, officially coming in at tropical storm strength and growing, he thought.

"Who was the woman involved in that childish fiasco?" Patricia said. "Not that girl at that bar, at the café, in the Grove bar from earlier," Patricia said, striking a defensive pose. "Her name is Brianna. I researched her."

"Not now," Cyra said, grabbing Patricia by the arm and guiding her in the direction of the Jeep. "That's also illegal by the way. But what else is new?"

"We're on a mission anyway," Patricia said. "Let's finish it."

Cyra took in the surrounding trees and shook her head. "It's really blowing."

They all looked around. Tips of trees began to move with more anger.

"It's not too dangerous yet," Patricia said, walking around, gauging the proximity of the storm. "But you can definitely tell the weather is deteriorating at a quicker clip now."

"We can still stand with no problem. But our hearing and vision are impaired," Cyra said, turning to Street. "Someone could be around. People could be around talking, lining us up in crosshairs and we wouldn't know." Cyra looked off into the woods.

Street looked at Cyra and then looked around for Patricia.

"Patricia, don't get lost. Let's get out of here. The storm is here," he said. "Let's go. Now." He jumped on the Jeep's running boards and scanned the woods. "The storm is here, and so are they."

"I figured you'd know when it would be time to leave," Patricia said behind him.

"Someone in the woods was staring at us but headed back to what I assume is a parked car back up the road. I couldn't make out who. We knew this would happen. We've only got a few minutes. Cyra?"

Silence.

"Cyra? Cyra let's go. They are here. In the woods. If we are going to take them out here, we need you here and armed. If you have a gun, whip it out. Otherwise, let's go!"

Patricia shouted, "Cyra, we're out of here."

Silence.

"Cyra? Cyra?" She looked around. Nothing. "Where did she go?"

"Yo, Cyra, storm's here. Let's go!" Street said. "Damn it!"

Street hopped off the running boards and peered into the swamp. The heavy cypress trees in the hammocks were whipping around and some deeper in the forest began to fall. Even the bonier bald cypress trees in the open prairie in the distance snapped around like skeletons engaged in some medieval dance of death. Street figured the eye of the storm was still east of Bimini, but the time to get back into shelter was running out. Loop Road could be flooded or choked with debris.

"Did you see her leave?" Street asked Patricia.

"No."

"Something's wrong," Street said. "She wouldn't just wander off like that."

"She's not going to advertise that she's peeing in the woods," Patricia said.

"She's a trained counterintelligence officer at the CIA and God knows what else. She knows how to communicate with her team," Street said.

They glanced around.

"Cyra? Come on," Street shouted. "Cyra, want to ride out a hurricane by yourself in the Everglades? Great! You're on your own."

Street walked across the road. He got down into a push-up position to look down over the wall into the culvert. He squinted across the creek and off into the distance, then pushed himself back up.

"Something is definitely wrong," Street said.

He knew exactly what was wrong.

"Cyra! Please hurry," Patricia was calling out a few yards away from the Jeep.

Then Street heard the inevitable: an angry shout from Patricia.

"Oh my God!"

Street looked a few yards in front of his Jeep. Cyra's body lay lifeless, massive trauma wounds across her abdomen and neck gushing blood onto the gravely road.

CHAPTER
58

"They're here," Patricia said, darting her eyes.

She stared at Cyra's body, and Street took note of her swelling anger.

"They may have gotten here, but they're not leaving here. Fuck! This is my fault. I knew they wouldn't kill me until they get their stuff, but I couldn't have said the same thing about Cyra," Street said, looking at Patricia. "Or you."

"Street, now is not the time to blame yourself," Patricia said.

Street grabbed a towel from inside the Jeep and covered Cyra's face. He picked her up and set her in the passenger side of his Jeep. He fastened the seatbelt around her with care.

"Did you know her well?" Street asked.

"No. But she was good," Patricia said. "I could sense it."

Street nodded.

"The wind is picking up. We didn't hear anyone snatch her," Patricia said, scrambling back into focus mode.

"They'll be out in just a few seconds. This is Brent and Ricardo messing with us," Street said.

He tied a few remaining green duffel bags down in the bed of his Jeep. He glanced around again, then snatched the shovel from his Jeep bed and paced. He couldn't see them, but he knew they were there. The shovel was the best weapon he had.

Patricia watched him walk away from the car as if it were some sort of safety base in a schoolyard game of tag, and the farther he walked away, the more danger he was facing. Then he threw the shovel down.

"What are you doing?" Patricia asked.

"They have guns on us. They are watching us to see how we react to Cyra's corpse. To see how many we are. Here they come."

"Where?" Patricia said. "From which direction? I can't see them."

"Trust me, they're here. You can't see them because you're out of your element. But luckily for us, so are they. They've got the upper hand, but only for now. There." Street pointed.

From the cypress trees on the north side of Loop Road, Brent Drum emerged with what Street guessed to be a Glock of some sort. Ricardo came after him with a knife in one hand and a firearm in the other. Both men were grinning. Juan Vicente Domínguez followed, looking a little out of place in gabardine slacks and fine leather dress shoes, though he appeared to care little about their condition in the mud, wind, and rain.

Two men emerged behind Domínguez, one short and stocky, the other tall and thin. Street stared at the thin man with wiry hair and green eyes. The man, who Street knew as Pérez, stared back at him. Both men held Street in their crosshairs.

"I've got an idea," Patricia said to Street. "Trust me."

Domínguez wasted no time. "I've got an idea too. Give me my stuff," he said. "Where's my uranium?"

"Uranium?" Patricia said.

"Don't play stupid with me. You know Street, here, stole my uranium out of *The Gateway* offices. Kudos, kid. You just proved again that the private sector does things better than big government." Domínguez turned to face Patricia. "Street probably bragged to you about what he had in this Jeep all along."

Domínguez walked over to back of the Jeep, snatched a green duffel bag, opened it, peered inside, and then glared at Street.

"What the fuck is this?"

"It's money," Street said. "My money."

"You sold my uranium?"

"Yes. I stole it and sold it about an hour later in the Florida Everglades during a hurricane. That's how these deals typically get done."

"Shut the fuck up. Where is it?"

A blast of wind nearly knocked Domínguez over. The winds were now steady between squall lines. Brent, Ricardo, Pérez, and Domínguez's other henchman, the short, stocky one, squinted up at the whipping canopy and moved closer to the center of Loop Road.

Street looked at Patricia and then at Brent, who had his firearm locked on him. Ricardo was staring at Patricia. Domínguez had tracked Street's lines of sight and was staring at Patricia as well.

"I don't know much about American football, but I do remember that defensive safeties track the quarterback's eyes to see where he will throw the ball," Domínguez said. "You'd make a bad quarterback, Street. You're an easy read, and you're in way over your head. If you don't want me to leave Patricia here alone with Ricardo in the swamp to suffer a fate far worse than that other bitch, then you'll give me what I came here for."

Street stared at the two security agents behind Domínguez. Pérez gave the faintest hint of a nod.

"All right. You win. Your uranium is right here."

"Street, don't," Patricia said.

"Take it," Street said.

He grabbed a green duffel bag from the back seat of the Jeep and walked it over to Domínguez. Domínguez grabbed it with surprising strength despite its uneven weight distribution. He unzipped it, looked inside, and smiled. Then he pulled out several canisters one by one. He stared at them, as if he were a lab technician reading the contents on vials, and then put them back in the bag.

A second later, a gray Nissan Altima approached. Street and Patricia didn't see where it had come from. A young man got out. Street recognized him immediately. The kid with the Boston T-shirt from Petare. The young man nodded at Ricardo, who kept a blank stare on Patricia.

"Nice timing," Domínguez said. "Hand me your keys. I'll take this car. Brent, you and Pérez and Pablo deal with these two, and then everyone meets me at *The Gateway* offices. We'll ride out the storm there and make plans for our future fortunes. And when I say deal with these two, I mean do it properly. I don't want any bodies washing up on this road or on hiking trails. And take all those other green duffel bags. Street's been stashing money out here, money from smuggling drugs, probably. Didn't we just witness that? Please tell me you guys knew about that."

Ricardo and Brent just shrugged.

Street motioned Boston to the duffel bags. Boston pushed Street aside and began loading them into the trunk of the Nissan.

"My God," Domínguez said. "You two don't deserve a cent of this windfall smuggling money, but grab it anyway and then kill these two."

"You son of a bitch!" Patricia said, running after Domínguez, managing to get a punch across his face before Pérez snatched her away. "We trusted you. I gave you intelligence on the Venezuelan government as well as on your competitors in exchange for letting me pose as one of your employees." She managed one more punch.

Pérez held her tight. He looked at Street. Street looked right back at him and gave Pérez the briefest of nods with a twitch of the head to Patricia. Brent took notice and squinted.

"Keep her off me!" Domínguez shouted.

"I've got this one," Pérez said, gripping Patricia tighter.

"Thanks," Domínguez said, slapping Pérez on the shoulder. "If only the rest of you were so decisive."

He grabbed a satellite phone and punched in a number. All watched him as if they were waiting for urgent medical news. Someone answered.

"Is this Pracy or Anderson?" Silence. "Whatever. You know who this is, Old Man Cornbridge himself. I'm going to hand you over to Mr. Ted Bullard. We're gonna make quite a trade on crude."

Domínguez handed Brent the phone and took a few steps back. Like an American football coach watching star linemen about to go through some full-contact blocking drills, Domínguez crossed his arms and watched Brent.

"Pracy?" Brent said, giving a thumbs-up to Domínguez. "Go to the office. You've got hours before the storm. Time to lock in a trade. We're going very long on crude. In fact, check your inbox. The details should be there." A silence passed. And it ended. Even the storm's building winds couldn't contain the loud explanations of disbelief coming from Pracy on the other end of the phone through Brent's satisfied smile. All eyes remained glued to the phone.

Brent laughed. "Yes, that number is correct. We're going long on a massive number of oil contracts, and, yes, I'm sure. Go through the email for the details, but you know what to do. Set it up now. I'll send you a text when it's time to execute the trade." Brent hung up. "It's done."

"Is the news story up?" Domínguez asked.

"It's ready to go," Brent said. "We can take photos of the uranium now as well," he added.

"Give me that satellite phone back," Domínguez said.

Brent handed him the phone. Domínguez took it, glanced at it, and shoved it in his pocket.

"I'm going back to Miami to check the markets one last time. Then I will upload the story from *The Gateway* back in civilization, and then the trade goes through. It has to be in that order."

"You will pay," Patricia said.

"Won't be paying any taxes for too long," Domínguez said. He walked off, stopping dead in his tracks at the sound of anger.

"Damn it!" Brent shouted. Heads snapped to face Brent, who looked white as he paced from one side of the road to the other. Then it hit everyone.

Street was gone.

Patricia smirked at Domínguez.

"Where the fuck did he go?" Domínguez said. "Find him!" he shouted to both Brent and Ricardo. He glowered at Patricia. "Kill her." He nodded to Pérez.

"Done," Pérez said, tightening his grip on Patricia's arm, jamming a gun to her temple. "This way," he said.

They walked toward the car Boston had driven and then rounded a slight bend in the road. The narrow road still allowed for some shoulder parking, and Pérez picked up his pace behind the cover of the Jeep and the Nissan and scurried farther around the curve. Whipping trees and howling winds gave Pérez and Patricia even more cover, auditory cover, especially.

"I'm Patricia. CIA. You're Pérez. Nice to meet you. Sorry for setting you up not long ago and making you think Street Brewer was a criminal. Apologies for all that."

"It's all good. Street knew Domínguez would put me in charge of eliminating you. That's why he bolted."

"It was my idea actually," Patricia said. "I punched Domínguez to distract everyone so Street could get away."

"Good thinking. Anyway, I'm here on direct orders from Hernán Bernal to end this shit."

"I'm with you. The problem is Domínguez has the uranium."

"We'll deal with that later," Pérez said. "I'm going to discharge my weapon. Be dead for about five minutes. Then we'll get out of here somehow." A shot rang out. Pérez didn't waste any time, firing into a nearby tree. "Stay crouched behind a tree. You may be CIA, but in the end there's not much you can do out here on a day like today."

Pérez emerged from the thrashing trees. Stone faces met him.

"She's dead."

"Stash the body deeper within the cypress swamps, farther away and on the other side of the bridge," Brent said. "We don't want her body drifting back on the road, which will happen based on where you left it."

"Got it," Pérez said.

"Bring me her head," Ricardo shouted.

"No time," Domínguez said. "I want all our energy on Street."

Ricardo shrugged.

Brent pointed to Ricardo, Boston, and Domínguez's other man, Pablo. "Go find and kill Street."

Pérez ran back into the swamp. He saw Patricia.

"Play dead," he said.

"I will. This whole operation is turning into amateur hour."

"Go with it." Pérez emerged dragging Patricia's limp body by her feet across the road. Her arms dangled. Pérez stared at her as he pulled her, wincing at one point when her shoulder appeared poised to dislocate.

"Remember there's a nice Lexus way up the road in someone's yard, in the house of someone who evacuated. Use it to get back," Domínguez said. He took the car Boston had driven and drove away.

Pérez nodded and eventually disappeared into the moving canopy of the cypress hammock on the other side of the bridge. Once under the cover of the canopy, he spoke.

"I think you've got a future in theater if espionage doesn't work out."

Patricia sprang back to life, crouched behind a large cypress tree, and took in her surroundings. "You need to take out Ricardo, Brent, and those other two guys right now. If they find Street, they'll kill him," Patricia said.

"I don't have a shot from here," Pérez said. "At least he got away."

Just then, Street jumped down out of a nearby oak tree and landed with a heavy splash. Pérez and Patricia snapped their heads in the direction of the sound. Pérez pulled his gun on Street immediately but instantly saw who it was and then withdrew it as fast as he had pulled the weapon. Both Pérez and Patricia released a sigh of relief.

"Told you my idea would work," Patricia said. "Nothing turns heads quicker than a woman hitting a man. It worked. Nice getaway, Street. See? You can trust me." Street nodded and winked at her.

"We don't have too much time," Pérez said. "I have about a couple of minutes to get back there. They think I'm burying Patricia here."

"Listen up," Street said. "I'll handle these idiots. They may be tough but out here, they're useless. You and Patricia just get out of here. Get back east just out of sight along the road in the woods and get to where there's cell phone coverage and call the police. Flag down a Miccosukee police car up the road if you have to. Tell them you saw Domínguez load up on something really suspicious. Maybe he's looting or something. Make some shit up. Just get the cops all over him, and I am pretty sure you've got contacts with local police here. Give me your phone," he told Pérez.

Pérez handed it to him.

Street dialed six digits and handed the phone back to Pérez.

"When you get back into cell phone coverage, look in your phone's notes app. You'll see six letters and numbers I just typed in. That's Domínguez's license plate. The one on the car that he just drove off in. Tell them he was loading up something from a boarded-up store, and that you saw him hitting a woman out around here. You heard gunfire—I don't know, something. Just don't let him get back to town. Get him pulled over."

"Done deal. So you want Domínguez arrested?" Pérez said. "Not killed?"

"You can't go gunning him down in the streets of Miami. Just get him pulled over and have them search the car. It may get that uranium off the street," Street said.

"Arrested? Done deal. I've got assets in the Miami-Dade Police Department as well as pretty much the rest of the municipalities here. Old friends who help me keep an eye on Venezuelan government sympathizers implanted in the country. And also since I am military, I spy on enemies of Venezuela, which would be the entire county. Like you, we spy on both friends and enemies. I won't even need to call 9-1-1. Not sure what they are going to hold him on, but I will do what I can," Pérez said looking at Street. "How did you remember his license plate?"

"Don't ask," Patricia said. Then she turned to Street. "What are you going to do?"

"Me? I'm going to take out Brent, Frog Legs, and Boston, and the other man from the detail."

"Frog Legs?" Pérez asked.

"The delivery man aka Ricardo," Patricia said. She glanced around. No one coming yet, but she knew it was time for Street to act.

"How are you going to take them out?" she asked. "They have training you don't have." Patricia then looked at Pérez. "That other man with you? Is he not here on direct orders from Hernán Bernal too?"

"His name is Pablo. And no, he's not with me," Pérez said. "You can go ahead and kill him too."

"Hernán Bernal?" Street said. "Direct orders from Hernán Bernal? Now who am I working for without my own knowledge?"

"Just go with it," Patricia said. She smiled at Street.

"Be careful, Street," Pérez said. "They're all armed, and they are all trained."

"Yes, but again, not in this neck of the woods. You two get out of here, and make sure Domínguez gets arrested. Walk or take my Jeep and go."

Street grabbed his car keys from his pocket and jammed them into Pérez's hand. He then took off through the thickness of the trees. The waters were cool and getting deeper and rougher. Storm debris began to coat the forest floor. He looked up at the churning canopy. Despite the bellowing blasts of wind, Street could hear Brent giving orders to Ricardo and Domínguez's other security official, Pablo, and Boston.

Street ran fast, knowing he could easily lose his footing on the rocks beneath the surface. The faster he ran, the less time his feet spent on shaky objects underneath, slippery ones especially. He jumped under the cover of a large tree. A brown water snake lay coiled next to him on a rock jutting from the water, as if it had found its spot to ride out the storm. He picked up the snake and tossed it into a nearby thicket of swamp, knowing full well it wasn't the water moccasin it resembled.

"Sorry, dude, but you'll find a better place to ride out this storm," Street said watching the snake slither away, a little angry at being forcibly evicted.

The road above was still visible, with whipping brush moving aside in short bursts to give Street a clear view. Small drops of rain pelted the men up on the road, forcing them to squint. Street eyed the rock where the snake had been resting. He picked it up, waited for a brief lull in the wind, and tossed it. It made a thud, snapping Brent, Ricardo, Boston, and the security detail to attention. They walked over and stared into the swaying cypress trees, leaving the bridge empty.

Can't believe they fell for that, Street thought. He bolted from the cypress hammock and darted for the small bridge. He looked back. Pérez and Patricia were following him.

"What are you two doing here? I told you to leave."

"Brent is having a word with his crew. They still have a line of sight on your Jeep, and it's getting too stormy to walk," Pérez said. "Oh, and I did get a bar on my cell phone. I made a quick text. Cops will be after Domínguez right about now, I'd guess."

"Keep up and don't splash," Street said, sliding into the creek. They followed suit.

Street headed toward the bridge. The water rushed through the culverts beneath, racing hard ahead of the advancing storm. It took an effort for Street to reach the mouth of one of the culverts, but he got to it eventually. The water was much higher than the last time he was there chasing an alligator inside. Street made sure he had solid footing and then reached out and grabbed Patricia's hand. He helped her and then Pérez into the culvert. Pérez and Patricia stood side by side, their backs to the opening. The water was chest deep, and they looked as if they were talking in an overturned raft in a pool. Street looked at Pérez and then pointed up.

"You've got the keys. Get her out of here when you can. But since they have line of sight on the Jeep and aren't leaving, they may be waiting for you. Go back to them first, Pérez. They are expecting you. Go and then sneak away with Patricia down here."

Pérez nodded and then backed out of the culvert and popped up to the street within seconds.

"She's dead and buried," Pérez said, surprising all four. "I say we forget Street and get back to *The Gateway* before the storm hits us full force. We'll take his car and leave him out here to die in the storm."

Brent stared at Pérez.

"How are we going to do that?"

"He left his keys in the car. I took them so he couldn't sneak back and get away."

"You did, did you?"

"Yes."

"Good thinking," Brent said.

"Thanks," Pérez said. He nodded to Ricardo and to the other man in Domínguez's detail.

"Good work," Brent said. Then he lifted his gun and fired. Pérez fell fast and hard. Even Ricardo was a bit surprised.

"I don't care if he's part of Domínguez's detail," Brent said. "I don't trust him, and I won't rest until I see Street dead with my own two eyes. Leaving him out here in the storm? That means letting Street live. What a fucking liar! How do we know whether or not the Venezuelan government implanted him on Domínguez's team? We don't. Toss the body."

Ricardo shrugged and ditched the body over the side of the road into thick vegetation.

"Street?" Brent shouted. "Mr. Brewer?"

Street huddled down below in the culvert with Patricia. He covered her mouth and looked into her eyes. "Stay in here," Street said. He looked up.

"Street? Your friend is dead, and you're next," Brent called out from above at the edge of the road. The water rushed through the narrow opening, though Street still managed to hear Brent's threat. Debris began to enter, slapping Street and Patricia. The added depth allowed Street some room to swim while grabbing the sides of the conduit to thrust himself forward quietly, holding on to Patricia's hand all the while. The deeper inside the culvert he swam, the less he could hear Brent above. Street waited for the team above to head off in search of him.

"Okay," he whispered to Patricia. "They're looking for me. I'm not sure Pérez is dead, so I have to try and save him. You just stay here in this culvert. Just hang on as long as possible. I know it's scary, but you've got to stay hidden. I swear to God I will come back for you. I'm going to distract them."

Patricia's eyes widened. She nodded. "You have no idea how I'm going to make this up to you when you get us out of here alive," she said.

Street smiled. "I can think of a few ways. But first, take this," Street said. He handed her a hunting knife.

"Where the hell did this come from?"

"Gifts from the culvert. I've got a few out here tied alongside bags I stash. Use it to defend yourself, if need be. And also, slash their tires if my Jeep is compromised. And make sure Cyra is properly cared for."

Street peered out. Metal wiring along the outside of the bridge served as a ladder. He climbed up to take a peek, and out he popped on the other side of the culvert. He looked up at the darkening sky, expecting to count the backs of the men out after him. Instead, he counted only one semiautomatic pistol, whose barrel was jammed right against his forehead.

CHAPTER

59

Domínguez sped eastward along the Tamiami Trail, back toward civilization. Civilization, however, was long closed for business. Shopkeepers had finished the last details when it came to boarding up their properties and had fled. A few stragglers were filling up their cars at gasoline stations that would be closed now that building winds were beginning to knock out power.

Domínguez came to a red light and waited in idle in the far right-hand lane. A car that had exited a nearby gasoline station pulled up in the lane next to him to his left. The window was down. A young family was inside. A woman in the passenger seat rolled down her window and motioned to Domínguez to do likewise. "Can we cut over in front of you?" she asked. "We need to get to that gas station to the right and get some milk for our baby. It's the only station that's still open."

"I guess," Domínguez said, rolling his eyes. He then frowned at them. They had tied plywood to the roof of their car. "Just boarding up now?"

"Yes. We both just got off work," she responded.

The light was still red. Domínguez shook his head. "You're too late. Wind is picking up and will carry those boards away in minutes. You should be more prepared like I am. Life would be easier."

"Asshole," the woman said.

The light turned green and Domínguez sped away, not letting the young family go in front of him. He headed toward Coral Gables with his precious cargo stashed safely in the trunk. Onward he sped. Eastbound traffic was basically nonexistent. He relaxed. His team could handle an unarmed Street, especially considering they had support from his own personal security detail. He turned on the radio, adjusted the dial to find some market news, and then lights flashed in his rearview mirror. Blue lights. He shrugged, pulled to the side, and killed the engine. He waited for the police officer to approach him. He stared at the strip mall. Cell phone stores, small businesses, and a sea of mom-and-pop success stories.

The officer approached. Domínguez felt a little uneasy when he saw three Metro-Dade police cars. Now four cars. Now five. What were they thinking? Other officers advanced. Hands on gun holsters. Radios chirping. Silent but glaring lights flashing. A dog barked in the back of one squad car.

"Hands outside where I can see them," the first officer shouted over the wind.

Domínguez rolled his eyes.

"Don't you guys have bigger problems to tackle than someone going five miles over the speed limit?" Domínguez asked. "Fine. Have a peek. Search the damn thing."

He put both hands out car the window, and dangled them there, a little bored.

"Driver, with your left hand, open the car door and step out of the vehicle. Keep both hands in the air."

Domínguez shrugged and did what they said. Like these guys are going to be able to know what enriched uranium looks like. It'll look like garden stones to them.

"Driver, with both hands in the air, stand with your back to the officers and walk back five steps." Domínguez did.

A few cars drove slowly, almost coming to a standstill just to his left to get a glimpse of the arrest in the wind and rain. Domínguez grew mildly annoyed at his audience.

"Driver, clasp your hands behind your neck and drop to your knees." Domínguez did, a little relieved that his elbows and arms covered the back and sides of his head, shielding his identity from the motorists around him.

Within a few seconds, he was cuffed and sitting against the hood of a police car but was told he wasn't under arrest, yet. The police searched him and found nothing of interest in his pockets. A cell phone and a wallet packed with cash and credit cards issued by US and international banks. They went through the car and found nothing in the glove compartment or between and under the seats. No guns at all. Domínguez had left them with his team back in the swamp. Hopefully, they were being used to kill Street.

"Anything in the trunk you want to tell me about before I search it?" a young Metro-Dade police officer named Díaz asked.

Domínguez noted the Venezuelan accent.

"Search it all you want. There are some lead pipes back there. Packages of engine washer rings, and maybe some concrete to make garden stones and statues and other stuff. There may be a jack for flat tires and some fishing tackle. That's it."

Díaz walked around and opened the trunk with the car keys. It rose. Domínguez heard muffled voices and bolts of surprise followed by laughter arising.

"Sir, would you mind explaining this?" Díaz asked.

"Explain what? I just did," Domínguez said.

Two police officers escorted him. Domínguez walked with authority anyway, though his confidence evaporated when he looked in the trunk. He saw the green duffel bags. Inside were some fishing sinkers and some stones. And the tennis ball canisters, though they weren't filled with lead. Domínguez stared at them with an open mouth.

Díaz spoke up. "Mr. Domínguez, I asked you if there was anything in the trunk I should know about. I gave you the chance to come clean. But the way we see it, there's enough marijuana packed in your trunk to book you on a major, major trafficking offense. You're under arrest."

CHAPTER

60

"Up," Brent told Street, ramming the semiautomatic in his forehead. Street had no idea what model it was. He knew nothing of the gun's specifics, the data, the numbers, the decimal points, bullet size, indicators of power and all that. He double downed on his guess that it was a Glock. Or a SIG Sauer. He couldn't be sure. Ricardo, backed by a sickening smile, had him in his crosshairs as well. Nothing more dangerous than the smile of an idiot with a shred of power, he thought.

"Come on, Street. Come out from down there," Ricardo said.

Street crawled out of the culvert. He glanced around. By the Jeep, Domínguez's other detail member, Pablo, stared up at the darkening sky and then down at the churning swamp.

Ricardo looked at Street. A blank smile came to his face. "Let's get all the drugs and the money," he said. "There's more left. I just know it."

"Not going to happen," Street said. "There's a hurricane coming. Too hard to go find."

"I need it now," Ricardo said.

Brent glanced up at the sky, around the swamp, and then back at Ricardo.

"Maybe Street's right. We detain him. Let the storm pass, and then come back out. Six or seven hours tops. Then we get the money and kill him," Brent said. Then he frowned. "We should also make sure we've got all of the uranium."

Ricardo threw a glare at Brent and held the stare. A lifeless stare. Empty. Brent's eyes widened then narrowed.

Conflict, Street thought.

Street avoided looking in the direction where Patricia was hiding, opting to focus his sights down the road. It was time to get the Domínguez gang away from Patricia and into the woods, while they were arguing with one another. Patricia could then check on Pérez. He spoke up.

"We ride out the storm and then get the stuff. We've still got a little time before the worst of the storm hits. If we leave too late, debris may block the road and trap us. Police might find us too. Better to battle the winds and rain than miss out. I'll show you where my windfall loot is. You need me. You won't kill me. You'll get everything you want. I walk out of here alive. Why would you care if I live? You'll be rich and far away. Or kill me now, never find the stuff and then ride out the storm all alone out here."

"Great," Brent said. "Whatever. Deal."

"No deal," Ricardo said. "You take us to the money right now. Then we kill you or that little girl of yours quickly. I think she's alive still. I don't trust having you two running around." He frowned at Brent. "And I don't really trust you." Then he stared at Boston. "Go find that girl!"

"Where the fuck am I going to start looking?" He took in his stormy surroundings. "Out in this shit?"

"Just find her," Ricardo said.

The kid rolled his eyes and walked down the road to where Pérez had originally faked her death.

Street focused on aggravating the conflict and tried to stall them to see which one would take command, either the renegade but trained spy or the massive, powerful but psychotic Iranian delivery man. Conflict bought him some time.

"The girl is dead," Street said. "I saw her dragged across the street."

Ricardo stared at him, just blinking.

"Whatever," Street went on. "Here's how this is going to pan out. I get you the goods, and I walk. I'll give you a cut."

"Not gonna happen," Brent said.

"We're in unchartered waters here. I'm the only one who can get the money," Street said.

"I'm getting out of here with that money. Period," Ricardo said, turning to Brent. "You and Domínguez are going to screw me out of my share of that trade you got planned. I can feel it."

Brent glared at Ricardo, and Street caught onto the growing conflict. Keep it between them and away from you as long as possible.

"Do either one of you think Domínguez is going to give you a cent of this money when this fucked-up price-fixing nuclear scare deal goes through?" Street said. "He's using you both: a two-bit research assistant and an illiterate courier. Both of you are just a bunch of errand boys in his eyes, entitled bureaucrats. He's been calling the shots all along. In fact, he'll have you both taken out once the deal closes."

Street walked to Ricardo and stared up into his face.

"You're not even employed by your people like Brent is. You're just some Iranian intelligence reject. Domínguez will pay scores of professionals, seasoned mercenaries definitely, to make you disappear, maybe with the help of Tehran. So you can call some shots here and walk away with some smuggling money but under my rules."

Brent laughed. "You're bluffing. You've done something to Domínguez, haven't you?" He walked toward Street, sizing him up. "Where's Domínguez? You know something. And I know more uranium is still out here somewhere." Brent looked around in the whipping wind. Street stared Brent in the eye and then gazed out at the Everglades.

Brent shouted over the wind. "Ricardo, you stay with me. You get your way. We get this money and everything of value out of this swamp right now, eliminate Street, and then end this. Street, we walk now. Pablo, go find that Lexus. We'll need to get out of here somehow."

Pablo left.

Ricardo's black T-shirt ruffled in the wind. He stood there, comfortable in short shorts but still visibly angry at taking orders, even though Brent appeased him by agreeing to look for the money that instant. A lull in the wind allowed for everyday noises to return if only for a couple of minutes.

Water rushing under the bridge. Footsteps on the rocky road. Bugs chirping in the canopy. A pistol cocking. Brent held his gun firmly on Ricardo.

"Ricardo, we're aligned now. But you need to follow my orders still. We take this money and any leftover uranium now, and then we need to regroup with Domínguez, hopefully," he said, staring at Street. "Even if Domínguez is compromised, the trade is already ready to go if not already executed by now. I can do it myself. Don't listen to Street. I can get Cornbridge Capital to pay us out. I manage the fund, for Christ's sake!"

Ricardo rolled his eyes and followed Brent.

Conflict, Street thought again. Brent's in control now. Not Ricardo.

"Follow me," Street said.

Ricardo reached into his pockets and withdrew some thin nylon pants and put them on over his shorts. He followed.

They paced down a small berm on the edge of the bridge and down to the back of the creek, heading deeper into the swamp. They pushed through the woods and came out onto the wet, grassy prairie, and Street broke out into a jog. He looked left and right, and moved ahead. Brent and Ricardo fell behind, unaccustomed to the wet, rocky bottom, but kept up, a little relieved to see some open sky and short cypress trees.

Street shifted his eyes left and then right again. Nothing but cypress trees carrying on their skeletal dances in the winds.

Ricardo spoke up. "You better not be guessing. I'll fucking kill you out here. Or rape you, cut off your dick, and let you live like that. Turn your mind into your worst enemy."

Street focused on one cypress tree in particular and stopped. He took three steps and jammed a hand into the water. He rooted around and pulled hard, as if something under the water, rocks, and mud were pulling him down. His arm popped out with a large green bag attached to it, thick and heavy gobs of mud dripping off. He tossed it to Brent, who unzipped it, looked in, and smiled at the money.

"There are a couple more out here," Street said. He ran off in another direction. Brent and Ricardo followed.

"How are you remembering this? Do you have a GPS? There're no markers out here," Ricardo asked.

"Just shut up and follow me," Street said.

He stopped and glanced around him. Nothing but whipping cypress trees in all directions. Two minutes later, after a solid trek across a stretch of grass, Street stopped and scanned the ground. He darted back and forth and looked into the shallow dark water, as if he were examining a problem deep within a car's engine under an open hood. He took a knee, drilled his arm into the ground, and retrieved another green duffel bag. He threw it at Brent.

"Looks like you're going to get your way," Brent said to Ricardo. "But keep in mind this is small potatoes compared to when we go long on oil."

Ricardo shrugged. "Like I'm going to see a penny from that deal. What are you going to do? Deposit it in my account at a US bank's branch in Tehran?" Ricardo eyed Street. "And you? How do you know where these money bags are?"

Brent shook his head. "It's not that hard, chief. He's using a GPS device."

"Bullshit," Ricardo said. "Let's just kill him and get on with it."

"There are still a couple of bags left, and, yes, some have uranium in them. Domínguez doesn't have it all. So don't kill me right yet. You'll need me to get them," Street said, staring at a nearby hammock. He edged toward it. Then he heard the click of a handgun.

"Don't even think about heading toward that hammock," Brent said.

"Take us to your next stashes slowly, and maybe you'll live," Ricardo said.

"One more stop, and that's it," Brent said. "The weather is getting worse, and we've got enough cash. We leave now."

"I'll stay out here with Street and collect whatever's left, while you get rich before announcing to the world that Venezuela is stashing uranium."

"Ricardo, or whatever your name is. We're getting out of here right now. We're going back to *The Gateway*. We have enough of what we need."

"I may be stupid in your eyes, but I do know you and Domínguez are going to cut me out of this. I'm getting as much cash as I can get out of this deal, and then I'm leaving. You should do the same because you're probably going to get cut out of this thing as well."

Brent pointed his firearm at Ricardo, who smirked.

"I'm in charge here," Brent said. "And I tell you what. Over there in that hammock where Street keeps staring, you'll find a fine Venezuelan woman hiding out all scared and alone. Little Patricia, CIA officer, and upper-crust of society is a babe in the woods out here but still alive and capable of contacting someone. Can't believe we didn't check the culvert where Street came out of. She was probably hiding in there with him. Fucking morons."

"Bullshit," Ricardo said. "Pérez killed her."

"I'm not buying that at all. So, either we stay out here and argue over pennies or go back to *The Gateway*, make sure that story is on the website, text Pracy to execute the trade if he hasn't already and then bingo! We collect our fortune. Just look at this weather. It's time to go."

Ricardo stared at the sky and then nodded. The tension between them fell. Conflict, Street thought. Bring it back up.

"You guys still don't have all the uranium," Street said. "When Domínguez gets back to the office and finds some is still missing, he's going to flip, and guess who's going to feel the heat? You two."

"I knew it," Ricardo said.

Brent shook his head. "Domínguez isn't—"

"Would you rather get it now, or when the full force of the storm strikes, or afterward, when Domínguez finds some is left out here? Decide."

"Fuck it," Brent said. "Let's just get it all now."

Street pushed ahead, moving closer to a patch of cypress trees. After a few minutes, he stopped to look at a bony cypress canopy. He zigzagged a few yards and stood at a nondescript spot in the grassy prairie between the thicker hammocks. He took a knee, jammed a shovel into the ground, this time in thicker soil, and he came up empty-handed.

"Are you joking?" Ricardo said. "Nothing?"

"It's like exploring for oil. Some wells are winners, some are duds," Street said, and ran off.

Ricardo followed closely, checking out the trees. He was searching for signs like paint on a trunk or ribbons tied to branches. Nothing.

"So what kind of technology are you using out here? How old is it?" Ricardo asked. "Is it several months old? Several years?"

"Several centuries," Street said. He looked up at the bowing bald cypress trees. "There's another bag over here. About two hundred yards that way. There's your uranium."

Brent shook his head and spit into the wind. Then he grabbed Street by the neck and jammed the barrel of his firearm into his throat.

"Tell me how you do it."

"Fuck you. Go ahead and kill me. See how long you last out here," Street said. "Kill me and then drive off to safety."

"I'll find and kill Patricia if you don't tell me," Brent said.

Street flinched.

"You see?" Brent said, turning to Ricardo, who shrugged. "Street's body language just gave it up. She's alive."

Street shook his head. The clouds continued to rush in off the Atlantic, getting darker and lower as they approached. Why not, he thought. Tell them.

"Certain branches point down. They look like elbows. I use them to mark the spot." Street pointed to one.

Brent released him.

"They're called trail trees," Street said. "Native Americans for centuries grafted the branches to make points that would define trails throughout the Everglades. I'm just piggybacking on their methods to stash the money in here, normally where those elbows point down. Big rocks jutting out from the surface of the water help mark the spots as well. I use GPS waypoints only as a backup in case something happens, like a brushfire. The next bag is up here."

Street sloshed through the fresh water and came to a cypress tree with an arm that was jutting downward. He followed the branch's lead, jammed the shovel into the thick soil, and then an arm into the water and grass.

"Who wants it?" he said, rooting around for a minute.

"I'll take it," Ricardo said.

"You got it," Street answered. "Because you deserve it."

He yanked his arm out of the wet ground. A silver flash streaked across the gray sky. Street stared hard at Ricardo, who probably thought the silver flash was a bolt of lightning before he realized that a five-inch blade was plunging between his ribs. Big problem for Ricardo.

Street jammed the metal hard into Ricardo's midsection, thinking he had made a clean stab. Big problem for Street. Ricardo had moved at the last second. The blade plunged through him as if his body were a stick of margarine left sitting out on a kitchen table on a summer day, though it stopped short of a rib or the vital organs beneath. The wound was minor, an annoyance more than anything that would slow Ricardo down for only a moment at best.

A slab of arm and muscle led by pointy knuckle bones pummeled Street in the jaw, and he fell back into the cool water of the Everglades. Street moved to regain his footing, but a kick from Ricardo lifted him into the air and back into the river of grass. Both hands slid forward as he tried to break his fall, and his palms sliced open on sharp rocks underneath. Another kick from Ricardo slammed down on Street's head. Water entered the nose. He tried to lift his head but couldn't. Thoughts raced as the air rushed out of his lungs. A brief flashback to the microwave in Venezuela. To the waters of Biscayne Bay. Images of his smiling parents, of his childhood friends, and of Patricia flashed in his head. His life in review was on display in his mind's eye.

Then Ricardo's onslaught of kicks stopped. Street lifted his head an inch and let the air flow into his lungs. He heard Brent laughing and saw the barrel of a firearm. A firearm extending from Brent's locked arm. Ricardo was laughing too.

"Maybe I should have my way with him out here before the storm comes. That'd be a great moment, a lasting memory to cherish on his way to hell."

"Do it," Brent said.

Street looked up at the racing clouds and back at the trees. Ricardo had kicked him along the floor of the Everglades for about fifteen feet. The cypress trees reached upward and were snapping in the wind. One tree, an older one, stopped its dance and seemed to stare down at Street, an elbow dipping low. It was the last thing Street saw before a kick from Ricardo slammed his head back under the shallow water. A hand grabbed his head by the hair and yanked him up. Ricardo leaned down over him, his mouth in his ear.

"You want a new job? Well, so do I. Come here, boy."

"Go rot in hell," Street said. His right arm, from down deep in the earth, soared to the heavens, a fresh hunting knife from a submerged bag leading the way. The blade landed deep in Ricardo's crotch and found its way into the man's femoral artery. Warm blood poured down Street's arm like hot urine on a cold winter's day, draining the color out of Ricardo's face with it as Street yanked the blade out of the large man's body. The ogre of a human being dropped to both knees within seconds, fell facedown, and died. His massive body bobbed in the rising waters.

Street knew he had to take out Brent that instant, and he wasted no time. He jammed the knife at Brent's throat, but Brent saw it coming. He dodged the blade and fired his pistol at Street, but dodging Street's blade had thrown off his aim. The bullet missed Street and plunged into Ricardo's enormous back. His body made no twitch or reaction at all. Street saw the missed opportunity, jumped at Brent, and took another stab. Brent moved, but not far enough. The blade cut Brent's shoulder, but then it fell into the water. Street had lost his weapon.

"Motherfucker!" Brent screamed. He fired in a wild, uncontrolled, defensive manner, but Street was already out of the path of the handgun, regaining his balance and flailing on Brent's face.

"Die you fucking psychopath! Die!" Street screamed, pounding away.

He grabbed Brent's throat and shoved his face under the shallow waters.

"No placebos out here! This is real," Street screamed. "Drown you motherfucker!"

Brent thrashed about, but Street held his grip. Then a click of a gun chirped out in the wind, barely audible but loud enough to steal Street's attention and stop his punching. A barrel of a pistol jammed against Street's temple.

"Let him up," a voice said.

Street turned his head. It was the other security agent from Domínguez's detail, Pablo. Patricia was standing next to him, her mouth wide open, staring at Street with a how-did-this-happen-to-us expression on her face. Somehow she had escaped Boston, but Domínguez's detail had found her.

"Found this pretty young thing trying to escape from out of the woods on my way in search of the Lexus," the man said, turning to face Street. "Up," the man said.

Street released his grip on Brent's throat.

It took Brent about two or three seconds to fully regain his bearings and catch his breath. He burst to his feet and gave Street a hard kick to the ribs. He then grabbed his gun and aimed it at Street, who spoke knowing he had just a second to bargain for his life—or Patricia's.

"There's still some uranium out here. Let Patricia go, I'll take you there."

"Not going to happen," Brent said.

"I've also got the evidence of your involvement in Olivia's death, and I know about your massive insider trading scheme. Everything. You let Patricia and me go, and I'll give you the evidence. It's with the uranium. And when I say uranium, I mean all of it."

Patricia frowned at Street. He looked at her and shrugged. Then he faced Brent. "Everything up to now was bullshit. I knew you would follow me, so everything leading up to now was one big show to throw everybody off. A red herring. Truth be told, I was stashing rocks earlier, including what Domínguez had in his trunk. So we get it all, and then we walk. I'll take my chances riding out the storm in the Everglades. Or you risk arrest and life in a supermax prison."

"If there's evidence out here, it will get washed away with the storm alongside your corpse," Brent said. "No one will find it."

"What are you more worried about? Evidence, or the uranium? If it's evidence, maybe I sent a text to someone telling them exactly where it is should I fail to return. Maybe it has a transponder on it. Or maybe I stashed it here a couple of days ago. Same goes for the uranium, which won't get washed away. Want to take that chance?"

Brent stared at the ground in thought and then nodded.

"Okay, Street. You deliver, and then you and the girl get quick deaths. Also, you tell me right now what this evidence is before we go any further."

Street smiled. "I have my own audio recordings and a video, compliments of the US and Russian governments, saved on a flash drive—it has you and some blonde woman talking about killing people and getting rich before the CIA announces Venezuela has joined the nuclear club. In fact, I stashed it here earlier when I was walking with the two women and my cousin, and they didn't even see me doing it. That's the beauty of pee and vodka-stashing breaks. There's some good footage of you saying aloud that I might suffer the fate of Olivia Crawford. Talk of a second phase that makes you rich as well. I already know what that's all about."

"Let's go," Brent said.

Street led the way. Patricia walked by his side. They walked for about two minutes when Patricia spoke.

"What are we going to do? What's your plan?"

"Don't have one," Street said. He turned to face Patricia. "Don't you have one? Don't they train you guys to get out of situations like this?"

"There's no way you can train for a situation like this."

"No, but you can get out of a situation like this by doing something crazy," Street said, adding, "something crazy like this."

He turned to the outside and came in hard with a left hook, knocking Pablo against the jaw. The man went limp and toppled into Brent. Both men fell backward into the water. Street turned, grabbed Patricia by the arm and pushed her ahead. He ran hard shoving her forward as if he were an American football running back pushing a pulling guard to block for him as he bolts to the end zone. A couple of feet later, he had her at the edge of a large hammock. She turned her head to face Street, and her eyes widened. Street took note of the sudden fear in her eyes, which let him know Brent was back on his feet and taking aim. He pushed her into the hammock.

"Disappear into the woods and then escape. Run! Go tell the world what happened here. You'll find a pair of flash drives with evidence under my sink. In my top drawer in my room, my sock drawer, you'll find a paper with login details to find more info on the cloud, stuff that I uploaded. If I make it out, I have copies buried out here, so we are backed up. Find the keys to my Jeep. There's an extra set in the glove compartment. I always bring extras when out here. The way out is that way," Street said, pointing to Loop Road marked by a line of trees. "Go!" He gave her a quick kiss and pushed her into the lush darkness. He heard her footsteps splashing water as she ran deeper into the cover of the trees.

Then he heard the sound of different footsteps. Heavier. Behind him. Street turned and punched Pablo. Street began to wail on him, though Pablo pushed him back, getting enough space between himself and Street to take aim. Street pushed Pablo's gun aside and managed to trip Brent as he ran alongside Pablo to get at Patricia. Brent slipped on Street's foot and almost fell, though he regained his footing quickly, but not quickly enough. Patricia was gone.

"That's enough," Brent said to Pablo, who was lining up his crosshairs at Street who was side-stepping him. "Put your gun down and don't fight him. It's a stall tactic. Let's get back to our task." Brent took one last look at the trees where Patricia had disappeared. "Damn!"

"Game's over," Street said. "Patricia is safe."

"She won't make it out of this alive. Let's just get out of here," Pablo said.

"There's a campground not far from here," Street said. "We can ride out the storm in the restroom facility. It's a solid building. Plus, the evidence you're looking for is pretty much in that direction."

Brent peered into the roiling hammock where Patricia had disappeared. The wind knocked him off-balance, and Street could see the resolve to find her ebb.

"Okay, let's go," Brent said.

"We have to kill him," Pablo said, taking aim.

"Not until I have that evidence and I am sure we have the uranium," Brent said.

"What makes you sure he has any evidence?"

"I just want to be sure," Brent said. "I want to see what dirt he has exactly, and maybe I can figure out who was onto us, you know, who sent Cyra after us. Whoever it is, I don't want him or her hunting me forever."

Walking back toward the road was difficult. Blasts of hurricane-force winds lashed at the three men. Branches from dwarf cypress trees that grew in shallow soil whipped the men over and over again. Street led the way, Pablo brought up the rear, while Brent held the middle. Both men kept their guns on Street, darting glances all around in the whipping wind.

"We're lost," Brent said.

"I think so," Pablo echoed.

"I'm not lost. It just seems that way," Street mumbled.

He looked up at the stormy skies. The roar of the wind got so loud and the winds so strong, that eventually all eyes focused on the ground out of protection. Then a lull in the winds brought some calm.

Brent screamed out to Pablo. "Keep up back there. Keep an eye out for Patricia making a break for cover. And make sure Cyra's body stays in the Jeep when we get back."

Pablo began to pick up the pace. A break in the winds allowed for the sound of Pablo's wet boots sloshing in the water to echo across the prairie. The squishy steps resonated loudly for a few minutes but slowed to a longer crescendo, as if he was sliding and no longer walking normally.

Street and Brent turned to check on Pablo, who plodded forward but in an unbalanced manner. His slow footsteps came to a stop, and he just stood there with glassy eyes and blood streaming down the side of his face, syrupy red drops taking flight into the wind. Pablo looked up at Street and Brent, his eyes losing all focus.

"Shit," Brent said. "Pablo, snap out of it. Let's go."

"Branch to the head," Street shouted into the rebuilding winds, grabbing a dwarf cypress to hang on. "A nasty blow, too. Shoot him. Put him out of his misery."

Brent stared at Street. Then he turned and fired his semiautomatic. Pablo fell dead. They both marched forward, and five minutes later, Loop Road grew as visible as it could. It should have taken about ten minutes to reach the road, but it took twenty. Both Street and Brent fell in the blasting winds and then walked with difficulty onto the gravely road.

"You stagger ahead first. This campground better be close," Brent said.

"It's close enough. There will be some more hiking but not much."

The winds held off just long enough for them to make it. They found a few cooking grills, picnic tables, and parking spaces. Sure enough, up in the distance, a squat, new brick restroom facility stood firm in the howling winds. A flash of dull-green lightning lit up the campground's features. Winds picked up even more, and cypress trees not only whipped about in the air but began to fall like twigs. The trunk of a pine tree shot past Street and Brent. They dove inside the entrance to the restroom facilities. The doors to the restrooms themselves were locked, but the facility breezeway offered enough protection from the wind and the rain.

"Where's the evidence, Street?" Brent shouted, barely hearing his own voice.

The howling winds seemed to snatch his words and carry them off. Street ignored him and sat down against the men's restroom door and examined the cuts across both arms. He didn't need a mirror to know his eyes were black and blue from fighting and from tree limbs battering him during the trek back to Loop Road.

"Who took the videos?" Brent asked again, with growing impatience.

"I don't know, Brent. You guys killed Cyra, the only person who did know."

"Where were the films taken? You sneaked in and took them, didn't you? Even if you did, who tipped you off? Trust me, there are no cameras in my office or home. I know how to find them."

"Again, I don't know. Nobody does. I have my audio evidence, but I didn't film you."

"Well, you do know that you're never going to see Patricia again," Brent said, holding the semiautomatic up to Street. "I'll find her after this and kill her if she's not already dead. So just sit down there in the corner. I want some distance from you."

Street moved deeper into the breezeway of the restroom facility and stared out at the winds that were just inches in front of his face. He was mesmerized by their screaming speeds. Then he stared at Brent. "You're not going to find her," Street said.

"Doesn't matter. I'm out of here once this storm passes, and I'm leaving this hellhole forever."

"Miccosukee police will want to know what a middle-aged white man is doing limping out of the Everglades after a hurricane," Street said.

"I'll tell them that I got lost birdwatching or python hunting," Brent said. He checked his firearm. Loaded and ready for use. He clicked the safety off.

"That'll work."

"I'll think of something. Anyway, Street. We've won, and you—"

Brent snapped his head to the side. His eyes widened. A palm tree whistled into the breezeway, shooting in tip first like a missile correctly meeting its target. It exploded into the wall separating the men's and women's restrooms, destroying a drinking fountain. The blast of the trunk and the twisting and grinding of the metal men's room door giving way was deafening. A frond whipped sideways, slapping Street into a corner of the breezeway. Though caught off guard, Street saw an opportunity. He jumped up, dove over the trunk of the palm tree, and buried a fist in Brent's jaw. Street jammed a foot on the palm tree's trunk, giving himself leverage to wail on Brent, who covered his head like a defensive boxer. Street pounded again until he felt a sharp pain on the back of his head. A hook of light like a camera flash blinded him for a second. He fell to the ground, taking a moment to regain his senses. A couple of seconds later, he turned over and faced Brent standing beside Boston, who had punched him hard on the back of the head with the butt of his handgun.

"Guess a microwave won't work out here, but we'll find something," Boston said.

"This has gone on long enough, Street. Tell me where everything is," Brent said, acknowledging Boston with a nod.

"Why do you care if you're leaving?" Boston asked.

"Less evidence out there means there's a less chance of Special Forces coming for me," Brent said. "Plus, the uranium is nearby. Everything up to now was just bullshit, right?"

"Go to hell," Street said.

"I'll let Patricia live if you give me everything. I'm sure she's hunkered down back on Loop Road, probably in your flooded-out Jeep, but she'll take the same way out as we do after the storm," Brent said. "I'll blackmail her into compliance somehow."

"Fuck you," Street said.

Exhausted, he stared out into the blasting storm. The swamp whipped in the roaring winds. Hopefully Patricia was safe somewhere in the Jeep or under some sort of cover. If there was any doubt in his mind that he was too afraid to take risks, it was gone with Granville's winds.

"Just shoot him, Brent. And then let's just get out of here," Boston said.

"Not until I get that uranium and evidence. Maybe it will lead us to whoever is really after us. If that person lives, he'll find us."

Boston rolled his eyes. "Great. We go after the storm." He looked at Street. "Shoot him in the leg to make sure he can't bolt out of here."

"Jesus you're an idiot! If he can't walk, he can't lead us to the evidence." Brent stopped to think, rubbing his stubbly skull with the palm of his hand. "If it's close, we walk in the storm."

Boston just stared blankly at Street, who peered out into the hurricane, into the black, roaring winds. The sun had long set, though Street could still see raindrops spraying sideways. The wind rushed south, sounding like a large waterfall flowing steadily as it goes off a dam. Then, as if someone closed a spigot, it all stopped. The Everglades calmed, as if its torturer had taken a break and left the trees room to lick their wounds. The air was calm and quiet except for a breeze or two.

"The eye," Brent said. "We've got a window. Let's get the stuff and then get out of here."

"It's too dangerous. It's dark out now and with all the debris, someone's going to turn an ankle. Hopefully, that will be you two," Street said.

"Up," Boston said. "We go get what he wants."

Street nodded. "It's this way."

Street walked out of the restroom facility and stepped over some fallen trees. The open areas set aside for campers were littered with shattered tree trunks and debris. Grills for cooking remained firmly in place. Street walked to the edge of the campground and into the swamp. The water was much higher. He walked about fifty feet out, bent over, and pried his arm deep into the muck. Not a couple of minutes later, he came back with multiple bags, two of which weighed down heavily across the back of his neck and shoulders, resembling slain game.

"That's it? You stashed it right there? Just a few feet away?" Brent said, crossing his arms with the handgun dangling from his side, looking more like an angry mother with a skillet than a corrupt spy ready to clean house and cash in. "Again, you mean it was right there all along?"

"You've got everything now. As long as Patricia lives, I'll take my chances."

Brent opened the bag. Peered inside. Garden stones and fishing weights. Money and a manila envelope were sealed together in a waterproof plastic bag. Inside the envelope were two blue flash drives. Street's old cassette recorder was inside as well. And a bottle of vodka.

"Vodka?"

"My cousin's. I added it to the pot earlier."

"Our mystery friend got this to you?" Brent asked, frowning at the flash drives.

"Her boss did," Street said. "It all implicates you in Olivia's death and planning Molly's death as well as my own."

"Okay, let's go for a walk," Brent said.

"Kill him now," Boston said.

"By a campground? Are you stupid? People will be back here in a day or two. I want it done deeper in the swamp. I think we have some time before the second half of the storm hits once the eye passes," Brent said.

"Fine," Boston said. "I'll lead the way." He walked into the swamp, and Brent and Street followed.

"Oh, and son, one more thing," Brent added.

"Yes?" Boston said.

"Bye," Brent replied.

He fired his gun into Boston's back. The young man fell instantly.

"That kid is off to Venezuelan hell, and you're off to, well, whatever."

"Go ahead and do it," Street said. "Patricia is safe and will make sure you walk this earth looking over your shoulder like the coward you are."

"On your knees, or this will go messily," Brent said.

Street shook his head. He scanned the forests he loved so much one last time, closed his eyes, and dropped to his knees. He spit and raised his arms in the air, hands behind his head. Execution style.

Street felt the barrel of the pistol ram against his head. He closed his eyes. The sound of gunfire was quick, painless, and deafening.

CHAPTER

61

The ringing in his ears let Street know he was still alive. Feelings started to spread across his skin like water, cleansing away the numbness that had frozen him seconds earlier. He opened his eyes and looked around. The restroom building stood there, firm over a chaotically strewed bed of debris. The storm's eyewall stood encased in soft moonlight shining from above. The circular clouds resembled a massive stadium that managed to seal off the fury of Hurricane Granville, roaring spectators held at bay and in silence for a few minutes, as if a crowd went breathless. When the first blurry visions came deeper into focus, Street jumped up and glanced around. There was nobody. Just Brent's lifeless body on the ground not far from Boston's. There wasn't much left of his head, while Boston's storm wounds appeared like small moons orbiting a massive hole where Brent's bullet made entry. The pistol remain locked in Brent's hand.

Street grabbed the firearm and stood with growing confidence. He grabbed the bag with the flash drives and his old recorder as well. He kept the heavy bags by his feet. He cocked the firearm and squinted in the darkness around him. There was nobody, nothing but trees appearing to be sucking wind during the halftime of a game they were clearly losing. Still, somebody was definitely out there.

Then his thoughts gained speed. Did Patricia find a gun and somehow come back to him? She would have rushed out to him by now. Someone shot

Brent, but was that someone his friend? Or did Brent have more friends around and the shooter was waiting to see who emerged from the swamp?

"Who's out there?" Street said in a matter-of-fact tone, darting the gun into the dark hammock, numb from the day's ordeal. Then logic quickly shot through his nerves on the coattails of an adrenaline surge, and he dove behind a barbecue grill for cover. Someone was still out there, someone with a good aim, some serious firepower, and no problems killing people.

"Stop thinking so much and drop the gun," a man's voice called out. Street didn't recognize it.

Street looked up over the grill. He relaxed a little. If the person wanted him dead, he would have killed him. Still, he said nothing, aiming the gun in all directions.

"Seriously, relax. You're safe. For now at least. The other half of the hurricane will hit soon," the voice called out. It was a neutral American accent. Probably Midwest, Street thought.

"Who are you?"

"You're boss's boss's boss's boss."

"Fuck off," Street said. "Don't think I won't use this gun."

"I believe that," the voice answered back. "You're probably not as good a shot as I am, though."

"Are you a cop?"

"No."

"Do you know who I am?"

"Street Brewer, an unknowing spy for hire."

Street felt more resolve. Not only would he protect himself by killing whoever it was in the trees ahead, he'd also likely walk out of the Everglades without being charged or even tied to this unbelievable mess of a crime. Then he realized he had a valuable tool, more valuable than a gun. His old cassette recorder. He pressed record. All was live and now being documented on tape. All he needed was to make the voice talk.

"Why did you kill Brent?" Street shouted out.

"Am I being interviewed?"

"Call it that."

"I killed him because he was bad. Bad for the agency, bad for the country, and bad for Worldwide Oil & Gas. They were horrified one of their own, Domínguez, was involved in this uranium smuggling ring. The CIA was horrified too."

Hope the tape player picked all that up, Street thought. "So, you're with the agency. Who are you?" he asked.

"I told you, your boss's boss's boss's boss. We are a large bureaucracy, after all. If it's all right, I'd like to come out. I'm not going to hurt you, and feel free to keep recording with that relic of a tape recorder. Oh, and by the way, my name is Roman Decker. I'm with the agency, and I'm not alone out here." The voice paused. "Fellas? Want to show Street here how many of us are in the hammock?"

A spattering of gunfire erupted. Around a dozen bursts of muzzle fire flashed through the thick of the canopy, perforating he corpses of Brent and Boston. Blood spewed out like small geysers and then quickly subsided. Then the noise stopped.

"We can be pretty sure they're dead now," Street said. "Military? SEALS? Green Berets? CIA? I don't give a fuck at this point."

"Some of them here were SEALS. Any former Special Forces here?" Roman shouted from the trees. Street heard chuckles. Roman went on. "Couple from the Marines too. Most are retired military working as out-sourced security contractors. Today they're brought to you by Worldwide Oil & Gas. Corporate headquarters in the US was happy to provide them to me. You see, when I informed them of Brent's Placebo Agenda and Domínguez's role in Venezuela, they were horrified. They want this to disappear, just like I do."

"You guys want me dead too?" Street pointed the gun down. "Fuck it. Do it. As long as Patricia's safe."

"We're not going to kill you," Roman said. "I'm going to come out and talk to you."

"You'll admit you killed this psychopath?" Street said, motioning to Brent's corpse. "You'll stay five yards away, and I keep recording?"

"Yes."

"I'm going to publish this."

"Great. But to print anything you need to have someone talking to you," the man said. "You'll need a credible source. Otherwise, you'll be another jackass calling himself a journalist spouting off unfounded opinions. We've got enough of those."

"Okay, come on out." Street held up the gun with resolve. "If I see a gun, I'm shooting. I've had enough of this shit."

Street saw the image of a human being emerging from the trees. Several men followed suit. Soldiers in fatigues. Rifle barrels pointed to the ground. The sound of footsteps in water followed. Street heard a few clicks and flood lights burst into the middle of the swamp. There the man stood. Roman Decker, all but five-feet-seven inches of him. Street knew him the instant he saw him—the handyman from *The Gateway*'s office building.

"Expecting someone bigger? Chiseled chin? A gruff spy with a chip on his shoulder or something like that?" Roman asked.

"Wait. You? You work for buildings and grounds back at the office. Always tinkering on the electrical, the lights and stuff. You don't speak English. That was you?"

"Do I work for buildings and grounds? Or is that what you thought you knew?"

"Who do you work for?"

"The CIA. I told you. And you know that."

"You knew Brent?"

"Yes. But he didn't know me."

"So you were keeping an eye on him," Street said, lowering the gun.

Roman slowly approached Street. A few men collected Boston's body. Street heard one give orders to search for the bodies of Ricardo and Pablo and to hurry, as they were short on time before the second half of the storm hit.

"Yes, I was keeping an eye on him. I was spying on him. You know we put agents in fake companies overseas and even embed some in real companies. But at the end of the day, we collect the intelligence. We don't send innocent people into harm's way to do it for us while we manipulate markets. We've done similar things in the past, like asking people to pass along casual information, but nothing like what you went through."

"What I went through? You knew all along that I was being used as some sort of mule?"

"No. Not all along. It took some snooping. But you did your job and found out that a rogue Worldwide Oil & Gas executive, rogue CIA agents, and a rogue Venezuelan government were stashing weapons-grade uranium in a plan to drive up oil prices. With Brent botching an already-screwed-up operation, I needed someone on the ground to verify what's going on and see who was involved. You did that."

"And Patricia?"

"She was being used by Brent, who threatened her to go along with it. She's safe now. We scooped her up not too long ago. She didn't do half-bad spending an afternoon in the swamp during a hurricane."

Street said nothing. He was still digesting the entire ordeal, a little proud of his tenacity.

"You know I'm going to write a story saying that the Venezuelans were stocking up on enriched Iranian uranium. Rogue oilmen and spies stole it and squirreled it away in the US to attack the United States or anywhere else for that matter if need be, and I helped them do it because I was an agent, but, hey, I didn't know about it. Oh, and by the way, they slapped an insider trading deal on top of this agenda."

The handyman named Roman Decker shrugged. "That's up to you. But if you do, then this might help out."

He dropped an envelope into Street's hand. Street didn't open it but knew what he felt, a couple of flash drives and a key.

Roman went on. "These flash drives contain more of our work backing up and verifying your own intelligence. You have a conference call of all involved discussing the details of this operation, including Brent's boss, who recently had an unfortunate accident in northern Virginia, as well as the president of Venezuela. You also have satellite and other info on Russian arms stashed in Venezuelan slums via Ricardo plus imagery of Iranian uranium arriving in a posh Coral Gables neighborhood via yacht. Some nice info on a base going up in La Orchila Island. Details on their trades to go long on oil. The entire cast makes an appearance, with names, phone calls, emails, bank accounts, trading positions, and everything, so go public with it. You deserve it. I always respected you. Human intelligence matters most of all, did you know that? More than anything else, despite all our technical advances in the field. No technology in the world out there can gauge what goes on in the minds of flawed human beings and all their convenient, transient loyalties, their irrational fears, and equally irrational dreams. You think you know someone, but you never will. You proved it."

Not bad. Not bad at all, Street thought. I think I found my quote. "Can I use your name?"

"Just say US intelligence sources told you."

Street nodded. "This is going to blow up. What if I need your help? What if I have more questions?"

"I'll be around," Roman said. "Publish the story. Horrific publicity will be good for the agency. Give us a kick in the ass to clean house. A little disruption is a good thing. A massive disruption can be a wonderful thing."

"Won't people be bugging my phones and every move? Including you? Do you think I trust you fully?"

"For a while. We'll go analog when it comes time to chat. I'll find you. Maybe out here. Listen, this story is going to shake up the US intelligence community. There will be congressional hearings, market swings, high-profile firings, and a lot of focus on you. But it will subside. I guess in the meantime, you'll need a little sanctuary. Something a little better than that apartment. There's a key in that envelope too."

"Is that a key to a safe house where I'm going to hole up?"

Roman laughed. "Nope. You'll have to pick out your own place. What's in that envelope is a key to a safe deposit box. Go see what's inside it. I think you'll find that your financial problems will go away. Your legal problems are over as well. Jenkins's too. We take care of our own, especially since we're going to use Cornbridge Capital to short oil and not go long on it. Ain't that right, Applewood?"

A dazed Applewood appeared from the darkness, dressed in full military fatigues but looking seriously out of place in them.

"Applewood? What are you doing here?" Street asked. "You should be back in the Kesselman offices not hiring anyone!"

"Like you, I was working hard to stay in the loop," Applewood said. "Roman contacted me not long after our coffee. Hernán Bernal hired me as well to keep him up to speed. Look, I can help you out. I can be the middleman between you and Roman. I'll keep you in the loop."

"Bullshit," Street said. "I'll keep you both in the loop. No one here has insight into that country like me, save the Venezuelans of course."

Both Roman and Applewood laughed, bringing some relief to a seriously skewed tension. "No foreigner, of course."

"Applewood, here, did a great job working for Hernán Bernal to see what was going on, including your role in this. He was, in a sense, a contracted spy for Venezuela, but on our side. He had the pleasant task of confirming to Bernal what the president had feared, that Caracas had been double-crossed. The world is changing, the energy world especially, and oil prices aren't headed in the direction that Domínguez and Brent wanted. We'll be in touch," Roman said.

He made some sort of commanding hand gesture to the hammock. About twelve heavily armed men in full combat gear plodded back to the road, where a string of SUVs waited, their lights shining through the darkness. Street looked at the tape recorder and turned it off.

"If you're going to help me going forward, I don't want you on tape. I want everything analog. Nothing, not even a cassette that people can steal." Street paused. "I guess I'll have to trust you."

The maintenance man known as Roman Decker smiled and looked down at the tape recorder.

"Save it for your notes. Then destroy it. I trust you. Do you really trust me? Can you ever trust an institution again?"

Street said nothing.

"That's your call to make. Anyway, somebody has to clean up this mess. That would be my job. Lord knows I can't have anyone else involved. You can't be here for this, so off you go. You're a brave man. Christ, you took us through the Everglades and in the Big Cypress National Preserve in a hurricane, which by the way, is ready for round two. How did you learn how to do that?"

Street just stared at him.

"It's okay. We all have our secrets, you know, little things we smuggle away hoping that nobody knows about," the maintenance man said. "We can shake on that."

Roman held out his hand.

Street looked at it. Conflict or trust, he thought. Take a risk, he thought, take a risk. Trust your gut and trust this man. Street shook his hand.

"One last question," Roman said. "Where's the rest of my uranium? We need everything you've hidden out here, and I mean everything. You'll get what's yours. I'm taking all the uranium though."

"There was a little in Domínguez's trunk. A small bit out here as well, but—"

Roman Decker grabbed the two bags at Street's feet and opened them. He shined a flashlight inside them both and shook his head, laughing.

"Street, this is not uranium. These are actually real stones and fishing sinkers."

"If you'd let me finish," Street said with a smile, "I was going to tell you that the bulk is in my parents' pool. Safe and sound. My cousin Jenkins had it, not knowing what he was carrying," Street said.

Roman laughed again. "You're getting good at this. You've come a long way from eavesdropping on Brent and Karen in that little office."

"One last question," Street said. "Who are you? Where are you from?"

"Just some man from the Midwest, as far as you know. You'll never guess my ethnicity. But you'll have to admit I'm a pretty good actor, aren't I?"

"You're quite the spy. In fact, if you're my boss's boss's boss, why close this up yourself? Do you have time to be a cleanup man?"

"The fewer involved in this mess, the better. Plus, if you want something done right, you have to do it yourself. You know that. And with Hernán Bernal involved, via his spies on the ground—Applewood and Pérez, of course—I figured I should get involved as well and stop sending Cyra in for me." Roman sighed when he mentioned Cyra. "I will always regret that. Anyway," he said, catching Street somewhat off guard at how quickly he compartmentalized his emotions, "go be a good journalist and report on what you think is important, and not for some media company big or small with an agenda. Now that you've risked your life, go reap all the rewards. And speaking of life, don't spend yours seeking a job you settled for, trading time for dollars to help others get rich off their dreams. Create and produce for yourself. Tell the world what happened in your own words. Keep everyone accountable. Give us all something we're seriously lacking, and that's a truly independent and reliable media source." Roman turned and walked away.

A distant rumble began to build to the east. The second half of the hurricane was bearing down. The torturer was back from its break, ready to whip the trees and the grasses.

"We cleared the roads, so these guys will take you back," Roman shouted to Street over his shoulder. "Patricia's with them, already en route back to safety—and for some questions and debriefing, of course. We've taken good care of Cyra as well." He turned and continued walking.

Far ahead, his men pressed forward, carrying Brent's and Boston's dead bodies. Others arrived with the bodies of Ricardo, Pablo, and Pérez, who stirred.

"This one's alive!" a man shouted.

"Pérez!" Street shouted, running over to the fallen man. "Make sure that one lives. He's one of us," Street shouted at a large soldier, who knelt down to check on Pérez's vitals.

"Street, asshole. The Venezuelan government sends its apologies," Pérez said.

"How about free gasoline for life and make that apology official?"

"Can you beat me in a boxing match?"

"Guess not," Street said. "Get well soon, my friend. Something tells me your Christmas bonus will be a little bigger this year."

"You're always welcome in Venezuela."

The large soldier checking Pérez's vitals nodded at Street, letting him know his friend would be okay, but it was time to move.

Street pressed forward, following the four men carrying the wounded Venezuelan spy master. All men entered the four black SUVs. Street closed the door, and the wind began to pound the procession, this time from the other direction. A Miccosukee police officer escorted them through Loop Road in the building winds.

Hours later, Street was back home, and his Jeep, while wet and wind-whipped, was parked safely outside. Houses were opening up from the storm. Groggy people, coffee in hand and eyes on the clearing skies, walked in the gray light to survey damage. Time to go on with their lives. Street's apartment building was fine. So was his parents' house. The pool was noticeably clean, a little odd after a hurricane. He laughed, and looked up. Streaks of blue were breaking through the gray as the clouds fled northward.

Street looked at the light to the east. His eyes were open and he could see. Sunrises would get even better for him from a new, three-bedroom condominium overlooking the Biscayne Bay in Coconut Grove in a few months' time. The paperwork and files on his new securities portfolios were all safe in his new bank deposit box.

He needed some rest before it was time to get to work.

62

Back in his one-bedroom apartment, Street opened his eyes. He stared at the ceiling. His entire body was throbbing in pain from his weary bones and from the cuts on the surface of his skin. All his muscles ached as well. His room was dark and hot. No power. He sat up in his bed. Something was off. Off, but in a good way. A very good way. There was a scent in his room. One that shouldn't have been there, but one that was more than welcome—the scent of shampoo. He grabbed a flashlight from his bedside table and clicked it on. The light beam caught sight of a woman's crossed legs. His heart skipped a beat when the beam revealed soft, golden skin void of any lingerie. No panty straps across the hips, no bra concealing her chest. Just her. Patricia's face came into focus, no makeup, just wet, disheveled hair. And those beautiful eyes.

"Shh," she said, touching his chest with her finger. "Lay back. Relax."

"Patricia, thank God. I love you."

"And I'm in love with you, Street Brewer."

She moved on her hands and knees across the bed. Street looked into her eyes and let his gaze move with confidence across her hips and legs. She was perfect save a bruise on her left knuckles from when she clocked him on the boat and Domínguez in the Everglades. He loved her even more. She kissed him, softly at first, then deeper, faster.

"Now it's my turn to take care of you." One knee remained in place while the other rose and she straddled him.

Several hours later, they lay there in bed. Patricia handed Street a cold beer. Bags of ice, a hot commodity after a hurricane, and a bottle of imported Polish ale had mysteriously made their way into his apartment.

"What time is it?" Street asked. "Isn't it a little early for beer?"

"It's four in the afternoon, big boy," Patricia said. She looked around. "I kind of like this place," she said. "It's you."

"Are you hungry?"

"So starving!" Patricia said.

"The Grouchy Grouper is open, I'm sure. Want to see what I can hustle up?"

"That would be awesome," Patricia said.

A few minutes later, Street walked into the Grouchy Grouper. No power, but lots of people were hanging out drinking fine craft beer from kegs in a cooler kept ice cold by a generator. Street walked up, ordered a beer from a gorgeous bartender. Black hair. A cascade of tattoos covered her arms, a little too many for Street's taste, but on her, they looked good.

"What's up, Street?" she said. "Jesus, you look horrible! What happened to you? Not all of those bruises are storm-related, especially the ones on your knuckles. Trust me, I can tell. Did you get in a fight, sweetie?

"Something like that. You should see the other guy. Got any cold brews?"

"Sure thing."

"I'll take that craft IPA everyone likes, a six-pack of those bottled beers people are always ordering and whatever sandwiches you can whip up."

"The charcoal-fired barbeque outside is heating up all the burgers so they won't go to waste."

"That'll work. Two to go."

"Dinner for two? Now we're getting somewhere. You got it, sweetie. Give me a second. Oh, and by the way, the last time you were here with those two girls, you left your backpack. I kept it here during the storm. I'll get it for you."

The woman walked across the bar and grabbed a backpack from a nail on the wall with two hands.

"Man, this is heavy! What's in there? Dumbbells?"

Street grabbed the bag and swung it over his shoulder. "Some lovely garden stones. Just enough in there to really brighten up our city. A little insurance policy I knew would be safe here during the storm. Something I need to get rid of eventually."

"Whatever," the woman said, smiled, and walked away.

Street left the bar. Whatever, he echoed the bartender. It's all whatever.

He hopped in his car, which was parallel parked just outside the bar. He looked over his shoulder. A police car was behind him. He could see the officer in the driver's seat, though the officer had no interest in Street. The cop was looking down, obviously reading something, either doing paperwork or texting.

"Keep your head up and be a little more vigilant, officer," Street murmured. "There's smuggled weapons-grade uranium about ten feet in front of you. Enough to make a bomb. It'll stay safe unless someone comes after me." The cop remained fixated on his paperwork.

Street grabbed his phone and checked his messages. He was surprised to see that there were many missed texts and voice mails that had arrived, now that he was in the Wi-Fi range of the Grouchy Grouper. The first one was from Applewood. He read it.

> **Street. Just wanted to let you know if you want a solid-paying job here at Kesselman, you got it.**

> **Thanks, but I think I will be okay working on my own. But I appreciate it. I mean that Applewood.**

> **Anytime.**

The next text was from Texas, someone named Arthur. Street read the text.

> **Street, this is Arthur Morgan. President, CEO and Chairman of Worldwide Oil & Gas. I understand you had some issues with our man in Venezuela.**

> **You could say that.**

Well, Worldwide Oil & Gas is forever in your debt. Anything you need, be it full-time job, work, projects, consulting gigs, environmental protection and climate change projects, whatever, I am professionally and personally at your service.

Thank you. I appreciate that and look forward to working with you.

Call when you need me.

Street saw he had yet another text. This one came from Wallace Lockwood, owner of *The Gateway*.

Street. We have never really spoken, but this is Wallace Lockwood, Brent's boss. I guess we need to delete these texts after reading. I wanted to write and say thanks for including me in this trade on oil prices going south. Appreciate it. I am deleting this text. Don't respond.

Street laughed. What oil trade? Thanks Roman, he thought. Making a buck on all of our troubles and giving me the credit for it. Low oil prices, he mused. A new reality.

Another message loaded up. This one a voice mail.

"Street? May name is Sebastián Ledezma, CEO of Tarapacá Mines in Chile. I was an acquaintance of Olivia Crawford, and heard of her unfortunate death. I was also told you brought her killers to justice. Anyhow, I was told to contact you by a young woman named Ana Patricia Osorio Harding. Lovely voice. She told me to talk to you about some freelance writing on port activities across the Americas. Call me at this number. I have some projects for you related to my port and copper mine. Nice to be finally dealing with someone at CIA with integrity."

Street responded via text.

Thank you. I will indeed, and I'm not with the CIA.

Next text. This one also a voice message.

"Hi Street, it's Catherine Burnett. Some people contacted me and told me what happened to Pennie and Roland. They told me what you went through to find out. Don't worry. Your secret is safe with me. Oh, and to say thanks,

the Rybovich is yours. I'm putting it in your name. There is docking for it in Coconut Grove. That's on me as well. Fuel and all services and captain fees for life as well. Enjoy. And most of all, thank you."

Street said nothing, letting his jaw and phone drop. He looked up and stared at the parting clouds above. He let that sit for a while, processing Catherine's message. He played her message again. For sure, he was the owner of a large Rybovich. This was bigger than busting a multinational nuclear smuggling ring, he thought. He replayed the message for a third time. After about three minutes lost in the sky, he snapped back to Coconut Grove's storm-battered reality. A Rybovich. All mine. More surreal than anything I've gone through.

Next text.

Street it's your old friend Pérez. Time we hung out under better circumstances. I get it you are busy tonight with your girlfriend. Drinks tomorrow? You and Patricia? I'm a little beaten up but in a safe place. Let's have some fun. You can drink my beers. But no touching my painkillers!

You got it. We'll be there.

Then he noticed a white piece of paper protruding from his glove compartment. He snatched it out.

Street. Roman Decker, your boss's boss's boss's boss. Hope you're feeling better. Anything you need, the agency will get it for you. I'll see you around. Trash this paper and any text messages or voice mails. PS Molly Wells included in our recent capital markets transaction. PSS The uranium came up a few pounds short. Nice try, and stop thinking so much. Leave the rest in the trash outside the Grouchy Grouper. One of my operatives is en route to get it right now.

Fair enough. Street ditched the leftover uranium in a plastic trash bag in a garbage bin on the street corner. He made sure no one saw it. In a matter of seconds, a City of Miami sanitation worker emptied the bin and left. Street never saw his face.

"Trust in the US government restored," Street mumbled. But what about the Venezuelan government? I guess we can't win them all, he thought. He was about to crank up the engine when another text popped up on his screen. It was his lawmaker buddy in Caracas.

Street? I guess Venezuela owes you one. After all these years the president is finally out. He's fleeing with his tail between his legs right now. On his way to Cuba. Good riddance. It's all because of you. We're being briefed on what happened.

Street checked his phone and did a quick scan of the headlines. It was all over the news. He nodded and texted back.

When it's time to go, it's time to go.

I'm hearing through the grapevine you're working on a story that will tell the world what happened. If you need anything from Venezuela, just ask me personally. No matter what you're working on, just count on me.

I appreciate that. Guess you're in a position to make things happen in Venezuela.

Thanks Street, It's looking that way, isn't it?

Looking that way? It's all over the news. You're the new president of Venezuela!

Yes, I am. I'm getting good support from our base, and surprisingly, from the past administration, Bernal especially. It's a new day for both of us. I owe you one. Thank you, Street.

Gracias, Señor Presidente.

Street turned the ignition. The sound of the engine startled the cop. He looked up and stared at Street. Street nodded to him via his rearview mirror. The cop nodded back and then returned to whatever he was reading.

Street pulled onto the small road and headed home.